NOVEMBERFEST

NOVEMBERFEST

Theodore Weesner

ALFRED A. KNOPF *New York* *1994*

THIS IS A BORZOI BOOK
PUBLISHED BY ALFRED A. KNOPF, INC.

Copyright © 1994 by Theodore Weesner

Grateful acknowledgment is made to PolyGram International Publishing, Inc., for permission to reprint from "I Will Survive" by Frederick J. Perren and Dino Fekaris, copyright © 1978 by PolyGram International Publishing, Inc., and Perren-Vibes Music, Inc.

Library of Congress Cataloging-in-Publication Data

Weesner, Theodore.
    Novemberfest / by Theodore Weesner.
        p.   cm.
    ISBN 0-679-43099-7
1. World War, 1939–1945—Veterans—New Hampshire—Fiction.
2. Man-woman relationships—New Hampshire—Fiction.   3. College teachers—New Hampshire—Fiction.   4. German teachers—New Hampshire—Fiction.   5. Middle aged men—New Hampshire—Fiction.   I. Title.
PS3573.E36N68   1994
813'.54—dc20   94-14507
                                                                CIP

Manufactured in the United States of America
First Edition

For Janet

And in memory of Richard Yates

ACKNOWLEDGMENTS

Special thanks to Gary Fisketjon. Added thanks to Alexia
von Gültingen. Long-term gratitude to Jim Silberman
and Peter Matson.

1

OVER THE ATLANTIC
Fall 1987

1

Leaving the vintage Volkswagen in the empty lot, they make their way through head winds to the seawall, father and daughter here to take in a November storm coming off the Atlantic. At fifty-two, Glen Cady may be on the downhill side of things, but his four-year-old, Alice, keeps close beside him in her corduroy cap and trusting way.

Moisture from the swollen sea is already misting Glen's old wire-rimmed glasses and he uses a handkerchief to wipe the lenses. He touches Alice's small shoulder as he lowers himself and then her slack weight, in both hands, to the loose sand below. Alice's fingers are like stubby, moist pencils and keep trying to return to his own.

Hand in hand they trudge along until they reach smooth sand, then wet sand closer to the surf, where their footprints fill with water. A late starter in all ways—he is an assistant professor of German language and literature, untenured—Glen likes being away from the troubles of his job, and likes also, now and then, to send a stray thought over the Atlantic to the distant past.

A sense of escape looms as they approach the noisy water. The weather inland was darkening into the afternoon, as Portsmouth State entered its first hours of the Thanksgiving break, and the pressure Glen feels, not from teaching but from being squeezed out of the profession, has been receding since he picked up Alice at nursery school. Moments now are free and touched with pleasure.

A quietness in Alice has them pausing, however, where the

flat beach begins its downward slope. Their feet begin sinking into the sodden sand, and as another wave comes rolling in, Glen draws her back to keep water from sloshing over their shoes. Flirting with waves is a little game they enjoy both winning and losing, but today Alice seems unimpressed. Quiet Alice. The stubby pencils sticking to his hand are telling him she is either uninterested or exhausted. Usually she strays, crouching quietly to inspect pebbles and shells before rushing to catch up, as if tethered to his angle of exploration. Does she ever cry or shout? Glen cannot remember the last time she raised her voice.

They go along with the breeze and the ocean's roar at their side. Sandpipers and gulls lift and flutter, and in the distance a lone jogger is coming their way. Under the rolling sky—it's barely four o'clock—it's too dark to tell if it's a man or a woman. Glen notices another figure standing and staring over the waves.

"How far is Europe?" he asks.

Alice knows to tease by asking, "In miles or kilometers?" but he can see only the top of her corduroy cap as she pokes along at his side without saying a word. Lifting her under her arms—she has the weight of an empty gym bag—Glen places her on his shoulder and says, "Are you tired, sweetheart?"

Again there is no reply.

"No falling asleep!" he adds, to goad her into making fake snores, but nothing is working today and he cradles her to his neck and shoulder. The empty gym bag seems to be filling with sand as he walks, and thinking she is too subdued, he reverses direction to trace his way back to the seawall and his car.

Kleines Liebchen. Glen never meant to be a doting father, but always has a diminutive for the tiny person for whom he has known only affection. Never anger or impatience, never disappointment; joy alone has been his discovery. His response is an older father's, he is aware, yet it's a vein of gold he's pleased to accept.

Alice comes around some as he buckles her into the passenger seat, and she touches his arm as he cranks up the old VW and circles out of the empty lot onto 1-A. Shy with strangers, his daughter will chatter at him like a squirrel, will scurry about at times and joke and play the tomboy, and Glen wonders if she senses his growing job difficulty and shares his fear.

Being an older father has gathered force in him since Alice's birth and is never far from his mind. Teachers and clerks and nurses keep reminding him in the way they say "Oh." Playmates' parents, too, who are always twenty-odd years younger. "Oh, you're the father," they say, and glance about his face. Even friends offer tabulations. "When your daughter is ten you'll be fifty-eight," they say. "When she's sixteen . . ." "She'll keep me young," Glen responds. He tries to ignore the remarks, but Paige, twenty years younger, is always offended.

Alice has removed her hand, and driving, Glen reaches to touch the frizz of her hair beneath her corduroy cap. "Wanted to ask you about Mrs. Ouellette saying your father's an older man," he says. Alice's teacher's remark has stuck in his mind since Paige mentioned it earlier on the phone. "You don't mind having an older father, do you?" he says.

Mrs. Ouellette is no spring chicken herself, he'd like to say and—as Alice would be sure to ask—would include a definition of the term, but she remains lethargic. Verbal give-and-take has become one of their pastimes and again he worries that she might be sick.

Parking in front of the Hampton bank where Paige is having a job interview, Glen removes Alice from the seat belt and presses his cheek to her forehead. She doesn't feel warm and he is reassured when he asks again if she feels okay and she mumbles, "Dunno."

"Dunno?" He'd like to tease her into saying more, but knows she isn't in the mood, so he cradles her and watches the rain-swept entrance to the bank. Paige and her job applications. They both know this has less to do with a wish to return to work than with the threat that her husband—the older man she married a decade ago—might not have a job much longer. It's what they know but have yet to admit.

However slim he knows his chances to be, Glen hasn't given up, and will go to his office later this evening. While Paige and Alice return home to prepare dinner, he'll spend another hour or so on an article on East German privatization he's translating, new work he's found oddly satisfying. They're not going to save his job—he knows it if Paige doesn't—but the translations are worth modest professional credits and a few hundred dollars now and then, and they distract him from the impending disaster.

What he'd really like to do—just now, after hearing sea sounds speak of age and of time passing—is slip away to the library and

browse *Stern* and *Der Spiegel*. Keeping up on events in his field
of study could be considered work of a kind, but the appeal of
the Periodicals Room has long been one of wistfulness and escape.
Mind trips into the past, glances at magazine photographs, really,
on the wild chance he'll see a woman he knew in Germany long
ago and be able to verify that she still exists.

"I think she does have a fever," Paige says when she's in the front
seat and Alice is in her arms. "Do you feel warm, sweetie?"

"I think so," Alice says.

"I'll take her temperature when we get home," Paige says.
"Nursery school's been frantic, with Thanksgiving and building
up to Christmas—she's probably exhausted."

Glen has driven into Portsmouth and across South Bridge to
the campus—its streets and lamplighted walkways deserted even
of parked cars—and pulls up in front of his building. Home is
ten blocks away, back over the bridge, a distance he always walks.
He turns off the motor, then he and Paige exchange key rings
and fix Alice into the passenger seat. "I'll head home by six or
so," he says. "Alice, if you want to go to bed before I get there,
go ahead and I'll see you in the morning. Feeling any better?"

"I think so," Alice seems to say.

"I think she's pooped," Paige says.

"By the way, how was the test?" Glen says. "I nearly forgot."

"Oh, I wouldn't mind working part-time, but having to go
full-time just as Alice is starting kindergarten isn't real exciting.
I hope this tenure stuff doesn't throw us for a loop."

Tenure is a subject they agreed to keep private, and Glen is
surprised. "I thought, you know, we'd agreed when and where
to discuss that," he says.

"Good Lord, Glen, she can't be protected from everything."

Glen doesn't want Alice to see how rankled he is. "I don't
mean to," he says. "It's a little embarrassing, okay?"

"I know what you're talking about," Alice says.

"I'm not surprised," Glen says. "Anyway, it's nothing we need
to make worse than it is."

Glen is outside the car, Paige behind the wheel. "There's one
thing I really *would* like to say," she says through the opened
window. "Don't count on me moving to East Jesus, Texas, or
someplace. I'll tell you right now there's no way I could do that."

Glen is a little shocked. "Let's talk about it another time."

"I'd just like that understood," Paige says.

"Understood—fine. What the hell happened at that bank?"

"Well, maybe I saw the light," Paige says. "I've *been* there, you know. The likelihood of going back to that, *every day*, turns me off." On which word the window is rolling up, and on a wave from within, wife and child are rolling away in the old car.

Glen stands watching the car's red taillights shrink, and there is such surprising hurt and fear in his chest he could almost weep. Everyone has predicted repercussions to the tenure issue, and here they are, right on time.

Still, as he walks to his building—the library is closed, its escape cut off to him—he'd have to admit that his marriage hasn't sailed along without problems. Not only age, but background differences. At times Paige has pointedly regretted marrying a man twenty years her senior, though it wasn't so in the beginning. The twenty-two-year-old bank clerk near the Rutgers campus smiled readily at the forty-two-year-old postdoc when he inquired about opening a NOW account. His father was a lifelong blue-collar auto worker, as Glen was for nine years, until community college night classes led to a teaching assistantship as a graduate student, while Paige's father is yet today an independent business-man with his own real estate agency. No, he'd have to admit, tenure may not be the problem at all.

His semidarkened building has its empty feel. The downstairs departmental offices are closed, and he can tell from the silence that anyone remaining in the building is reading or writing soundlessly behind a closed office door. It's an old building with a three-story wing attached, and his office, on the top floor of the addition, is the size of a jail cell. The desk has drawers on one side only and the conference chair always blocks the door. Still, it's his and he likes the privacy and his books and the hum of his computer, likes—however slight and cheap the furnishings—being a professor.

The room's only window, a bubble on a slanted ceiling, receives light as the sun lifts from the nearby Atlantic. A trapezoid of yellow fire descends the wall above the room's lone bookcase—ersatz wood veneer, like the desk—and slips up the wall and out again before midday, returning the room to shadows. Shadows at noon, Glen likes to think, as the title of his life. Still, however much he may be in trouble overall, he enjoys closing himself into his small space with his books and papers. "Savors" is the word, even as it evokes another, "loser," which Glen heard a smart-ass young TA use—in reference to his age, he fears—and which he's been unable to eradicate from his mind. In spite of the commitment he brings to teaching, dates of birth are factored into academic achievement, and the remark stabbed, he knows, with its degree of truth.

At an age by which most who try are tenured or have gone on to other things, Glen is into his sixth year as an untenured assistant professor. Next year it is up or out. As the product of a factory town, he is, as Paige likes to say, a soldier boy who, serving time in Europe, promoted himself from American private to German major. Now, after three decades of catching up, he is tenure-track but probably untenurable. His particular flaw, besides starting so late, is not unusual: articles but no book. A mere two articles at that, pieces on his secret hero, Thomas Mann, extracted from his dissertation. Otherwise, nothing accepted, nothing expected. From the moment he decided, age twenty-four and in his third year at Chevy, to take night classes, he's been swimming—as Paige also likes to say—straight into the oncoming tide of reality.

"To be candid, your trajectory is slight," the dean said to him hardly two weeks ago.

Administrators and their words; they found new ones every year. The meeting was identified as a preliminary discussion of the year's tenure cases, and Glen didn't go to the dean's office prepared to defend anything as ominous as trajectory.

"Why in the world did you take this turn so late in life?" the dean asked. "And taking a doctorate in a field that's been declining for years?"

"Well," Glen said to the younger man who had come to the deanship from public policy. "The truth is, I developed a kind of romantic interest in the literature and I didn't calculate my prospects in quite that way. I was a young man—not that young, it's true. I'd been in the army and was working in a factory in the city where I'd grown up—the same plant where my father had worked. Chevrolet Assembly, Van Slyke Road. Prior to that I'd spent two and a half years in Germany, prior to which, in fact, I'd been a high school dropout. It wasn't the academic part of high school that gave me difficulty, by the way, but life in general.

In the army, I discovered reading and education, and back home, going to work at Chevy, I started taking night classes, which led to courses in German, and before long I was kind of swept away. I began to live for literature and the language lab. It's true I excelled, but I wasn't 'calculating' a career."

The dean was looking at him. "You did go on to graduate school."

"It was offered to me. I ate it up."

"Offered?"

"In a sense, which is a problem I have with what's happening now. The message I'm hearing is that the profession doesn't have room for me, but back then every door was opened and I was invited in. Fellowships, grants, teaching assistantships—I worked hard, it's true, but everything was made available."

"I guess that's a reasonable argument."

"I did excel, and I still do, to my mind. My credentials are as good as most others who've been tenured, here and elsewhere. I love it; all these years it's what I've been compelled to do."

"Nonetheless. What you say is interesting—"

"I worked incredibly hard just to master the language, let alone the literature. The hours I put in, for years, thousands of hours in language labs alone. In a certain accent I'm all but undetectable to natives. That's rare for an American who didn't grow up with native speakers. My trajectory—I really don't believe it's slight, just a little tardy."

"In any case—and I agree, tardy may be what it is—still you see the position we're in. Tenure is an enormous investment for the university. Frankly, and this is off the record, if you were twenty years younger and . . . well, neither race nor gender points are in your favor either, as I'm sure you're aware."

"A couple of things shouldn't be overlooked," Glen felt he had to say, not to be angry with himself afterward. "I'm a proven teacher—I'm a good teacher. And it isn't just tenure for me now. It's sink or swim at my age, as you well know. This is a brutal system."

"Indeed it is. And true, you are a proven teacher; your evaluations are among the highest in the college. And the argument that you were encouraged to commit to the profession, that's also compelling. Still—"

"My translations. I've only been doing them for a year or so but I have five, well, four pieces to my credit—I'll have a fifth before long—and one of them is up for a translation award."

"Translations are fine, they give the university visibility. But as you know, the guidelines make it clear that translations cannot count as publications. The guidelines also state that at least one book is required for tenure, especially for a literature professor."

"A comparable number of articles."

"Two articles a book do not make, I'm afraid. I wish they did, because I like you and I'd like to pull for you."

"I'll say again," Glen says, though he doesn't want to, "I was invited in—not that I minded giving up my seniority at Chevrolet. All the doors were opened to me, and I've served the field well, in all categories. Now, at my age—I also happen to be father to a young child—I'm being shown the door. I'm fifty-two years old, and I'm not sure this is ethical."

"You make a persuasive case," the dean said. "At the same time, the decisions were yours and, of course, it was your decision, without tenure, to have a child."

"My appointment was tenure-track. The future looked okay. And, of course, time was pressing."

A pause seemed to indicate a conclusion to the visit, and feeling he had said what had to be said, Glen got to his feet. Against his better judgment, shaking hands, he heard himself add, "I saw Thomas Mann once. On a sidewalk in Stuttgart, in 1955."

"The author?"

Struck with regret for uttering something he had mentioned but two or three times in his life, Glen felt too distracted to answer.

"You do mean the author?"

"Yes, but it doesn't matter," Glen said. "My commitment is real, that's all. I've been around, and my commitment to the field is real. I do a good job, I work extremely hard."

"I wish your chances were better," the dean said, still moving toward the door. "I'd be misleading you if I said they were. Still, the vote isn't in yet, and until it is . . ."

Glen knew as he left the administration building that the vote was in. Only in rare moments—at daybreak, or in the evening under the influence of glasses of wine—did some mechanism of mind and heart allow him not to know. Tenure would be denied, and fighting it would gain nothing. Articles but no book. If the rejection itself did not destroy him, contesting it could.

Might he nonetheless have tried to make more clear to the dean how, returning from Europe and going to work at Chevy, there came a day when the alternative to language studies would have been to no longer possess meaning in his life? To remain in the factory—on the treadmill of the living dead. To forgo ordinary thinking and dreaming. No, he thinks, he couldn't have told that to the dean, no more than he could have told of the experiences he had coming of age in Germany, experiences with the country and with a married German woman, how they informed and even enticed his own students today. What better reason than lost love to set out on a course of study, and did the dean not understand being seduced by Europe and returning to work in the auto factory where one's father worked and drank and died, where, but for night courses and study, one might simply cease to exist? Did the dean imagine that a person consumed language and literature for purposes of landing a job? What in the world would such a person have to teach?

Sitting at his desk, computer glowing, Glen realizes he has been running through his mind yet again the dilemma which has come to preoccupy both him and Paige. Paige's advice seems sensible to her, unrealistic to him: Take your case to the president. Tell him you have a wife and a child not yet five years old. Return to the dean and invite him to dinner, to lunch, and lay it out again. Hint at a lawsuit.

Such moves won't work, he has told her. Not only would they be blatantly shameful, they would make things worse.

She told him about an acquaintance of her father's who went to the home office, demanding to be heard by the company president, and gained whatever it was he wanted. Glen listened calmly while looking at the floor, and felt that his manhood was being questioned. When she cited the example a second time he lost his temper. "I made my case!" he snapped. "It isn't a fucking sales job," he added, and left the house for a long walk.

Now Paige has declared she will not move. But wasn't she tired when she made the remark, tired and depressed at the prospect of returning to work, even as she has said she looks forward to having another job? Does she have any idea how guilty he feels at the prospect of her having to return to work? Forget what she said, he tells himself. Look ahead. There's this year and your year of grace. Then the telephone rings, startling him.

It's Paige, apologizing. "Being in a bank like that called up the drudgery of it all," she says. "What I remember most about my job is having lunch with my friends."

Glen feels relieved. "I understand. Thanks," he says.

"It's not the only reason I'm calling. Alice's temperature is over a hundred. I called Dr. Beal's and they say he can work her in at the end of office hours, about six-fifteen—"

"I'll take her."

"Could you? Then I could get dinner ready while you're gone."

"No problem. I'll be there in plenty of time, about an hour."

If he got a job in a prep school, at least Alice could get a good education as a faculty kid. Or are languages dying out in prep schools, too? Would he be considered too old? And would Alice be embarrassed having her older father on the faculty? He wouldn't let her, he thinks as he tries to return to the task at hand, article number five. He'd work hard, make her proud, make her laugh at such things. Ironic, he thinks, to find his job threatened just as he could be settling into a life of reading and teaching, of teaching German and French to Alice, too, and telling her funny stories.

Work, he tells himself, and looks down at *"So seien in den ersten neun Monaten des Jahres 1987 ..."* His urge is to get the privatization article in the mail to the New York agent who works with East German publications and intellectuals. Labor to some, translation has been turning into creative work for him—Paige calls it the kraut mentality—and however little they will add to his case, he takes pleasure in seeing his name in print, albeit below the author's, so much so that he limits himself to no more than two or three hours of translating in any one day.

"Is piecework and peace work, you know," the agent, a refugee from East Berlin named Magnus Klein, has remarked on the phone. "You work from my stable—who knows? Ralph Manheim as exclusive Günter Grass translator is earning one of the author's ten points. Is not chicken feed."

Translating is not very different from explaining something

to Alice, Glen has realized, which approach has become his strategy—to generate English of such clarity that even Alice would
have a sense of what is being said. Occasionally he asks for his
four-year-old's response, calls her on the phone not just for the
fun of it but to ask what sense a certain phrase makes to her.
Untangling convoluted German, he thus takes liberties of a kind
which, as it turns out, draw repeated praise from the New York
agent. "You stand up to abstraction!" Magnus Klein says to him.
"You stand up to precious language—this blows my mind!"

Glen checks his watch and sees he has forty minutes left. He trusts
that Alice is fine, that the visit to the pediatrician is the right thing
to do—check throat, nose, eyes, ears—and that the doctor will
prescribe something to kill the bugs. Glen taps along, tries one
phrase and another, then Paige comes to mind and he resolves
not to be bothered by her threat even as her words worry him
faintly still and invoke the awful question. God, what will he do
if—? What will he do *when*? his frightened heart wants to know.
    A phrase he translates, *"deutlich verbessert,"* shifts his thoughts
elsewhere, and in the next moment—in his mind's attic, as his
fingers continue—he is processing again his telling the dean of
seeing Thomas Mann pass on a sidewalk in Stuttgart. Over thirty
years ago: 1955. Did the dean think he was slipping? What if he'd
told him about the time he took Thomas Mann's daughter, Erika,
to dinner in absentia? Was it youthful passion? he wonders. Loneliness? Missing, as he so missed her then, the woman through whom
he had glimpsed that other world?
    Whatever was guiding him, he did it. Living alone, working
second shift at Chevrolet Assembly so he could drive to Ann Arbor
for day classes, he read of a performance in East Lansing in which
Erika Mann was scheduled to appear in *Tea and Sympathy*, and
seeing his idol's daughter took him over. Not seeing the play, but
seeing her—for in his mind it was as if he would be able to call
up something he'd lost and left behind. He ordered a ticket, made
plans to take a sick day from work, and began to fantasize not
only watching Erika Mann perform—he knew nothing of her—
but meeting her, even falling in love with her, as she would prove
to be a variation of Hedy, last seen a couple of years earlier. They'd
walk together and he'd tell Erika Mann of seeing her with her
father in Stuttgart three months before he died. He'd tell of the

married German woman who had introduced him, a teenage GI, to life in that other world and with whom, for the first time in his life, he had had a love affair. Erika Mann would like him and find him young and strong; they'd like each other and would go to dinner and to a hotel, and would meet again, and he'd make her happier than she'd ever been, and would leave Chevrolet Assembly and move with her to . . . What a wonderful dream it was, he thinks.

Erika Mann wasn't so young, as it turned out, was quite a bit older than Hedy, but she was beautiful and he was affected by the lovely character she portrayed in the play. In truth, she took his breath away, and he thought to look for a stage door where he might present himself and launch his dream. But it was a theater-in-the-round within a field house, and when the play ended and the audience stood to applaud, and when Erika Mann was called forward to curtsy within a circle of light and he rose to applaud with the others—his only occasion of infatuation with an actress—the cast dashed away into darkness and the impossibility of what he was doing held him back.

He took her to dinner nonetheless. Dressed in a suit he had had made in Germany, wearing the watch and bloodstone ring given to him by Hedy in Baden-Baden, he drove to a hotel restaurant in Lansing in hopes of seeing her there. His only acquittal, he thinks, gazing over the glowing words on his computer screen, was that he did not order a meal for his imaginary guest, although he did, he recalls, go through two bottles—as a sudden *knuk-knuk* sounds on his office door and his heart jumps beneath his shirt.

He had heard no footsteps, nor can he hear anything now. A ghost could have floated along the darkened hallway and tapped on his door. "Yes?" he calls.

Silence holds, while the hair on the back of his neck remains aloft. Pushing from his chair, he reaches to open the door, expecting—even as he knows he heard a knock—to see nothing.

A figure stands in the darkness, a student he recognizes from his sophomore German lit class.

"Fräulein Owens?" he says.

"You *are* here," she says.

"Not for long," he says, trying to see her face in the shadows. She is his favorite student of the year, a bright young woman and native speaker who has been helpful in class for her expertise in colloquialisms and slang. "You're looking for me?"

"I am, yes," she says.

"Come in. I was sitting here daydreaming and you startled me."

"I'd like to talk to you."

"I do have to leave in just a few minutes. Ecki, right? May I call you Ecki?" He gestures toward the chair.

"Ecki, yes, please," she says. "May I stand?"

"Of course. May I sit?" He does so, smiling, wondering what this young woman is doing here at this hour of this day, acting so strangely.

"I may remove my jacket?" she says.

"Is there some problem? I thought everyone had left town by now. The building's deserted, isn't it?"

She removes her jacket, hangs it over the chair, and her blouse, he sees, is unbuttoned several buttons, revealing—hair on his neck stands for the second time in minutes—the naked V of her chest. His thought is to ask if she isn't cold being so lightly dressed on a damp evening in November. "Please, sit down," he says, as something about her continues to seem confused.

"The problem . . . ," she seems to ask herself as she steps around the chair to sit. "I am *Frau* Owens-Reiff, married but separated. Someone has told me you are often here so late. Not someone exactly. Kathleen Maris, who is also married but separated."

"Hmm," Glen says. Kathleen Maris and the woman before him are older than most of his students; he knew that Kathleen Maris was married and addresses her as such in class, but he didn't know this of the young woman before him.

"We live upstairs and downstairs—are friends, out of class— in Married Student Housing," she says nervously. "We are active in MDC, both, although neither is exactly married, yes?"

"MDC?" he asks, finding it difficult not to pass his eyes over the naked V and shadows of breasts more or less looking him in the face, maybe wishing to see if seeing all the way is possible.

"Mothers of Dependent Children. We're single parents, in college on a wing and a prayer. Kathleen is more active in MDC than I, though she has two children."

"You have children?"

"One. I have more time than she, but she is more active. Actually, we were speaking of you. Often we speak of you."

"You do?"

"We believe—in class—you use a secretive language. A double language. You have in mind added meaning, which regular students are not always comprehending, while we are."

"Well, you and Frau Maris *are* more experienced than regular students."

"We feel this every time. Actually we are both in love with you, you see, and what we talk about at all times is what you are like in bed."

Glen laughs, as the light goes on for him, and he says, "You're here to seduce your old professor!"

She is smiling. "It's true, yes. My mission. I was hoping, I think, you are *not* here. But . . . please help me."

"Gee," Glen says, flushed and smiling. "It's flattering. But I'm a happily married man, you know. What can I say?"

"May I show you—one thing?" she says.

Touching fingers to the lapel of her blouse, she hesitates, and seeing what she is about, Glen is shocked still again.

"I was going to show my breast," she says. "Now my nerve has deserted me."

While he smiles, Glen is flustered with embarrassment, and says, "Probably just as well."

"In the key moment I have lost my nerve," she says. "I suffer disaster."

Glen smiles, feels sympathetic at the same time that he is wondering by now how to contain what is happening.

"Kathleen has said when I am doing this, I should arouse you to passion and win you over. She has said . . . men are always . . ."

Glen laughs, though flushing with added embarrassment.

"She has said, you would want to kiss me here."

Ecki's face appears open. His own remains aflame; he's been attracted to this young woman but isn't prepared for this. "You guys should have better things to do with your time," he tells her.

"I am twenty-seven," she says. "You know this age? I've been lonely for so long. All is going wasted, and my life is such a predictable theme. Goodness, it's your word, how have I forgotten this?"

Glen remains at a loss, swallows.

"I don't want your marriage," Ecki adds. "Nothing like that, believe me. I only want to have love with someone I admire, and who understands. It's what I've never done, although, believe me, I've been with lots of guys. My life—well, Kathleen said if I did not offer I would never know. This is my offering. I want you to come to me, to my place. Tonight. Tomorrow afternoon. Pure love is my offer. My son is with his father for Thanksgiving. I am desperately lonely, it's true, and maybe it makes me a little crazy like this. But women may ask today, isn't it so?"

"It may be so, but this could get me canned in a second," Glen says.

"That's not going to happen," she says. "Not with me."

Glen keeps to her eyes, keeps himself from looking for the fulfilling nipple. "I'd like—of course I find you attractive," he says. "But I love my wife. And I've never been unfaithful. I'm a little on the old side, too. Where were you when *I* was young and lonely? There have been times in my life, believe me. Well, I'll tell you something true. You can't simply go to bed, make love, and get up and go on your way. Feelings always come in, don't they? Anyway, I'm flattered. I've always liked you in class, I've liked you a lot, but I'll have to decline."

"May I tell you what I know to be true," she says. "You *shall* be unfaithful to your wife; it is a given fact. Why not with someone who likes you as I do? You will go to a convention, you know, and to a hotel room with stale cigarette smoke and filthy carpeting. You will have too much to drink and will not even *like* this woman. Nor will she like you; she may, in fact, be disliking you. Thinking back, then, you will wish it was this loving person, who knows you in the daytime, with whom you are being unfaithful. Yes? You cannot say I'm wrong."

"That's neatly put," Glen says. "I believe you know what you're talking about. The time comes, I'm sure—well, regret is everyone's demon. Time does come, maybe I'll give you a call. Right now, though, and this is also true, I have to leave. My daughter, who's four, right now her temperature is over a hundred, and I'm taking her to the doctor."

"You must leave in this very moment?"

"I have to," he says.

Standing, reaching for his book bag, he glimpses Ecki standing and holding her blouse together as she lifts her jacket from the back of the chair.

"I may walk with you downstairs?"

"Of course."

"I hope I haven't made you late," she says.

"I'm sure I'll end up waiting, I always do. Ecki—how long have you been in this country? Your accent is wonderful." He has his parka on, book bag in hand; she is zipping her jacket.

"You won't think I am fraudulent?" she says as he turns off the lights and closes his door.

"Fraudulent? You've been excellent in class, from the very beginning. If you're going to say you already knew the literature, I guessed that early on and it doesn't make any difference."

"You do like me," she says. "As I like you. I've sensed this and listen to all you say, and study immensely, as does Kathleen. In this way we know that others but half understand what is said."

Glen smiles. "That's nice to hear."

"You will continue to like me, now that I've embarrassed you? You won't find me foolish?"

"Don't worry about it. I've done some unusual things myself, we all do. I'm pleased that you like my class. Don't say I said so, but I put a lot of myself into it." At the doorway to the stairwell, he holds the door open for her.

"You will change your mind and come to me later?"

Glen laughs. "I'd love to, but I'm afraid I have problems of my own."

"Life is like a bad film sometimes, isn't it?" she says.

"One that flops at the box office," he says. "But this is something, well, I'll remember this someday when I'm down and out."

"Now I am embarrassed," she says, as they descend the semi-darkened stairway.

"Don't be, maybe I shouldn't have said that." At the first floor, he adds, "How old is your son?"

"Robert is soon to be six."

"He's gone and you're alone at Thanksgiving?"

"Yes."

"Kathleen's out of town?"

"Has gone to London, Ontario."

"I have just one child, too," he says.

"I know," she says. "Your wife is a housewife."

They step into moist and dark November air at the rear of the building. "I'm going to South Bridge," Glen says, indicating the lamplighted footpath.

"May I walk with you to College Road?" she says.

It's okay, he thinks. At College Road, he'll turn toward the bridge that leads to the city's residential district, away from the restaurants and shops downtown.

"I am born in Berlin," she says. "Nor is Owens my surname, but the name of my husband. My name at birth is Karin Reiff, while I am known always as Ecki."

"Your English, your American, it's remarkably good."

"Oh, English is my best subject always in school. In Berlin, growing up, I fraternized also with American soldiers, it's true. I married an American officer, you see, Lieutenant Owens. Six years ago, but it seems now to be forever. In this country then I watch television every day with my parents-in-law, in Harrisburg, PA. They are retired, and life is altogether miserable for me there. Because of having no money we live with his parents, who are suspicious and watch both me and television all day. So it is not American English but soap opera English which is my language. Perhaps a soap opera heart, too—is this what you now think, *Doktor Professor?*"

Glen laughs. "I don't know. I never see daytime soaps."

They walk for a while in silence. The campus appears entirely deserted. "I love it when it's like this," Glen then says. "When everyone's away. Pressure's lifted. Thanksgiving has always been my favorite holiday—fall weather—and none of the baggage that you have at Christmas. I love it."

"I see this," she says. "It is lonely for some, though, and for some there is the baggage of the turkey, yes?"

The lampposts are far enough apart that they pass through spots of full darkness under great, fragrant pine trees. Across the river, amber-lighted houses beckon with their warmth in the damp autumn darkness.

"You will not dislike me in the morning?" she says.

In a moment Glen says, "You sound like you're going to feel bad. Please don't. There's no way I'd dislike you, so don't even think about it. You're a wonderfully bright person, and, believe me, there's no way in the world I'd ever do anything but like you."

Approaching College Road, where their paths will diverge, they follow a macadam path under more great black-green trees and pass beside another brick building.

"Will you grant me one small favor?" she says.

"Probably."

"Kiss me, please—so I will not feel like a total fool?"

It would be a mistake to kiss her, and could be a mistake not to, he thinks. "I feel like a friend," he says, "but not that much of a friend."

"Please. This is so hard."

"One friendly kiss," he says.

They pause, and her tongue touches his lips and he goes ahead and kisses her. The faint taste takes him back in a rush to Baden-Baden, to Hedy, and he thinks how German it is, her approach.

"Some kiss, Frau Owens—Fräulein Ecki," he says, as her eyes glisten in the dark before him.

"I am passionate, and have no interest in frivolous young men," she says.

Glen waits, then says, "I do have to hurry. You take care. I'll see you on Monday."

"You are positive?"

"Good night now, Ecki. See you in class."

As he crosses the street, walking away, a car's headlights appear to dim as it passes to the right, and he wonders if some security guard just saw two people exchange a kiss.

The adjacent residential streets are dark and quiet. Warm light reaches from living room windows across lawns, through webs of branches, and down over South Pond. He wishes for snow, imagines the wonder of its silent beginning adding silence to this favorite evening and favorite weekend of the year, cushioning, for a day or so, the weight of rejection with which he's been trying to live.

Wow, he allows at last. He's heard of such things, and an occasional young student has made suggestive remarks, but no one has ever been bold in the style of Ecki Owens-Reiff. Or so tempting, he thinks. *Ecki aus Berlin.*

Why him? he wonders as he walks along. A married father, an assistant professor whose influence reaches about as far as his students' grades. Or did she in fact like him for the literature he teaches, and for his experience and understanding?

So maybe he's not *that* much on the downhill side of things. His confidence has been taking a beating recently, he'd have to admit. And his vulnerability is taking him by surprise. He'd always believed he was much tougher than he's turning out to be. At the same time his rejection is explainable, is the work of a handful of self-interested persons, and there was a time not long ago when he knew himself to be confident, aggressive, imaginative. He has a quick smile still and something of a wit, at least in the classroom, he thinks, starting down the far side of South Bridge, as car lights flash from behind and he angles to the side of the road.

The car pulls over, though, slowing beside him, and when the window rolls down, Ecki is there, and something turns within Glen Cady, as if within an old movie. Her face, her glistening eyes, a new smile, the memory of her soft lips. "Thought I'd give you a lift," she says. "So you won't be late."

As he enters the car, Glen knows with rising hunger that everything is different now. "Right down here," he says. "South Pond Road, then you take a right."

Driving on, Ecki says, "I enjoyed kissing you."

He doesn't respond at once, which he knows to be a new response. "You took me back," he says.

She makes the turn onto the darker side street.

"Next left," he says.

"I know where you live," she says.

Nor does he respond to this, even as he knows he is lost to her now. Thirty yards from his house, before a dark vacant lot, she pulls over, stops, and turns off lights and motor.

Glancing her way, there is the glistening reflection of her eyes. As she moves toward him and he takes her, receives her, and kisses her as she kisses him, he lets himself go and kisses cheek, chin, throat, wants to ask her to do what she was going to do in his office. There is her warmth, a smell of broth, the salty taste of her, her pressing and offering, and a flutter of laughter from her as she swoons and sighs, crying into his hair.

"Come to me tonight," she says. "You must come to me!"

"I don't know—God, I don't know."

"You must, please. Telephone me—say you will come to me."

"I'll call, I will."

"As soon as you come from the doctor, please."

"I'll try. I'll do what I can. I'll try. I want to."

"Tell me this, yes, you want to, please."

"You have no idea," he says. "I've always wanted to, all my life. Where were you?"

"I'm in the telephone book," she says as he opens the door. "I'm in the telephone book, and you will call?"

Nodding, book bag in hand, he backs out of the car and closes the door. As he moves away in the dark, the engine starts behind him. In a moment the car rolls past, and only then do the red taillights come on and reflect through the misted air.

2

"Alice Cady," Glen says into the waiting room window, removing Alice's corduroy hat and stuffing it in his pocket.

After this, after dinner, will he telephone Ecki Owens-Reiff? Will he go to her, a student, and devour her, as he wants to? On what pretext, what explanation to himself?

He's never cheated. Doesn't he love Paige? There's no doubt he loves the child in his arms. They'll have but one child—Paige's disinclination has settled the question—and he's been discovering hopes for Quiet Alice, and for himself, that keep expanding. Helping Alice grow is his future.

Adultery is terrifying and exciting, he thinks, and these feelings of desire are part of it. Isn't Ecki right in saying it will happen someday? Infidelity. For the millionth time in his life, he thinks of that first night with Hedy in Baden-Baden so long ago.

Some things refuse ever to go away, and though he'd been an inexperienced teenager at the time, that first night lingers as both a wonder and regret of his life. Hedy was slighter than Ecki and even more attractive. Through a moist summer night they wound along a path to her hillside home from a brookside cafe in the forest. They kissed, wandered on, kissed again; high on Rhine wine, they wandered and stopped to kiss again. A married woman, a beautiful young mother, she whispered, did he want to do this? she'd like him to do that, did he want to do this to her? to which he replied with added kisses and crazed hands because he did not know she was making love to him with words, did not know how to make love with words in turn, part of a failure of the night which has taxed him always—yet again now—with regret.

Oh, Alice, he thinks on a charge of guilt. If only—he'll allow himself the thought but once—if only his precious child were not so sick.

"Alice," a nurse announces from an opened door.

Glen carries her along an interior carpeted hallway and, as directed by the nurse, into an examination room. He settles her into a sitting position on the stainless steel table, holding her all the while with one hand as he works with the other to remove her padded snowsuit. Her face is flushed, her eyes glassy.

As he holds Alice's arms, the nurse takes her temperature with a digital device, which reading Glen doesn't manage to see. After pressing two fingers under each side of Alice's chin, the nurse leaves the room.

White-haired Dr. Beal enters moments later, nods but doesn't speak or make eye contact as he positions his stethoscope and listens to Alice's small bare chest—bony, flat, no larger than a sheet of paper—and feels her neck, thumbs her eyebrows back to gaze into her eyes. Another instrument in hand, he tells her to look at a rabbit decal on the wall as he aims a beam of light into her liquidy pupils, then—"Open wide"—studies her throat and, stepping back with another instrument, cradling her head of curls in one hand, leans close to explore inside her ear.

Standing upright, placing the ear instrument on a cabinet, wiping his hands on a paper towel, he says, "We've got a sick little girl here, I'm afraid. I'm going to admit her to the hospital, for a while, a day or two."

Standing beside Alice as the doctor steps back to take a throat culture, Glen, surprised, says nothing. Depositing the swab into a glass cylinder held by the nurse, the doctor looks at him. "One night," he says. "Maybe two or three."

"The hospital?" Glen says.

"Yes," Dr. Beal says.

"It's that serious?"

"She's going to be fine, but I think she has some pneumonia, probably a throat infection. Her temperature is at a hundred and two. Were you objecting?"

"Oh, no."

"I'll give her something to bring that temperature down, and we'll start working to knock out the infection. In the hospital she'll be watched closely and I'm there a lot—I'll keep an eye on things."

"Okay," Glen says.

"Believe me, this is a very sick little girl."

"You want me to take her over right now?" Glen says, to let him know, in case he thinks otherwise, that he's also on Alice's side.

"Yes, take her right up to the children's ward on three, tell the floor nurse to admit her, and say I'll be over in a while. We'll give her something strong to see if we can turn this around."

"Shots?" Glen says, knowing at once that the word has to be alarming to Alice.

"Hmm." The doctor nods, wiping his hands again.

"Daddy, what?" Alice gets out.

"Well, you're going to have a bed in the hospital," Glen says as the doctor and nurse leave the room. "One of those mechanical beds that go up and down at the push of a button."

Refixing her undershirt, he adds, "Don't worry, sweetheart, everything's going to be fine. The doctor wants you in the hospital where he can look after you, to make sure you get better in a hurry. But I'll be with you, understand, little bugaboo?"

"Shots?" Alice says, to return to the point of things.

"I shouldn't have said that," Glen says. "Still, we're going to do whatever we have to. So you'll get better. Besides—you're a tough kid, aren't you? You need shots, you'll take all they have and ask for more, won't you. They say four, you'll say make it five, my name's Alice Cady and what do you think I am, some kind of wimp?"

Her liquidy eyes blink and she gives little response. Carrying her from the waiting room, pulling her hat back on her head, he whispers, "I'll be with you all the way, so don't worry," and takes her into the chilled night air and along a brief roadway to the hospital's emergency room entrance, a hundred yards away. Her face is close upon his neck and he holds a hand to her cheek and forehead as he carries her. She is his, he thinks. This small shy creature with strawberry blond curls who is quiet and reserved outside the house, and who talks to him within, listens to him, who reads books and stories, laughs at even his foolish jokes, and telephones him in the office merely to say hello, over which exchanges he will catch himself smiling thirty minutes later with happiness he had not known existed. He had no brothers or sisters, had no childhood girlfriends, and nothing has prepared him for the surprise of being father to a daughter. A father now carrying his daughter into an antiseptic-smelling, beige-tiled emergency room, where a nurse moves to intercept him.

"She's a regular admission," Glen says without stopping. "Dr. Beal's admitting her—he'll be over in a few minutes. I used this entrance because it's closest."

"Where's Dr. Beal now?" the nurse says. "Just a minute, sir. If that child is an emergency room admittee—"

"She's not, and he'll be right over."

"Sir, you can have a seat if you like. We'll have to have confirmation from Dr. Beal before—"

"I know what I'm doing," Glen says, going around a corner.

"Sir!"

Glen ignores her, continuing into the hospital where Alice was born and which he knows from previous visits. At a set of elevator doors, he asks a passing nurse, "Children's ward?" and she says, "Three." As the doors open, he enters with Alice on his chest and knuckles 3. "No need to worry, *kleines Liebchen*," he whispers. "Everything's going to be fine."

Then Alice is gone and Glen is standing at the nurse's station, where he asks to use the counter telephone.

"There's a phone in her room," the nurse tells him.

"I don't want to disturb her right now," he says.

The nurse makes an expression granting reluctant permission, and he dials his home number. Ecki's number, it occurs to him, would be in the telephone book on the counter. After he has explained to Paige the severity of Alice's condition, she wants him to come and get her, but they finally agree he can't risk missing Dr. Beal and that he'll pick her up afterward, when they both might return to the hospital. "I don't think there's any pressing worry," he says. "The doctor says she's going to be fine."

Alice is asleep in the only bed in the pea-green room. It is past eight and Dr. Beal has yet to appear, although he called the nurse's station and Alice has been given two shots by a tall nurse, the second to the side of her tiny seat, and Glen has called Paige from the phone in the room to say he's still waiting.

He holds the railing, watching as Alice lies in feverish sleep.

With the backs of his fingers he feels her hot forehead. Just then her lips part to take in air, a belated catch, nothing more. Awakening with her temperature reversed—in the morning, perhaps—she will be clearheaded and will recognize him at once, he thinks, as he stands before her.

His offshoot, he thinks. With whom his record is good. No offenses. When she awakens, he wants her to know the security of seeing him there. For he wants above all else to be a good father, and decides, no, he won't make any calls tonight based on old regrets and half-fulfilled desires.

At a minute before nine, Dr. Beal turns into the room. From the other side of the bed he reexamines Alice—her hospital johnny all askew—listens to her bony chest and under each arm, checks her pulse at her ankle. Her eyelids move feverishly as her limbs are moved about, but she doesn't appear to entirely awaken. They share the task then of returning her garment to her small shoulders and legs, repairing her dignity.

The doctor gazes at the child lying between them and says, "I think she'll be fine." Stuffing his stethoscope into his suitcoat pocket, he adds, "She's one of my favorite patients and I've never seen her as under the weather as she was in my office."

"Thanks for seeing her like you did," Glen says, surprised at the man's declaration.

The doctor continues gazing down at her. "You're lucky to have such a healthy, wonderful child," he says. "This little girl is remarkably intelligent."

"You think so?"

"Oh, I know so."

"You have children?" Glen says.

"A son and a daughter," he says. "Both grown now and gone."

"Well, thank you," Glen says. "Thanks for these long hours."

He nods, though only after a grudging pause, and Glen knows all at once that the doctor had disapproved of him as Alice's father, perhaps because of his age.

"I'll see her first thing in the morning," Dr. Beal says, moving toward the door. "You'll probably be asked to leave before long, when the night nurse comes on. Don't worry. They'll call me if anything comes up."

Glen has no intention of leaving, but doesn't say so as they exchange good nights. Gazing at Alice then, he wonders if something just happened. Had the doctor, realizing how much he cared for his daughter, perhaps *because* of his age, admitted him to some inner circle?

As before, he touches Alice's forehead and smooth cheek with the backs of his fingers. She's still warm, but not as hot as she was before, and standing over her, Glen recalls an incident at her birth that still amazes him. Her obstetrician, a burly and somber German immigrant, had all but growled whenever Glen joined Paige on prenatal visits. Doctor or not, and however gently he treated the ballooning mother, the side of himself he presented to Glen was more that of a rattlesnake. His manner hadn't changed when Paige's time came and Glen put in the call and drove her to the hospital. But then Alice came forth with frosted hair on her egg-shaped cranium, and a peaceful expression on her face. Birth without trauma by a kraut perfectionist. What surprised Glen, though, was looking up to see the burly doctor in surgical garb, tears of inexplicable joy in his eyes as he cried, "Is a girl! You are fasser to a girl! Oh, thanks be to God!" so smitten with joy that he raised tears in Glen's eyes, too.

"She was okay when you left?" Paige asks for the second time as Glen eats reheated chicken-fried rice at the kitchen table.

"I'm sure she's still sound asleep."

"What if I called the nurse's station?"

"We'll be there in twenty minutes."

"Anything can happen in twenty minutes."

"Go ahead and call. I'm sure they deal with hysterical parents all the time."

"You should talk," Paige says, then calls—ten feet away at the kitchen desk—and learns that Alice is asleep, that the nurse answering had looked in on her just minutes ago. Returning to the table, she says, "They couldn't have been nicer."

"She'll probably sleep till noon, she's so full of drugs."

"I'm sorry I said what I said about the bank," Paige says then, and Glen knows without looking at her that she's in a tender mood.

"Thank you, dear," he says.

"It's what I really want to do—have a job."

Glen looks at Paige with bemused affection, and she catches his glance. "You think I'm crazy, don't you?" she says.

"Not at all." He considers raising the subject of her also taking courses toward her B.A., but the added subject of tuition remission for a faculty spouse is too close to the tenure question, and he leaves it be.

"Anyway, I'm sorry," Paige says, then adds, "So please stop looking at me!"

They laugh. He could tell her that he finds her switching from one strong feeling to another endearing, and would mention, if he could, that a student came on to him at school and has him excited. "I probably shouldn't mention this," he says. "I've been thinking what fun it would be if I got tenure and we could spend a sabbatical year in Europe, or on a Fulbright, maybe do a year at a German university."

"No," she says, "I guess you shouldn't mention it."

"You'd have a chance to see Europe."

"You're dreaming, Glen. Besides, I'm not sure I'd like to stay someplace like that for a whole year."

After dinner, they both return to the hospital, Paige to visit and Glen to spend the night. She will spell him in the morning, and see Alice through the strangeness of waking in the strange bed and room.

Perhaps an hour after Paige has left, Glen hears Alice's small voice utter, "Daddy," and moves to the bed railing to see her liquidy eyes opened just enough to see him. "Potty," she seems to say.

Lowering the railing, he says, "Number one or number two?"

"Number one."

He slides both hands under her to pick her up, finds her hot where she is partially naked in his hands, and there is a warm child smell about her as he lifts her to him. Carrying her through the open door to the toilet in an attached room, he positions her on the seat and helps clear her johnny so its tails are in her lap. As she squirts into the water he holds the small apple of her shoulder, and as she finishes he unrolls toilet paper and places petaled wads in her hand for her to use as she will.

With Alice resettled in bed, he leans over the railing and looks into her eyes. "Want me to tell you about Blackie?" he says, wanting to tell his dog story to himself as much as to his daughter. There is no reply, rather her eyes have already begun to drift, and he caresses her silken hair.

———

At four a.m., another nurse comes into the room to take Alice's vital signs. Glen awakens, but as he gets up from the vinyl chair he can see that Alice, though a thermometer is placed under her tongue and her wrist is lifted, will remain undisturbed. "Ninety-nine plus," the nurse whispers as she slips away.

At the railing, Glen gazes again upon the snoozing sprawl. He sees how deeply Alice is sleeping, feels her cheeks with the back of his hand, and touches her cooler temple. Alice will outlive him after all, while in an earlier era she might have been feverishly clinging to life one breath after another.

At the room's window he blinks his wired eyes. The first sign of breaking day is on the horizon, and he recalls that it's Thanksgiving. The view is to the northeast—from the third floor, like his office—where he glimpses a ribbon of cream above the Atlantic, promising clouds and maybe chilly sunlight. Hungry and thirsty, he decides to rinse his face and slip downstairs in search of coffee, to begin his way, after this night on the town, back to reality.

In the first-floor lobby, a woman at the switchboard tells him the cafeteria doesn't open until seven "and the machine coffee's foul." Along the road to the right, she says, there's a Dunkin' Donuts open twenty-four hours, and outside the overheated hospital Glen sets out walking. He appreciates the bite in the New England air and the massive body of nearby cold water, while his thoughts slip back to tenure and survival.

How is it, he wonders as he pushes along the shoulder, that he who has worked so hard and long is coming up a loser? Does everyone lose sometimes, or is this simply the politics of the times? It hurts almost too much to think that he may be told now, at age fifty-two, to empty his desk, that he no longer qualifies. What is he to do? He has no prospects at all.

The coffee is fresh in any case, and the cinnamon roll he chooses is still warm. He has Alice, he sees as he gazes away, and he could have missed this time with her. He could have missed what she's been telling him, of what it is at last that one lives on.

He sits and stares and then decides to carry two rolls back with him, one for Alice when she awakens and one for Paige when she returns to take over. His quiet daughter, he thinks. She's been telling him things every day and he hasn't been listening.

2

BADEN-BADEN

Summer 1953

3

On a summer day in the French Zone, strolling a sun-dappled path around the Baden-Baden casino, he nearly bumps into an elaborate baby carriage. "Sorry," he says, glancing at the young woman—the mother, he assumes—guiding the carriage along the path. She gives no reply, though she seemed to nod. Glen is not yet eighteen and he glances over his shoulder as the woman pushes her Daimler-Benz of a baby carriage down the semi-shaded path.

Free from duty, as on any Saturday afternoon, he has taken a train to anywhere, selecting the French Zone—from a motor pool wall map—to be away from other soldiers back in the American Zone. In stripeless summer khakis and khaki cap he wanders the narrow city streets adjacent to the casino and Kurhaus. There are sidewalk cafes here, too, as in the garden park, and aromas of tobacco, perhaps of cognac, of fresh baked goods and steamed wurst, of geraniums in flower boxes and banks of red and yellow tulips bordering walkways, perhaps even of the old cobblestone streets. He strolls along looking in windows, listening to a language far less guttural than he'd heard in movie theaters at home—of a mind, as a soldier in the occupation, to be a good visitor.

At a wooden bridge over a shallow stream at the edge of town, he pauses to watch shadows of trout play over the sandy bottom and the less visible spotted trout themselves, holding in the cold water, repositioning and holding. Fish twelve, fifteen inches long. He thinks how he'd like to tell someone about the precious trout and the stream clean enough to swim in on this warm summer day—telling someone is an impulse born of being alone and being in a foreign country—and how he'd like to stroke over the bottom with his eyes open and go for trout bare-handed, surface and turn and backstroke to another town downstream in the Black Forest.

It has the feel of paradise, and across the bridge he follows a dirt path and meanders streamside into a forest of great pines. There are few people here by the trees, then none at all, as he continues along the path. The trees reach beyond two hundred feet and block the sunlight but for cathedral-like shafts, while the forest floor is as cool as night and scented with pine needles. Birds chirp and move elsewhere. Chipmunks and squirrels and other animals scurry from tree to tree, and he imagines the creatures' forebears having had roles in Grimm's fairy tales.

In a forest clearing, he discovers logs stacked artfully and carefully branded. Like other things he has seen so far in Germany, this contradicts what he expected to find in a country only recently ravaged by war: items of quality and mystifying beauty that are both seductive and intimidating. And while most West Germans he sees on trips off post go about their business as if the soldiers did not exist, others have been helpful, some even humorous, and a few, as a courtesy, have volunteered to speak English. Growing up in a large factory city, he never imagined himself to be naive, yet much of what he sees is surprising and keeps teaching him that what he assumed he knew of the world he hadn't known at all.

From the forest, walking on a paved country road, he crosses another bridge and turns in a direction he believes will lead to Baden-Baden and the train station for which his round-trip ticket applies. The road is barely used—an occasional VW or Mercedes diesel rattles by, once a bus—and soon he enters a small town. The dusty town square is deserted; then an elderly woman in black crosses on a bicycle, and he sees two elderly men on a side street. The town is simple in contrast to Baden-Baden, and its dry barnyard smells say it is a farm village.

In the middle of the square is a war memorial, two infantry soldiers in glossy, forest-green bronze, as deeply green as the baby carriage he saw earlier. One soldier wears a helmet, the other holds his helmet in hand. The two gaze in the way of statues, but as he looks at the cutaway holes which are their eyes, they appear alive after all, and the feeling that moves through him is unlike any he has known in the presence of a statue or painting. Did one of the two just move to gain his attention? He thinks to startle them by banging a toe or giving a military command.

For a moment there is no other sound or presence under the motionless blue sky, and he senses three soldiers standing together, one young and alive and two if not dead then removed from the world of the living. Feeling for them, reading the plaque, he's surprised to see that it's a World War I memorial:

FÜR
Deutschland's Freiheit
Starben
212 Söhne Lichtentals
Den Helden Tod
Im Weltkriege
1914–1918

For Germany's freedom, he wonders, when Germany was the aggressor? Two hundred and twelve sons of Lichtental. The number is astonishing—all the sons, all the men, he'd guess— and would the town's nearness to France and the front account for such a loss? Is life here so cheap? Couldn't have been, he thinks, for he has never seen life treated as carefully as in postwar Germany. Where he grew up, parts of the city were resigned to hanging doors and broken windows—for newly arrived auto workers, his father once among them—and even if there existed a regard for life, the care with which the Germans looked after themselves was not lost on the occupying soldiers.

Would the added numbers of World War II be too embarrassing to include in the town's memorial? And what of the slaughter of the Jews?—the question every occupying soldier seems to face in the first weeks here. How, he wonders, looking to the statue's eyes, how could these people have done that? These people who treated life so preciously and were so educated and accomplished? How, in all of history, could they have done what they did? In odd reply a town bell begins tolling the three-quarter hour, and while he turns away, the enigma of life and death and slaughter hangs in the air.

———

In Baden-Baden the attractive mother is sitting on a bench in the shade in the garden park, her hand on the carriage handle. More than pretty, she appears beautiful, eyes angled into the carriage; then she glances up, and here in the French Zone and against all warnings, he speaks. "Hi, hello," he says.

She looks at him without noticeable expression.

He stops there opposite her; it's the most spontaneous thing he has ever done. "Sorry I bumped into you. Earlier."

She doesn't respond, but perhaps she does; the faintest of smiles is in her eyes. "No harm," she says.

"You speak English," he says. "I guess I didn't think of that."

The woman makes an expression, as if to say that speaking English is not so unusual. She says nothing more, however, and more than looking at him seems to be keeping an eye on him.

"Well," he says, feeling he should move along. "I just wanted to say something. Your carriage, it's nice-looking."

"Forgive me?" she says, her words and faint smile holding him in place. "My baby is not so nice-looking?"

Glen needs a second to see that she is being clever, and another to say, "What baby?"

She laughs. His little joke came out okay and her laughter is gratifying; at last he is speaking to someone, to a German, and the experience is exciting.

"Have I been rude?" she says, surprising him. "I have not meant to be. It is quite forbidden, you see, to speak to a stranger, certainly to a soldier. You have surprised me. Not forbidden exactly—taboo."

He stands there, aware that, yes, it is taboo and altogether satisfying to speak to an attractive German woman, one with green eyes, a faint smile, a quick sense of humor. "Can I look?" he says, nodding toward the glossy carriage.

"I think you may," she says, smiling as before.

He takes a step and extends his neck. The baby, dressed in white and surrounded by eyelet white cotton, lies on its belly, head on its side, eyes closed in restful sleep; a wisp of hair is on its head. "A girl?"

"Very good, yes, a girl. Why have you said this? Do you know that everyone, the men, they always say 'A boy?' Women, too, I think. How is it that you say a girl?"

"Well, I think it—she looks like a girl," he says, realizing that this woman might be as receptive to casual conversation on this quiet afternoon as he is. "She's really pretty. Has pretty hair."

"Pretty hair. Yes, thank you. She has pretty hair, it's true."

"It's nice to talk to someone," he tells her. "I've been walking around—I came on the train—and haven't said a word all day."

"Yes. It's forbidden in Germany, is most scandalous that I am speaking to you."

"I'm not causing a problem?"

"It is less a scandal, speaking here to an American. In the American Zone it is forbidden, among certain classes, while some young girls, I think, defy this taboo."

"It is different, here in the French Zone," he says, even as he fears she has been mocking him. "I thought I'd take a train ride and get away from all the troops. In Stuttgart, where I'm stationed, near Stuttgart, in Böblingen."

"This is a town?"

He tries for better pronunciation. "Buurb-lean-genn," he says. "Everyone calls it Bubblegum."

"Ah, *Böblingen!*" she says. "Yes, in the vicinity of Stuttgart. But bubblegum, this is—?"

"Ah, chewing gum, the kind that . . . bubbles."

"*Kowgummi!*" she exclaims, and laughs. "This town the soldiers call *Kowgummi!*"

"Bubblegum."

"Chewed in the manner of cows, yes."

He laughs with pleasure, laughs more than he thinks he should. Then, as if to explain, he says, "A while ago I caught myself nearly talking to the fish in the river."

People strolling by stare at them, even hesitate as if to eavesdrop, and a middle-aged couple actually stop and turn to watch from twenty feet and do not proceed until he stares in turn. "I see what you mean," he says.

"It is rude, but is not, I think, so uncommon in Germany. It is okay—no harm is done to me, I assure you."

"Something could happen?"

"Nothing, no. It is—what?—indiscreet, a concern for appearances? It isn't proper, you see. If we are acquainted, it is acceptable. Nor is it so much that you are a soldier in the occupation and I a German citizen. No, it is that you are a stranger and have not been properly introduced. What is clever is to act as if we have known each other many years. At university. Columbia University, in Morningside Heights, yes!"

Glen nods and smiles, though it's the first he's heard of the location of Columbia University. "You won't get in trouble?"

"Trouble? No. This town is more of strangers than neighbors. Many visitors. Still, they are of a certain class and come for the mineral water, and health. Some stay a long time—Russian, Swiss, English, not so many French. No Americans come here, I think. The taboo is more to do with class than soldiers, is a taboo which is within a person and defies logical examination."

Again she is being clever, and her slight smile has him wondering if he's being teased. He tries for cleverness in turn. "Would it be daring if I bought you coffee or something? There are all those tables. If we sat there and talked?"

She hesitates. "A wonderful idea," she says then. "Of course, it is the best strategy. You will see, if we are sitting at a table in this way, we shall no longer be stared upon as if breaking the law. Yes, we may sit for a drink if you like."

Astonished, he merely nods.

"We shall walk there as if friends for a long time, from university, or family business in America. Yes, a good strategy. If only— it is my concern—if only *kleine* Ilsedore is not wishing also to be heard."

They follow the path leading to the outdoor tables closer to the casino, and an unfamiliar self-consciousness comes up in Glen. He asks questions: How old is your baby? How do you spell Ilsedore? Do you live in this city? How long have you lived here? Questions he withholds have to do with her husband, and he sneaks a glance as they leave the path, and remarks to himself once again how striking and sophisticated this woman is, and older than him, for sure. Well, it's just a friendly way to pass some time. How could it be anything else? And thinking it might be funny, he says, "I could push the carriage; that would fool them all."

Her laughter is genuine and he feels more confident in her presence.

"Would I then be eligible for American aid?" she says.

Glen laughs, and keeps smiling as they move over crushed rock to take a table under the trees. As she positions the carriage to one side of the table, he removes his cap and pauses before sitting in a chair opposite her.

"Enjoyable," she says, looking toward him. "And, you see, we are now ignored."

The colonnaded casino is fifty yards away, surrounded by banks of flowers, and the hardwood trees above them—perhaps sycamore—deflect the sunlight and create shadows which move now and then with the breeze.

"A nice day," he says. "Not too hot, not too cold."

She is smiling, surrounded by soft voices, tinklings of glass, a violin in the summer air, touches of laughter, and puffs of smoke. "It's enjoyable to have conversation," she says. "As with a friend."

He unbuttons one of his shirt pockets to remove his Camels and matches. "Mind if I smoke?"

"Of course not—may I also?"

"Oh, sure, yes, sorry."

They discuss American cigarettes—as highly regarded as French brandy or perfume—until a waiter appears. In a different voice, she takes charge of the transaction, orders, and the waiter bows faintly as he withdraws. To Glen she says, "You are providing the American cigarettes, I shall provide some German wine."

Glen has barely tasted wine in his life, but there are her soft green eyes and smile. She leans his way and he strikes a match to light her cigarette, glimpses her hair, her tanned wrist and fingers, lights his own from the same match. He doesn't know about women or love, but realizes that something is happening.

She looks up, smiling; there are her lips and her even white teeth. "When we are friends from university," she says, "it is likely we know each other's names."

"Ah, Glen Cady," he says.

"Yes, Glen Cady. I am Hedy Andreas. I am at home in Baden-Baden not yet two years. I shall call you Glen, yes, while you shall call me Hedy—this is acceptable, in the American style? May I ask how old you are, to be in the United States Army?"

"Ah, twenty," he says, an age which seems mature to him, and three years older than his own. "I won't ask your age. It would be indiscreet."

She smiles. "Well, I am not so old, in a larger consideration— it is not so old to be in one's twenties," she says. "And *kleine*

Ilsedore," she adds, "as a lady, you are allowing your age to be known to Mr. Glen Cady?" The woman named Hedy reaches a hand into the carriage. "She has awakened," she says, looking at Glen. "And discretion be damned," she adds, "Ilsedore will have it known she is presently seven months, fourteen days."

"What does—where's her father?"

"Yes, while we are casting aside discretion, it is okay. My husband, he is in, do you know Firenze, Flor-ence it is called, in Italia? Flor-ence?"

Glen nods. "Yes. In Italy."

"He is here a broadcaster—you know this? For radio, in the sport of English football, soccer, yes, to Americans. He will be heard from the radio tomorrow presenting a contest between Germany and Italy. Do you understand?"

"Yes, a sportscaster," Glen says.

"Yes, it is so, a sportscaster."

"That's a big deal in the States," Glen says. "Can be."

She smiles, perhaps amused again. "Yes, he is well established, my husband—is older. I may say this, in our spirit of indiscretion? I think so. May I say that I enjoy speaking with a young American soldier who is so able to smile."

"I'm not *that* young," Glen says, trying to please her.

"This is enjoyable, and I would not offend you. You are youthful and not so always serious. Twenty is *not* so young, I agree, it is very old." She smiles again. "I am teasing, of course. You are so indulgent of my teasing, forgive me if I cannot help myself." She seems so clearly to be enjoying herself that Glen cannot help smiling in turn.

"Your husband—he's how old?" he dares to say.

She laughs. "Now that is most indiscreet," she says. "You are both discreet and indiscreet. My husband, well, he is many years already a professional person," she adds, smiling and looking again toward the carriage. "Forty-six years, what do you make of that?" she says. "It is terribly old?"

Glen returns her glance and shrugs.

"May I," she says, pointing. "Another wonderful cigarette from Norse Carolina?"

He lights this cigarette as he did the first, almost touching the slim tanned hand presenting it to him. They talk and laugh, sip from their glasses of wine, and she now and then leans into the handsome carriage to tend to Ilsedore, who begins to gurgle and draw more of her attention. Glen is finding the experience remarkably pleasant but also natural, even as he knows that by sundown he'll be back in the midst of the army and that an outing like this will seem like something he dreamed. He looks at the baby carriage as if in anticipation of telling friends in the motor pool of its chrome springs and silent rubber wheels, its crisp white-on-white interior and deep-as-water green enamel body, and the beautiful infant within. Who would believe what he is doing when he can hardly believe it himself?

Hedy Andreas declines, then accepts, a second glass of wine and a third cigarette. "It is only when my husband is away that I spend such time," she says. "It is also true that I have not had so many chances to be so young. Does this make sense? It is said that because of the war there are few young men in Germany today. It is also true that others have not been so permitted to grow up in this time—not permitted to be young. You understand? It is not my glasses of wine?"

"I understand."

"Of course you do. Forgive me. What it is, young Germans coming of age today are fortunate to have an opportunity to be young. This has not been so for one just my age. As a girl I was in school but also not in school, you see, while boys this age have been of the last in the war and in the end, many have fallen. Very many. Therefore we have missed in this time to be youthful, and so am I enjoying this occasion—invoking a strategy upon *die Bürgerin von Baden-Baden*."

"I'm really enjoying this," Glen says.

"Which is also to say that I must now leave," she says. "Darling Ilsedore has been more than good. She is kind to her mother as she indulges herself a little, though I know she will not accommodate much longer and I must be on my way. Please, walk with me just to the first street—I will show you. Appearances shall be proper to the end. As friends we shall say goodbye, while at home I shall recall you as I listen to phonograph recordings from Sarah Vaughan and Louis Armstrong. They are my favorites, too, and shall remind me of an American friend who is at once discreet and indiscreet, yes. A pleasant time to be able to talk some and smile, for which I thank you."

The waiter is signaled. Glen insists on paying and then walks the woman named Hedy back along a garden path to an intersection she indicates, sensing the approaching end of something, sensing, too, that she is a married woman, after all a mother, is six or seven years older and not the pretty German schoolgirl or shopgirl he has dreamed of meeting.

Their parting occurs more quickly even than he anticipated. At the first intersection of paths she offers her hand. "Again, a pleasure to laugh a little," she says.

"Would you—could I give you these cigarettes?" he says.

"No, this is not necessary," she says.

"I don't know what to say. If I were here again, and you, do you—"

"I am not always living here," she says. "Often I go to my family near Duisburg."

"Well," he says, to say he understands.

There is her faint smile and a brief silence. "I may give you a telephone number," she says. "When you are here once more, when you are not pursuing young girls—I tease, forgive me— perhaps it's possible we may speak as friends."

From her purse in the carriage she removes a small pad on which, with an equally small pen, she writes numbers. She tears the sheet free, hands it to him. "Goodbye," she says. There is her lovely face and a glimpse of her eyes.

When he has walked a few steps, he glances back to see the slim woman going away with her glossy baby carriage; then he turns toward the train station, letting her go, telling himself, Well, that was some cigarette break for a teenage jeep driver. And assuming he'll never see this woman again, he thinks of Stuttgart and of the Crossroads movie theater, where, if he makes it back in time, maybe he'll meet a shopgirl impressed by his uniform.

From the station—he has a two-hour wait before the next train leaves—he explores narrow side streets and window-shops, then turns into an ordinary restaurant and again is surprised. The *Gasthaus*, operated, the menu says, by Familie Heller, is beautifully furnished throughout with polished, lightly colored hardwood and framed black-and-white photographs, plus illustrations of Black Forest animals, and a tank with live trout. There is an inner patio, too, where he chooses to sit, and the *Wiener Schnitzel* he orders is served on a heated plate and placed upon a crisp white tablecloth with heavy polished silverware. The setting and food, not excluding bread rolls and beer—nor the waitress, whom he imagines to be a daughter of the Heller family—are all more attractive than anything he has ever seen and perpetuate his amazement at what is happening to him on this magical day, with what he is seeing and learning. The cost of the meal, about a dollar, is another unbelievable item to store away for the motor pool or mess hall, or to include in a letter home to his mother back in Michigan.

Walking again, he feels curious contentment, and only then does he wonder if he blundered in trying to give the woman his cigarettes. Oh well, he thinks, she seemed to like them. And he meant no harm.

The contentment continues throughout his train ride, most of which he spends standing at an open window in the aisle, taking in the warm evening air. And once he arrives, not visited with early Saturday night urges to prowl the city, he bypasses Stuttgart and returns by bus to his base, Panzerkaserne, passes through his largely empty barracks, and walks to the post theater in time for the eight o'clock movie, *From Here to Eternity*, which touches him more than he would have expected.

Nor does he stop by the EM Club after the movie to sit with friends over glasses of beer. Before his wooden wall locker, in his eight-man squad room, he removes his necktie and empties his pockets before unbuttoning his khaki shirt. As always, he leaves his hat until last, as the image amuses him. There on his wall locker shelf, with other items from his pockets, is the sheet of paper with her number written in blue ink. No name. A married woman older by so many years, and, he thinks, the most attractive woman he's ever talked to. He wonders how many days will pass before he'll forget her name.

4

Thursday is the last day of the month and not only payday, which is an army holiday, but Glen's birthday. He'll turn eighteen. If this isn't enough, on Tuesday at the 0800 Work Call, First Sergeant Thatcher himself stands formation and announces to the four platoons lined up in the company street that a promotion list has been posted on the company bulletin board, that concerned parties have until Work Call tomorrow to have new stripes sewn on all uniforms or concerned parties will suffer the consequences of having their promotions rescinded.

It's an army game Glen has heard about, and knowing he's due, he checks the list and experiences the charge: promotion to PFC. It means more money, even as it imposes this pressure of having stripes sewn on by tomorrow morning. He removes an armload of uniforms from his wall locker and heads to the basement. Little Mutti—the troops' name for her—is a seamstress who works full-time for Message Center Company, as other companies in his battalion also employ nationals as seamstresses, dishwashers, and barbers, and Glen works to explain to her that he has to have the stripes sewn on by the end of the day. *"Ja ja,"* she says, smiling a near-toothless smile. *"Ja, selbstverständlich, genau."*

"You like *Kaffee*, Mutti, from the PX?"

"Ach, ja!" she says. *"Kaffee ist köstlich!"* Missing key teeth or not, the woman's smile is engaging.

"Mein Geburtstag ist Donnerstag," Glen says, deciding to tell Little Mutti, alone, of his birthday, and have it done with.

"Ah, ja, gut—wie alt wirst du denn?"

"Achtzehn," Glen says.

"Nein. So jung—nur achtzehn?"

"Was für Kaffee, Mutti—Chase and Sanborn?"

"Ja, gut, sehr gut!"

Mutti smiles throughout, and Glen feels pleased as he goes on his way, thinking not to forget to stop by the PX with one of his coffee rations.

And, he thinks, so much for his birthday. All along in the army—nearly all other privates and PFCs are draftees in their early twenties, in for two years while he is in for three—he has been made to feel embarrassed over his age. To be so young, to have enlisted—how, the draftees always say, could anyone do such a thing? The less generous among them put it more strongly: How could anyone be stupid enough to join the fucking army? Fucking RAs have to be out of their fucking minds.

Draftee wrath may be one of the reasons Glen is something of a loner. Some of the RAs *are* out of their minds—witness First Sergeant Thatcher and forty-year-old PFC Dusty Rhodes in the supply room, and most mess sergeants he's ever seen—but they seem no less stupid to him than draftees who endlessly count their days remaining. "Hundred and twenty-seven days to go," Nute Nutter, a fellow driver from Columbus, Ohio, offers as a greeting every morning when Glen arrives at the motor pool.

"You're bad for my morale," Glen sometimes replies.

"Fuck your morale. You asked for it."

"Someday," Glen kids him on occasion, "you're going to look back and see these were the happiest days in your life, and you were too fucking stupid to know it."

"Bullshit!" Nute always says, and Glen will turn away to work on his jeep, or take it on one of his courier runs to Seventh Army HQ in Vaihingen, Patch Barracks in Heidelberg, Patton Barracks, Robinson Barracks, Fliegerhorst Kaserne, to Munich, Ulm, Darmstadt, Frankfurt. He says nothing more of the waste of counting days because he knows it is too true not to sting—although draftees do not hesitate at all when an RA's jugular may be visible.

———

On payday, Work Call is over in seconds. "Comp-nee, tensh-HUT!" Sergeant Thatcher bellows side-to-side. "FALL OUT FOR PAY CALL!"

Everyone shows up on payday as it is acknowledged, from top to bottom, that duty is on hold. Payday's singular duty is cash money and all that money implies, paying debts and bets and laying in supplies, getting laid and paying up shackjobs, gambling it all away in an afternoon and a night of pinching cards and sweating bullets, going with a whore after all at prime prices—"I told myself I'd never do that again"—or getting bruised and battered in a barroom or *Bahnhof* brawl, sliced by a knife along Bubblegum's main line of hillbilly hangouts or along its side street of black hangouts, dying in a drunken fall from a bridge or train or hotel balcony, a wrong turn on the Autobahn after dark, a daybreak tree-meeting with motorcycle on the back road to Ulm, taking a punch to the mouth—in dependent quarters as likely as in town—sent along by a woman scorned. A day for the ages.

"Time to raise hell," Glen says to Nute Nutter as the formation breaks.

"Fuck the army," Nute says. "Hundred and twenty-five days to go."

Nutter, Glen thinks, entering the building, caught up in the fever as he falls into pay line, Nutter is so full of resentment he wouldn't know a good thing if it walked up and touched him between the legs. In the midst of which thought, hearing his name bellowed from Thatcher's raspy throat—"PRIVATE FIRST CLASS CADY!"—he is stabbed with resentment of his own.

"Yes, Sergeant!" He turns to face the red-cheeked, black-eyebrowed top sergeant.

"Wanna keep that stripe, Private First Class Cady?"

"Yes, Sergeant, wanna keep it!"

The man's large yellow teeth coming into view could lead to a smile or snarl. Unaware of charges against him, Glen senses at once that his holiday is in jeopardy. Nothing elaborate; he's thinking of taking a bus, say, to Tübingen, another small city he identified on the wall map in the dispatcher's shed, looking around and buying something maybe to celebrate his birthday and promotion, to see what there is to see, and heading back to base in time for the eight o'clock movie or, maybe—he'll decide at the time—to risk twenty bucks in one of the irresistible sessions, across two-foot lockers covered with a blanket, of dealer's choice.

"Get your sorry ass in line with your grade, PFC, or mark that stripe 'Return to Sender'!"

"Yes, Sergeant!" Glen leaves the line of stripeless privates, the bulk of Message Center Company, and moves ahead to join the PFCs. The pay line inches along and Glen continues to wonder what he might do, where he might go, for the rest of the day. On payday last month he signed up for a two-day trip to Berchtesgaden, over which weekend, he recalls, he became entranced with a German girl, although at a distance. One of a family of dancers in a Bavarian floor show at the army hotel where he stayed, the fifteen-year-old Heidi with hemp-colored braids was a combination of shyness and exuberance. As she danced, skirt and lace petticoat twirling, she seemed to make shy eye contact with him— perhaps with other soldiers, too, although he hadn't seen it that way—and gave him sensations which for days afterward had him tracing fantasies of returning to the mountains and stealing her away.

The corporals are done and the PFCs have made it to the pay tables. Glen, the last of them, checks his uniform, brass, and shoes before squaring himself in front of the first table. "PFC Cady reporting for pay call, SIR!"

He sidesteps along tables then with his stack of MPCs and coffee and cigarette rations. One ten-dollar bill returned, Soldier's Deposit. One dollar, Company Fund. Four dollars, Company KP Fund. One dollar, Company Barber. Near the last table, he's inserting bills in his wallet—next stop, PX American Express across post, to exchange forty dollars for D-marks—when his name is bellowed yet again by the first sergeant. Glen's heart sinks as he turns to face the monster dog. "Yes, Sergeant!"

"PFC Cady, report Company Commander on the double!"

"Yes, Sergeant!"

"Soldier—sound off like you got a pair!"

"Yes, Sergeant!"

Along the first-floor corridor Glen is struck with fear. Being ordered to report to the company commander is serious business. What now? he thinks. And: Goddamn army. Draftees are right— army's a pain in the ass. His urge, his desire, is to punch the red-cheeked first sergeant in the mouth.

———

In the Orderly Room, Glen ducks under the counter. He readies himself, and uses his knuckles to rap on Captain Skaggs's door.

"Enter," comes from within.

Glen obeys, steps into place before the captain's desk, snaps to, and salutes. "PFC Cady reporting as ordered, SIR!"

"At ease."

Glen shifts a foot, overlapping his hands at the small of his back, but is not, to be sure, at ease. Maybe it was his slipping away early from the Guard Barracks a week ago. It's become his scheme: Show up early enough to be in the first row for first shift, finish first the next day, and, rather than wait around the Guard Barracks, steal away for half a day of freedom.

"Private Cady, you been in Message Center Company how long?"

"March 7, sir. Four months, sir."

"Four months. You consider that a long time?"

"Well, yes sir, fairly long. Depends, sir."

"Where do you come from in the States, Private Cady?"

"Michigan, sir."

"Have family there?"

"Yes sir."

"What's the makeup of your family, Private Cady?"

"The makeup, sir?"

"Parents and siblings, Private Cady."

"Just my mother, sir."

"Just your mother. What about your father, where's he?"

"Died, sir."

"When did he die, Private Cady?"

"Year and a half ago, sir."

"Year and a half ago. No brothers or sisters?"

"No sir."

"How'd your father die, Private Cady?"

"Heart attack, sir."

"Sometime thereafter you enlisted, Private Cady?"

"Yes sir."

"Leaving your mother alone, Private Cady?"

"Yes sir."

"Your mother work for a living, Private Cady?"

"Yes sir, AC Spark Plug, sir."

"She a secretary?"

"Works on the line, sir."

"I see. Mother lives and works state of Michigan, holds factory job, father deceased, you, an only child, enlisted U.S. Army sometime after father succumbed heart attack—have that about right, Private Cady?"

"Yes sir."

"Dropped out of high school?"

"Passed the GED, sir."

"Passed the GED."

"Yes sir—qualified for OCS, sir."

"I see. Passed the GED and qualified for OCS. I assume this suggests you know how to read and write, Private Cady?"

"Read and write, yes sir." There it is, Glen sees, as the captain says what he knows he's going to say.

"When's the last time you wrote home to your mother, Private Cady?"

"Ah—don't remember, sir. Been a while. Guilty in that department, sir."

"Received mail here, from your mother, Private Cady?"

"No sir, haven't, sir."

"Why's that? Assume your mother likewise knows how to write. She guilty in that department, too, Private Cady?"

"No sir. Yet to write home, sir, to give her address. Been meaning to, sir, just—well, no excuse, sir, just haven't gotten around to it."

"You love your mother, Private Cady?"

"Yes sir."

"She love you?"

"Yes sir."

"Wrong about one thing, Private Cady. Have written home—once. Time in European theater have written one-each postcard, arrival Bremerhaven March 5, 'proximately four months ago. Aware of that, Private Cady?"

"Yes sir, am now, sir."

"'Yes sir, am now, sir.' Let me tell you something, Private Cady. Battalion Headquarters received inquiry, via USO, via Pentagon, Washington D.C.—via Right Honorable Congressman

Charles B. D. Kinder the Third, State of Michigan—concerning whereabouts one U.S. Army Private E-2 Glen Cady, whose family has not heard word one since said individual arrived Bremerhaven 'proximately one hundred twenty days ago! Explanation for this, Private Cady?"

"No excuse, sir. Been meaning to do it, sir, but my free time I've been taking trips, here and there, sir, just haven't done it. Tend to it right away, sir."

"Better believe you'll tend to it, Private Cady. Don't tend to it, price you pay will be greater'n you ever dreamed possible. You are hereby restricted to post, twenty-four hours, during which time you will produce four-page letter—one page each month of delinquency, Private Cady—which letter will be on my desk 0800 Work Call, tomorrow, unsealed, stamped, envelope addressed, which pages, my capacity, company commander, will examine but not read for content. Failure your part to do so will result disciplinary action—understood, Private Cady?!"

"Yes sir!"

"Know what will happen you fail to produce said four-page letter, Private Cady?"

"Have an idea, sir!"

"Sure as hell better have an idea, Private Cady. Summary court martial. Reduction in grade. Restriction to company area, thirty days. Your ass will be converted to buttermilk—make myself CLEAR?"

"Yes sir!"

"DIS-missed!"

Snapping to, saluting, and about-facing, Glen exits, recloses the captain's door, and ducks back under the counter. Back along the corridor—pay call is over and the building is largely empty—he is able to curse only himself. His poor mother. He's hurt her, though he never meant to, and could at least have sent home a note with his address. A poker game is under way in his squad room and he pauses to watch. His rarely used letter-writing folder—a PX purchase in basic—is in his wall locker, but he lingers to see if Corporal Rusk, a black assistant cook, has a straight or is bluffing. He guesses Rusk is bluffing and too lightly, when he raises a dollar. Hit back with a five-dollar raise, Rusk folds and Glen guesses he folded the winner with something like two pair. He waits until Rusk says, "Shit, I folded the winner," and moves on.

In the USO, on the second floor of the Service Club, a gray-haired American lady—she resembles his mother, intensifying his guilt—asks if he needs assistance.

"Assistance?"

"You know how to write a letter and address an envelope?"

"Sure."

"Honey, sorry to offend. Some of the boys don't."

"Those're sergeants," Glen says, and gets her to smile.

"Some of them," she says sweetly.

Well, I'm doing it, Glen thinks. But he isn't writing what he would try to say if he were home again or with a friend, drinking, say. He'd talk then about the cafes and zither music, the special intoxication of German beer, the enchantment he seems to feel riding the trains and the new hunger he's experiencing at every turn, and the classical music and old violin waltzes that play in parks and beer halls, music he's come already to love as if it were alcohol and he were addicted.

He makes no attempt to explain any of this—his mother would think he'd gone queer—and instead writes about his job, and the mess hall where two German civilians do KP, the war damage and bomb ruins. He tells of an incident he witnessed in a GI hangout where an old German pulled a Nazi flag from under a counter and waved it, shouting indecipherable spittle, only to be laughed at by the soldiers, one of whom called out, "Martin Bormann lives—washing dishes at the Texas Bar!"

It's after 2200 and, his letter finished, Glen is lying in bed in the darkened side of his squad room; two other soldiers are in their bunks, leaving five out on the town with their new money. So far he's resisted the siren call of the pasteboards. The game in this room is over, one of the low-stakes games which always gave way to the pot-limit games—maybe one per barracks—which could be found by walking hallways, following smoke-filled light to quiet pauses that occur when a bet of twenty dollars occasions the reply, two players later, of "Yours and fifty more." In Wire Company, rumor has it, thousands of dollars are won and lost in the highest stakes first three graders' game on post, to which an occasional poker-wise corporal or PFC gains admission.

Glen lies in his bunk, thinking of being that corporal or PFC. It's a warm summer night and sleep remains far away. There has always been this pull of the night. Poker, alcohol, and sex on one side; education, sleep, and travel on the other. He likes both. In daylight it's easier to do the right thing, but when the sun goes down and the cards are being dealt, not to be in the game is like saving pennies and watching life pass by.

Still, he doesn't stroll into the hallway with a smoke in his mouth, as he might have in the past. He lies staring into space and sees in time that tonight poker isn't so magnetic. What is magnetic tonight is the woman from Baden-Baden. She might be out of his league, but he's taken with her in ways that won't leave him alone.

5

Placing a call turns out to be easy. Friday, in the Service Club, Glen notices a sign at the foot of a stairway: POST TELEPHONE EXCHANGE, and thirty minutes later, recovering the slip of paper from his wall locker and returning, a German woman at a counter looks at the number and directs him to "Booce number four."

Closing the door behind him without knowing what is going to happen, he takes the receiver down and, after a moment, to test it, says, "Yes? Hello?"

"Yes?" a woman's voice says faintly.

"Hello?" Glen says.

"It is Glen?" the woman says.

"Yes," he says, surprised it is Hedy. "Yes, it's me."

"Glen?"

"Yes, you remember me?"

"I've been afraid you won't call."

Something happens, a blink throughout his system in response to her words, and he hears himself saying, "I've been thinking about you, all the time—I want to see you again."

In turn, she says, "I've thought it's best you do not call. I've thought of this more than anything throughout the week. And you've made me wait until the last moment!"

He didn't know what he had expected—perhaps that she would search her thoughts to remember him, or would, embarrassed, put him off. "I wasn't sure I should call," he says. "I didn't think I should."

"You should not, it's true. Yet, I have wanted this. I've been faithful to my husband, always, but all week I've waited to hear from you. It is dangerous. He left only this morning. I—may I not speak of him now? I shall change my mind."

"Is it okay—if I visit? Could I come see you tomorrow?"

"Yes," she says. "I would like this. It's terribly forbidden, yet it's what I would like. I've been afraid all week you are not going to call!"

"I'll come on the train, tomorrow, like I did last week."

"Yes. My husband, he's in Frankfurt at this time. It's okay. Fraught with questions, and risk, yet it is what I wish."

"You're sure?" Glen says, not entirely understanding what he is asking, or the risk she refers to.

"May you not wear your uniform, but appear as a civilian? It's possible? Is it allowed?"

"It isn't, but I can do something," he says, thinking to buy something cheap at a German store and change on the train.

"You will telephone when you reach Baden-Baden?"

"From the station. Tomorrow afternoon."

"At which time, do you know?"

"About three, in the afternoon."

"Until then, Glen. Young sir."

"Yes, until then. Hedy."

Replacing the receiver, he pauses before stepping from the booth. Once he's paid and is outside, he cannot believe that what just happened actually happened. "Young sir"?

The beautiful woman in Baden-Baden. Is it so that he's going to see her tomorrow? Hedy Andreas. She was so pretty when he met her, more than pretty, beautiful. And educated and funny. And, strangely to him, he likes talking to her.

The sleek train with its clear windows and polished wood is gliding into another Saturday afternoon, and Glen is at a pushed-down aisle window, taking in the air of the countryside. His awol bag, in an overhead rack in the compartment behind him, holds a carton of Camels as well as the civilian pants, belt, and short-sleeved shirt he bought an hour ago in a Stuttgart department store. His plan was to buy clothes in Stuttgart, change on the train in the French Zone, and change back again before reentering the American Zone. The danger is real, given the seriousness with which dress code violations are treated by the army, not to mention the many warnings about CIC operatives lurking in civilian clothes.

Can he get away with changing in a WC? He wonders, too, how the gift of a carton of cigarettes will be taken. If it feels wrong, he thinks, he'll just leave it in his bag.

Is this the French Zone? he wonders in time. Uncertain of the boundary, he proceeds anyway with his plan of entering a WC from one direction as a PFC and emerging, going in the other direction, as a civilian. Awol bag recovered, he moves through two, then three cars, enters a WC, and turns the lock to *"Besetzt."* Removing his necktie, unbuttoning his shirt, he realizes that he could end up in the stockade. Quickly, he strips to his GI underwear and slips into the civilian pants and shirt. Removing his army cap, he ruffles his hair. He selected the clothes by holding them up to himself, tan pants and a blue short-sleeved shirt, but trying to see what he looks like in the small mirror he already misses the comfortable khakis, even the necktie he was always happy to loosen. A train explodes past in the opposite direction, startling him into uncertainty, and he moves to the side of the clouded window as if to think things over.

Don't think about it, he tells himself as he folds and packs his uniform. He swiftly unlocks the door, slips out, and moves into another unfamiliar car, feeling detectable each step of the way. The pants feel too loose, and he knows he has to be recognizable as an imposter. He has GI hair and shoes, and wouldn't fool anybody.

Taking a seat next to a window, he visors his eyes with a hand. He looks only to the window side, to avoid anyone's eyes, and in time, pulling into Baden-Oos and deboarding to change trains for the ten-minute shuttle into Baden-Baden, keeps his eyes averted. He's definitely in the French Zone, he knows, as he sees two French officers in their upside-down saucepan hats at a distance. Relief. Word has it that French soldiers earn five dollars a month, hate Germany, and on liberty always return home across the Rhine. Should he encounter an American officer, he thinks, they'd have to move like lightning to catch him.

His next task will be to manage a German telephone on his

own. What if an operator says something he doesn't understand? If he gets through to Hedy, will she meet him in the park? Is he really going to see her? It's hard to believe, and exciting. He's on a date. Glen Cady, PFC and jeep driver, is going on something of a date with a beautiful German woman, one who just happens to be married.

In the busy Baden-Baden station he feels glaringly out of uniform, in violation of serious laws, and disoriented by the flimsy clothing. The pants legs flap as he walks from the station and approaches a yellow telephone booth. He enters and, without thinking, drops in two ten-pfennig coins. Then, after a woman speaks *auf deutsch*, he recites in his best German the numbers on his slip of paper. Nothing happens; the coins return. He tries again, this time dialing Hedy's numbers, and a ringing sound follows. He seems hardly to breathe.

She answers, and he says, "I'm here."

"You are here in Baden-Baden?" she says.

Something in her voice seems distant. He says he's at the *Bahnhof*. "The clothes didn't turn out real good," he adds, laughing, but she doesn't laugh with him.

"This is the address to give to taxi driver," she says. "Nine and thirty—thirty-nine, you understand?—Chekhovstrasse. Yes? Chekhovstrasse. Please, Glen, allow me twenty minutes?"

Off the phone, Glen repeats *"neun und dreissig Chekhovstrasse"* to himself, and, at a short row of taxis, where the driver of the lead car is coming around to open the passenger door, utters the difficult words. In the next moment he's in a Mercedes—pinned in turns to the leather seat—as the driver downshifts and the car rockets through town and along a two-lane road, and pulls onto the shoulder and stops.

Have three minutes passed at sixty miles an hour? They're in the country and Glen says, "Here?"

The man points across the road to the side of a hill. *"Neun und dreissig Chekhovstrasse."*

Glen pays and gets out, though no houses or buildings are in sight, and, as the Mercedes blasts away, fears he's been had as a GI, or is known to be flirting with a married woman and has been dropped on a country road as a joke or warning. He realizes yet again that he doesn't really know what he's doing.

He looks up through trees across the road. Fifty yards up the steep hillside, panels of glass and walls of cream-colored stucco are visible between leaves and branches. At the roadside, he deciphers a shrub-covered wall and gate, and to one side the panels of a two-car garage of the same dark brown color as the gate. A stairway zigzags up the hill between shrubs and flowers while his impulse is to return at once to where he came from.

Well, he tries to tell himself, she's just a friend, a woman whose English is better than his, and walking into his fears to overcome them, he crosses to the gate. Its steel handle won't move, and spotting a button, he presses, and presses again.

"Ja?" a voice replies from a pattern of holes by the button.

"It's me," he says.

"Moment."

A buzzer sounds, and this time the steel handle turns and the heavy wooden gate opens freely. He starts up a zigzag walkway through a rock garden, feeling, bag in hand, like a delivery boy. Join the army and see the world, is all he can think.

At the top there are landings and terraces at two or three levels, and before he has taken more than two steps, a glass door opens within a shadowed overhang and Hedy is stepping out to greet him, smiling and faintly foreign. Over her skirt and blouse she has a half-length blue smock of the kind doctors wear, and is more striking even than his fantasies have had her.

They shake hands in the German style, and this formality and awkwardness lingers between them when they are inside. Her house, its views, his clothes (they are okay, yes), the whereabouts of her baby (with a friend), how quickly he has arrived from the station (not in twenty minutes but in five!), the cigarettes (*Wunderbar!*), even her blue smock (last-minute cleaning)—all this makes up their embarrassed conversation, and only when she has excused herself and returned without the smock does he seem to recognize the woman from the previous Saturday afternoon.

"I'm nervous," he says.

"It's natural," she says with a sympathetic expression. "Shall we take a stroll? Here below in the forest it's pleasant to walk. And we shall leave nervousness along the pathway—yes?"

"Sounds fine," Glen says, trying to relax.

In the vestibule, amber glass panels let in golden light where she pauses at a closet door. "The question: Shall I take a light

wrap?" Turning, she looks at him as if fondly, and—it's more
her move than his, as he will know down through the years—in
the next moment they kiss. Their heads turn, there are her eyes,
their lips meet, and it is a kiss which shoots into him and arouses
him for no less a time than forever.

They walk on a forest path. She's right, his awkwardness *is* being
left behind, only to be replaced by anticipation. He'd like to look
at her, and touch her, and he glances but keeps his hands to
himself. As they walk and chat, he remains confused and almost
stricken by what is happening. His mind skips around, clouding
his senses; he'll need time to know what his senses have taken in,
will need time, too, to learn of intimacy, as his own inexperienced
heart continues to be stimulated and pleased. God, he could lick
her, could do anything.

The civvies feel more comfortable, and he walks as if he's
another person. In the forest, as on his last trip, it's cool in the
shadows and the smell of pine tar is everywhere. The path runs
alongside a stream, and now and then through wooded clearings
of sunlight and sudden warmth. They talk as they walk, and Glen
feels more relaxed the farther they go. Before them then is a rustic
tavern, Gasthaus zur Blauen Forelle—"Tavern of the Blue Trout,"
she translates—and she asks if he'd like to have a glass of wine.

Two cars are parked close by, and a dirt roadway leads out
through the forest. In the late afternoon sunlight, they pause on
a deck, part of which extends over the stream, and look for the
shadows of trout holding above sand in the tea-colored water.

She excuses herself and he thinks she's going inside to use a
bathroom, or to summon a waiter, but returning, she says, "No
one is here to whom my husband and I are known. Shall we sit
inside?"

Within, walking through several empty rooms—only two tables are occupied—they enter still another room and sit out of
view of the doorway. When a waiter appears, Hedy looks to Glen.
"Wine is okay?" she says, and he nods. She orders and the man
withdraws.

"In the time I have known you," she says, looking at Glen,
"even in this week as you have kept me waiting like a schoolgirl,
many things have been wonderful and perfect. Do you know this?"

He only smiles, although they have the room to themselves.

"A lovely place for a rendezvous," she says.

The waiter returns with glasses and a decanter of white wine on a tray and makes a friendly remark as he places them on the table. Then Hedy pours modest amounts and they take up the glasses. "I've imagined all week seeing you," she says, by way of a toast. "When you called I was deeply relieved, and pleased. I believed fate was acting in an appropriate manner. May we therefore drink to fate acting in an appropriate manner?"

They tap their glasses and drink.

Glen dislikes the wine for perhaps two or three sips, then the alcohol seems to add pleasure to mind and heart. "Fate is doing a good job," he says.

She smiles. "I must tell you one thing," she says. "One thing I wish you to know. In spite of appearances, I am—I have, for a long time, been unhappy. Not unhappy on the surface, but unhappy at heart. Do you know this expression?"

Glen nods, looking into her eyes.

"While otherwise I have all reason for contentment, certainly in contrast to many others, especially in the aftermath of the war, when so many have lost so much. Yet I've been distressed—oh, not with melancholia, but with, I'm not so sure, desolation? Does this make sense, desolation, this frame of mind?"

"I think so," Glen says.

"Out of the air you have appeared, and for the first time in memory I know some happiness. Happiness only of moments in the park, but happiness which is quite full."

Glen would respond, but a man appears, approaching with a smile. The man speaks, laughs, gestures toward the decanter, and Hedy laughs in turn. "Glen Cady," she says. "Herr Günther, the proprietor."

The man extends a hand, nods in a near-bow, indicating with his other hand that there is no need to rise. "How do you do?" Glen says.

"*Mein* pleasure, *mein Junge*," Herr Günther remarks, and after another laughter-filled exchange with Hedy, he bows and backs away.

Glen says, "What was that about?"

"This man is—what do you say?—an ironic man. He is the proprietor, the owner. He has asked if we wish to have the light on, and when I have said no he says something of the light glowing later. He is, he indicates, an admirer of the Americans, but not of the French, who are too bossy in this district. American soldiers he admires, because they are humorous and casual, and are not in this district"—at which remark she laughs herself. "Even with others, with you there is pleasure," she adds. "It's wonderful."

In another moment Herr Günther is back with another dew-covered decanter of the golden wine and two fresh glasses. Smiling, half bowing, he says, "Is vine from this locale, private vine, you say." Glancing toward Glen, he adds, "You are having in Chermany a goot vizzit?"

"Yes, yes," Glen says. "Having a nice visit, thank you."

"Goot, *ja*. I am hoping srewout a goot vizzit, *ja*?"

"Thank you," Glen says.

"Likewise," Herr Günther says, giving a nod and taking away their used glasses and decanter.

"He is fond of you," Hedy says. "He is not so familiar like this when you are not American. When you are French or English—or German, you may be sure—he is not familiar. But it is you, dear one. This freedom I have also felt with you."

"This is something," Glen says, excited by "dear one." "I've never felt like this. I'd like to kiss your hand," he hears himself say.

She laughs with him, and offers her hand. He feels it on both sides and kisses, as if to be romantic, not the back but fingers and palm.

She continues to smile, and to look into his eyes. "Herr Günther, he is fond of the American style and is wishing to give it a trial. As do I. I've been fond of you at once, and wish you have felt the same for me."

Glen looks at her eyes and sips his wine. "I have," he says. Are they—Hedy and this man—fond of him? He wonders if it's true, and if it's his own ignorance, his lack of decorum and taste, the foolishness of kissing her palm that would have them liking him? Or is it simply that he is even younger than they know? They drink and smoke, look at each other and talk. She touches his hand with both of hers as he holds a match, and he says, "I love this, it's exciting—though I think I'm already a little juiced."

She laughs. "So am I," she says.

"You may be fooling, but—" he says.

"I am not fooling," she says.

"You aren't offended, well, that I brought you cigarettes?"

"Should I be? No, certainly not. I am pleased, only I must hide them from my husband. You mean offended as if I am trading affection for cigarettes?" She is smiling. "As if I am your street girl?"

"That's what I didn't want to mean," he says.

"I shall be this for you, if you like," she says. She continues to gaze at him, and to appear amused. She leans his way, looking into his eyes. "All this time I am wanting you to like me, can you understand? It has nothing to do with cigarettes."

He looks back at her and sips more wine. "Let's go back," he hears himself say. He wants to hold her and kiss her. "I want to hold you," he says.

She smiles. "Soon," she says. "As it is growing dark. Soon. This is so pleasant. I feel—I want to ask you—you have read the English novelist, Mr. Lawrence?"

"I don't think I have."

"*Lady Chatterley's Lover*, the work of D. H. Lawrence."

"I've heard of it," he says.

"In this novel, it's as you are to me. As I wish to be with you, to know you and have you know me. I wish to be free with you, do you understand?"

"I'm not sure," he says. "I think I do."

She studies him with her faint smile. Leaning forward, she whispers softly, "You will not be shocked, only surprised."

Uncertain whether she's telling him something or asking, he doesn't reply, and looks into her mischievous eyes.

"We are so much together here now," she says. "It's wonderful to me. The wine has me a little tipsy, true, but we are almost as one. It's what I have wanted and dreamed all week, what I have believed possible only in dreams."

He looks at her and, unsure what to say, says, "I've felt that, too."

"I have wanted, when you are parting last time, to kiss you. To have you kiss me, and to kiss you, too. Has this been your wish also? May you tell me?"

"I did, and I want to kiss you right now."

"You may, then," she says. "It is what I want you to do."

She closes her eyes and turns her face, and he touches her lips lightly with his own, as if to tantalize her.

She opens her eyes. "Glen, you will be my lover?" she says.

"I'll be anything you want."

"Just to kiss you, when you are parting. You cannot know how I wanted this, as if all my life."

He looks at her, again doesn't know what to say.

"You are young, and I'm happy you are so honest. You have never had a young girlfriend?"

"Not really."

"Nor I, really, a young boyfriend. Only a husband."

For no reason other than that he wants to, he lifts his hand and touches her temple, moves his fingers over her hair.

"You give the appearance of both a young man but also of a boy," she says. "It's okay, is not a problem. It's wonderful to possess such characteristic."

Again, he doesn't know what to say.

"I will tell you something, my dearest darling," she says. "A gift of cigarettes, from you, does not offend me. Nor does it offend me that you have spoken to me and I am with my baby in the park. Many would be offended, as one is taught in Germany."

"I wasn't sure if I should."

"I am thrilled as a schoolgirl that you have spoken to me. You are young, and I know at once you have spoken only as there is attraction. I am also at once attracted, in part I think because you have responded to your feeling but not to the rules of society. Can you appreciate this? I think it is so German, and English, but not so American. I've felt affection for you—may I say love for you— in an instant. In the time we have walked, and are sitting next to each other, I've only looked at you and felt in this way. It's wrong, I know, and I tell myself—that day in the park I tell myself I am not to say where I live or may be reached, that I must never see you again, because there is nothing more in the world I want so much. Then you have asked, and I have gone against my judgment, and through the entire week have grown every day more afraid you will not call. What will I say—I do not know—when my husband is there? And when the week is passing and I'm certain you will not call, and when my husband is leaving only that morning, then it is that you call. It's as it should be, Mr. Lawrence would be in agreement with this. You have captured my heart, and it is destiny. It's the wish of the stars and I am alive in my life at last, where there has been the war and I have never been alive before. In you, at last, I am alive. You cannot know."

As darkness settles on the stream, with no more light than is provided by lamplights, they make their way along the unoccupied forest pathway. They kiss and embrace wildly, stopping here and there. Glen had believed himself knowledgeable—he's been with teenage girls at home, necking at the drive-in, has never known failure—and only later will he recognize his ignorance, however unbridled the passion that seizes him now. Stopping along the path, all muscles alive, he moves his hands up over her legs one at a time, ankles to knees to thighs, feels her abdomen, presses her pubis with both hands, lifts her breasts, squeezes her breasts and shoulders, kisses her neck and ears, sifts her hair, and raises her from the ground by her seat to hold her to him, presses to her center with the bulge in his pants.

"I want you to eat me," she says. "Do you want to eat me? Say this to me," she says, and he responds by kissing her mouth and eyes, licking and biting her neck, draws her neck into his mouth, bites her breasts through fabric, takes them as much as possible into his mouth, but doesn't know quite how to answer her question.

In her house high on the hillside, they fall like teenagers to a couch in the unlighted living room as he continues—his head swimming with wine—to kiss her and kiss her, running his hands over her clothing and body until, and he feels foolish for not having acted sooner, she says, "Do you want to take me in there?"

He knows that "there" is a bedroom—she nodded in a certain direction—but is already beyond his experience. He rises, lifting her in his arms, sustaining his embrace as he carries her toward the bedroom, bumps his shins into a bed near the center of the room, then settles her onto the bed, sensing that she is already unbuttoning her clothes.

He does the same—pushes off shoes, rips at buttons and clothes—and has never been so excited, and is okay still as he reaches to touch her naked body, her small breasts and alert nipples, her ribs and belly and patch of damp fur, moving at once to connect to this married woman who is opening to him. But when he brushes, touches her leg, he loses control, howls in confusion as she cries, "Oh no, please don't come."

They awaken in daylight to strangeness. Naked, she slips from bed into a bathroom. Not knowing what to do, he waits his turn. When she emerges, showered and wearing a white robe, she stands at the foot of the bed, smiles, and asks if he will have coffee.

He lingers in the bathroom. There are chrome gooseneck hoses, mirrors, glossy white ceramic fixtures. He showers head-to-toe, uses her toothpaste on a finger to brush. A hint of wine squeezes his skull, but he's had worse hangovers and remains afflicted more by his failure in bed.

They sit at a small wooden table in her kitchen, sipping strong coffee and nibbling rolls with butter and strawberry jam. She smiles as before, faintly, fondly. She must go soon to recover her Ilsedore, she says, and wonders if he prefers to walk or to have a taxi carry him to the station. "Oh, I'll walk," he says. Summer sunlight glances through windows into her hillside home, and the prospect of being out in the air, walking, perhaps of leaving behind some degree of his failure of the previous night, perhaps of leaving and never looking back, appeals to him.

She gives him an address—the friend who is caring for Ilsedore—in care of whom he can send letters. "Please write to me soon," she says. "You will not make me wait each day of another full week to hear from you?"

"I'll write," he says, even as he wonders if it matters now.

"May I see you Wednesday?" she asks, holding one of his hands. "Is it possible I may drive to you, to the gate of your camp? I think I will very much like to see you before a week has passed. May you telephone, by Tuesday, to tell me of a time when I may drive to you? Tuesday afternoon my husband is at his work. Monday he is here, but on Tuesday may I hear from you by telephone?"

"I'll call," he says. "If not during lunch hour, if I'm on a run, I'll call. Before three on Tuesday."

He's eager to be outside and away, to walk in the summer air, and gets to his feet. "I'm going to hit the road."

"We have ten minutes still."

"I should go," he says.

In the vestibule again, as he is ready to escape, they hold each other. He kisses her temple, her forehead, and says, "I'll call." Giving her hand a squeeze, he opens the door and leaves. Glancing back, he sees her standing outside the door and waves, then slips down the hillside to freedom.

Hours later, back in uniform and at an open window in the aisle of a train speeding west out of Karlsruhe, relief of a kind seems to have entered him at last and he wonders if he will ever return. An outing, and a certain adventure. Sensational, but regretful. For after all, and however lovely, she is married and is a mother. No one would ever believe what has happened, and he wonders if it's anything he'd ever try to tell.

3

SNOW SQUALL
Winter 1988

6

Snow picks up partway through class, coming in off the ocean to scratch the windows as if with sand. The darkening sky seems to make all the more real Mann's *Death in Venice*, which the class is discussing, and no less real the feeling the professor harbors for the twenty-seven-year-old student sitting extreme left, third from the front.

Is *Death in Venice* a "homosexual" story, and if so, to what extent? This is the turn the discussion has taken, no surprise to Glen, as he's been trying to lead the students in hopes that they will say yes, okay, but also see—has it ever happened in a room of undergraduates?—that the sexual vein in the story implies a larger, similar theme. In any case, he feels at his best at times like these, even as he knows that lights have to ignite within his students and not merely be flashed upon them by an erudite figure standing in front of a room.

German Lit in a wooden-ribbed classroom in the old part of the building. On these winter days, under dramatic skies, the old globes hanging from the ceiling are milk-yellow with warmth, and when he is good, Glen feels, the room becomes serene, even sacred, with Heine and Rilke and Schiller visiting wisdom upon them, and Keats, too, in an underlying poetic of truth being beauty being all one needs now, or ever, to know.

"Let's hear it," he says to prod them. "If it's a gay story, does it mean von Aschenbach wants to make some move? Is it pure love—or is he a dirty old man? Does the story elicit a sexual, or a homosexual, response, from one's private little psyche? Let's get serious here—aren't we grown-ups?"

"I don't have a homosexual response, Professor, how about you?" an ever self-congratulating male student offers, followed by a line from one of his friends, "No doubt in my mind he was an old queen hanging around a hotel in Venice."

Glen is more pleased than they know with the prickly comments and is moving to counter, shifting to the front of the table when, to his satisfaction in being able to speak her name, a hand is up and he says, nodding, "Yes, Ecki."

"No, von Aschenbach, I don't think, is necessarily homosexual, not in a carnal sense," Glen hears her say as he looks to the floor, and his heart travels to her. "Certainly he's in love with the boy, but it's existence which has him stricken. He's going to die now, as he knows, and is grieving for human beauty. And what is more beautiful than an innocent child? It's sexual, yes, but only as sexuality and eroticism—" some in the class giggle at the latter word—"as they are the apex of life and therefore also beyond—"

"Go on, Ecki, please finish," Glen says as the snickers from a couple of boys seem to unnerve her.

"Poor von Aschenbach," she says. "At once he is loving the eternal and the temporal, but who wouldn't, facing death? The success of this as literature is that it has an awareness of both life and art. It is, I'm sorry, nothing so simple as illicit sex which is the subject—even as the story *includes* this element. Isn't the erotic one of the wonders of existence? Why else are my classmates amused and, yes, aroused? Thomas Mann clearly believes the erotic to be an affirmation of the species, and I believe poor von Aschenbach is mourning the passing of erotic life on erotic earth."

The class is shocked with regard, not least of all Glen, who utters "Bravo!" as he begins clapping. "Brilliant, a brilliant reading, Ecki, good Lord, I applaud you." Others join in, as applause and laughter and good feeling fill the room and make the class one of the most memorable Glen will ever know.

Snow still pings the cloud-darkened windows, and Ecki—it's the first time since the night before Thanksgiving that he's spoken to her—is standing at his table while other students are leaving. "Way to go, Ecki," a boy says in parting.

"For sure," Glen says to her. "That's the best moment I've ever known in a classroom, absolutely the best."

"I came to love poor von Aschenbach, I think as the author also loved him," she says.

"I guess we all love him," Glen says with odd emotion.

"Of course it's my professor who has taught me to read also from the heart," she adds.

"How nice of you to say that. Thank you."

"I've taken you at your word," she says. "And all this time I've missed you," she adds, though a last student within Glen's view is gathering possessions.

"Me too, and I'm sorry," he says as if in code. "Excuse me," he adds. "Yes, Fräulein Wells?"

Even in Ecki's presence—to whom his attention if not his eyes remains directed—Michelle Wells tries to cajole him into disclosing the contents of the impending final exam. "Just the general areas, please," she says.

"Michelle, you know I've told everyone what's going to be on the exam. Three times. Review everything we've done in class."

"Everything?" she says with a dash of spleen.

"Texts, lectures, everything—it's the idea of a final exam."

"It can't *all* be on there."

"That's right, it can't."

"You won't tell me more than that?"

"What do you think?"

Looking down then, Glen pauses as the student strides from the room. "Sorry," he says to Ecki. "On the heels of your brilliant remarks, which isn't to say that most of them didn't get it, because they did."

"Fräulein Wells has the soul of a potato," Ecki says.

Decorum allows Glen but a smile.

"May we talk?" Ecki says. "In your office, later?"

"Sure."

"This evening?"

"No. How about in an hour, around four?"

"You haven't been angry with me all this time?"

"Not at all."

"That I acted as in a soap opera?"

"I haven't been angry at all. Well, maybe a little, because you stirred up my life. But not real anger."

"You have stirred up my life in the first place."

His eyes look to hers again. "You say some of the nicest things," is all he can think to say.

"Three months ago I, too, would have laughed over von Aschenbach, you know, as just a dirty old man. You've given me this, and I feel now that nothing I've ever learned is more important. I see all things differently."

He only looks at her, impressed all over again.

"To be with someone who understands nothing, as I have always been—is to be with a farm animal. I seek something else, if just once in my life. Until four," she adds and starts away.

Glen doesn't allow himself to look her way as she walks from the room. He'd like to glance over her figure, just as a moment ago an urge was in him to touch the back of her hand where it rested on the desk.

He takes his time preparing to leave, stacks his materials, and wipes away the phrases from *Death in Venice* he'd scratched on the board. Did he ever really believe that anyone would understand what he was trying to say about that story? However many times he's led students through the novella, in both languages, not one of several hundred ever recognized it as much more than the story of a dirty old man. Now this. To have Ecki see, too, that sex, even when it touches on the forbidden and tacky, is not without meaning.

Entering the hallway, he knows that if there was any doubt of his feeling for the young woman who slipped into his life a few weeks ago, there isn't now. She has him, as she said in the front seat of her car, and he's excited by her, while the thought alone is regarded as illegal. An undergraduate. Out of the question.

At the same time, whatever his anxiety about adultery, and about harming his small family, and whatever his awareness that it's the same old professor/student story, she is so appealing, so much a part of his old dreams and regrets. . . . Upon which thought, reaching his floor and sidestepping students, he feels a new affinity with old Professor Unrat of *Der Blaue Engel*, who heard Lola-Lola sing "Falling in Love Again" as she offered her love, and heard her sing it again as she took it away and left his life in ruins.

Just steps from his door he is signaled, with smile and partial bow, by a large colleague waiting there. Otto Gentz, tenured full professor, who resides not in a cubicle high in the modern addition but in a windowed office on the first floor of the old wing. Gentz, whom Glen believes—despite the man's smiles and European manners—has disliked him from the beginning. Nothing personal, Glen imagines, merely the ram-on-the-hillside syndrome: women who fawn are courted by Professor Gentz, hands are kissed and elbows fondled, while men of lower status are dismissed out of hand and venomously slandered. University life. No one, Glen imagines, is more devious than old Otto.

"I am assigned as your advocate," Gentz announces with a smile.

"My advocate?"

"*Jawohl.* I shall present your case. I have been assigned, and have wholeheartedly accepted."

"I see," Glen says. "Am I to participate—"

"My good fellow, of course not. Senior members only. From here, with our recommendation, and a separate recommendation from the chair, one's case goes to the dean and the college. From the dean to the president. A drawn-out process. You will participate, to be sure, in the *gathering* of materials, in which consideration we must soon put our heads together and plot our strategy, as it were. These things come on one quickly. *Ciao, Kamerad.* I shall be in touch."

With a near-gleeful smile, Gentz is gone. Intrigue, Glen notes, turns him on.

Glen settles in at his desk. Otto Gentz, of all people. If he retained the vaguest hope, it has to be dispelled by this. How could Monica assign such a man as his advocate?

Ecki taps on his door at ten past four. For five minutes Glen has feared her arrival, and feared even more that she wouldn't come at all. Then the object of wonder is inside his door, as he says, "Please, have a seat."

She does so, smiling a little.

"So what can I do for you?" he says, and adds, "You were really impressive today."

"I follow my teacher's instructions."

"You're kind of funny, aren't you?" he says.

"I hope so, if it makes you smile."

"It does."

She sits looking at him.

"I think we should clarify things," he says.

"My feelings haven't changed," she says.

When he doesn't respond, she adds, "I accept that you are married and have a child. I would not be a problem. I wish only to be close to you at times. To learn from you. Not to hurt you."

"You know, maybe I'm supposed to be the strong one here, but it occurs to me that I could be the one who'd have difficulty with this. What do you think of that?"

"I think, well, I must leave now. Sorry to be abrupt." She is on her feet, about to leave. "I should have said at once, it's a difficult time as my son is just now home from school. Today he stops with a friend, until ten minutes from now."

Glen is on his feet, too, wanting to have something decided. "We can be good friends," he says. "Maybe have coffee in the union, like professor and student."

"You would like more than this?"

"I'm not going to say what I'd like."

"You know I'm in love with you. It grows worse for me; still, I don't want to cause difficulty, only at times to be close."

"You're always surprising me in what you say."

"I *must* go now. Only wait until we may speak again. Please. Now give me your hand."

Almost dumbly he does so, which hand she takes in both of hers, raises, and presses to her breast—the sudden sensation is one he's never really known, of touching the off-limits, sweater-covered breast of a pretty high school girl—as she is saying, "Wait until we talk again. Please don't be angry with me."

She is gone, the door left ajar, and he stands in her aftermath, confused and excited. The feel of her breast; did she pull him in and undo him, just like that?

"I'd like to think you're on my side in this," he says to Paige that night in the kitchen.

"Why do you say that?"

They're about to have dinner and Paige has just surprised him by saying, as she added sauce to Alice's spaghetti, "If Otto Gentz didn't like his advocate, he'd have been in Monica's office five minutes later."

Sitting down then, Paige says, "Of course I'm on your side. Don't be so sensitive."

"You say something like that, Otto standing up to things, it puts the blame on me, and that isn't fair."

"Glen, let's face it, okay, you haven't gone about this in a sensible way. I don't see, myself, how anyone ever gets tenure if they don't campaign and politic. I'll never understand academics."

"Kissing ass is not my style."

"Say what you want. Everyone knows it's political. You want to get along, anywhere, you have to get along with the bosses. You neglect to do that, how can you say it's their fault?"

"You do blame me, don't you? Tell you what: Let's forget it for now."

"It's just—"

"Let's forget it, Paige. It'll spoil everyone's dinner, and if you want to know something, I don't like talking about it. And don't be putting me down in front of my kid."

Paige makes a gesture of conciliation, though she appears ready to fire another round. Of course he's sensitive, Glen is thinking. Who wouldn't be? His job is being taken away, at his age, with a wife and child to support, and there's not a thing in the world he can do about it. Kissing ass wouldn't have done any good, and sucking up now would only make things worse, especially for his own dumb psyche.

What Paige doesn't know is that he's more of a wreck than he ever guessed he'd be. He's been self-confident all his life, and never would have believed that something like this would bring him down. But it has. Besides, as feeling for Ecki jumps up in him, he retains a fear that Paige *wants* him to be denied. For years she's played the pragmatist to his role as dreamer, and his failure would give her leverage in the old power struggle and prove she's been right all along. At the same time, he cautions himself not to get carried away with such thoughts.

At bedtime they clash again, however, and again he's surprised at the turns Paige seems to be taking. At issue is a story Glen tells Alice while Paige is in the master bath, getting ready for bed. The story is the one he occasionally tells about his childhood dog,

Blackie, as a way of defining love, for one night, when he told her he loved her more than anything in the world, Alice said, "What's love mean, Daddy?"

She knew, he was convinced, even if she didn't know she did. And tonight again, knowing it fills him with pleasure, she just said, "Tell me how you loved Blackie."

Her bedroom is dark, his eyes all but accustomed, and he lowers himself to the floor and, as usual, rests his back against Alice's bed. He could not be more willing than he is tonight, as love and loss are close to the surface, and he readies what has become their favorite opening line. "I was eleven and Blackie, my best pal of all time, was four," he says into the darkness.

The details hardly vary, and tonight, again, Glen tells how Blackie wanted to go with him wherever he went, even to school. It was a problem every morning when he left, and a couple of times Blackie showed up barking at his school, a mile from home. Usually Blackie stayed locked up in the kitchen, but when his father didn't work overtime and came home early enough to let him out, Blackie always raced to a hilltop corner a block from where they lived and sat waiting for him to appear.

Turning the corner, ever on the lookout because Blackie was his best friend, Blackie would take off down the block and go crazy trying to jump up on him and lick his face, which he'd let him do. Sometimes, depending on the weather and how much he was carrying home, they'd roll on the ground, which Blackie also loved to do, unless he squeezed Blackie too hard, which he sometimes did, even as he knew and regretted the meanness of it. Then Blackie would cry and he'd let him go. Mad or not, Blackie always forgave him, and he felt the same way about Blackie, because he got mad at him at times, too. Whatever happened, the next day Blackie would be sitting on the hill waiting for him.

Blackie slept on a rug beside his bed, but when he was a puppy, for a month, he slept there in a cardboard box and whimpered like a baby whenever Glen lifted his hand from the box.

He also refused to mind sometimes, like someone else he knew, he always tells Alice. He'd tell Blackie to stay home or to stay on one side of the street, and he wouldn't do it. And his all-time favorite game of mischief, in the winter, was to race along and snatch Glen's hat as he was sledding down the hill. He'd drop it and stand over it, daring Glen to make a move, when he would snatch it up and run, only to put it down again, even when Glen was really mad at him and wanted his hat back. The only thing that worked was to tell Blackie he wasn't going to play with him and to turn and walk away acting dejected, when Blackie would come along with his hat and try to give it back as a way of saying he was sorry and wanted to make up.

Whatever their ups and downs, as he always tells Alice, he loved Blackie more than anything in the world. And of course the time came, as maybe it does with dogs allowed to be what they are, the time came around four on a summer day when Glen was riding his bike across the street and Blackie was chasing after him, and even as he fell over with his bike, shouting at him to stay back, Blackie was hit by a car, hit hard, and he ended up lying on the curb next to Blackie, ordering him and begging him not to die, but Blackie went ahead and died while he rubbed his head and eyes and told him he'd let him come to school anytime he wanted, bled from his mouth and died anyway, and, as he adds each time, he loves Blackie still and always will, no matter what, which is how he loves her and which is what it means to love someone more than anything in the world.

"You told her that story again, didn't you?" Paige says as he enters the bedroom, quietly closing the door.

"My Blackie story, yes, I did."

"I don't think it's right to keep telling her a gruesome story like that."

This is new, and Glen takes a moment. "Why do you think that?"

"I just do. I told Mother about it—she thinks it's sick to tell a child a story like that. So do I, as a matter of fact."

"Sick?" Glen says. "She likes the story because it makes her feel loved. It isn't sick. It makes me feel love for her, too, when I tell it."

"I'm not surprised," Paige says.

Glen is hurt, having assumed Paige found the story endearing. Then he says, "Are you unloading on me because I'm down?"

"God. I should have known you'd say something like that."

"If I weren't having a hard time, I don't think you'd have said that."

Paige turns away with her magazine. Now she is angry and, as on other nights, they will go to sleep without speaking.

He should resign, Glen thinks as he lies there. The thought comes to him in his inability to find the way to sleep. Beat them to the punch, he thinks. Losers hang around and piss and moan. They cry and sue and appeal, and in the end they lose everything, even their self-respect. The hard fact is that men move on, so be a man, he tells himself. You don't have the goddamn publications, it's true, and they have you by the balls. Others have slipped through on less, but they're ass-kissers one and all, so tell them to take their tenure, and their emasculating year of fucking grace, and stick it up their collective ass. Resign. Be a man. Pick yourself up and take a new run at life.

Ten minutes later, in a state of panic, he sits up on the side of the bed and doesn't know what to do. He'd like to turn to Paige, but she's turned her light out and he couldn't appeal to her now anyway, and he sits there breathing unevenly. There's no doubt about it, they're going to do it. They're going to put him out of his job.

7

Ecki comes to his office. He's just returned from a faculty meeting and her timing is good; he's free until noon, when he must attend a lecture by a visiting scholar.

"Do you have time to talk?" she says, looking in his door.

"For you, yes."

She enters, closing the door gently behind her. "Time for me? It means we are having an affair?"

"A friendship affair."

"So bland."

He shrugs and smiles.

"I know wickedness remains in you," she says.

"Wickedness?"

"Life's seasoning, Professor. Must I teach you everything?"

He enjoys her liveliness, and tries not, as he thinks of it, to recall the feel of her breast.

"You have nothing to teach in turn, with your experience?"

"You're in a devilish mood," he says.

She appears happy in a way he hasn't seen before. "You tease, but nothing more is forthcoming," she says. "What is a woman to think?"

"That you're too full of tricks for your own good?" he says.

"How else am I to present my case?"

"Your case?"

"The winning of your reluctant heart. I want to be your mistress."

He sits back, weighing how impossible things are with this clever young woman. "Before you said pure loving sex, which I took to not include the old ticker. Anyway, bland or not, friendship's the best I can do. I like you—a lot—more than I should. You're sweeping me off my feet, you know. But I'm a father, I'm married. And I'm in an awkward position concerning my job. Besides, I'm too old for such things."

"Not so old—you only say this is so."

He laughs and they sit there smiling. His thought is to say less than he has been saying, however bland she may believe him to be. "I have to review for my afternoon class," he says.

"What I want—I know you are busy, I won't take long. I want to tell you about my husband, the man from whom I am separated, and I want to say a small something, about my experience of aloneness, as I think of it, in this country."

"As a friend, okay, I'll indulge you for a few minutes, as long as you don't try to exploit my weaknesses."

"Which you obviously wish me to do. But—honesty as a basis. I like the term of 'friendship,' and accept in spite of other desires."

He sits looking at her.

"What I wish to say: I do not wish to return to Germany, not just yet. It would be such a failure for me. But all this time in America I have felt not so much new experience as aloneness. All this time. Until, that is, I've been in your class, when I've begun to no longer feel as an exile. It's not just studies, of course, but you. You understand, dear professor? Of course you do. Loneliness and aloneness. Thus I have understood the state of the exiles who left homeland and language in the thirties."

Glen sits watching her, thinking again how bright she is.

"I've seen in your heart that which is in my heart, yes? Does that explain why I wish to be with you? I know you know about aloneness, and not being able to resist the longing which takes control of one. It's in the things you say, and in the literature you teach, and it is this to which my heart has responded." She smiles. "Believe me, I'm not so easy in all ways as you may think. It isn't a daily habit to offer love and sex to my professor. I'm in love with you. I can't help it."

Glen sits looking at her, and says at last, "I'm flattered, which is all I can say."

"You know German, as I know English, but it isn't this, rather it's the contents of hearts, the communication which exceeds language. Yes?"

He doesn't confirm or deny, just looks at her with admiration.

"My husband, the first lieutenant I married in Berlin, and with whom I have traveled to live in Pennsylvania, he hasn't learned more than ten German words, I think, in all this time. In eighteen months in Berlin he has not learned ten words. I have spoken for us in all instances. Yet, I have been in love with him, and we have married and have a child. But they are youthful mistakes, and I've come to realize that what he feels—is nothing. There is no language within his empty heart." She laughs, while her eyes have glossed over.

"He is spoiled, by his mother, I think. Now he writes only once in two or three months to his son. He doesn't care that his son is growing without a father, just as he hasn't cared to learn more than ten words in eighteen months. His heart is hollow, of this I feel little doubt. His heart is hollow and yours, I know, is full. It's what I know."

As, pausing, she looks at him, Glen says, "He's young, he needs time."

"I think his selfishness will never go away."

"That's why you separated?"

"He is no *fun*, too, you see. When we are in Pennsylvania he has no humor, no sentiments. One needs to laugh and cry a little. I have seen the look in your eyes when you are standing before the room to write something. What does life mean if you don't laugh and cry a little, if you are so spoiled by your parents that your heart is left empty?"

"I've been emotional lately, but it's not what I want to be. And I'm older," Glen adds.

"There is some passion in your voice, and caring for life, not just foolish things. You *know* when someone has no caring, and in this husband, I tell you, there is caring only for himself. Not music or poetry, not people or children or history or politics, not even business or money—no, there is caring only for himself. I tell you—in films, when there is cruelty, when there is—what do you say—I'm not sure, false courage? This he cares for. False courage and cruelty. This alone calls forth in him feeling which is strong. What kind of person can this be?"

Glen sits looking at her, fondly, thinking it is right to let her say what is on her mind, to let her, if not him, be free of frustration. What she does next takes him by surprise yet again, as, all at once it seems, she is standing with her hands around his head, pressing herself to his face.

He doesn't pull away, hardly has room, and thinks to persuade himself that this, too, the warm smell and feel of her, the feel of her breasts against his nose and mouth, is not something he should challenge. Her head bent down over him, she whispers, "Please, I want to give you pleasure with my mouth, even here in this room."

She embraces him, and he barely moves. He'd like to reach his arms around her—she has him aroused—while his merest capacity of mind is telling him to protect himself. "No," he hears himself say. "I don't want that. No." He moves his neck to disengage himself.

She stands looking at him. "It's distasteful to you?"

"No," he says. "I'm married. And I'm your teacher."

"Propriety keeps you back, not your feelings?"

"I think you're taking advantage of our friendship."

"I am a Berlin girl," she says with a smile. "I have long ago learned to be tantalizing in all ways to the man I wish to make happy; this makes me happy."

"Well—" He goes silent upon a sudden rapping on his door, and calls out, "Yes?"

The door opens and Otto Gentz's eyes move from Glen to Ecki. "I am interrupting?" he says.

"She's just leaving," Glen says.

"Yes," Ecki says, and proceeds quickly to duck her head and depart.

Otto glances after her. Returning his gaze to Glen, his eyebrows jump. "Dear colleague, I advise you, the office door must be left open with students at all times, male or female. If tenure is your concern, it's the new law of academe."

The heavy man is nearly winking, but Glen is too aware of Otto's devious reputation, and returns his smile with but a thin, red-faced smile of his own.

"In any case," Otto remarks, "I'm here to see how things are proceeding—letters of support, copies of publications. Are we getting our materials together?"

"I have the translations I've done recently," Glen says.

"You know, of course, how I feel about translations."

"I guess I don't, no."

"More harm than good. Original work is the key. Translations are so clearly an admission of a weak case, you see, they're better *not* to include. You make a little money, true—"

"They count for something."

"Nonetheless—"

"Otto, tell me the truth. Is this all a waste of time? I don't know if I have the heart for it."

"Your case is not easy, that's obvious. In fact, it is most difficult. Still, I assure you, it's in your interest to put it forth as strongly as possible. You don't *know*, for one thing, how it will be received. So can we meet again soon, to discuss merely a checklist of items? Recommendations, committees, even former students, especially if they have gone on to some success, say, in reputable graduate schools. May we meet, say, Tuesday next, to go over all this?"

Glen nods. "Including the translations."

"As you wish," Otto says, and again raises his substantial eyebrows. "Remember: open-door policy." He slips into the hall then, smiling happily.

At home that evening, Paige tells him she has advanced to the next level of job interview—tomorrow, at the main bank in Dover, fifteen miles away. The other news is that the job has been redefined from a full-time bank position to piecework at home for six months, evaluating mortgage applications. In all probability this would lead to the title of mortgage officer at the bank at the end of the trial period. "What they don't realize," she adds, "is how perfect six months at home would be for me, with Alice starting kindergarten by then."

"That's great," Glen says. He doesn't mention, and hasn't in weeks, that her job prospects seem inversely related to his own.

"I'll need the car tomorrow—you won't mind walking Alice to school?"

Glen shakes his head, to say no problem. He'll work at home in the morning, walk Alice to nursery school, go on to his office, and pick her up after his afternoon class.

"You won't forget to pick her up?" Paige says.

"No way," Glen says, and by way of confirmation reaches to touch Alice's shoulder, low beside him in her ordinary chair, and leans down to kiss her hair. Suffering a degree of guilt over Ecki's visit that morning, he's resolved to be a good husband and father.

"The pay could really help," Paige is saying. "Then, in the fall, if I get the full-time position—I see no reason why I shouldn't—there are benefits, too. It's exciting, really, though I'm sure there'll be drawbacks. Punkin, you won't mind if Mommy goes to work, will you, when you go to kindergarten?"

Alice shakes her head no—of course not, how silly of you to ask, her expression says—and her parents take in their child's agreeable nature, and her ability to deliver such neat, if silent, one-liners in a toss of her eyes.

"It's good of you to be so generous about this," Glen says to Paige.

"The timing just couldn't be better. That's what has me feeling so hopeful. It's the kind of work," she adds to Alice, "I was doing when Daddy came along and slid a note under my cage like a bank robber." She slips Glen a smile.

"What I didn't know at the time," he says, "was that Mommy could have stepped on an alarm button and had some cop blow poor Daddy to smithereens."

"When we first met," Paige tells Alice, "Mommy was working her tail off at First Guaranty Trust, being *very* careful about the customers she gave credit to, though she did notice a certain customer taking looks and even lining up at her station when old Mrs. Pace had no one in line at all. Then, one day, on her slab of marble, Mommy finds a note, and she probably should've stepped on the alarm. You know what the note said? 'Armed with hungry heart eager to steal your affections. May I treat you to a glass of wine after work? Glen Cady, Postdoc.'"

Paige and Alice laugh, while Glen titters in embarrassment over the inclusion of his status at the time.

"Not pressing that alarm is probably the biggest mistake I ever made," Paige says, and they all laugh. "Anyway, Punkin," she adds, "it's something I know how to do, and doing it at home wouldn't get in the way of anything."

"I've been thinking I should resign," Glen says, surprising himself.

Paige gives him a look. "I can't believe you said that," she says.

"I'll get shot down anyway," Glen says.

"Even if I get the job in the fall," Paige says, "we couldn't get along on what I'd earn, not in this house."

Suddenly the situation seems confused, and Glen says, "I shouldn't have said that. I'm a little rattled these days, you know, as in mentally deranged. Forgive me."

"I just hope you're not serious," Paige says.

" 'Mentally deranged'?" Alice says.

"It's going to happen. That's all I know. But let's drop it for now."

"You don't *know* it's going to happen," Paige says.

Glen says nothing, then the telephone rings and Paige, who usually answers the phone, begins to get up. But there isn't a second ring. "What other job would give you time to look for something else?" she says, sitting back down.

"I don't know. I could write letters on nights and weekends, but I haven't really thought about it."

"What's 'mentally deranged'?" Alice says.

"Everybody has to swallow their pride sometime," Paige says.

"It means losing your ability to think straight, sweetheart, and I've *been* swallowing," Glen says.

"And that's why you're not eating?"

"Not eating?"

"Glen—" The telephone rings again and they wait to see if it will ring a second time, and it does. "I know when you're not eating," Paige says, rising from the table.

"Hello?" she says into the receiver.

She makes a face at Glen. "Hello!" she says. "I know you're there," she adds and hangs up. Glen has an idea who it might have been, as Paige, sitting down, says, "You fooling around with someone?"

"Because of that?"

"I wasn't born yesterday," Paige says.

"Was probably a wrong number."

"Preceded by a one-ring signal, and you're sitting here faint-hearted and not eating. Have you fallen in love?"

Glen laughs. " 'Fainthearted and not eating.' That's pretty good—where'd you get that?"

Paige almost smiles. "Don't change the subject. You'd think people would learn, but it's always the same. Is it one of your students?"

"I'm changing the subject. Don't be ridiculous. Tell me where you came up with 'fainthearted and not eating.'"

"Glen, I can read you like a book. I know when you're being strange, and this is one of those times."

"World's coming down on me, I can't help it. Can we drop this, in any case."

"Beryl," Paige says then. "She's always saying Amy is faint-hearted and not eating over some boy at school. But look me in the eye and tell me you'd lose your appetite over Otto Gentz. Look me in the eye, come on."

"You'll see what you want to see."

"All I know is you work all day with those pretty young things."

"Come on yourself, and lay off," Glen says, looking to Alice. "I'm getting it from all sides, except from Little Peashooter here."

There is no response, from either of the women in his life, and Glen returns his attention to his dinner plate in hopes of having this new threat go away.

"Maybe it *was* a wrong number," Paige says. "I don't know."

They're lying in bed in the dark, and several of the quiet moments which lead to sleep have slipped away.

Glen had begun to drift. "Phones ring like that, don't be so suspicious," he says.

"You may be right, but you have been acting strange."

"It's a strange time. I'm surprised myself."

"You don't eat. And maybe you dote a bit too much on Alice."

"That's what you think?"

"My father sure never carried on like that with me."

Glen doesn't respond.

"I'd mind less if you doted on me, too," Paige says, seeming to joke as a way to change the subject.

Glen, however sleepy, feels desirous at least of lying close, and he reaches a hand over Paige's rayon-covered ribs and slides it down to her belly. Not sure if he is aroused or simply needy, he whispers a line close to her ear—hoping to be both funny and provocative—including the phrase "dote on some dirty words?"

Under his hand, Paige tenses in disappointment.

Stillness follows, and Glen knows he's spoiled the mood.

"Do you really have to say things like that?" Paige whispers.

"I guess not," he says at last.

"It just isn't exciting to me," she whispers. "It's the opposite."

"I thought, well ... I'm sorry."

Silence gathers. Glen would like to talk, would like to not be at odds, but doesn't know what to say. Disappointment, anger, frustration—all are familiar and close at hand once again. He could sit up and cry tears of disappointment, could say, directly, that he yearns for, would give anything every once in a while for, uninhibited sex—adult sex, is how he's come to think of it—and that its absence throughout a decade of marriage has become one of his deepest regrets. He could say, too, that he is deeply in trouble and needs her help, and knows he can't.

His thoughts swirl as he lies in the dark in fear and silence, and Ecki comes to mind. It wouldn't be like this with her, he thinks. And it wasn't with Hedy.

8

In the morning, leaving for her interview, Paige is beautifully dressed and beaming with hope, and her appearance persuades Glen all the more that he, or his age, is the problem. He's confounded that a woman can look so sexual and be so inaccessible. Is she conditioned to respond to a nice-looking right fielder, while her husband more closely resembles the coach?

He steps over Alice on his way to the ringing telephone. Lying on her belly, face resting in her hands, Alice is reading; Glen was grading papers, in an armchair, and he thinks, Quiet Alice, who knows what goes on in that ball of reddish-blond curls?

Paige's friend Beryl is on the other end, and though Glen thinks to ask about "fainthearted and not eating," he explains that Paige has driven to Dover for an interview.

"I thought it wasn't until this afternoon," Beryl says. "You're baby-sitting Alice?"

"Sort of," Glen says. "We're off to nursery school at one. We both have afternoon classes."

"You're up to baby-sitting?" Beryl presses.

"Gee—we're sort of candid here this morning," Glen says. "Guess it's what I've always liked about you." However playful he means to sound, he's surprised by what she just said.

"I guess I shouldn't have said that," she says. "Ron would go nuts if I asked him to stay home with the kids, especially when he has problems at work. Sorry to offend."

"Beryl, I can't imagine you offending anyone."

"Listen, if you grew up with my name—well, I'm sure you understand. Tell Paige I called, will you? And again, no offense."

"What an old radiator that woman can be," Glen mumbles, stepping directly over Alice on his way to his chair.

"Who's an old radiator?"

"Nobody—somebody."

"Who?"

"The old toilet bowl I was talking to," Glen says.

Alice lets it go and returns to her reading. Of course he's up to taking care of his daughter, Glen thinks. What an idiotic thing to say. But can he support her, he wonders, and what of the old man he'll be when Alice is a teenager? "Sweetheart," he says with a degree of fear, "what are you reading?"

"Green Eggs and Ham."

"You've read that before," he says.

"Hmm," Alice says.

"How many times have you read it?"

"Don't know."

"Alice, don't say you don't know," he says. "It's like saying you don't care to even think about something."

No response. Absorbed, Alice continues to read. Gazing at her, Glen feels amused that she didn't respond, believing it's because she's comfortable with him.

Then he wonders if Alice is being so good because she was instructed by Paige to be on her best behavior. Could Alice be afraid of him? Of course not, he thinks.

In time, absorbed in grading papers, he realizes that Alice is at his side, and he looks into her face, which has been called old-fashioned by friends. Someone said she appeared to step out of an old tin poster, a way of implying, he has guessed, that she *is* different, more cute than glamorous. It's a face he adores in any case—Paige is right, he's been doting on his daughter—and he allows her time to say whatever she came to say.

"Thirteen," she says, then pauses. "I think."

Glen smiles. "You run out of other books to read?"

"Reading it upside down."

"Upside down."

She stands there and he looks into her gray-blue eyes. "You always this good, even when I'm not home?"

Her brow wrinkles some in consternation, and her lips purse, but she doesn't say anything. It's as if she doesn't know what he's talking about, or perhaps she does, and her response, as usual, is silence and something of a face, although not to the extreme—fish lips and crossed eyes—among her favorites.

"Sorry," Glen says. "Of course you are. You're not afraid of me, are you?"

"No," Alice says. "I like you."

Melting a little, Glen draws her to him, kissing and whispering into her frizzy hair. "I like you, too, you little tulip bulb. I'm crazy about you."

His task is to deliver Alice to The Learning Tree by one and pick her up when the session ends at four-thirty. He gets her into a zip-up playsuit left on her bed, then into her jacket and cap, allowing half an hour for the six-block walk. "We'll just putz along," he tells her.

They do, and not in a straight line. The air is sunny and warm for December, and most of the time he holds one loosely mittened hand like a leash while she twists and turns, lifting, one at a time, the miniature denim sneakers whose pink laces, in defiance of his offer, she tied herself.

One of her steps, he guesses, is a third of his, and given her zigzag pattern, her circles and studies of ground, the ratio is closer to four to one. Nor is her pace anything like rapid. In time he asks, "How's the view down there?"

"Counting cracks," she says, pulling to the side.

"Counting cracks?"

She offers no follow-up.

"So you won't step on them?"

"That's Mr. Twenty-seven," she says, pointing.

"Mr. Twenty-seven! You can count that high?"

"Yes!" she says, perhaps irritated that he doesn't know this about her.

There is her small face, her corduroy cap, as cleanly yellow as a rose. "Like a ride?" he asks.

Lights go on in her eyes, and he wonders if the leash routine was a setup all along.

Does she weigh thirty pounds? He's losing track of these things, he thinks, as he lifts her and lowers her to a seat on his shoulders. He grips the grainy one-and-a-half-inch pipes of her legs—she wears beige tights—and resumes walking. "Comfortable?" he says, tilting his head upward but unable to make eye contact.

She doesn't say.

"Kind of hard to count from up there," he says. "Must be like riding an elephant."

She gives no response and he plods along.

"You know, sweetie," he says, "there are hawks that fly up high like you, and their vision is so good they can see a mouse, on the ground, more than a mile away."

She doesn't respond; nothing. Quiet Alice.

"How much do you weigh?" he calls skyward after a moment. "Do you know?"

"Thirty-three pounds," Alice says.

"When did you last get weighed?"

"This morning."

"You weigh yourself every morning?"

"When Mommy does," Alice says, floating along, and Glen envisions the two women checking their weight on the bathroom scale. Does Paige *know* this little thirty-three-pound mystery?

At The Learning Tree, entering the fenced-in yard, Glen lifts Alice down, stretches his shoulders, and looks around for someone to whom to make delivery. As they enter the main room, where three or four children are working at a table, two women appear, a young woman from behind a partition and a middle-aged woman in a white smock from an office.

"Alice's father," he says to the woman in the crisp medical smock. "We may be a little early."

"Oh—Mr. Cady?" the woman says.

Glen nods.

"I see Mrs. Cady often but we've never met. Mrs. Ouellette."

"How do you do," Glen says, noticing that Alice is regarding the world from beside his leg.

"No reason to be afraid," the woman says to Alice, smiling with expanding eyes.

Glen, surprised by the degree of Alice's shyness, touches fingers to her hair. "Go ahead and join the other kids," he says. "I'll see you after school."

Glen smiles apologetically at the woman, and is about to leave when Alice says from the side, "Daddy, see my cubby."

Glancing to the woman as if for permission, he follows Alice around the partition to a wall of orange-crate-sized openings painted different colors. Alice is hanging her cap and jacket inside a red space. A label across the upper board reads ALICE CADY, in her writing, and it is as if she is suddenly someone in addition to the person he has assumed her to be. He glances at a jar of Magic Markers, her yellow cap on top of her jacket, but mainly it is her name he sees. ALICE CADY.

Crouching, he says again that he'll see her after school. "Alice Cady," he adds, and gives her a kiss on the cheek.

Near the door, however, Mrs. Ouellette says, "Might I have a word with you, Mr. Cady? Just a couple minutes?"

Glen nods, looks to Alice again, gives her a waist-high wave, and steps past Mrs. Ouellette.

Closing the office door, she says, "Sometimes it's good to talk to the fathers about these things, too."

"These things?" Glen says.

"We're a little concerned about Alice, frankly. We're not sure she's progressing in socialization the way we think she should."

"Socialization?" Glen says.

"Getting along. Interacting with peers. They're among the main objectives of nursery school, and Alice—well, she's shy and slow in this area. You saw how reluctant she was to leave your side just now?"

"Well, she's only four years old," Glen says, his ears burning at the word "slow."

The woman smiles in a faint way he likes even less. "Children are often shy when they first start here," she says. "But they soon get over that, most of them do, I assure you."

"Alice *is* a little shy," Glen decides to say. "And she's quiet, but I don't see that as a defect."

"It's her progress that concerns us. Most boys move in quickly and stake claims on things, as do any number of girls. But Alice, as a matter of fact, has held back a bit more than we think she should. I don't like to be the bearer of unpleasant news, Mr. Cady, but many parents—well, you're at the college and I'm sure you understand what I'm saying."

Glen has a feeling he's betraying the child he carried here on his shoulders, who, an hour ago, told him, directly, that she liked him. He says, more firmly, "I think, well, she's not a boy. She *is* shy, and quiet. Don't you have other kids who are quiet?"

"I only wanted to call it to your attention."

"You're concerned?"

"We just wonder if Alice is developing in these areas. She's been having difficulty, too, with one of the boys in class."

"Really. What kind of difficulty?"

"Well, they just don't seem to get along."

"Is there some reason why?"

"Not exactly that we've been able to pin down. A question that comes to mind, of course, is Alice's general, well, reluctance, in getting along, in participating."

"Gee," Glen says, "that's not what would come to my mind. Maybe the boy's been poking her when nobody's watching?"

"We don't really know the reason."

"Well, I don't mean to be defensive, which I guess I am. And I'm sure Alice is capable of doing things she shouldn't. She could be poking *him* in the ribs."

"Before the term is over, it's something I would like to discuss with Mrs. Cady. As I'm sure you'll agree, we want our girls today to get as much attention as the boys."

Glen nods. "I'll tell her mother about your concerns."

Leaving, he sees that Alice, in a group of several children, is watching for him to come from the office. "Later, alligator," he says to her.

She waves her hand as he waved his earlier, from the waist, and he leaves smiling.

But outside, walking away, his mind spins with the term "slow." Jesus, talk about an old radiator, he thinks. Does that woman have something against little girls? Is Alice resented for being quiet? Isn't a four-year-old just a four-year-old? Could it be, dear God, could it be that something is lacking in the little complication that is their one and only child?

Ecki doesn't come to class and Glen's heart does an about-face. A year of feeling as he feels now—heart knotting when a young woman doesn't show up for his class—could short-circuit whatever self-confidence he has left. He might as well quit.

He starts without her, glancing now and then at her empty

seat, and knows he's failing as a person. Relinquishing the year of grace might give him the strength he needs to go on, instead of watching himself fall further in some sort of charade.

The class ends—his teaching has been uninspired—and her seat remains empty. One of his rules is that students give notice in anticipation of absences, and as the afternoon proceeds he imagines her absence was calculated to do just what it has done. It's the psychology of infatuation: whatever his age, he knows he's falling into the old feverish sway. Needing to see her, he wonders if he might call her at home on the pretext of a missed assignment?

He has forgotten Alice! The one thing he meant to keep in mind has slipped away and, on a panicked grab at his watch, shocks his heart. Four-thirty, already dark. At once he's on his feet, stuffing papers into his book bag as he gets an arm into his parka, and a moment later is hurrying along the corridor as his office door slams in his wake.

A mother and child are just leaving, and Alice—his heart is immediately becalmed—is playing at a table with two other girls. She greets him with a smile, but no words. "Hi," he says as, from the side, Mrs. Ouellette says, "Professor Cady, might I speak with you once again?"

Following the woman's ominous tone and gesture, still recovering his breath, Glen enters her office.

"I'm afraid our little problem has gotten out of hand," she says. "Kevin Baker, the boy Alice has been feuding with—he became quite upset this afternoon, and so has his mother, over Alice calling him a name."

"Alice called him a name?" Glen says, still trying to catch up with himself and with what he's doing here.

"What she called him, more than once—his mother thinks it's to suggest he isn't clean, which he certainly is, is Toilet Stool."

Glen can't help laughing. "Toilet Stool?" he says, and coughs to get himself to stop smiling.

"It's not a flattering name to call a person, Mr. Cady. None of us believe it to be terribly amusing."

Glen looks at her; she's serious. Still, he can't help feeling relief for the second time in several minutes. "I think," he says, "maybe there's some jumping to conclusions here. I'm sure this name has nothing to do with this boy being clean. It's wordplay. That's all. She was playing."

"I'm sorry to tell you it was not taken as playful."

"Is there a chance this boy deserved to be called a name?" he says. "Alice is a little girl who weighs thirty-three pounds. I don't think she's going to hurt anyone. How big is Kevin Baker?"

"This isn't a championship fight, Mr. Cady," she says. "You may call it wordplay. To us it is name-calling. It's certainly not positive behavior, as I'm sure you'll agree. We don't want children passing through nursery school thinking it's acceptable when in fact it may be hurtful, and even damaging."

"Okay, I'll talk to her," he says, trying to keep himself under control. "I'll say this, though, because it's something you seem eager to overlook. Maybe this little boy was the instigator. And the name still strikes me as harmless, no matter how you wish to characterize it. It's something we do at home. Wordplay."

"Kevin was clearly upset, in any case."

"Okay, I'll talk to Alice," Glen says. "I don't want to say anything else right now, because to tell you the truth I'm getting a little heated up here. I wouldn't want Kevin's feelings to get hurt, but if he can't handle a little—" No more! Glen says to himself. "Sorry—I'll talk to Alice," he says.

Stepping back into the main room, he helps his small child roll up a damp finger painting, helps her into her jacket and cap, and takes her small hand in his own. Mrs. Ouellette watches from her office door.

"Good night," Glen says, then adds, softly, "Alice."

"G'night, Miss Ouellette," Alice says.

"Good night, Alice."

Outside, when they have walked fifty yards or so at Alice's pace, Glen asks if she wants a ride. Is this what mothers go through every day, he's wondering as he lifts Alice—hugs her, feels love for her, in the process—and lowers her into place. Fending off humorless windbags who've never seen a playground? And the name continues to amuse him, even makes him a little proud. Pretty sharp, really. You little Toilet Stool.

No, he thinks, he won't even hint to Alice that she might have done something wrong. But as they walk, and as the day around them descends into full darkness, something more elusive than the day itself is slipping away, and he grows oddly emotional. The sweep of things. Why does so much seem to be slipping from his grasp?

9

No word from Ecki. Days between classes pass slowly while Glen hopes to hear from her. But nothing—no excuses, no inquiries about missed assignments. He has become taken with her, it's clear, and the grip of desire is at once thrilling and maddening. Why now? he wonders. Other times he tells himself how fortunate he is to be coming alive again as forces around him are trying to put him down, that it's lifesaving to be emboldened by schoolboy feelings of love.

Still, nothing from the object of his youthful dreams. No visits, notes, or calls. He guesses she's wise to the psychology of love she's visiting upon him, and his infatuation only thrives, as does his admiration for her.

Midmorning, Friday, the day of their afternoon class, he sees her at a distance walking toward the library and he looks upon her as long as she's in view. She's wearing a waist-length jacket, a flowing flowered skirt, and a beret or tam-o'-shanter, affecting a funky Berlin style all her own.

He goes on his way, hoping she's cramming and cutting classes in preparation for finals. She is, after all, an exceptional student, however else he imagines her. What a crush he has on her, he realizes as he enters his own building. Hedy. Paige. Is it but the third time in his life he's felt such rapturous desire? Is so small a number a curse or a blessing?

———

Ecki misses class again, the third in a row, and it's clear she's sending him a message. He doesn't know if her message is one of caring or of not caring, knows only that he misses her and doesn't want to lose her. Whatever their relationship is or might be, she's reconnected him to dreams he imagined were no longer his. Doesn't she know that he has made no friends in his decade of marriage and hard work, that he adores her and needs her?

She knows, he thinks.

He has to get through the weekend, but that night in bed he clashes with Paige when he tells her at last of the tiff in nursery school days earlier.

"Which boy was it?" Paige wants to know.

"I was afraid that's what you'd say," Glen says. "It doesn't matter."

"Of course it matters. What are you so angry about?"

"I'll tell you in a minute," he says. "It has to do with Alice, that's all I'm saying, and how quiet she is, which Mrs. Ouellette sees as a shortcoming. It isn't just about the boy."

"She *is* shy. My gosh, calm down."

"I dislike the word 'shy.' I reject it out of hand."

"There are times myself when I wish she'd speak up."

"Well, I never feel that way, and I don't like hearing you say you do. Is she 'slow,' as Mrs. Ouellette would have it? That's the word she used, 'slow.' Or is she simply not loud? I believe it's the latter, okay, and I'm beginning to think there's an objection about Alice merely because she's a little different. She's not strange, but she *is* a little quiet. She's private. Look how well she reads. She loves to read, I bet she's reading way above her grade level, and I don't see any problem that she's not some little monster bashing the walls for attention."

"She still needs to learn to get along."

"Let's give her a chance, folks. She's four years old. You know what she called this kid? I really like it. Toilet Stool! What a name. Can you imagine? I think it baffled the kid is what it did. Only his mother apparently thought somebody was saying her little schmuck wasn't clean."

"What kid, what mother?"

"Don't you think Toilet Stool is pretty imaginative?"

"I'm sure you do. What kid?"

"Kevin Baker, but that's beside the point."

"Tom and Tracy Baker. He's the new internist at North Shore Douglass."

"Yeah, well, fuck him, I don't care who he is. Alice is the point here! She's a little girl who weighs thirty-three pounds and who happens by nature to be quiet, for which reason people are calling her slow and shy. Her mother included. It's pissing me off, in case you haven't noticed. This, too: After I saw the way her teacher, of all people, regards her—what are that old sow's credentials anyway?—and the way you seem willing to join in, then I think something's being foisted off on my kid, and I've been coming around to the conclusion all week that I'm not going to stand for it."

"God, Glen, what is with you? Good night! Go to hell!"

Glen lies there, steaming still and checking himself against giving in even more to his confused feelings.

"When am I supposed to see her?" Paige says, facing the wall.

"See who?"

"Will you stop being so horrid!"

"I don't know, whenever."

"Boy, who's wound you up lately?"

"World's unloading on me, that's all I know. As a matter of fact, I'm sorry."

"Why aren't you so tough about tenure?"

"That's a little different. But thanks for your support."

Paige says nothing more, and unable to let it go—knowing he is going to say what he decided a moment ago not to say—Glen adds, "The way I've seen women treat one of their own, trying to mold her into a preconceived little phony, Alice may be goddamn lucky her father happened to stay home and take her to school."

"Well hoopty-do for Clint Peckerwood," Paige says to the wall.

Glen's eyes have filmed over, and silence gathers like a small cyclone in his chest. On a thought of Alice, a rising of his small child to his heart, he slips from bed and from the room.

Along the carpeted hallway, hesitating, he enters her room. He'd like to just sit on the floor and have quiet words in the dark, speak of animals and oceans, or tell stories and talk about words. He'd like to speak of Blackie tonight, for his own benefit.

As he leans over her bed, however, he sees something other than that her eyes are closed and she is asleep. What he sees is that she appears to be a person he's always wanted to know—a small girl character from a great book or from a great foreign film in black and white. How could anyone want to change little Alice?

He leans down, as he often does, watches for a moment, to be certain of her breathing, kisses the frizz of her hair, and moves to slip away. As he touches the door an uncertain voice says, "Daddy."

His heart breathes and he looks back. "Hi," he whispers. "You're awake?"

"I heard you and Mommy," she says.

"Boy, you have good ears—it's why children hear everything."

"Over a mile," Alice says.

The hawk. He wasn't sure she'd understood, and now this slow child is making a joke of it. "You don't miss much, do you."

"You and Mommy were fighting," she tells him.

"I guess I got a little loud," he says. "Did I wake you up?"

She doesn't say and he wonders if her reticence has to do with people speaking foolishly to her, for obviously he'd awakened her. "We weren't quite fighting," he says. "I was, sort of, telling myself, well, that you're my daughter, and that I see it as my duty to stand up for you. Because I love you—do you know how much your father loves you? And I'm not going to let any old used auto parts keep me from believing in you."

He's surprised when she says, "Miss Ouellette?"

Glen laughs, then laughs some more. "Case closed," he says. "But we'll be nice to everyone, at all times. Right? We'll travel the high road."

Alice doesn't respond to this.

"I'll let you go back to sleep," he says. "I just, well, I wanted to see you, but I'll see you in the morning." He doesn't want to leave, but leans down to kiss her again, to touch her temple, and backs away. When he was young, his father—coming home after a few too many—would get him up to have hot dogs and talk, and he sees now that his father was looking for ways to tell him he loved him. And in the hall outside Alice's door, he pauses as if to take in a prize he has won.

Monday arrives at last, with wet snow needling in off the sea as he crosses South Bridge to the island campus. If Ecki doesn't show up today, he's decided to call her at home—out of genuine concern, he tells himself. He's not going to give in and cross over to her, but he will ascertain that she's okay.

His morning class slips by, then he attends a meeting and reviews for his afternoon class, all the while pondering Ecki's nature. A sexual creature, a reader of literature and hiker of Alpine trails, and perhaps the fulfillment of old dreams—none of which characteristics, he thinks, it would be fair to expect of Paige. But wouldn't it be something, perhaps everything, if Paige were less inhibited?

The time arrives at last and Glen leaves his tiny office and proceeds down the stairwell and through the hallways to his classroom, where a scattering of students awaits him. They go through routine greetings—*"Guten Tag,"* and *"Guten Tag, Herr Professor"*—but the seat to which his eyes and heart are drawn remains empty. Materials placed on the table, door left open, he writes a line on the board, the text, he always calls it, for the day's sermon.

> The real purpose of my work?
> I say simply: Joy.
> —T. MANN

Eyes down, he busies himself with papers before looking up. Well, she's rejecting him, trying to make him pay and succeeding, he thinks. His only reprieve is that he now has a reason to call. Then, as he opens his lecture folder, he realizes someone has entered from the side and he turns to see Ecki.

"I must drop the class," she says. "Please, you will sign this card—to say I am not a failure."

She appears distraught and what he'd like to do is touch and comfort her. "You can't drop a class this late in the semester," he says in a near-whisper. "Why would you want to?"

"I've petitioned the department head and it is acceptable, upon your signature. Please."

"I'm not signing," he says, trying still not to be heard by the others. "The credit's already yours; you don't want to drop now."

"You refuse to sign?"

"Of course I refuse."

"I cannot be forced to attend." She turns to leave.

"Ecki," he says. She pauses and he steps toward her, touching her elbow to guide her into the hall. "Excuse us for a second," he says over his shoulder to the class, and once outside, looking into her eyes, says, "I'm sorry you're feeling bad, but this isn't necessary. If you want my attention, you've got it, so you don't need to do this. I thought we were friends—it's what I want."

At last she says, "I make such a fool of myself, I must do something—"

"This would just waste what you've done all semester. You don't *have* to do anything. Everything's okay."

"Will you never let me have my way?" she says.

"I guess not," he says. "Just come in now and sit down. We'll talk about all of this later."

"Not just now, I cannot—Forgive me."

"You're forgiven."

She moves away. Glancing after her, Glen reenters the class-room and closes the door. *"Meine Damen und Herren, Verzeihung . . . ,"* he says by way of beginning.

When class ends and Glen leaves, eager to reach his office, hoping Ecki may be there, he is intercepted by Otto Gentz.

"News," Otto says with a frown. "Not very good news, I'm afraid, but I am obligated to report it to you, and also a little advice. May we stop in my office?"

Within Otto's large first-floor office, he gestures toward a chair and Glen shakes his head. "Have an appointment right away," he says.

"The news, in two parts," Otto replies. "One, the preliminary vote by senior members, all six in attendance. This is not a binding vote, but a checking of sentiment, to see what work lies before us. A straw vote, you know?"

"Yes, a straw vote."

"Six-zip," Otto says.

"Six-zip?"

"Yes, not that all the senior members are dead set against you. This is only their impression of your chances, as it were."

"I see. The problem?"

"Your case is not promising, that's the problem."

"That's not what I meant. Did they say *why* they felt my case was so weak?"

"Certainly. Articles but no book."

"Most of them haven't published any more than I have."

"Well, entering is one thing, admitting others is something else. Plus the usual arguments, declining enrollments and so on."

"This means you didn't vote for me?"

"I must also see added materials, persuasive evidence, which is why I'm here. To keep you informed, and to bolster your case with stronger materials."

"You don't think that your voting against me—as my advocate—undermines my case?"

"In no way. Understand that my final word will mean nothing if I have not established credibility at the outset. Given credibility *now*, a recommendation will carry weight *then*."

"There *are* no other materials, Otto, as you know. If they're going to vote me out, why don't they just get it over with."

"Bitterness will not help your cause. I must warn you, in an official capacity, that a poor attitude in one institution will make it difficult for you to receive appointment in another, ever."

"I'm sure. The other news?"

"The other—well, it's less news than personal advice. There is a student in one of your classes, Owens-Reiff? Yes?"

"Yes."

"I have seen her leaving your office recently in a certain state, my closed-door advice—you recall? Now, as it happens, I am privy to her petition to drop your class at this impossibly late date. She has appealed to Monica to grant the request, and Monica, in her capacity as chair, has inquired of this comely lass if there is a problem with her professor, and even as the young woman has replied in the negative, the suspicion is there—as is my own, quite frankly. Thus, without asking you to reply, I want again to call your attention to the volatile nature of situations of the kind. Be very careful, is what I'm saying. A *hint* of impropriety could tarnish your reputation beyond repair."

"How can she be allowed to drop at this late date?"

"Glen, really. Woman to woman, any request is granted today, where have you been?"

After a pause, Glen says, "Anyway, there's nothing—"

"Please—no reply is necessary."

"I'm going to reply: There's nothing between me and this student. Nothing. She may be going through—"

"Please. Wake up! Do you think there needs to *be* something to create a case?"

"Fine," Glen says. "Fine," he says again, then turns and leaves.

He blinks in exasperation as he enters the stairwell to climb to the third floor, and, entering the small corridor, sees that his office door remains closed and locked. Ecki cannot be here, and he had hoped against hope that she might be standing near his door.

He closes the door behind him, and has a thought of turning to a friend, but nobody comes to mind. Could he try Paige, he wonders. Call her and try to explain the loss he's experiencing, and the risks they're facing as a couple and family? He knows, feels certain that she wouldn't be sympathetic and he'd end up feeling worse. Suddenly he realizes the only person he might turn to is Alice, and he feels undone.

The afternoon is fading and he's still at his desk, trying to clarify the defeat his life is suffering, when the telephone rings.

"I'm so sorry for my display," Ecki blurts out. "I am so confused."

"It's okay. Nothing happened, there's no need to be sorry."

"You are angry with me?"

"I was disappointed—but not angry. There's just no need to drop my class. You're the best student I've ever had."

"I'm in my apartment now, while my son visits a friend. May you visit me here, only to talk?"

"No, I can't do that. I'm in too much trouble as it is."

"You know where I live?"

"Yes."

"Please."

"I'd like to, because I like you. I like you a lot. But a lot's at stake for me."

"If I beg, will you come to me?"

"I'll see you in class Wednesday. You come to class and finish the semester. There are only two classes left."

"I will."

"Just throw that drop card away."

"I wanted to hurt you, to gain your attention, it's true."

"Let's forgot all about it. We'll be friends forever."

"Darling, please come be with me. I want to hold you."

"I'll see you in class on Wednesday," Glen says, and hangs up.

He stares at the phone, then swivels his chair to look at the article lying beside his computer, which he switches on. What was he doing when the phone rang? He starts reading the article, but is too rattled to make even three or four words fit together. Why is all this happening?

Downstairs, he taps on the door of the department chair, Monica Beniquez, and, after a confused exchange, is sitting in a chair by her desk. "Sorry to walk in here like this, Monica. I'm not sure I even know what I'm doing."

Monica looks at him across her desk—kindly, he thinks—but says nothing, merely looks.

"Otto told me about the preliminary vote, and how slim my chances are, as has the dean, and, I don't know, I just thought I'd stop in. I guess I'm in serious trouble. Monica, we've been friends, you know I'm a good teacher—do you have any advice?"

Monica continues looking at him with her sad expression. At last she says, "I'm really sorry, Glen, because I don't know what to say."

"I'm probably a goner, I know that. I'm not asking for support, it's not like that. I'm—what's a person to do?"

"Well . . ."

"Really. No punches pulled. I need some help."

"Well, in the profession—it seems brutal, and this is certainly off the record—I think you have to accept that it hasn't quite worked for you. Nor do I know if you've tried to make it work, to tell you the truth."

"Fair enough. Chances of hooking on elsewhere?"

"Slight. I'm sure you know we haven't—and this is *strictly* off the record—we haven't *looked* at an application from a man in over five years. The department, the university, is top-heavy with men. What can I say? It's an adjustment that will go on for some time."

"Just like that, I'm out—everywhere?"

"I'd like to tell you otherwise, but you asked for some hard truth. You might pick up a replacement job, and you might try prep schools. As for being a candidate for new positions, well, the likelihood is hardly promising. You wanted the truth, I'm afraid that's it."

"I knew things were bad, I didn't know they were that bad."

"For women and minorities, frankly, they're not so bad. Young women. Most positions get redefined as entry-level and are going to young women just earning their degrees and just beginning to publish. That's the reality of academic life."

"I'm not sure that's fair."

Monica's expression tells him there isn't much else she'd like to say. He nods, thanks her, and leaves.

Paige answers on the second ring and, hearing his voice, says, "This'll have to be quick, Glen. I'm just driving Alice to nursery school—you know my final interview is this afternoon."

"Well, go ahead, it's okay. I'm just a little rattled here, but it can wait."

"Glen, what is it?"

"Same old thing, I guess—middle-aged male being shown the door."

"You sure?"

"I'm sure, and I'm thinking I ought to resign. The best defense, you know, being a good offense. I keep thinking that if I don't, they're going to—well, that I could lose it all and end up a basket case, you know, sitting on the curb with my hand out. I'm sorry, maybe I'm losing it already."

"Glen, you don't mean that, you're just upset."

"Somewhere, on the periphery of things, I know I need to do something forceful, I have to—"

"Glen, I don't think we can talk about this right now."

"No, of course not."

"What I don't see—I do have to go—what I don't see is how we could manage through all of next year, or how you could find something else, if you resigned. You'd really be out in the cold."

"Let's talk about it later. I'll let you go." By now Glen wants her to hang up and leave him to himself.

"Just don't worry yourself to death about it," Paige says. "We'll talk tonight."

Maybe twenty minutes later, in windblown December air and rain mixed with snow, Glen is walking in a direction away from home. His heart knows where he's going, even if he's trying to keep it from his mind. He tells himself he doesn't care and knows it isn't so.

At Married Student Housing, the stairways and corridors are external, covered but open on the sides, and the stacked units remind him of military dependent quarters. Scattered plastic toys tell him to go home to his wife and daughter, but he goes on.

B-21 is on the second story. He taps and the door opens, and Ecki stands there, in stocking feet. She appears surprised, maybe shocked, then steps back and he is inside her warm apartment, saying, "Sorry to surprise you."

"Of course—no, I mean it pleases me." She's smiling, and with steps and hand gestures is directing him into the living room, to a couch, a hostess receiving a guest.

"No, no, your coat, please," she says. "Excuse me—yes, I'm taken by surprise."

"This is okay?" he is asking. "You're sure?"

She places his coat somewhere and returns. "I don't mean to bring you my problems," he says, faltering. "I'm not sure, I just wanted to talk to someone, to you. Do you ever want to, well, to be with somebody?"

"Me—want this? Of course, never."

They laugh. Her eyes are as glossy as his, and then she reaches a hand to his arm, is saying something, and he raises a hand to her shoulder, feels her shoulder under the slippery fabric of her blouse, and she moves into his arms. His face, eyes, lips press to her neck and hair, stick to her face and throat as he tries to swallow and cannot have enough of her.

4

THE BLACK FOREST
Autumn 1953

10

She asks him not to call her baby when they make love. Her request comes with a smile. Unsure if he's being criticized or merely informed, he smiles in turn. She's behind the wheel of her VW and he's in the passenger seat. Love is riding with them, is in the sunlight ricocheting between the great trees all around. It's a time when he'd do anything for her, would climb the branches of one of the giant trees if it would impress her. Should it amuse her, he'd leap from treetop to treetop and yodel like Tarzan.

She wears dark glasses and he misses her eyes. When he looks her way his attention is drawn to her lips and mouth, and the words they form. Love is new to him, and he says, "Maybe there're some things I have to learn."

His words are so cocky they make her laugh. They have talked of what is happening to them, and he has confessed that while he had a crush on a girl in high school, it was a one-way street. When he worked up the nerve to call the girl, she politely rejected him; he never called again but remained infatuated all the way into the army. It was puppy love, he knows now. He's never been where he is now, had never quite known that sex and love might go together. "I love your forehead," he says, to get her to laugh. He thinks to say he loves her pussy, but doesn't dare, not yet.

" 'Baby'—as in popular songs," her lips offer with a smile. "There is no poetry in 'baby.' I prefer poetry and Mr. Lawrence. You like to kiss my forehead?" she adds.

He smiles at the windshield. If only he'd said "pussy." Her capacity to speak of things sexual has taken him by surprise, and is titillating him. He's handicapped by ignorance and immaturity. "Me and my shadow," he says, unsure what he means to say. "One thing I'll never do again is call you baby when we make love," he gets out, and sees her smile again.

Baby, baby, as in every song. What he wishes is that she'd come right out and talk to him about talking dirty, for it's occurred to him that talking dirty is what she likes to do, in his language or, apparently, in her own. He likes it, too, and saying "pussy" to her, "fuck" or "cunt," makes him instantly hard. ("Oh no, don't come," she said on the occasion of his sad misfiring, and he will wonder always how she knew the phrase so well in English.) Should he try a word or two? He's uncertain how it might go and maybe so is she—except when they're drinking. He longs to say "fuck" as he looks into her green eyes and touches her breasts, longs to feel their sexual excitement compound itself.

All week at base, she seems never to leave his mind. He can almost taste her and hear her over the distance of ninety kilometers. To be without her is an idea he's incapable now of considering. How can it be that she loves him as she says and writes? This beautiful woman, whose husband is a big-shot sports announcer who drives a big Mercedes and has it made. How is it that she loves not her husband but a teenage GI who has cried "Oh, baby" when they make love?

"You may kiss my forehead if you like," she says.

Her offer makes her more sexual, hotter, as in childhood when forbidden show and touch were unbelievably electric. "I'll have to read this Mr. Lawrence," Glen says, and they howl with laughter as he leans and kisses the smooth, fragile curve above her eyebrow.

When he's with her he knows that love is what has him in its grip, for when he's away and fears losing her, the mere possibility feels unbearable and could have him committing any crime to see her, or just to hear a word from her on a telephone. This is what love is, he thinks. Talk about joining the army and seeing the world. Oh, baby.

In her green Volkswagen, they trace a secondary road through the Black Forest. Autumn covers rolling valleys and expanses of coniferous trees; the air is warm in sunlight, cool in shadows. September nights are chilly, the days dry and aromatic. He glances once more at her smooth forehead, for the excitement it allows. Hedy. Nylons cover her legs, exposed above the knee as her legs work the pedals. Her legs are tanned, the same smooth tan of her forearms and fingers, and he remains ablaze with sex and love.

"I have something special to tell you," she says, "but we must first arrive in a special place."

"A special place?"

"In this moment it doesn't exist. Only as we find it will it come into being."

The macadam road she follows turns and climbs farther into the trees. As green as her eyes, the car rolls through valleys where patchwork patterns of cultivated brown and beige rectangles reveal contours of land; the patchwork stops neatly at forest walls and is punctuated here and there by timbered farmhouses. People are rarely in sight—but for those in an occasional Taunus or VW passing in the other direction. There are farm smells, too, of manure and cows, of cut wood, pine tar, all satisfying. Everything is sexual. Life is sexual, as he knows she wants it to be, and he's amazed to realize that in the past he did not know this. "Making love" was a polite woman's term for screwing. Now, as the sky keeps opening for him, making love touches everything.

"In daylight I prefer to be in the country," she says. "When it is growing dark, the city will do nicely."

More than happy, she seems as excited as he is. Leaving her hillside house—backing the VW onto the road from one side of the dark-doored hillside garage, the other side standing empty— she drove them into this deep countryside, working gears and pedals; her glances his way are affectionate and mischievous. They both know that she has him within her web, even if she has insisted all along that he has her in his.

Wanting to touch her, he kisses his fingertips and touches them to the back of her hand on the steering wheel; she reaches the back of her hand to her mouth and then to his. Kissing the lightly veined surface, he swoons a little.

"You're a hot number," he manages to say.

missing the last chance he thought he might ever have. A fool in aimed toward intersecting walls of high dark trees. "I am crazy with love, it's true," she says, removing the dark glasses. "For you. This week I've sought to imagine a special place we may visit."

She turns onto a one-lane dirt road, which calls up maneuvers for him, and he says, "You haven't been here before?" He loves the smooth dirt road and pine aroma of the forest, loves the dappled shade and privacy like existence itself.

"In my heart," she says. "In other ways, not exactly."

"I'm on fire for you," he gets himself to say.

"We musn't ignite the forest," she says.

She smiles and in reply he kisses his fingertips and this time, taking a chance, reaches to slide her skirt over her thigh, and touches the grainy nylon surface, and her thigh and its inner curve. He touches the silk-covered sponginess between her legs as she drives, and her pelvis moves forward a little to meet his touch, and he knows his chance-taking has carried and that she is on fire, too, and wants to play love and make love. He slips his fingers back over smooth skin to the nylon and back again between her legs as her center meets him in turn and her eyes blink and she says, "Yes, darling, we must hurry to locate our unknown place. I am crazy with love, yes, and want to bite you. Darling, you are telling me please what it is you want to do, whisper to me as I look for place to park, please do this."

He is free to tell her, and his face moves to her ear, kisses, licks, penetrates her ear, which she offers, whispers that he wants to fuck her, wants his cock in her cunt fucking her and fucking her forever after.

She whimpers, and he is nearly undone. She turns her head about, shoots a look into his eyes, kisses him quickly, then negotiates the smooth dirt road, then brakes and leans her head toward him and whispers, "I want you so to be fucking me, darling, yes, I want it so much." He moves his hand under her skirt to the swollen wetness between her legs, and roughly pulls his other hand over her breasts, squeezing them, and as she wails he wraps his arms around her fragile head and hair and pulls them to his chest and throat.

She turns onto a logging road hardly wider than the car, and onto an overgrown path where any semblance of road disappears and rolls the car between trees over pine-needle carpet, nosing to a stop. She switches off the motor, and they pause and glance. For a moment they are silent, then she reaches behind the seat and retrieves a blanket.

Leaving the car from both sides, they walk ahead into the quiet world of rough columns and, once the car is out of view, they embrace and kiss, walking with arms wrapped around waists, turning here and there until they come to a depression between massive tree roots, where she lays out the blanket and they settle knees-first to the ground.

She glances around before lying down with him, face to face, and he is desperate to pull off her clothing, but she slows him with a touch to his lips, and whispers, "We lie still a moment, darling, in the company of elves and enchantment." She looks at him close up, lifts her hand again, a momentarily threatening gesture, then touches his ear and twines his hair with her fingers, smiles, and kisses him lightly.

He looks into her eyes, sensing relief and safety. Even if someone came upon the car, they wouldn't be seen where they are. They'll have a time finding the car themselves, he thinks as he settles close enough to give her neck and cheek and lips light touches and kisses, to see in the green specks of her eyes that wherever she might have ever been, she is here with him now.

He relaxes even more and, raising to an elbow, reaches a hand to caress her fragile, complicated forehead. "Sometimes," he says, "I don't know if I can satisfy what you want." When she smiles, he adds, "Maybe I shouldn't say that."

"I love for you to speak truthfully."

"I'm afraid, sometimes, when you say you'd like to visit me on post, to go to the movies. I'm afraid I'd go nuts because with all those guys, I wouldn't stand a chance. It's like a nightmare. Some lieutenant would pull rank on me, some college guy with a little Austin-Healey you'd love, he'd order me to repair to the ammo dump and stand guard, and you'd go off with him. That's the worst part. You'd go and then I'd have to kill him. Which I'd do. It's how crazy I am about you. I'd have to go awol forever, and we'd have to go together because I couldn't stand not to be with you."

She studies his face from inches away, her own face resting on her forearm. "You love me," she says.

"I've got it bad," he says. "Something could happen, you'll go back to your husband or something, and I don't know what I'd do. I might as well step in front of a truck."

She touches his face. "You know I love you in turn, beyond all reason."

He doesn't know, and just looks at her. "You'd do anything for me?" he asks. "I'd do anything for you."

"Anything, I think, yes," she says, looking into his eyes. "There is my baby, for whom I would also do anything. You understand this?"

"I love you like they do in all the songs," he says. "Even the ones that say 'Oh, baby.'"

This gets her to smile, but he still feels as if he's at a dinner and doesn't know which utensil to use. It's what he's trying to have her know, as she gazes at him, that he doesn't know what to do or say. He extends a hand and, because it's permitted to him, feels her breast, then the side of her face and her hair, then feels her breast some more for the pleasure it gives him.

"We have this special place," she says. "We have it come into being now and belong only to us. May we have a cigarette? I would love a cigarette. It's certain smoking is expressly forbidden, but we shall be very careful, not to be imprisoned."

They share a cigarette. As she takes a turn, he feels her breasts from the sides and leans down to nip at them. She looks at him, leans toward him, and whispers, "You wish to make love now?"

"I do, yes," he whispers back.

"I'm so hot again. I've been waiting all week for you. It's doubly satisfying in this way. I've not known this feeling, you know, a passion of love and making love. It was my hope, to make a special place and not be rushed. Still, I'm afraid to remove clothing . . . you don't mind if I am removing only some things?"

"I don't mind," he says.

"Will you kiss me now?"

He kisses her.

"I've arrived at a decision," she says. "It's not to frighten you, though it's true I'm in love with you and you are in my dreams like nothing else."

Perhaps he feels a twinge of alarm, as he slides his fingers along her throat, unbuttoning the top button of her blouse, and she reaches out to touch his forehead.

"I shall separate from my husband," she says. "I can see this has always been going to happen. Don't be frightened."

Not knowing if he is or not, he says, "I'm not."

"I tell you this in the hope we may be together someday, but, to be sure, I have no wish to frighten you."

"You haven't."

"I wish only to say, in another way, how it is I love you."

"I've never known this before," he says. "It's the first time, the way I feel about you."

"The first time—it's stronger the first time, darling, more painful in a pleasant way, I think. Pain and love are so close."

"I don't like it that you were in love before," he says.

She smiles. "Not with such passion, I assure you."

He leans and kisses the point of her brassiere as she holds the cigarette. "When will you separate?" he says.

"This I don't know. I know only that I shall."

He rubs out the cigarette in dirt and buries it, and leans back to face her, touching and kissing.

"Don't be frightened at what I now say: But only if you have not nearly walked into me and spoken to me, my life may not be changing in this way."

"Could it have been anybody?" he asks.

"I've thought of this, you know. You are younger, and perhaps not so ready. I know we may be all things to each other, that we have—I know this—that we have deepest possible chances for happiness. To grow together. I believe it is you, your freedom of spirit, and, no, not because love has been denied to me as a girl. Of course it's difficult to believe otherwise, but I believe it is you alone. No one else is coming close to bumping into Ilsedore and making me wait a full week before telephoning. Though when you have telephoned, I know already that I'm in love with you. I'm sorry if that is too quick, but it's true. I knew this in the moment I give you my telephone number."

"It's true for me, too," he says as they lie gazing just past and at each other. "I felt that way when I looked up and saw you, although I felt like it wasn't allowed. When we sat at the table and drank wine, I wanted to touch you and kiss you."

"It's not a simple decision. Believe me, I've thought of nothing else, every minute, but that I must separate. It's a marriage for convenience, for family and financial reasons. My marriage has been an error on a grand scale, for it is based not on love but on my father, also my mother, and convenience, and I shall correct this error while there remains a chance."

He finishes unbuttoning her blouse, pulls away its tails, and reaches his hands around her back to unhook her brassiere. He takes one of her small breasts into his mouth. But as he begins to move over her she turns to her side and shifts back to him, twisting her face over her shoulder. "Slowly now, darling, slowly," she whispers. "Yes, be inside me, but do not move, yes, like this, only lying still, yes, hold tight like this, you see . . ." And as he settles some she says, "Yes, fucking me now, yes, yes, darling, fucking me now, yes, can you say you love me, please, say to me please, yes . . ."

And in time she whispers, "Do not leave me yet, remain with me, I know you wish to leave, I know it is hurting, but we may relax . . . and now, darling, please, yes, grow in me again, you see, oh yes, like that, yes," and he does see beyond treetops as she gasps and cries and tucks her chin and he has no fear of finishing, goes on unimpeded as he kisses her bruised, twisted chin, kisses her shining wet temple, kisses hair sticking damp over her forehead, which is as smooth as a brown egg above her closed eyes, as he continues as requested in under her leg, up into her, caressing her breasts and filling her over and over, pushing up into her over and over, stretching his neck to flick his tongue to her lips and mouth in the upward, unpredictable journey on which they have embarked.

11

A time comes when he doesn't call her, a time of merciless confusion. His promise is to telephone Tuesday at midday after chow, when her husband will be away, so they may speak, if only for a moment, hear the other's voice, and reaffirm that they will meet over the weekend.

But he doesn't call, and doesn't know why. He does know that on a recent Sunday, returning from Baden-Baden and bypassing the taxi stand to walk up the long hill to Panzerkaserne—a balmy October afternoon walk of three kilometers—he longed for the simplicity of army life he had known before he met her. Foot locker, wall locker. No worry about what to wear, health care and no bills to pay, a pocketful of money once a month and an identity as a soldier, being a modest somebody after having been a nobody. At the same time, he realizes that everything he knows evaporates at the sight of the married woman from Baden-Baden.

For whatever reason, he puts aside calling. Today is Tuesday and though little besides calling her has occupied his mind, he lets the time go by and doesn't do it. In the mess hall he eats a little, then wanders down to the motor pool as if to take a look at his jeep, and at 1300 reports to the company street for Work Call. He knows she's waiting, knows he's being cruel, but does nothing about it. Her given name is Hedwig, but she's been known all her life as Hedy, and he doesn't know why he's trying to hurt her.

In the afternoon he makes a run to Patch Barracks near Heidelberg, feeling relieved and pained at once on the Autobahn as, side curtains removed, brisk autumn air pours through the jeep. He returns to base, turns in his trip ticket at the dispatcher's shed, looks to the wall clock for retreat to arrive as he shoots grease into axle points, and leaves for the barracks at 1700 to wash up and join the line shuffling into the mess hall for evening chow.

This night as on other nights he goes to the post theater for the 1800 movie and stops at the EM Club on the way back to have a beer or two. Sitting with Nute Nutter, he experiences flashes of missing her and returns to his barracks, where he lies in bed and reads from a dog-eared paperback copy of *From Here to Eternity* he found on a windowsill at the end of the corridor. What is he doing, he asks himself. He knows only that he doesn't know.

Closing the book, hoping for sleep, he tries to worry over Prewitt in the book's pages, while Hedy, and what again that day he didn't do, looms larger than the night.

Thatcher's voice blares in the hallway.

Drunk and belligerent, the first sergeant has apparently joined the CQ in the sounding of First Call. Glen turns his feet from bed to floor, his pattern each morning at 0500, and sits listening. It could be his father coming home drunk and hell-bent on disaster. Glen usually slips on wooden clogs and clacks into the hall with towel and toilet-articles kit as one of the first into the gang shower. Now he waits a moment. Then, hearing nothing, he rises to leave—only one other soldier is sitting up, while the rest cling to sleep and pillows—and entering the hall walks almost directly into the first sergeant's staggering, rheumy-eyed gaze.

"You outta uniform, soldier!"

The CQ, a corporal about a year older than Glen, stands behind the many-striped figure, shaking his head. On a gamble, Glen moves past the first sergeant.

"Private, I'm talking to you!"

Glen stops—has to—and turns back.

"Front and center, soldier! Goddamnit, talking to you!"

Uncertain of what to do, Glen stands rigid with growing anger as Thatcher closes in on him.

"Talking to you, soldier!" he says into Glen's face.

"Hear you, Sergeant."

Thatcher, cap peaked nearly to his nose, stands eyeing him. "Defying me, soldier!"

"No, Sergeant."

The man's drunken face is adrift on a wobbly neck, and Glen is wondering if he's obligated to obey a drunken noncom. "Gotta take my shower, Sarge," he says.

"What the hell is that, you talking back to me?"

Thinking, Screw it, Glen moves away, and at his back there comes the expected roar: "SOLDIER, YOU DEFYING MY OR-DER!"

Glen doesn't falter, and only as he is turning into the washroom does something containing "candy-ass fucking PFC" come his way, which he strives to ignore.

He's on a roller under his jeep in the motor pool when somebody shouts, "Cady, report Orderly Room immediately—Cady, Orderly Room, on the double!" and fear comes up in him.

Pulling himself out and checking the wall clock—just after 1400 hours—he leaves at a steady walk, pulse throbbing. Through the motor pool gate, heading for the battalion quadrangle and wiping his hands down his pants legs, he expects he'll be charged by either the first sergeant or the company commander for disobeying a direct order, or charged by the company commander for not reporting the first sergeant's drunken, illegal behavior. One way or another, and as it has a reputation for doing, he believes the army has him by the balls.

His surprise, checking down fatigues and boots on approaching the Orderly Room, is to see Thatcher sitting at his desk over paperwork and to hear the company clerk, Corporal Plourde, say "Cady, telephone," and nod toward a receiver on its side on one of the room's several desks.

Ducking under the counter, seeing that the first sergeant is holding his head in both hands—dead or alive, it's hard to tell—Glen steps over and picks up the receiver. "PFC Cady speaking, sir!"

"Oh, it is you?" a soft voice says.

His face flushes in surprise as he begins to twist the cord. "Yes—it's me," he says, wishing he could twist himself out of sight.

"You cannot talk? Darling, I'm so worried—I had to call. I'm sorry. You may not talk?"

"Not very well right now," Glen says.

"I must see you—it's so important. I must. May I come, not tomorrow, it's impossible tomorrow, may I come to you the next day? Friday, it's possible?"

"I believe so, yes."

"Darling, if I'm arriving at the gate, may you come to me there at three o'clock? Is this possible? Three o'clock?"

"I'll try. It's hard."

"There is no other time for me, and I must see you. Can you know? Is something wrong that you haven't called? I cannot stand that something may be wrong."

"Nothing's wrong. Everything's okay."

"All is okay?"

"Yes. Not right at the gate, down the hill."

"Down the hill?"

"A couple hundred meters?"

"Yes, darling—Friday at three p.m., two hundred meters on the hill."

"Yes."

"Must you go now? I have—perhaps I am too deeply in love."

"Me too—it's okay."

"Tell me only that you love me still, yes, please."

"I do, yes."

"I love you so much, please do not hurt me."

"I didn't mean to."

"Goodbye, darling."

Glen replaces the receiver and crosses the room to slip back under the counter, is a step away when he hears behind him, fiercely, "Cady!"

He stops and turns back. "Yes, Sergeant."

"Front and center!"

Thatcher's harsh whisper, Glen guesses, is to avoid being heard by the captain in his nearby office. Ducking back under the counter, he presents himself at Thatcher's desk. "Yes, Sergeant."

"She pregnant?" Thatcher says with a grin.

"Hope not," Glen says at last.

"Tell you something," Thatcher hisses. "Don't think yours truly not up to carrying out duty, meeting responsibility, first sergeant this company—*ever!* Make myself *clear?*"

"Yes, Sergeant."

"Got more time in the fucking army you have *breathed*, soldier! Don't forget it! Tell you this, too—anytime you think you man enough challenge *my* fucking authority, meet your ass the bulk-head, stripes on the ground, man to man! *Make myself clear?*"

"Yes, Sergeant."

"Want to meet at the bulkhead, soldier?"

Glen hesitates a second, as challenges of the kind always stab into him. "I'll let you off this time, Sergeant," he says.

"You gutless wonder, outta my sight!" Thatcher is grinning then, as if to say it's all a joke. "Move your candy ass—now!"

Guard duty. Rosters are posted once a week, and later in the day, when Glen happens to check the company bulletin board, it is with a sinking chill that he sees his name and day of assignment: Friday. He shivers as he stands there. He knew he was due, but is stunned that the overnight detail could fall exactly on the day he planned to slip away. How can he contact her now? If he stands her up again, she might never come back.

He wonders if Thatcher is responsible, realizing that he couldn't be. The roster was already out of the company clerk's typewriter when he stood in the Orderly Room agreeing to meet Hedy down the hill from the main gate on Friday. He hurt her, and fate is contriving to hurt him back. A letter addressed to her friend wouldn't make it in time, and a telephone call, she has told him, would have her husband answering. Getting a message to her isn't what he wants anyway; he has to see her, has to make it down the hill and be with her.

On a thought, he returns to the bulletin board and notes two soldiers listed for Thursday. Dolby and Garland, also PFCs. If he can trade days and not pull third shift, and—not a given—get off post, he'll be able to meet her as promised. Neither soldier, however, is anywhere to be found. When he locates Dolby, past eight-thirty at a table of soldiers drinking in the EM Club, the draftee of twenty-two or so bluntly refuses.

"I'll toss in three bucks," Glen says.

Dolby smiles thinly, shakes his head.

Glen increases his offer to four, then five. "Why not?" he says at last. "What's it to you if you pull guard Friday instead of Thursday? If there's an inspection Saturday, you'll miss it. You'll miss cleanup Friday night. It's a good deal."

"You want it, that's why," the soldier says with his thin smile. "Tell you, I hate the fucking army, hate fucking RAs."

Glen is a little stunned and all he can think to say is, "You're a good man, hope I can do something for you someday." He returns to his barracks, knowing he nearly said something about not wanting Dolby next to him in combat and is glad he didn't. It was a remark from basic training, and the draftees would have hooted.

PFC Garland is equally resistant. But when Glen reaches seven dollars, says "Thanks a lot," and turns, walking away, Garland says, "Okay."

Glen looks back. "You'll do it?"

"Paid in advance," Garland says.

"Yeah, I might ship out owing you seven bucks."

Lying in bed after lights-out, he considers that it's nearly settled. He still has to scramble, and will have to get off post without a pass. He'll have to be in formation before the Guard Barracks in time to pull first or second relief in order to be free, if not technically, by either noon or two the following day. Second relief is safest, he decides. An occasional sergeant of the guard perversely orders the formation about-face and awards first relief to those who show up last. And by now he cannot bear the possibility of not seeing her.

Throughout the day and a half following, all goes well. Glen polishes his brass down to the latch on his ammo pouch, cleans his rifle until the inside of its barrel glints in the reflection of a thumbnail, spit shines his combat boots until they reflect like mirrors. Then, taking his place in the formation before the Guard Barracks forty minutes early, he positions himself in the middle squad, and when the formation is called and inspection proceeds— missing supernumerary—is assigned to second relief.

Two on and four off. The next day, though weary from almost no sleep in the Guard Barracks, he pulls his final shift, 1200 to 1400, simply walks away from the guard truck and across post, and slips into his barracks through the bulkhead. There, after quietly checking in his rifle with the company armorer in the basement and slipping upstairs to his squad room, he undresses and moves along the hall barefoot—shower clogs make too much noise—to shower, shampoo, and shave. Back at his wall locker, dressing in clean Class A's, he is conscious that each move brings him closer to seeing her, and touching her. As he fixes his tie, bells from nearby Böblingen ring out the time: fifteen to three. On a last look in the mirror inside his locker door, squaring his cap, he locks up and slips back to the cellar and the bulkhead exit.

One last maneuver stands before him—eluding authority. His P-pass is locked in the pass box in the Orderly Room—until 1700, when duty ends for the day—and he's counting on not being stopped by the MP at the main gate, as MPs rarely stop soldiers leaving post, and to return later within a grouping of soldiers, when, in uniform, flashing even a package of cigarettes has always been enough to be waved through by an MP on duty.

But at the main gate—it has to be ten to three—the MP in the booth in the middle of the empty street steps outside as Glen approaches, and Glen's heart seems to falter.

"Let's see some paper," the MP corporal says from under his face-shadowing helmet liner.

"Oh, man, I don't have my pass," Glen says, pulling up. "Listen, I have to see someone down the hill in about two minutes; I'm just trying to get out of here a little early."

"Going nowhere without a pass, soldier."

"This is really—"

"About-face, soldier! Want me to put you on report?"

Glen turns, everything knotting up as he tries to think what to do. He sees no option but to walk back, away from her. Then, as if the setback isn't enough, Sergeant Thatcher is coming his way.

Glen nods in appropriate greeting and is hardly two steps past Thatcher before the man's voice sounds yet again at his back, "Soldier, hold it right there!"

Glen stops, turns back.

"What the fuck're you doing, Cady? I know you're on guard today, know you switched with Garland—what're you doing here, out of guard uniform minus your weapon? Wanna go to the fucking stockade?"

"Got a personal problem, Sarge," Glen says at last. "I pulled guard, I was just trying to get away early."

"What kinda goddamn personal problem?"

"Just personal."

"Personal my ass, what're you talking about?"

"There's a woman I have to see," Glen says.

"Woman—that what you said? Woman you hafta see?"

"That's it."

"Said she ain't pregnant, what the hell's the problem?"

"Supposed to meet her down here, Sarge."

"You in *love?*" Thatcher asks with a yellow-toothed smile.

Glen doesn't say.

"You fucking candy ass," Thatcher says.

Glen stands there.

"Got yourself a shitload of trouble, what it sounds like to me. Not to mention breaking rules and regulations. Sounds like momma-san's gonna have your candy ass, too," Thatcher adds with another smile.

Glen has no idea what to say, knows only that three o'clock is fading and Hedy is waiting down the hill, out of sight.

"When you 'posed to meet this woman?"

"Three o'clock. Now."

"You asking me to authorize a pass?"

"Not really, Sarge."

"Shit outta luck if you are." Thatcher stands there smiling. "Cady," he says. "Gonna say something you ain't hearing said, understand?"

"Yes, Sergeant."

"Under threat of death, understand?"

"Yes, Sergeant."

"Ever contrive, stand witness, saying any such thing, will prove you a fucking liar, will personally, to boot, see your sorry ass destroyed—*clear?*"

"Yes, Sergeant."

"Ammunition Dump A. South Post. Hundred meters past entrance, Ammunition Dump A, path leaves dirt road. Enters woods. 'Proximately one hundred meters barbwire-topped perimeter fence, running east and west. Guard on duty fifty meters west. Carries live ammo, which you oughta know, you candy ass. 'Proximately thirty meters right, small section fence may be lifted from ground enough to allow lover boy to pull his sorry ass under. Once lifted, fence must be returned to original position. Hear me say anything, soldier?"

"No, Sergeant."

"Get caught, soldier, ass is grass and mine remains in the clover, clear?"

"Thanks, Sarge."

"The fuck outta here."

Twenty minutes later, in a lather from having run and jogged over two miles, one khaki knee soiled with dirt and his left cheek scratched from pushing through brush, Glen climbs from a roadside ditch only to realize he's way too far down the hill. Pushing hard, he shifts into a gasping uphill jog, stricken with a nightmare anxiety of missing her.

Jogging up the road, he's passed by a car, then a jeep, both going downhill as the duty day is ending. Then, at a curve in the road, in shadows two hundred meters away, he sees the green Volkswagen, though it looks black, and his heart seems nearly to pop.

He waves in fear that she'll pull away without seeing him, then the car's red taillights come on and the nightmare seems real; she's going to drive away and he'll never be able to catch her.

The car is backing up! He can see no silhouette within, but the red taillights are bright within the shadows and the car is rolling his way down the shoulder. He stumbles, gasping to a stop, stands waiting, and in another moment is in the passenger seat, embracing and kissing her, crying and laughing about his fear and love and foolishness and the obstacles that had interfered with his escape, until Hedy—she has waited close to an hour, and he is all but kissing the life from her—joins him in laughter and tears and words of her own.

In no time—his breathing seems barely to have settled—she is gone, making her way back to husband and child, and he is standing on a corner in Bubblegum, feeling as if he had just survived a crazed ride in an amusement park. Four bells peal throughout the town and he realizes that he was with her hardly twenty minutes. His own reassurance is hard to grasp. She cried to him of her fear that she loved him too much. They held tight and she told how terrified she was when he didn't call, and how she had to see him, had committed her dreams to him, and would die for him. It was the first time he'd hurt her, she said, and she asked him to never hurt her again.

He stands on a corner. Twenty minutes of words and touching, kissing and feeling; they seem now not to have happened. What would he do if he had not gotten off post and had missed her?

He walks in the small city. Perhaps in time his appetite will return—he hasn't eaten since noon yesterday, before reporting for guard duty—and he thinks that a meal will return him to normal, will expend time, too, until tomorrow afternoon, when he'll travel to Baden-Baden to see her again. Near the small train station, he's propositioned a couple of times by prostitutes stepping from doorways. "Hey, *Schatz*, vant hot nookie?" "Sveetheart, vant some hot time viss me, come on, ten mark, come on, baby, hot to go!" It's the end-of-the-month price, but he feels no temptation. He walks, waiting for his heart and insides to settle enough so that he can eat.

In the past, he knows, he'd have been in a beer joint by now, pouring away one stein after another, perhaps on his way to a ten-mark quickie and a cab ride back to base to sleep it off. That was before he made the trip to Baden-Baden, when he had been a mere high school dropout who had taken the GED and enlisted in the army.

Soldiers are unloading here and there from taxis—corporals, sergeants, red-faced PFCs with hash marks on shiny uniforms indicating nine, twelve, fifteen years, lifers on their way to a cheap drunk—to the general invitation of the jukebox music drifting from doorways along the street. Glen considers stopping for just one beer, pauses in front of a *Gasthaus* to hear, ". . . you left me and you went away/ . . . you promised to return another day," then changes his mind as two sergeants push past him, one of them saying, "Blocking the door, son."

He remains too much with Hedy to want other emotions to mix with his own. Love is alive in him tonight like nothing he has ever known, and having no wish to dilute the excitement, he stops at a quiet *Konditorei*. Like most, the cafe is attended by a handful of Germans having coffee or desserts, reading newspapers on wooden spines. No other soldiers are present and Glen finds new pleasure in being on his own. He orders *Apfelsaft* and takes up a newspaper hanging close by to look over its words and photos.

"Können Sie Deutsch lesen?" the waitress asks as she delivers his order on a tray. *"Nein . . . nein,"* Glen says. "Just looking." He puts the paper down, but takes it up again in a moment. He studies and understands several phrases and captions before the waitress is beside his table again, smiling, asking how it is— he guesses—that he can read the newspaper if he cannot read German.

"Lot of words are nearly the same," he says, assuming she understands English.

"This is true," she replies in a schoolroom English accent. "Not a few are in common."

"Yes," he says. "Yes." He also smiles.

"Do you wish anything in addition to order?" the girl says, and he realizes she's flirting in her practice of English.

She is attractive, maybe sixteen, and thinking to be flirtatious in turn, he says, *"Nein, nein, danke,"* which has her smiling as she moves away. He thinks, sitting there, that at another time he would have been pleased to get to know her better, that she is the girl he imagined meeting, but his emotions are elsewhere and he has no added desire available in his foolish heart tonight. Leaving an extravagant tip, he slips into the evening without looking back.

Another unexpected experience awaits him, however, as he returns toward the bars, hoping to share a cab back to base. Not far from the *Konditorei* he passes a lighted entryway leading downstairs to Kino Starlight. He pauses and looks it over. The German theater displays no posters or still photos, only the title of a film playing. Then he ventures down the stairs and buys a ticket—of half a dozen prices, he buys the most expensive—and a moment later is sitting among others watching a black-and-white movie.

The language is impossible to follow, and he tries to sort out a story from the images. An elegant couple—on a honeymoon it seems—is in a luxurious hotel and having difficulty gaining privacy so they may make love, interrupted constantly by waiters, telephone calls, accidents they themselves cause.

Glen watches intently, and smiles when people around him laugh. Then he realizes what it is that's exciting him: The leading actress resembles Hedy, whose eyes, lips, and slim body are somehow present in the woman moving, stretching, kissing, talking on screen. Jealousy surges up in him. The male lead appears powdered and effeminate, but in his ease of using the language—as Glen imagines Hedy doing with others and with her husband—becomes a rival against whom Glen knows he wouldn't stand a chance.

He decides to leave, to rediscover his feelings from earlier in the evening. And as he walks along an old stone street, the buildings and stucco houses, the flower boxes and bicycles, a statue and water fountain, are making sense to him, are telling him he belongs.

12

She tells him a story. It's a rainy Saturday afternoon and they are lying in bed in her hillside house. The room is unlighted, and gray sky filters through rain-spattered windows.

A schoolgirl's secret, she tells him, and not a happy story. She has told it only once, to a girlfriend. Not to her family, nor to her husband. Only to him now, no matter what may happen in their lives.

It is wartime, the eve of 1943, and she's in Duisburg on holiday from school. It's Christmas and bombing is sporadic. On a Saturday at midday, a man approaches her on the street. At fifteen, she has permission to visit her friend, Hannelore. After months of seclusion at her girls' school, the danger is exciting, and she has romantic yearnings in spite of the war. All is threatened by flames, but she is an adolescent and perhaps her parents are remiss in allowing even this one day's freedom. Only later, when her brother dies and her family home and life are destroyed, will she know the grave cost of war.

The man appears at her side. At first he's clever, saying outrageous things about rationing and bombing, Hitler and the Nazis. For what he says one may be summarily arrested and face hanging or the firing squad. He's an artist, he says, a portraitist rejected by the military due to a heart defect. He says he is thirty-nine, had lived in Paris before the war, and that some of what he tells her will not be true. He says she's attractive in a way that had him following her ever since she'd walked by in the station, while he was on his way to buy bread, and now the bakery is certain to be sold out. A moment in the presence of beauty or bread—such was his dilemma, he says, and as an artist he chose the former.

This man's words impress her, this fifteen-year-old girl. If she were not so inexperienced and if the boys her age had not been called to the war, this appeal might have gone only so far. He tells her she is lovely in her youthfulness in ways she is incapable of understanding in this time of war, and that beauty is all that remains true in Germany. As an artist and as a man, he tells her, he was in love at once with her form and wishes to invite her to the hotel to spend an hour of life, that he may look at her and make himself a better artist forever, if his life is not soon taken on account of his irreverence toward the war effort. They will only talk, and drink perhaps one liter of champagne, he says, and he will give her all his money for bread if she wishes. Beauty and love are all for which to live in this time of madness—romantic love, family love, love not of Hitler, he says, but of Cézanne and van Gogh and, yes, he says, of the shape of her neck and face. Above all, he tells her, the hour in a hotel will be a secret never to be disclosed to another person.

The question: Does she go with this man? Something tempts her, though she has been well taught about strangers. But in wartime, nothing is normal.

He also says to her—she forgot to include this important part of the story—that not only may he die at any moment from a bomb falling from the sky but also that he could be arrested and charged on the spot with sedition, and executed by the Gestapo. This is a fact of life which has become known to all, not excluding fifteen-year-old schoolgirls, though they may not as yet have borne witness to such executions. In another year bodies will hang from light posts and doorways; in Duisburg, in 1945, she sees three bodies, a woman and two men, hanging from a railroad bridge. The local political officers know everything, and others as well are whispering to authorities. There is death and fear of death everywhere.

Still, the central question, even as it may confirm the narcissism, the amour propre, of a privileged adolescent: Does she succumb to this man's artistic and romantic entreaty?

The answer: Yes and no.

Yes, in that she decides to do so, though that is not the shameful part of her confession. He has seduced her quite successfully, and she makes the decision not merely to go with him and sip champagne in a hotel room but perhaps to allow him to see her and touch her, to make love to her. All things, yes, she decides, and not so much in innocence as in favor of such desire being made known to her, in favor of a certain education lasting one hour.

So it is that she makes her decision and then—what colors shamefully this otherwise childish encounter—the brief affair ends as he has said it might, which makes him an honest man, while it introduces her to the horror of the times. As the man has said, and perhaps he is seductive because he speaks with both kindness and conviction, something may happen in the next moment, and so it does.

Two men appear, and he is turning to run away at once. The two men are also running, and she sees the man has just reached the entrance to an alley when he is shot and falls to the pavement. Perhaps he is dead; she doesn't know, for she also runs away. She sees this man shot, perhaps she screams, and then she is in a hotel lobby, terrified and barely able to breathe, thinking that she might still be in danger for having talked with him, and only after an hour of trembling and hiding does she leave and board the streetcar, and that is the end of the story. She's never to know anything more of this man, though she'll always feel guilt over what happened, and for running away and hiding.

"Well," Glen says, "you were innocent."

"No one has been innocent—that is what this incident has taught me in time. And many things have happened at war's end which not many wish to remember. On all sides."

Glen doesn't know what to say.

"Well," she says. "I recall this story to have you know that you are the fulfillment of a dream that could not be, and perhaps a cleansing of mistakes in my life. Dreaming is cancelled in the war, and only after many years has dreaming again become possible. This man—I do not know what the charge was against him, or if it was, as I suspect, without merit—but this man's death has meant to me the end of dreams. I cried in sorrow and shame many times, and when years have passed and I see you in the park, I think—it's true—I think for an instant this man has returned, or my youth has returned. Only then have I felt at last a capacity to entertain something as elemental as dreaming, as being in love."

She washes him provocatively. Warm water and soap. A delicate, soapy touch as he is instructed to be cooperative. "It's something I wish for me even as you would appear to be the object," she says, and he has but a half-formed idea of what she has in mind, uncertain of himself in terms of sophistication and decency and eroticism. One thing he knows: She knows more than he knows. He's been in car seats and on baby-sitter's couches, but not in bedrooms on rainy Saturday afternoons, not that this makes him an unwilling pupil.

Once, in his first month in Germany, sent on field maneuvers as a courier, he ended up overnight in Nürnberg, where he spent perhaps an hour on a park bench in the dark with a young woman who was a complete stranger. He had been wandering through an old part of the city, and was in fatigues. There was a risk of MPs stopping him, whatever he might say to them about maneuvers. The young woman passed, and they exchanged a mere glance. Then, returning the way he came, he saw her waiting on a streetcar island in the street. This time she smiled faintly, and he paused on the sidewalk as a wooden streetcar rumbled toward the island. The woman stood in line, but as the others boarded and the streetcar began to move away, she stepped back and walked over to him. *"Komm,"* she said with a smile, and he walked with her. A few steps along she took his arm and they walked as a couple, although one whose communications consisted of nods and smiles. She led him into a dark and misty park, to a damp bench where they were hardly able to see each other, and without kissing him she unbuttoned his fatigue pants and masturbated him. He did not resist, but tried to hold and fondle her in turn, all of which she resisted. What she wanted and he did not quite allow—she asked by no means other than directing her head—was to use her mouth. Her urge confused him, and when she finished masturbating him, they sat for a time and then she masturbated him again. And again, as he was seventeen and arousal, like his lungs, had the capacity of quick recovery. On soft words then, she slipped away into the night. He followed to the street, but there was no sign of her. And so, mystified and sore, he made his way back from misty medieval Nürnberg to the U.S. Army.

No such soreness occurs here. Hedy teases him with tongue, bites and pinches, and also draws him to laughter and to points of hardness and desire which are just about unbearable. "This part is as an egg upon a pestle," she tells him.

"Hard-boiled egg," he is able to say.

"To devour for breakfast," she says.

He doesn't respond.

"May I devour this egg for breakfast?" she says.

"Yes," he says.

"But I am thinking—what would happen if I refuse this egg," she says.

He doesn't respond.

"Darling, you must insist that I am having my egg for breakfast—you must insist."

"You better have your egg for breakfast!" he tells her.

"I refuse," she says adamantly.

"Do as you're told!" he tells her.

"You insist I have this egg for breakfast?"

"I insist! Eat your egg! Do it now! Eat it!" To his surprise, the egg keeps enlarging.

"You order me?"

"It's an order—do as you're told! Eat that egg!"

"As you insist," she says, and proceeds as if to test the flavor, on this side, and that side. "Caress my hair as I am having my breakfast," she says. "This I like—that you caress my hair, and that I know you are watching me."

He keeps hardening. She takes her egg in its entirety and he caresses her damp hair and ears, her shoulders and her precious forehead, wipes hair from where it sticks to her cheeks, gives up directing his thoughts elsewhere as she appears transported, as she said she would be, and she doesn't look his way even as she draws greater ecstacy from depths of which he was unaware, informs him not merely of uninhibited lovemaking but of dying and going to heaven and of not dying after all.

In the aftermath of showering in the sparkling chrome-and-tile bathroom, they venture into the damp evening, the autumn air thick along the path through the forest. Leaves and branches sag and drip with water where they duck on their way to Gasthaus zur Blauen Forelle, but they ignore the rain and stop periodically to embrace and kiss.

She mentions marriage and his heart constricts with fear. At the *Gasthaus*, where they sit at their usual table, she says, "If we were to marry—it is only thinking aloud, and I remain a married woman as of today—is it permitted that I may live in this town, Böblingen? It is permitted, at your rank?"

Her eyes remain on his; he seems to have blinked. "I think, only first three graders can do that. Sergeants."

She touches the back of his hand. "Have I startled you, speaking of marriage? Of course I have."

"It's okay."

"It will be a long time before I'm free to marry," she says. "Who knows what our fate will be at this time? I only know that I shall separate from my husband, shall be divorced, this I know, and that I am in love truly for the first time. It's all I know. Many months will be necessary to reach agreement. Divorce is not so simple in Germany; is very complicated."

"Okay, you did surprise me a little," he says, and gets her to laugh.

"May we do this one thing—to speculate upon the possibility? Certainly it is you who fills my thoughts. A final agreement is— one year, perhaps two years away. You shall have finished with the army in this time, still it is you filling my thoughts as if for all time in the future. Do you mind that we speculate? Does this bother you? Is it correct? Speculate *upon* the possibility?"

"I'm not sure," he says.

"You must help me improve not only my English but my American."

"I think you could help me improve mine."

"You wish to make love with me, and we are enjoying to be together—yes?"

"Oh, a little," he says.

He notices in her smile the attractiveness of her eyes and lips. Even extremely beautiful women, movie stars, need to be loved and have husbands, is his confused thought.

"I do not ask that you are declaring to forever," she says. "I wish only—my Germanness, perhaps—I wish only to see something in its evolvement. We may talk like this?"

"Sure," he says. "Let's speculate."

"It's not easy what I shall do, and I'm needing to have an idea how I shall live, under what condition and how to care for Ilsedore. Might we be together in the town of Böblingen? It is permitted that you marry? Or if I am taking a flat, may we be together often? Is Uncle Sam objecting to this, that I am your girlfriend?"

"I'm really not sure," Glen says. "Sergeants are allowed to live off base, maybe corporals if they're married. Lots of privates are married, but their wives are in the States. One guy, his wife came over from New Jersey to visit and stayed in a hotel in town for two months. What it is, I think, is you have to be a certain rank, or have been in the army so long, to either live off post or in dependent housing."

"Of marriage, Glen—you are speculating upon this?" She struggles with a straight face before exploding into laughter. "I am teasing—to see your face decolor."

Glen is laughing with her, blushing. "Maybe I do want to get married," he says. "Maybe it's all I ever think about."

She smiles. "May we one day live as exiles in southern California?" she says.

"I guess we can do anything we want."

"We may, it's true. It's what is wonderful in you, you see. Still, when you are young, marriage may be frightening. Also when you are not so young."

If only she knew how young, Glen is thinking. "You know, I never ever *thought* about marriage before now," he says.

"There are flats available, in Bubblegum? It would be lovely, don't you think? Together in a small nest and becoming a father in the same day? Hmm? Again, I am teasing, although—another time—may we speak clearly of the future? It's helpful to me. Might we in fact speculate upon living in southern California? German exiles are living in this part of the world, artists and intellectuals. Thomas Mann, you know, is living in Pacific Palisades. There is sunshine, citrus fruits hang from trees at one's doorway, beaches and waves of the Pacific Ocean. I have to admit that I've dreamed of the happiness we are knowing in southern California. It fills me with happiness to say this to you, do you understand? Hold my hand, please, for the happiness it gives me to speak of being together in the future."

He holds her hand on the table, confused by what she is saying and certain that a happiness—of commitment, perhaps—is in him, too. She places her other hand on his and the agreement they seem to have struck, as he looks into her eyes, is as frightening and as exhilarating as anything he's ever known.

At dawn he opens his eyes to Rhine wine confusion in his cranium and looks to the rain-covered window to confirm his whereabouts. Shifting his head, he looks on Hedy where she lies asleep, partly uncovered. He looks on her slim, tanned arms and shoulders, her slightly opened mouth, an exposed lemon-sized breast. He pulls a hand over stubble sprouting from his face and returns his head to the pillow. Right now he'd welcome squad room and steaming shower down the hall, the familiarity of coffee, eggs, toast, the Sunday *Stars & Stripes* in hand and—most tables are unoccupied on Sunday morning—an unoccupied table in the mess hall. Right now he'd welcome the dream of a beautiful woman in bed as much as the beautiful woman herself.

He lies still not to awaken her, and senses a fear within himself. He loves her, doesn't he? Why does it feel so wrong? He lifts his head to look at her. A sleeping woman who has a child—a girl baby, looked after by a friend on certain weekends—and who has decided to divorce her husband. She seems to know fully what he cannot understand. If he *were* twenty, as she believes him to be, would he understand what he's getting himself into?

What he does know is that she is doing to him and his childish heart what he had not known until now even existed. A feeling of love is always on his mind, and a sexual feeling is always close by, one which has him growing aroused as he looks at the single lemon-sized breast, as he imagines leaning in and licking its pebbled nipple. This is what it is to be alive, he thinks. Alive with that which was forbidden and locked away and whispered about at home.

Angling his neck, he extends his tongue to lick the bottom of the exposed nipple. He extends his tongue, wants to have her now, is powerfully hard and wants to fill her to her heart, and twists his neck to take in more of the lemon-shaped organ—only to have her awaken angrily and pull a cover to her shoulder as she turns away. It's the first anger between them, and he shrinks back, shattered with humiliation.

Later, as they sit at the kitchen table, drinking coffee, she says, "Forgive me for being cross. You startled me awake."

"I guess I shouldn't have done that," he says. "I just wanted— I can see I shouldn't have done that."

They smile over his half-truth and the issue seems concluded, and spirits seeming restored by coffee, bread rolls, and preserves, she notes playfully, "Lessons learnt from Glen."

"That's wrong," he says. "It's 'learned.' "

"Learnt—?"

"There's no such word. You asked me to help you with your English."

"Oh, darling, it is English usage—'learned' is the American usage."

"Ah," he says.

" 'Learnt' is acceptable, I assure you."

"You know my language better than I do," he says.

"I've probably studied it more than you," she says with a smile.

"Probably," he says; he smiles, too, to say it's okay, he doesn't mind, even as he gets to his feet and steps to the coffeemaker to leave the subject behind.

She makes a call, to gain an added quarter hour before she has to pick up Ilsedore. At her suggestion, he packs his bag, so she may let him off near the train station and save returning here, gaining, she says, another quarter hour.

"You worry about running into your husband coming in on the train?" he asks.

"Oh, he would not be without his Mercedes to drive like a race car on the Autobahn," she says. "It's of others, who do come and go on the train, that I must be careful."

Driving his Mercedes like a race car: it's one of few images to emerge of the man whose wife has given all to him and is just then preparing to take him for a drive. As Herr Günther might say, he doesn't sound like a bad guy, and Glen feels a rush of sympathy for him, a rush of disrespect for himself.

November air provides a fresh beginning under rolling skies and they walk on a sun-lighted country road. Without time to linger in the forest, she turns from one two-lane paved road to another— surrounded by the patchwork of green, brown, even chocolate-colored rectangles where crops have been harvested—and pulls off the road where two or three cars are already parked.

The crisp air and country smells are bracing, and people walk here and there, couples and families with senior men in the lead, some women with pheasant feathers in their Robin Hood hats, some men wearing green loden capes and hats with the decorations the GIs call shaving brushes.

Hedy, for her part, wears a pale blue and white cotton dirndl under a sweater, white earrings setting off her complexion, and Glen feels she could not possibly—he who rarely notices women's clothing—be more lovely. She points out the Feldberg, capped in white, topping the overlapping ranges, the haze growing stronger over each succeeding range no matter how sharply blue the immediate sky.

She takes his hand, though at times they must walk single file to allow others to pass. Things continue to be confused for him, and he realizes there is a spirituality about the Germans in their walking. He finds this comforting—no more than he notices women's clothing is he given to such thoughts—even though he feels an urge to be back on base, playing football on the parade field, running wildly with other soldiers, shouting, tackling, cursing freely, and having no uncertainty whatsoever about language usage or absent husbands or the timely use of four-letter words.

"I'd love to play some football," he says. "That's what this weather calls up for me—football—not the kind where you kick a ball but where you tackle and run and pass."

"I understand this urge," she says.

"What do you like to do—on days like this?"

"Well," she says. "For physical conditioning, I enjoy cycling. Have I told you I am expert to a modest degree? You are surprised? It was my passion for many years, this and hiking in foothills and mountains, until I am becoming a mother. Sometimes I want nothing more than to climb long stretches, and to sail down lonely roads for a dozen kilometers. In California, perhaps, is such a dream allowed? We shall swim in our swimming pool and cycle the contour of the Pacific Ocean—a wonderful dream, hmm?"

Glen smiles as they continue walking, but he looks elsewhere to conceal a gloss over his eyes. He could not, if he had all day, explain what it is that has been constricting his heart all morning. Is it the strangeness, the nodded greetings, *"Guten Tag"* and *"Grüss*

Gott"? The feeling of being an unwelcome outsider pierces him at times. Something's wrong, but he can't make clear in his mind what it is.

They pass through shadows without saying much, and he looks at Hedy and knows that he adores her. She is lovely beyond belief, and it comes to him that he is what is wrong. He's living a lie. Nor would he feel this hurt if it were not wrong for him to love her as selfishly as he does. It's all so simple. He shouldn't be here. Someone else could be, maybe a captain who is twenty-seven and has college degrees and comes from a wealthy family in a state capital somewhere. A teenage jeep driver—he's in over his head and it isn't fair to her. Or to him. For he has his pride, he thinks miserably, and a touch of honor, too, which makes him feel guilty about her husband. Nor does anything lie before him with her— he can see so clearly here within the long shadow of the Feldberg— except being shown the door.

They stroll on silently and there, all at once, is her car, parked in a clearing. He had not known they were tracing a circle of walkways, while the confusion of all that is happening is raging in his mind and heart. At the car, as usual, she enters on the driver's side and reaches to open the passenger door. Glen doesn't enter, though, but reaches into the back and retrieves his awol bag. Through the open doorway—it seems the bravest, wisest thing he has ever done—he says, "I'm going to walk, I'm walking away. . . ."

"Glen, darling, what are you saying?"

"I love you so much," he says. "But it's all confused for me. It's all wrong. I'm saying goodbye."

As he closes the door, glimpsing her face in alarm and instant tears in her eyes, he's too far gone to turn back and moves away down the dirt road.

Nothing happens as he walks, though his mind continues in a swirl. The car starts behind him, but he immediately turns right onto another dirt road, to be out of sight before she can reverse direction and see where he has gone. Fifty yards ahead, there is yet another road, and he begins running toward it, as if to escape himself and what he feels, hoping he can disappear into the woods, where he knows there is no way he may be caught or seen. At the intersection, he lopes to the right and ten yards along jumps from the dirt road into the woods. He moves between trees, and what stops him then is doubt and regret. What a fool, he is thinking, as he leans back against a tree trunk. And God, by going back now he'll only look worse: she'll think he's run off to hurt her again and will see him, as he sees himself, for the immature fool he is. His only hope is that she will have driven off and left him, with good riddance.

Has anyone ever been so foolish? He begins to panic even more about what to do. His bag hangs at the end of his arm and he stands looking down. "What an idiot," he mutters, "what an imbecile." Almost mindlessly then, he begins to make his way between trees back to the road. Too humiliated to show himself, he sits down, his back to the roadside and his feet aimed into the ditch.

In time he hears a car, but is too ashamed to turn his head. He remains sitting, feeling the faintest relief as the car stops and begins backing up. The car is behind him, motor running, and he pushes to his feet and walks to the car, to the driver's side, without quite looking up, and looks at last into her bewildered eyes. "I'm sorry," he says. "I wish you'd drive over me and kill me so I wouldn't have to feel as stupid as I do. I don't know what it is."

She sits there crying. "Glen, why do you do this? I do not understand for the life of me—have I hurt you?"

His eyes blur, too, and he shakes his head. "I don't know," he says, "I just don't know what it is."

"Have I said something to anger you? Do you not love me anymore?"

"I love you. It's stupid—maybe I love you too much. I feel so dumb about everything. I'm just a private in the army. I have nothing to give you. Dreams about the future, I don't know if they're anything I can ever do. If I deserve someone like you. This is so awful."

She pauses. "Darling, please, can you understand that it is you I love? It is not a position you have. It is only you and because you are a person who is honest and can laugh at things, that is all. It's what I have never been allowed to know, a person who is *not* living only for success in business or money. Does it make sense? I have only affection for you, no one but you, only desire to be with you at all times. Don't you see, I love you in a way that I cannot help myself."

"California," Glen manages to say. "Swimming pools—I don't know if that's anything I'd ever be able to give you. But it's what I think you should have."

Her face appears to soften. "It's only talk, believe me, only dreams. You are not obligated to be rich and provide swimming pools in southern California—it's only dreaming. I'm sorry this has made you worry, I'm so sorry. . . ."

Stricken with embarrassment, he struggles to say, "I want what you want. It's why I left where I grew up. I want an education, and to know things. I'd like to have a swimming pool in California . . . to give you everything you ever dreamed you wanted. But I keep feeling like everything's wrong and impossible."

Her eyes appear so accepting that all he can do is shake his head to convey how helpless and foolish he feels. "Please, darling, get in," she says. "We must go back. Please."

He nods. "If you can forgive me for being such an idiot."

"Please," she says.

He misses his train. Hedy has dropped him off and gone on, and instead of being annoyed at missing the train, he welcomes it, as if the two hours he has to wait is time enough to work out the humiliation swarming in him still. He has until reveille before he's obligated to be present, and thinking he might walk off the shameful regret, he decides to walk once more to Lichtental. He'll exercise limbs and lungs, and visit the soldiers in the town square. They'll commiserate, he's sure, even as they may laugh and shake their heads, and might suggest, if it's all too much for him, that they'd be willing to trade places for a decade or two.

Once there, where the glances of the cutaway eyes seem to be studying the horizon, Glen begins to feel better. Well, he thinks, praise be to the troops who paid the big price. A salute, a toast with the five-star cognac and the beautiful women left behind to be looked after and loved. If he's taking their place, well, it's how the cards fell, and all he can say is that he'll do his best to appreciate all that he can, just as he imagines they'd do the same if the tables were turned.

He thinks of his mother, too, as he walks back along the road to Baden-Baden. What is she doing today, all the way around the world in Michigan's Thumb? A Sunday afternoon in November—she's probably in Fenton at Aunt Eileen and Uncle Jay's for dinner.

Uncle Jay is probably caught up in how the Lions will do today, and if he were there, Glen thinks, he'd be caught up in those things. Or would he—will he—if and when he ever goes back? How can his life ever be the same?

Aboard the glistening shuttle train to Baden-Oos and another train out of Karlsruhe, he's relieved to be back in his heavy uniform; civilian clothes have been authorized off duty and the spy business will soon be a thing of the past. Cap tucked under an epaulet, loose civvies in his awol bag, he gazes over the countryside while trying to gaze over his own fate.

His appetite is returning, and it comes to him how little he's eaten throughout the weekend. Love is exhausting, and as he enters the familiar and busy Stuttgart *Hauptbahnhof* his hunger and thirst are accompanied by the relief of arriving home.

At a tiny *Schnellimbiss* table, he stands over his *Bier und Brot und Würstchen*. It feels good to be a soldier, no matter what Nute Nutter and the others say. To be alone and on his own. It feels good, he thinks, as Hedy, forgotten for the moment, comes to mind along with the pain and desire of loving her. Hedy Andreas. His sudden need is so strong he turns his head against a feeling that his heart has been gripped. Just like that, he misses her and wants to see her. What he wouldn't give to be able to dial some numbers and hear her voice. He'd give a month's pay to hear her speak half a dozen words.

To know he hasn't lost her, to know he might be with her forever, he'd give anything.

13

"ALERT!"

Glen is lying asleep and words are jabbing his mind. He's awakening, lifting his head as he hears: "ALERT! SEVENTH ARMY ALERT! LET'S GO! FULL FIELD, DRAW WEAPONS, SEVENTH ARMY ALERT! HAUL ASS! REPORT TO STATIONS ON THE DOUBLE! SEVENTH ARMY ALERT! HIT THE DECK!"

On his feet, pulling on fatigue pants, shirt, socks, combat boots, his mind races between several things—equipment, jeep, weapon, assignment. Wednesday? It is Wednesday, isn't it?

S-3. Speed-lacing his boots, he reminds himself that his alert assignment is S-3, Battalion Headquarters. He pulls on his field jacket, straps on his ammo belt and canteen, makes up his bunk in two seconds, and grabs his helmet and backpack from the top of his wall locker.

Racing downstairs to the basement, he falls in behind another soldier drawing a weapon from the company armorer, Corporal Dunham. Thatcher stands to the side with a pencil, clipboard, and shit-eating grin, checking names to make sure everyone draws a weapon.

"PFC CADY—KNOW YOUR ASSIGNMENT?" he bellows.

"YES, SERGEANT!" Glen bellows back, then adds through the half-door opening to Corporal Dunham, "Carbine number sixty-three!"

"WHAT *IS* YOUR ASSIGNMENT, PFC CADY?" Thatcher bellows.

"S-3, BATTALION HEADQUARTERS, SERGEANT, JEEP AND TRAILER!"

"WAY TO SOUND OFF, PFC—CARRY ON! ROOSKIES MAY CHARGE OVER THE HILL ANY MINUTE—CARRY ON!"

Only as Glen trots through the gate to the motor pool does he see from the wall clock in the dispatcher's shed that the time is 0340. He runs on to his jeep, MC/5, its trailer hooked up, as always, in anticipation of such an event, unstraps the canvas cover and folds it into the trailer, adds his backpack, taps the gas can attached to the rear to be sure it's full, props his carbine beside the gear shift, and climbs in to crank up the motor. Deciding on blackout—as if following two dim flashlight beams—he pulls out of the lineup and heads for the motor pool exit. The alert was called at 0330 and they must intend to pull out at 0400. "MC FIVE!" he calls to a sergeant standing near the gate.

Other soldiers are running in the dark and engines are revving all around. Silhouettes pass before his jeep as Glen wheels around to the quad and pulls up in front of Battalion—one vehicle is ahead of him, HQ/1, the battalion commander's jeep, and several figures in helmets, the brass, are on the sidewalk—sets the brake and leaves the motor running, jumps to the pavement.

"PFC Cady reporting S-3, for Major Guptill," he says.

"Here you go, soldier, what's the name again?"

"PFC Cady, sir."

"Okay, good timing. Let's load up this gear. We'll be pulling out in about five minutes."

The major, joined by a sergeant first class, begins wedging duffel bags inside the trailer. They also load two small lockers and push things around for balance, as Glen begins to replace and retie the cover. The SFC and a captain, both wearing holstered .45s, are loading into the back of the jeep as Glen returns behind the wheel and they wait for the major, who is talking to the battalion commander, Lieutenant Colonel Knowles, beside the jeep ahead.

"Driver, what's your name again?" the SFC asks, and after Glen tells him, the sergeant, a man with a wide moustache, surprises him by offering introductions. "I'm SFC Doughan, S-3 Operations Sergeant. Captain Cohen, Assistant OIC, S-3. Done good, Cady, pulling in ahead of time. Word to the wise—Major don't stand for no incompetence, no slow-moving feet. Understood?"

"Gotcha," Glen says.

"He say shit, you squat," Doughan says.

"Shit and squat," Glen says, drawing a laugh from his passengers. All are high with the excitement of an alert as the major swings into the passenger seat. "Let's roll, Cady," he says. "Follow the colonel's jeep around to the main gate."

Glen, flattered that the man recalls his name, is already releasing his brake and accelerating.

"Stay on blackout for now," the major says. "Through the main gate, go to full beam—don't wanna run over some local on a bicycle."

"Yes sir."

"Know how to drive this jeep, Cady?"

"Yes sir."

"Good. When I tell you to drive it, I want you to drive it. Want your mind on driving. No smoking when you're driving. We're gonna wave the convoy past, and on the Autobahn we'll overtake and resume the lead—you can handle that?"

"No problem, sir."

Glen waits with his jeep then, just inside the main gate, as his passengers unload and wander back to talk to the company commanders whose vehicles are lining up. Lighting a cigarette, he steps ahead to where the colonel's driver sits behind the wheel, and asks, "Know where we're headed?"

The driver turns his head. "You the major's driver?"

"Yeah, what company you in?"

"Today's alert area is near Crailsheim," the driver says. "I'm in Headquarters Company—draftee, less than three months to go. You a college man?"

"Me—no," Glen says.

"You'll never be the colonel's driver," the corporal says.

Glen looks at him. "Breaks my heart," he says, and, after taking a drag, returns to his jeep, regretting his sorry attempt at conversation.

He knows about where they'll go and what they'll do; there was no need to ask. They'll commandeer a stretch of Autobahn, drive maybe thirty kilometers to a predetermined location, set up signal stations for radio and wire, and a field kitchen maybe a mile away, check out the stations, transmit messages, smoke and drink coffee, have a good time in general, make a pass by the field kitchen for a plop of bad scrambled eggs into a cold mess kit, attempt to clean the mess gear in garbage cans of tepid water, repack everything in trucks and trailers, and return to base by noon, then spend the rest of the day cleaning and repacking for the next alert.

All around there is the revving and coughing of motors, the shouting of orders and cackles of laughter, regulars having a good time, draftees moaning about sleep and food. Before long the captain and Sergeant Doughan climb back into the jeep and the major, coming to stand in the street on the driver's side, exchanges a salute with the colonel as the older man climbs into the lead jeep. The major turns then and bellows back along the line of vehicles, a message repeated at ever greater distances throughout the darkness, "CRANK IT UP AND ROLL IT OUT! RIDE 'EM, COWBOY! LET'S GO!"

As the major stands waving them on, jeeps and trucks, headlights going to full beam, rumble through the main gate, accelerating without hesitation. Near the end, when some thirty jeeps and trucks have rolled by, there come the secretive radio and crypto vans, the water and mess hall vans, the big generator trucks, and two dark wreckers the size of dinosaurs. Swinging into the passenger seat, the major says, "Let's hope, shit ever hits the fan, the Rooskies are a little slower than we are."

Down the long hill, Glen follows the convoy as, waved on by an MP with a lighted baton, it accelerates right. After several kilometers another MP waves them toward a ramp onto the Autobahn and salutes.

"Okay, Cady, time to earn your pay," the major says as they reach the highway. "Overtake the convoy and pull in behind the colonel's jeep. Do not, under any circumstances, drive carelessly. Let's see what kind of driver you are."

Glen hand-signals through the open side of the jeep and enters the passing lane. He understands the major's message: fast, steady, always passing but not too fast. He concentrates, rolls past one vehicle and another, maintains a speed of about fifty while the convoy moves at thirty-five. As he drives, his passengers talk— discuss a location unfamiliar to Glen—and remark about a Captain Cahill being a cowboy. After several miles of passing trucks and jeeps, Glen blinks his lights, hand-signals a right turn, slips in behind the jeep driven by a college graduate, and is surprised to hear the major say, "Good job, son. Told Thatcher to assign us a good driver and glad to see he did."

That sonofabitch Thatcher recommended him—after all the shit he gives him! Glen has to keep himself from laughing aloud. Then Hedy comes to mind and he realizes she's been just beneath the surface of his thoughts, that for a brief stretch of time he's been merely the eighteen-year-old PFC jeep driver he is otherwise paid to be.

A four-hour Seventh Army alert. Four hours is the word passing between soldiers, but few things in the army go as planned and nearly six hours have fallen away when the colonel appears carrying a briefcase, slips into his jeep, and is driven away in a direction that has Glen guessing they are jumping convoy. When the major, captain, and operations sergeant come from the van, and Captain Cohen salutes the major as the major and SFC Doughan load up, Glen is certain the colonel jumped convoy because it appears they are going to do the same.

"See you at base, sir, if not sooner," Captain Cohen says.

"Head out the way we came," the major says to Glen, and Glen follows the narrow dirt road taken by the colonel.

Half a mile along, directing Glen to turn right on a paved two-lane road, the major says, "We got a village here about five klicks. Visiting which village, our mission is to spot one-each *Bäckerei. Verstehen Sie*, Cady? More for Doughan's benefit than my own, I'd add, whereupon we're going to shoot cross-country about twenty klicks, pick up the Autobahn west of Marbach, kick it into sprint—okay?—and overtake the convoy north of Stuttgart, ride shotgun the rest of the way home. Think you can handle driving back roads?"

"Yes sir, no problem."

"*Sprechen Sie Deutsch*, Cady?"

"A bit, sir. I study a phrase book."

"Good—what we like to hear."

Moments later, rolling along an all but empty village street, they spot the key word, *Bäckerei*, in the midst of the town's shops, and Glen pulls over to park.

"Food stop," the major says, unloading.

As Glen deboards to follow, the major says, "Don't leave that weapon behind."

"Yes sir."

"Chances are it wouldn't be here when we come back."

Glen is surprised as the major and SFC, each wearing a holstered .45, wait for him to retrieve his weapon and slip the strap over his shoulder. "We'll scare the shit outta these people, but tough titty," Doughan says.

Inside the bakery—entering to a tinkling bell—two elderly women customers do appear alarmed by the sudden presence of three armed soldiers in field gear, and step quickly aside. The woman behind the counter, older and smaller and wearing half-glasses, says sharply, *"Bitte, Jungs?"*

" *'Jungs'!"* the major says. "That's cute. Whatta ya have, Cady?" he adds, taking a five-DM note from his wallet. "Apple turnovers are outta this world. It's on me."

"Bitte, sprechen Sie Deutsch!" the woman says.

"Telling us to speak German!" the major says, laughing. *"Warum—können Sie kein English verstehen?* Got us one feisty little lady here," he adds.

"Wir sind hier nicht in England, sondern in Deutschland!" the woman says, the faintest of smiles appearing on her old, wrinkled face.

"Jawohl, schöne Frau," the major replies. *"Verzeihung, Sie haben ganz Recht."* The major adds a partial bow, which brings a half-toothless grin to the old woman's face and muffled laughter from the two customers watching.

Glen is also smiling as having fun of this kind is new to him. The old woman brings him up short, however, as she says, *"Was ist so komisch, mein Junge? Sprechen Sie Deutsch? Worüber lächeln Sie?"*

"Ich kann ein bisschen Deutsch, Mutti," Glen says, as if speaking to the seamstress in his company.

" *'MUTTI'!"* the woman exclaims. *"Er hat mich Mutti genannt!"*

The three women are laughing and making a jumble of tittering remarks. Looking back at Glen, the clerk offers a rush of words, gestures, and smiles he does not understand.

"Bitte," he says. *"Kann nicht verstehen."*

"She's saying that if she's to be your mother," the major tells him, "you'll learn the language or go without supper."

"Well, I'll try," Glen says, surrounded by laughter. *"Ich—danke schön,"* he adds, not knowing what else to say. "I'll try."

She nods, but the fun is over and she turns back to the major and the transaction concludes with a stack of paper-wrapped *Apfelkuchen* and mock argument over the major refusing to accept change from the five-mark note and the woman refusing to accept a gratuity. The major simply leaves the change on the counter, insisting *auf deutsch* that the woman and her friends enjoy glasses of schnapps on the U.S. Army. The woman behind the counter waves them away like pests, calling, *"Gute Reise, Jungens!"* as they leave.

That night around nine, Hedy telephones.

Given last-minute duty as CQ, Glen is in the Orderly Room and answers the company phone himself. He had made the mistake, passing the many-striped figure in the motor pool, of thanking Thatcher for recommending him to S-3, only to see Thatcher point at his chest, tell him to eat early chow and report for Company CQ at 1700—a detail usually given to corporals, which consists of answering the phone and looking after pass box and book until eight o'clock the next morning.

"Message Center Company, PFC Cady speaking, sir!"

"Glen—it is you? I recognize your voice."

"It's me," he says. "I'm on duty here because somebody's sick."

"Everything is confused, darling. I may speak only one moment."

"Is something wrong?"

"You may *not* come to me this weekend—yes? My husband is at home. I'll explain all when I see you. New things have happened and I must see you. I may drive there tomorrow? Is it possible? I believe I may stay until morning—may I do this, as before, but not so quickly this time?"

"Sure. But it might be hard for me to get away. I have to make a run in the afternoon to Heidelberg."

"It's okay—later is okay—only tell me the time. I am able to speak only this moment."

"Five o'clock. Hill Road at five o'clock?"

"Oh, Glen darling, you cannot know how I long to be with you. I love you in such a way I cannot help myself. Until then," she says, and the dial tone begins to hum.

Glen stands at the desk holding the receiver. Around him, stray soldiers are picking up passes, still signing out to leave for town, and it will be his job to check them in throughout the night—and for the moment, in spite of or perhaps because of her declaration, his life again feels both exciting and impossibly complicated.

The night drags on. It's close enough to payday that many soldiers go into town, and though most return by midnight, others wander in at odd intervals. Each time Glen lies down on the cot provided for the CQ and begins to doze, more soldiers come in talking and laughing. Finally, at 0340, he sets the alarm so he can wake the troops for first call at 0500. Removing his shoes and pulling the blanket over him, Glen realizes that Hedy, of course, is the one who is trapped; and with his heart going to her across southern Germany, he finally gives way to sleep.

All of forty minutes pass before someone is drunkenly slapping the counter. "Charge a Quarters? Who's fuckin' CQ 'round here?"

It's Thatcher, no surprise, and Glen, sitting up on the side of the cot, holds his head in his hands. "Sarge, what the hell you want?"

"Ain't late signing in," Thatcher says, tapping the counter with one finger. "Not due fer duty oh-six-hundred, *kapisch*? Mess hall open? Old lady kicked my ass out, you believe that? What the hell the world coming to? Who'd blame her, I say. I'se her, kicked my ass out long ago." Thatcher stands laughing and weaving, keeping a hand on the counter.

Glen closes his eyes, says, "Sarge, go on and get some sleep. Don't know if the mess hall's open. Get some sleep. You got duty in about an hour and so do I."

"Don't tell me when I got duty," Thatcher says with sudden anger. "Don't ever tell me when I got duty."

He'd like to hurt the man, but Glen pushes under the counter and, taking a chance, he knows, props Thatcher up by the arm, and then Thatcher is cursing and swinging wildly at him. Glen glimpses the fist, ducks, and Thatcher spirals out of balance and into the counter. He hangs on, draped there, and Glen, nervous and angry, wants to hit him, would like to knock him out, and only then imagines he could face charges for doing so, no matter how drunk and belligerent the first sergeant is. His head partially raised, Thatcher hangs on to the counter with one knee on the floor, looking like a half-conscious boxer on the ropes.

At last Glen takes Thatcher's arm with both hands and pulls the wavering man to his feet. "Move it!" he says, but Thatcher isn't so much resisting as simply drunk. His eyes attempt to focus on Glen, and spittle slides from one side of his mouth.

"Don't say anything!" Glen says as Thatcher gives in to being guided along. "One fuckin' word and I'm calling the duty officer."

"Ole lady kick my ass out," Thatcher mumbles as Glen steers him with both hands. "Married United States fuckin' Army, death us part. Know what I mean? It's Tommy this an' Tommy that. . . ." Glen turns him into his first-floor room, pushes him down on his cot. "Goddamn, man, I get on your ass, know what I mean?" Thatcher says. "Don't take it personal."

"You're going to bed, Sarge—so just shut the fuck up."

"Good soldier, Cady, an' I know what soldiers're made of."

Then Thatcher falls silent, and Glen lifts him by the ankles and turns him onto the cot. He'd like to warn Thatcher, first sergeant or not, that he's flirting with trouble by drinking so much, but there's no way to give such a message and he decides to leave well enough alone. At the door, on second thought, he flips on the light. He's heard of drunks choking to death, returns and loosens the man's necktie.

Hoping to draw a cup of coffee for himself—the night is wasted—he walks toward the mess hall. Inside the doorway, however, a cook, Corporal Rusk, black as motor oil and said to be illiterate, shouts at him from the kitchen, where he and the two German KPs are preparing breakfast. "Mess hall's closed—CQ or no fucking CQ—stay the fuck outta here, man."

Though the room is unlighted, Glen can see the day duty sergeant at the first three graders' table drinking from a mug. He walks in, takes a mug from a tray, and suddenly explodes: "Blow it out your ass, Rusk! I'm having . . . fucking . . . coffee! I live here!"

Sergeant Gantos sits laughing as Glen fills his mug. "Rusk," Gantos calls over his shoulder, "you best allow the man his coffee, he's already got it in his hands."

Lifting a leg to sit at the table, Glen says, "Pass the milk, Sarge."

"Milk, sugar, I'll stir it and drink it for you if you want. How come you pulling CQ—Thatcher nail you for something?"

"Somebody got sick. I said something nice to that asshole and he put me on CQ."

Rusk comes around from the kitchen in his whites and white hat, draws coffee, and joins them. A mess hall routine: cooks and regulars at the first three graders' table, smoking over endless refills, trading gossip. "Don't be bad-mouthin' Thatcher, man," Rusk says. "He's got you down as his fair-haired boy."

Glen can only snort.

"Across this table, man say Cady the best soldier in the company, a thirty-year man. Say he got hisself a shackjob, too. That true, man? Got yoself a shackjob, fucking PFC?"

"Three-year man," Glen says. "No shackjob. I wasn't bad-mouthin' Thatcher either. All I did was say something nice to that prick with ears and he slapped me on CQ."

"Do three, they got you by the ass," Gantos says. "Miss kraut pussy so much won't be able to beat you away with a stick."

"Ain't never ZI-ing myself," Rusk says. "What I do in Birmingham, be the white man's nigger? Got no shackjob, though ain't to say I ain't been lookin'."

After two cups of coffee, Glen walks the hallway upstairs, hollering in someone else's voice: "Let's go, first call! Hit the deck! Drop your cocks and grab your socks! Reveille in thirty minutes!"

Only after midday chow, after making the run to Heidelberg and struggling to stay awake, does he recall that he had all but separated himself from the army. How is it that the army seems, more than ever, to have him back?

The green VW is down the hill and Glen's heart seems to inflate on sight of the car's reflecting windshield. She's here and he's going to touch her in one more minute. He waves his hand, though he can't see through the reflection, and removes his cap as he slips into the car on the passenger side.

Beautifully made up and beautifully dressed, she says something not quite decipherable as he embraces her.

"God, you look good," he says, and pulls back some to look at her, sees that her eyes are lightly filmed with emotion.

"Thank you," she says.

"You have any idea how good-looking you are?" he says. "I wake up in the night, I could go crazy you're so good-looking."

She smiles and kisses his forefinger. "May we sit a moment and have a cigarette? You can't know how happy I am to see you—I think I'm the one going crazy on days that I cannot see you."

"Everything's okay," Glen says. "Whatever it is, we'll make it okay."

"Yes," she says, smiling. "Okay."

Unbuttoning his jacket to get his Camels from his shirt pocket, he cannot help stifling a yawn, and she says, "Darling, you're tired."

"I am sleepy. We did an alert yesterday, then I was up all night—but it's okay, I'll be fine. How are *you*? You got me worried, when you called."

"There must be hotels in this town," she says. "Do you know of a place we may stay? I must return very early, to be back by six o'clock—this is okay?"

"It's fine," Glen says. "I don't have to be back until reveille, at five-thirty. It sounds great, staying in a hotel."

"In one hour I drive here," she says. "Therefore I must leave, I think, before four-thirty?"

"It's no problem."

"Darling, we must take separate rooms, you know. Everything has changed—it's what I must tell you. It's dangerous now. I must be so careful."

"What's dangerous?"

"Glen, I will separate now from my husband. He's moving to Frankfurt, only for two days, before returning Saturday to attempt to change my mind. He knows, of course, that I'm in love with someone and have a lover, he knows this, and if he can prove something it's possible he is attempting to take Ilsedore from me. This I cannot allow, not under any circumstance. It means we must be so careful until everything is finished. I'm in fear that he may have appointed someone to look after me. This is his way, there's no doubt."

"I guess I thought you were, well, thinking of moving out."

"The house, you see, is a gift to me from my father when we are married—he's not disputing this, I think. Oh, darling, may

we find this hotel and sit where it's safe and drink something—
that I may tell you everything from the beginning?"

Der Baron, a small hotel with a cellar restaurant, is across town
from the area of bars Glen knows. He pays in advance and they
are shown to separate rooms on the second floor, one at either
end, before returning downstairs. The restaurant is cozy, and only
one other table is occupied, though in just minutes a party of four
enters and takes a table. Hedy remarks that the wine here is not
as special as in Baden-Baden, but she selects a glass of the waiter's
preference. Glen orders beer and finds himself presented with a
half-liter dark brown bottle with a wire-attached ceramic cap and
red rubber seal.
    "Perhaps we must also eat something," Hedy says.
    Glen feels too nervous to eat, even though he skipped evening
chow to shower and make it down the hill on time.
    "I, too, am overly excited to eat," Hedy says. "Perhaps later."
    As they smoke and drink, Hedy relates the accusations which
led to the crisis. Her husband confronted her over withholding
affection, and this time—she had not, as she had imagined, prepared a speech—she told him directly that what he perceived was
true, as it was true that their marriage had been an unfortunate
mistake from the beginning, and she had determined, without
possible reconsideration, to separate and have a divorce. To have,
she told him, some happiness in her life at last.
    Then he packed and drove to Frankfurt, where he has the use
of a flat near his office. "He could return tonight," she says. "It's
not certain. Ilsedore is with my friend, and I'm so desperate to
see you. If he returns—this will tell you of my madness—I've
left a note indicating Ilsedore and I are visiting my family in
Duisburg, where I'm certain he is not to call."
    Glen is into a second half-liter of the dark beer, while Hedy,
relating her experience, nurses her initial glass of white wine. He
asks questions—what he said, what she said, why it was that he'd
try to take custody of their daughter—as he sips more of the dark
beer, and zither music floats pleasantly from the back of the room.
And as he hears what has happened in the past days, the beer
seems to give added clarity to what Hedy is saying and to the
music itself. Pouring the last of a bottle into his glass, he tries to
recall if it's his third or fourth bottle.

"Good beer," he hears himself say. He blinks, and hears her say something about *"Festbier."*

"Perhaps we should eat something," she says. "Is there something you'd like to eat?"

"Not sure, I don't think so," he says.

"Darling, you are okay?"

"I'm fine, I think."

He knows, minutes later, when he is making his way to the rest room, that if something isn't wrong—nothing *seems* wrong—it is different. One leg feels longer and looser than the other, or perhaps the floor is uneven, he can't tell. He enters a brief hallway, wondering why the zither continues to sound in his ears. "Glow little glowworm, glow and glimmer," he sings softly. Is he still on the troopship, he wonders foolishly as he stands at a urinal singing softly to himself. It seems he cannot help singing as he shoots a stream into the drainage holes, scoring a steady bull's eye. "Gotcha," he says, buttoning up, and turns to see a man waiting his turn.

"Didn't see you," Glen says.

The man says nothing and steps past as Glen turns to sink and mirror to wash his hands. "You are drunk," he whispers to the image before him. Lifting cold water to his face, he sees the man slip past and leave, and he turns, thinking to apologize for lingering over the sink, only to see another man enter. "What the hell's in that beer?" he hears himself say. This man laughs and, as he stands over the urinal, says something in German. Glen stands swaying, trying to dry his face on a paper towel, and recognizes but one word: *"Festbier."*

On his way back to the table—he's certain it's in this direction—he tries to concentrate on walking evenly, but the floor keeps tilting and he has to pause to keep from sailing out of balance. He hears laughter—is he being laughed at?

Darkness, soft bed. There is tapping on a door and a male voice calling in a harsh whisper, and Glen's mind begins at last to take in fragments even as he doesn't entirely awaken.

There is the sound again, and again the harsh whisper.

Glen gets his head to lift an inch—the banging continues—and hears himself say, *"Ja!* I'm up!" in the approximate direction of the door.

The voice adds something, retreating, and Glen puts his feet on the cold floor and stands in the dark, bladder nearly bursting.

Dear God, something in his head is saying as shame washes over him. Oh God. He can barely admit the images coming to him and making him feel sickness, regret, shame. He lets his head drop, trying to escape his misery, but no escape is possible.

Finding a light switch near the door, he finds a toilet stool and pisses. Then, sitting on the side of the bed, he wonders what time it is, knows he must return to his feet, knows he has ruined everything, can see in his mind the awful things he has done—did he pass out?—and things he cannot bear to see. He's alone, that he also knows; still, he reaches a hand under the comforter on the chance she is there.

He forces himself back to his feet, and weaves as nighttime scenes blur before him—a drunken attempt to pull her into bed, a drunken loss of control and a drunken sexual mess all over her beautiful lingerie. Has she gone away and left him? He hopes she has, and that he may die at once, not to have to face her ever again.

There's a tapping on the door. "Glen," she says, and relief races through him that she is speaking to him.

"Yes," he gets out, stumbling to his feet, toward the door.

"Please, at the car," she says. "Please—I must return now!"

He gets the door open only to see her walking away. "Hedy!"

She turns. "At the car!" she whispers. "Please!"

She goes on as he stands there—in his GI underwear, he realizes—gazing into her wake along the dimly lit hallway. Back in the room, he closes the door and stands against it for a moment to sort out what he has to do.

At the sink, washing his face and the back of his neck, he runs a finger over his teeth and gums, rinses his mouth over and over with water. Then, knowing the eruption is on its way, he holds the sink and tries to keep it down, and fails as an explosion of bile splatters the sink.

She came to him with her news, he thinks, dressed for him in her beautiful clothes and silken undergarments. . . . Dear God.

Cold, dark air. Is it December? Then he's in the dark car, shivering badly and trying to control his trembling. She's driving; the Volkswagen labors as it climbs the long hill to Panzerkaserne. Their headlights pass—no view could be worse—a sodden sergeant staggering up the shoulder of the road, laboring to make his way home in the freezing predawn darkness.

Silense rides with them. "I'm sorry," Glen gets out.

No response. The car labors, its headlights passing through layers of fog.

"I don't even know how I got to my room," he says.

The car is approaching the turnaround space before the flood-lighted main gate. All is quiet and draped in fog, and no taxis are waiting at this hour. She pulls over.

"That beer," he says. "I'm sorry—"

"I'm so damned tired, Glen, all I can think in this moment is I must return quickly. Please."

He decides not to risk trying to kiss her as he exits the car, but reaches and touches her forearm as he gets out.

He stands in the chilled darkness then, watching the car's taillights circle into the fog and go out of view back down the hill. He wants her to beep, to give a sign that all might not be lost, but no sign is forthcoming.

The weekend passes without a word from her, and he wonders if she's trying to find a way to say goodbye. Finally, she had a glimpse of his true self—an immature GI who can't handle booze and mauls her when drunk. He posts a note to her friend's address: "I'm so sorry and I don't know what to say. All I know is that I love you and would give anything to live that night over." He makes jeep runs to Heidelberg and Darmstadt, stands formations, and sleeps in fits of sad regret. He begins to dread the coming of another weekend, in fear that he'll hear nothing from her and won't know what to do.

By Saturday she has neither called nor written. The troops drift away into the weekend, and Glen is struck with fear. To have the CQ know he's there, in case a call should come for him, he stands around the Orderly Room counter chatting about the weather. Most of the time he sits on his bunk in his squad room. The building empties, except for a soldier sleeping here or there, leaving him alone in the quiet Saturday afternoon of an early winter day. He waits, hating waiting, in hopeless hope that she might call.

Returning to the Orderly Room, despising himself for what he's doing, he says, "Any calls for Cady?"

The CQ shakes his head without looking up, and Glen wanders the first-floor corridor. As long as he hangs around, so weak and foolish, there's no way she'll call. Nothing ever works that way. Still, it's Saturday, and the thought of going to town and finding out later that he missed a call is unbearable. But by waiting, he thinks, he's making an even bigger fool of himself, so he is shocked, sitting on his bunk, when the CQ knocks on the door. "Cady— call's on the line."

He hurries downstairs, where Thatcher is sitting at his desk, writing something. Taking the receiver from the CQ and turning his back on the open-ended room, Glen says, "Hello."

"Glen? It is you?"

"Oh, I'm so glad you called."

"I'm happy now to hear your voice," she says.

"Me too—to hear yours."

"You are not free to speak?"

"Not too much, no." He glances up, but Thatcher is absorbed in whatever he is writing.

"Darling, you may not speak more loudly?"

"A little, yes," he says. "I'll try."

"I know it's not a good time to call. I may not see you now this week, or next—is it okay? I'm sorry. I know you are feeling bad."

"I'm glad you called. I've been worried."

"I'll write and explain. In one moment, I must return. I'm happy to hear your voice. Do you feel this, too?"

"Yes, do I ever."

"I'll write soon—and I love you."

"I do, too."

She's gone again, but has said she loves him. Now he might walk outside, and go to the PX or snack bar without fear of missing the last chance he thought he might ever have. A fool in love, he thinks. Too far gone to know what to do.

5

MARRIED STUDENT HOUSING

Spring 1988

14

Alice is with him, making a supermarket run to pick up Raisin Bran for breakfast, and they pass the street that leads to Married Student Housing. He comes this way for the thrill of nearness. He's kept himself from returning to Ecki's apartment through the first weeks of the new semester, and passing close to where she lives helps him call up the pleasure of his infatuation. They made love that one afternoon, he heard her cry out and was smitten, but since then has engaged her only in his mind.

Driving by the street where she lives is one small pleasure and so is thinking of her as he lies waiting for sleep at night, or walking to school in the morning. The thoughts are no more real than dreams, and no harm is done, he tells himself. It'll pass. He slipped that once and will make it up to his small family. Hedy incarnate. If he could find a way to tell Paige of his curious dream and that part of his life, would she ever understand?

He glimpses Ecki in a flow of students. Classes just ended and she's moving downstairs within the mob, going outside. Going, maybe, to the coffee shop to look over notes and chapters, or maybe to flirt with someone, maybe a young student whose head has been turned. He hopes so, and hopes not. Jealousy, desire, the forbidding laws of his job—he knows all the old, conflicting emotions. Seeing her has stirred him and he's thrilled that her feet touched the floor where now, a moment later, his own are touching. After all these years, love is visiting him again, although at the distance of a film on a screen.

Another day, leaving the department office on the first floor, he sees her again, going away down the empty hallway. He follows, seized by a certainty that she will see him and pause to talk. He studies her hair, her shoulders, hips, and ankles, returns his gaze to her hips, but keeps himself from following and takes a stairway he has no reason to take. Lets her go.

Then, at last, she stops by his office. He knows from his fantasies that he must resist his desire, but feels helpless in her presence. He wants to lift her breasts and rub his face in them.

She smiles nicely, standing with her back to his office door. "May I stop like this?" she says. "You've said we may be friends, but I miss you and you never call or write. Is it permissible that I visit my favorite professor?"

"I have to tell you the truth," he says after a moment passes. "It was wrong of me to go to your place. I was in bad shape, and probably it was wrong saying we could be friends. I'd like to, but I know I can't quite handle it. I know it would be wrong."

"I must leave now?" she says.

He looks down at the top of his desk, says nothing, and hears the door opening. In the next moment he's on his feet, pushing to the doorway. "Ecki, just a minute," he says, "come back a minute," and no matter what eavesdroppers along the hall might have heard, as she returns behind his door, he cannot resist embracing her and pressing his face into her hair, reaching his hand around her head and neck and whispering that he is sorry and kissing her ear and face.

Walking over West Bridge, he stops at a stationery store for no reason and buys her a fountain pen made in Germany. He charges the gift to Visa—a risk he knows he shouldn't take—and returns to the icy winter air stricken again with guilt over his betrayal of Paige and Alice, stricken with fear, too, of being caught. Paige, working at home, is the one for whom he should be buying gifts, and thinking of how he would feel if the tables were turned, he resolves yet again to conclude the affair he's resumed. He has to quit once and for all, before he hurts others, and destroys himself.

He'll save the pen for Alice. He'll show it to Paige and put it away—say it's something he wanted for Alice for her fifth birthday, in April. An expensive instrument with a gold nib, he'll say, full of magical words. No need to worry about the card charge arriving in the mail, by which time he'll have extricated himself from this midlife madness.

Ecki calls, as she does every Monday, Wednesday, and Friday after his Intro to Modern German Lit class. The pen remains in his parka on the wall hook, and glancing that way, he knows that he must move to break with her, that he cannot risk losing or hurting his family. Ordinarily he would say he missed her over the weekend, and that he has a gift he wants to give her tomorrow afternoon, but this time he is distant.

She tells of a class for which she's been studying, of her son, of a letter from her estranged husband in Harrisburg. Too much is at stake, Glen wants to say as they talk. If found out—and how can he not be found out?—it isn't as if he'd be chided for having a mistress, rather he'd be summarily fired, would be ousted from the only profession he knows, and probably divorced to boot. It has to end, he's telling himself as she is describing an exotic coffee she bought for him, as her habit—once they've made love and showered in the afternoon, when it's time for her son to come home from school and Glen is about to return to his office—is to serve small, carefully brewed cups of gourmet coffee. It has to end before all is lost, he's thinking, as he tells her goodbye for now, see you in a while.

His hands slide over her hips and waist and over the damp small of her back. It's just an erotic affair, he's trying to tell himself, a forbidden physical adventure in which he's been given a last chance—is seizing a last opportunity—to act out fantasies suppressed over years of solitary work and a decade of an unfulfilling marriage. A merely physical affair doesn't have to hurt anyone, is as harmless in its way as twice-weekly handball, isn't it? What a joke, he thinks, and how nice it would be to experience an unconditional smile or two.

Worry about Otto Gentz, about your integrity as a teacher, worry about Paige, he's urging himself as, over the ratty ottoman on the living room floor of her apartment, he's into Ecki from behind. Her slippery hips are under his hands and he pulls back enough to glimpse nature at work, and returns to consideration of his hopeless tenure case, whatever will keep him from the brink, but then Ecki is extending chin and closed eyes and begging, "More story, please, more words," and he takes them into a narrative along a foggy cobblestone street in Munich, up a stairway and into an anthology of scenes he has filed away, scenes Ecki has been appropriating as protégée, coauthor, performer. He whispers hard four-letter words as he directs her into a role as a beautiful street-walker underneath the lamplight, swirling her long black coat in presentation of garter-belt-decorated naked ass and naked patch of fur, a scene and words she has said "work a miracle" for her, leads her up the winding stairway to the "whore's red-lighted room," has her uttering syllables known to one language and another as they strive toward the narrative's climax.

In the aftermath, as always, intimacy is gentle and without embarrassment, while behind his eyes guilt is virulent. In her cramped kitchen they sip her tiny cups of coffee and joke and smile while he tries to ignore the troubles raging within him.

"Insipid," Ecki is saying, in reference to Goethe's remark that a woman's disposition is akin to art. She is not in Glen's class this semester, on which account alone his life is made easier, but she likes to discuss with him what she's studying with Renate Leonhard, one of his tenured colleagues.

Glen is getting to his feet. He must return to campus, while she awaits the after-school arrival of her son, whom Glen has no wish to encounter, fearing it would unacceptably compromise his relationship with Alice. Anxiety is in his throat and he knows little more than that he is about to lose control and has to move. "I have to hurry now, I'm sorry, I'm feeling really anxious," he says. "It's not you, it's me. The guilt's too much at times and I can't bear hurting my wife and daughter. I'll talk to you soon. I just have to go."

His last glance is of her sitting at the small table. Then he's pushing hard along the sidewalk where snowflakes have begun to blow from a heavy sky, disliking himself for his apparent cowardice and confusion, hurrying on before he changes his mind and runs back, then disliking himself all the more as he pushes on.

Days later, along the first-floor hallway, he hears Otto Gentz's voice at his back, calling his name, and his immediate fear is that he's been caught and will be prosecuted at once on charges ranging from infidelity to professional wrongdoing to cowardice and cruelty in a love affair.

"It's gone up," Otto says. "I'm not sure if you wanted to be informed of these little details."

Glen is looking back at him. "What's gone up?"

"Your case—from department to college to dean."

"My case? I didn't know it was through the department."

"Of course. I haven't told you this? I was certain I had."

"When?" Glen says. "When did it go up?"

"I'm certain I told you."

"You didn't tell me! *When* did it go up?"

"Oh, only a matter of days, to the dean. But I'm *certain* I told you."

Some small vein is being pinched in Glen, and he says, "You're wrong, Otto. Last thing you told me—last thing—a preliminary vote in the department, six to nothing, remember?"

"Well, I certainly *thought* I told you," Otto says.

Glen holds as students and instructors stream about them, glimpsing the scene, and Glen knows he's already on the other side of a line he shouldn't have crossed. "Otto, why are you sputtering such horseshit? Who in the fuck do you think you're talking to?"

Otto's back clearly stiffens. "In any case, it has gone up."

"The department voted? The college committee? *What's* gone up?"

"At the recommendation of the committees, of each committee. Again, I couldn't know if you wanted to be informed of each little step along the way."

"Little steps! The little steps that will put me on the fucking street?"

"Look, Cady, if you are going to assume—"

"Come off it, Gentz. It's your job to tell me! You haven't, so don't say you have!"

"I refuse to stand here and hear such abuse, I assure—"

"Otto, I'm going to Monica, right now, and to the dean. And I may file a lawsuit against you, personally, on grounds of gross negligence. How does that sound?"

Staring down the hall, Glen sees that among a dozen bystanders are two English professors. "Don't mind us," he adds. "Foreign

Languages—the usual stuff." This, to his satisfaction, draws a snort of laughter from one of them, a man, while the woman glances the other way as if she hadn't been witnessing the nasty scene in the first place.

"Consider yourself informed," Otto says.

"Tell me what the vote was, Otto. Believe me, I can handle it."

"I have no choice but to report this incident to Monica."

"Tell me the fucking vote, asshole."

"The fucking vote, Dr. Cady, was six to nothing."

"There—that does it. That wasn't so bad, was it? Now, was it six for or six against?"

Otto glares at him, and nearly smiles as he turns and walks away.

His family, Glen thinks. If he can retain his family, he'll not lose all. It doesn't finally matter if he wallpapers walls or sweeps streets, as long as he has his family to work for and go home to. To walk Alice to kindergarten in the fall. To be able to buy her a new pair of shoes, or a book to read. Walking Alice to school on a September morning, he thinks, is as much happiness as anyone might ever reasonably expect.

Nonetheless he'd like to hold Ecki in his arms and rest his head on her shoulder. But he's letting time slip away now and hasn't dialed her number and has avoided her calls for many days. He knows, too, that Paige's final interview is scheduled for nine in the morning, and that he doesn't want to cause her any more anxiety than he already has. Do something, he tells himself. If it's the translation of one sentence, even if it takes an hour, just do it.

So it is that he forces himself to swivel his chair and push the switch on his computer, to gaze at the snowflakes hitting his skylight as the machine hums and beeps. The line he turns to is red-checked from when he last worked on the piece—what, three days ago?—and doesn't even require him to reread the paragraph. Still, he tries to call up his maxim of making his translations clear enough for Alice to grasp: *"Am 17. Januar war grauer Himmel über Ost Berlin."* Straining his eyes, he forces himself to experience gray skies over East Berlin, continues, *"Tausende und tausende von Arbeitern verliessen die Fabriken und demonstrierten,"* hearing the rumble of a massive gathering of long-deceived, pent-up factory workers. . . .

Glen sits at the kitchen table, writing checks and paying bills. Anxious still, he's doing anything to justify his existence. Simple math and check-writing are tasks he can handle—even as they call up the fear that, losing his job, he will not be able to pay bills—and he sits adding and subtracting carefully. He proves the sums, as he learned in third or fourth grade—it seems two lifetimes ago—when he was himself as open to the world as a blank check.

Paige is a dozen feet away in the kitchen, preparing dinner. Alice is behind him in the sunken living room—where, earlier, Glen ignited some logs in the fireplace—lying on her belly reading. Television has not been forbidden and she watches "Electric Company" and "Sesame Street," but her pastime remains reading, for which, as always, he adores her.

Glen knows he's taking sustenance wherever he can find it. He writes a check to Visa—Paige has hit the cards hard lately, outfitting herself for the bank, and Glen avoids acknowledging how much they may be in debt.

He seals the Visa envelope. Snow floats down outside and all could be well with him and his family, despite even the threat to his job, he thinks, but for the shards of betrayal and lovesickness lurking within him.

Paige, taste-testing spaghetti sauce, catches him gazing her way. "No trip to the store tonight?" she says.

"Hmm?"

"No urgent errands?"

"It's snowing."

No response.

Looking to the torn envelopes, he begins to put things away. Then an image of Ecki enters his mind—how can you make feelings for someone stop?—and he blinks as if to will it away. Paige is suspicious; this much is obvious. He's losing weight, and their conversations are ever more riddled with accusation. Out of guilt and fondness, he volunteers to make a salad.

"Go easy with the seasonings," Paige says. "You'll make Alice sick to her stomach."

"Make Alice sick? I never have before. Alice?" he calls, in one of their regular routines. "You like some croutons?"

"*Yes!*" Alice snaps in mock irritation, keeping her eyes on the book.

Suddenly reinvigorated, Glen says, "I'm going to get Alice started in German—Latin, too. I can't believe we're letting these good years slip by."

"Well, let her turn five," Paige says. "Don't you have enough on your mind these days?"

"Five's too late," he answers, as if even his small hope for Alice is sinking away.

Once the salad is prepared, Glen opens a can of beer and sits down at the table. "Have some news," he says. "Not very good, but not surprising either."

Paige looks at him. "What news?"

Glen gives a watered-down account of his exchange with Otto. "Six to nothing, he finally admitted. From both committees."

Paige is still looking at him.

"I'm sorry," he says.

She only shrugs.

"I thought Monica might call, or the dean. I'm sure Otto will file a report."

"Where were you earlier?"

"Earlier? Oh, I walked some, hid out in the stacks for a while—I kind of knew this was coming."

Paige looks into the living room. "Honey, wash your hands," she calls. "We're going to eat in five minutes."

She knows, Glen is thinking, even as he's been keeping his distance from Ecki. But what she says is, "I understand how hard this is for you. I don't know if I did before."

"I still wonder if I shouldn't get out of teaching right away, get started on something else sooner rather than later."

Paige places Alice's glass of milk on the table. "Well, I'm sure I *will* be going back to work," she says, and Glen senses either an absence of sympathy or that they're talking at cross-purposes. "Alice will be in school and we'll have to get along," she adds. "So I see no reason why an entire year should be given up when it doesn't have to be."

"There are other reasons," Glen says, as Alice enters.

"What other reasons?" their small child says.

Her parents look at her. "Nothing," Paige says. "Something we were talking about. Let's eat, I'm about to starve."

"Bitte," Glen says. *"Die Hände, Liebchen."*

Alice steps before him and presents her palms; it's a small game they play, and is oddly important to him now. Studying the weightless hands held in his own, he says, "Microorganisms by the millions," and gobbles at her fingers, getting her to squeal and making himself blink.

"Believe me, I do understand," Paige says as they lie in bed in the dark. Then she says, "That's the most spaghetti we've ever had left over."

Glen doesn't respond. He's frightened and wants to feel close to Paige, wants to return to their being partners and accepting each other. His thought is to tell all at once, to apologize and convince her how sorry he is, and start over again.

He touches her silken waist. "Thanks for trying to understand," he says. "It really helps."

She lies there, and a confused amorous need stirs in him as he slides his hand over the inside of her forearm. He'd like, really, to move his hand over her belly and ribs, over her hip and over and under her breasts, and at the same time he knows she is unlikely to reciprocate for one reason or another.

She surprises him now, however, by saying, "I can't seem to get warm."

"Come over here, then. It's a winter night out there."

One surprise is followed by another, as she lifts her nightgown under her arms.

"Why, Paige Sims," he says, "whatever has gotten into you?"

Their hands move about each other in an uncharted sequence of lovemaking. He senses that she is almost too eager, at the same time that he knows any remark might derail her delicate scenario. He wonders how much their tender exchange had to do with what is happening, or with the snow still falling outside. Then, as she is aroused and giving of her naked self, an arm circling around his neck with her face on his shoulder, she tightens her grip.

He turns his neck to free his windpipe, attempting not to disrupt things. He continues losing his breath, however, as she moans and squeezes harder. He can neither speak nor swallow, and at last has no choice but to force his head and neck free and gasp, "Honey, please! I can't breathe."

However soft his tone, and as he feared, she gives up and sinks away.

"Don't go away," he says. "Come on."

"Forget it."

Glen, gasping still, says, "I couldn't breathe. You were squeezing my windpipe."

Silence accumulates in the darkness and, not knowing what to say or do, he reaches for her and says, "Please, come back here."

"Glen, for God's sake!" she says, pulling away.

15

Daybreak. The snow is six or eight inches deep, but spring is present in the sunlight and clear blue sky, and Glen is feeling some hope on this glorious March day.

In hat, gloves, and sweater, he has pushed snow from porch steps and driveway and is in the kitchen fixing coffee, while Paige is upstairs preparing for her deciding interview. When the kitchen radio announces that school closings will be read in ten minutes, at seven, Glen races upstairs to urge Alice into her small housecoat and slippers. "Who knows, maybe The Learning Tree will make the list," he tells her. At least for its morning session, he figures, since they're always the first to close, and this small thrill for Alice will be the same for him. The late New England snowstorm that came sweeping in yesterday—especially since the new day has broken blue and cloudless above the shoveling and huffing of snowplows—takes him back to his childhood in Michigan but also to the Alps, to Garmisch, Salzburg, Bad Tölz, Lenggries, the other stretch of time he spent growing up in a snowy climate.

After the morning session is canceled, they start breakfast and, when Paige makes her appearance, they look her over. She does a turn, hands posed—the incident of last night ignored. Made up, decked out with high heels and nylons, she fills out the blue suit nicely and looks attractive and confident. Glen recalls being attracted to her in the bank over a decade ago and wonders if in giving up her middle-class ways she feels now that *she* is the one whose life has gotten lost. Hooking up with an older man, an academic and a dreamer. A man with whom her sex life is—well, who knows, maybe she'd have a much easier time with someone her own age.

Glen returns outdoors to sweep snow from the car and shovel some more, tasks he more enjoys than endures on a day like this, while tension over his own disrupted day waits close at hand. All is ready then for Paige to back out and drive to the main office in Dover, by which time Glen has Alice in her snowsuit and pink rubber boots and they stand beside the car and wave as Paige rolls away.

Alice packs a snowball, and her light toss topples a cascade of fresh snow from a bough, and Glen understands her intoxicated excitement. He'd like nothing more than to play in the snow with her, but feels rattled with pressure: school, the translation he hasn't looked at in days, his confusion about Ecki—might she call, should he call her and apologize, will she ever have anything to do with him again? So it is that when Alice uses the broom to knock his hat off, and grabs it up, he snaps at her, "Come on, Alice, I've got a lot to do."

She ignores this, stuffs snow into his hat as she moves around, and he gives in to the occasion and absorbs a barrage of snowballs, but ducks to avoid what looks like a roll of toilet paper taken from his hat. In response, though, he gathers a double handful which he side-lobs, only to see it meet Alice squarely in the face and almost knock her down. He moves to comfort her, but suddenly she's whipping snow at his face—is she about to laugh or cry?—in handful upon handful, to pay him back, and then some. Taking a blow or two, relieved that she gets some revenge, he finally grabs her and gently carries her over to the porch steps.

"You got me," he says, sitting down with her in his arms. "I'm sorry, I overdid it. But you really shouldn't lose your temper like that. Is that how you beat up that boy at school?" he adds, hoping to make her smile.

"I didn't," she says, blinking back tears, then crying, "You said you liked playing snowballs with Blackie."

Glen is stunned that she'd cry and mention Blackie, and holds her close, cheek to cold cheek. "I was just joking, Alice, I didn't mean I believed it. And I love playing snowballs with you, believe me, I love it more than anything." He sits rocking her, wondering what she knows of what is going on, even if she isn't aware she knows.

They enter the house to the ringing phone and, answering, Glen thinks for an instant that it's Ecki. Then he realizes it's Monica Beniquez, chair of his department and professor of Spanish.

"Glen, I'll have you know I braved the storm."

"Meaning you've heard from Otto?" he says.

"You might say so, and I'm afraid it's a disturbing report."

"Well, you've heard his side of the story. You know Otto—his version of reality is always exclusive."

"I do think we have to meet and talk this out, before it gets out of hand."

"The two of us?"

"For now, yes. I need to hear your version."

"Fine with me, Monica. When would be good?"

"This afternoon? I'm free at one and after four-thirty."

"One's fine."

"Glen—one other thing, while I have you on the line. One of our German majors—Karin Owens-Reiff—filed a late-drop request at the end of last semester. Did that get worked out?"

"It did, yes. She changed her mind."

"She did? Okay. I did make an exception there, granting permission so late in the term."

"I guess she was having a personal problem. But she worked it out."

"Good. I'll see you at one."

She worked it out, all right, he thinks as he hangs up. He also thinks that Monica would go for the jugular if she knew of the affair. No matter that Monica herself married, and later divorced, her own professor twenty years ago at about the same age, though, like many others, as a graduate student. Was she feeling him out, mentioning it at this late date?

At The Learning Tree, Glen half expects Mrs. Ouellette to joke with him. It will be their first meeting since their clash a couple of months ago.

"Mrs. Ouellette, how are you," he says as she suddenly appears in her white smock.

She doesn't say and Glen can see that the hatchet is not buried at all, but poised. "Mrs. Cady isn't ill, I trust?" she says.

"She's fine," Glen says. "I assume Alice is doing fine, too."

The woman hesitates, then says, "I don't really like to discuss a child's progress in a casual manner."

Glen decides to say nothing more, and turns to see Alice appear around the wall of cubbies with one boot and sock already off. Stepping over to help her change into her sneakers, he hears Mrs. Ouellette say, "No bare feet in nursery school, Alice," and anger shoots up in him.

He restrains himself, but whispers, as he leaves, "You be tough now, no crap from anybody," drawing, he thinks, a knowing look from Alice.

Then, as he walks, he wants at once to return and save his child—the urge is so strong that he pauses before crossing the street. He could simply remove her, he thinks, take her to nearby Beach Hill, where there is sledding and skiing. Or have her spend the afternoon with him in his office, even in his class. But he doesn't turn back. Alice will fend for herself, he thinks, and he has antagonists of his own. If things were right in his life, though, nothing would keep him from rescuing his daughter.

Six years ago, in his first year at PSU, Glen was a distant witness to another man being denied tenure. Preston something, in political science. Glen was too new to know him personally and recalls only the depth of anger surrounding the case, as it was discussed on campus and written about in the college biweekly.

Preston Littlejohn was his name. He held press conferences, rallied students, appealed, and sued, all to no avail. In the years following, Glen heard he'd formed a wallpapering business, then that he was working in a boat works in South Portland, then selling shoes at the Kittery mall, then that his marriage had broken up, and at last that he had died of exposure, north along the coast of Maine.

Here you go, he says to himself as he taps on Monica's door. Then he steps across the room to accept her hand. "Monica."

"An unfortunate situation," she says, waving him into a seat. "This is the part of the job—well, I'm sure we've all heard that remark enough times."

"I wonder if it isn't the part some administrators like the

most," Glen says. "A dean goes home, says I had to fire old Smith today, honey, but let's have our steak rare tonight."

Monica is smiling. "In any case—Glen, my gosh, we started here together." She alters her smile to one of helplessness.

"I'm sorry we have to meet like this," he says. "And sorry if I sound bitter. I don't mean to, not to you."

"I'm sorry, too."

"I did lose my cool with Otto," Glen says. "What can I say? Some students were around, and some English faculty. So, do you want an explanation—or does it even matter? Which isn't to say I didn't have a right, given what Otto was trying to unload on me."

"Well, I do need an explanation. Otto claims—this is his most serious charge—he claims you threatened him physically."

"Well, he may have *felt* threatened, but I didn't threaten him."

"You didn't?"

"No. That would be Otto rearranging reality to suit his purposes. And that's exactly what was at issue in the exchange we were having."

"Which was?"

"Well, he wants to argue that he's kept me up to date on my tenure case—as my advocate—when he hasn't at all. I don't know if I blame him. It isn't very pleasant news to pass on. Anyway, he didn't tell me. So I challenged his claim and we had some words. That's it. Having tenure might let him think he can repaint the world, but words are all that transpired."

"Well, I sympathize. With your overall situation. And you may be right—Otto may merely have *felt* threatened."

"I am right."

"In any case, what's to be done?"

"I don't know. I don't see why anything has to be done." Glen sits there. He has always liked Monica, he thinks, even as he is aware that administrators always express sympathy and that she herself named Otto as his advocate and, as a friend, was one of the six to vote against him. When she doesn't say anything, he adds, "Stringing it out is one of the most taxing things about it. I'd like it gotten over with, so I can get on with my life."

"The dean—or the president, either one, could turn your case around, you know."

"Fat chance—not with two six-love votes on the board."

"It doesn't look good, I agree. Still, it isn't over, not quite yet."

Glen is aware it's time to leave, yet—maybe in reaction to Mrs. Ouellette—hears himself say, "Monica, I'm going to say something I probably shouldn't: You could've said yes, you could've voted for me. So why didn't you? That's something I really don't understand."

"Glen, I simply couldn't do otherwise. Your publication record is weak and—although I consider you a friend—I have to follow guidelines like everyone else. I wouldn't be doing my job."

"You could have granted me status as an exceptional teacher, which you know I am and which is supported by the evidence. You could have done better than assign Otto Gentz as my advocate, which you had to know he never could be."

"Your teaching record *is* excellent," she says, looking down at her desk. "It was taken into account. At the same time, as you know, one has to show strength in the three areas. You've known that from the beginning."

"My publication record is hardly different from yours, Monica, I'd point out. Nor is it different from at least three of the other five senior members. The majority. And in the case of my student, to whom you issued a drop card on the last day of classes—which guidelines were you following then?"

Monica looks at him and doesn't speak for a moment. "Maybe these are things you shouldn't say," she says, and adds, "Glen, I'm sorry you feel this way—it's all I can really say."

"Fine," he says, standing, and at the door adds, "Sorry to embarrass you, Monica—not that you don't deserve it," and even though he tries, neither of them entirely smiles.

Back in his office upstairs, he dials her extension. "Monica— I'm sorry if I seemed to blame you. I'm sorry."

A moment passes before she says, "It's no problem."

Hanging up, disappointed and frustrated with everything, he resolves from now on to reach for some dignity, some bearing, as he departs this phase of his life.

Sitting at his desk, he tells himself he will keep Ecki, if not from his mind, from his heart. He'll hold firm. Even as his colleagues treat him unfairly or foolishly, as he hungers for her, he'll hold his own. It's his only chance.

One of the odd losses he stands to suffer, he realizes, is just being here, in this building and in his small office. He loves his books, has loved sitting here—especially at daybreak and during evenings and weekends, when the building is empty—with Goethe, Schiller, even Günter Grass, Peter Handke, Christa Wolf. It's a love over which Paige has always shaken her head, but not unkindly, and with his guilty, regretful heart going out to her, he takes up his phone.

"How did it go?" he says. "Did they say when they'd say?"

"Are you ready for this?"

"I hope so."

"I got it!" she says.

"You did? That's great. Congratulations!"

"It's only at home, of course, for now, but I'm still so happy I can't say."

"Well, I'm happy for *you*. That's wonderful."

"You know—I *was* confident. I do have the experience, but I just wasn't sure. Then they told me right away."

"Let's celebrate—let's go out to dinner."

"Gee, maybe I better earn some money first," she says.

"We can manage it. We'll all three go out. No baby-sitter—would you like that?"

"I'd love it, to tell you the truth."

"So we'll just take an entire booth at Pizza Hut!"

"Oh, I'd love a pizza. I'd love just to be waited on."

"We'll do it. I'll get some more work done—this picks me up, too, you know—and pick up Little Pumpkin, on the way home. We'll even belt for extra cheese, do it up big."

Hanging up, Glen turns to his desk. Though an ache lingers, he feels a sense of hope, too. If he works hard, takes one small step and another, perhaps he and his family might emerge free and happy on the other side of the jungle he's led them into. He has papers to grade and classes to prepare, not to mention the article to translate, and picking up Alice at four will squeeze him from the other end of the afternoon. To sustain a foothold on sanity, he should work until six-thirty or seven, but the sense that Alice needs him is the strongest and simplest thing he knows.

Hardly ten minutes have passed before his telephone rings. He looks at the phone, and wonders if it could be Paige calling back as he takes up the receiver.

"Hi," Ecki says.

"Hi."

"Are you going to talk to me and tell me what is happening?"

"I'm sorry for not calling. I've just been having a terrible time. The truth is, I'd love to see you, I'd love to see you every day, but I can't do it anymore."

"Not even as friends?"

"I wish I could, but it doesn't work. I like you too much."

"Just rarely then, so friendship will not die."

"I just have to say goodbye," Glen says then. "I don't want to be unpleasant, but I have to say goodbye."

"Can you say you don't love me anymore?"

"No, I couldn't say that."

"Then let us talk once in a while, only as friends."

"I can't do that. I have to get my life straightened out. I can't deceive my family anymore. I just can't."

"Robert is angry with me, too," she says, her voice beginning to break. "For I have met the bus today as it is letting him off—"

"Ecki—" he says.

"Last year he is angry when I have *not* been meeting this bus. I'm unable to understand these men in my life whom I wish only to love. Can you tell me if I have done something so wrong?"

"You haven't. It's me. I shouldn't have gotten into this in the first place."

"You know I love you," she says.

Feeling he must allow no openings to either of them, must even cause her to dislike him, Glen says, "The truth is, I'm so behind in my work I can't talk. I have problems at school. I'm sorry, but I have to catch up or I'm done for. I just can't talk with you like this anymore."

"Goodbye then," she says in a moment.

He holds his bowed head in one hand as the dial tone sounds, and finally replaces the receiver.

16

One week, and another, then a new month slips by. He finishes the translation and Magnus Klein agrees to send another his way. Glen finds this as satisfying as any work he's done, other than teaching, in months. In recent days he's been able to catch up on his course work, and his concentration seems finally to be returning. He strives to give more of himself to the translations and continues to invoke Alice as copilot, so that he may make the work his own.

When he sees Ecki pass one day in a corridor, he turns away. Periodically he has dreams of her that awaken him in the night, occasions when it's clear to him he loves her still, in all ways, even when he'd like to ravage Paige as she lies innocently sleeping. More than once he's wandered downstairs through the darkened house with a persistent hard-on, gazing from windows out over the yard and driveway, and jerked off like a teenager in the first-floor half-bath.

Increasingly, from his office, he telephones Paige for brief exchanges. "Any word?"

"No, how about you?" she says.

It's become their regular exchange. Paige is putting in twice as much time as intended into the work-at-home phase, waiting to hear if she'll be selected for the full-blown office position in the fall, when Alice starts kindergarten. For what she has inadvertently learned, and waited a week to confess to Glen, is that she's one of three candidates, only one of whom will be hired. Or, as Paige has remarked, "two of us are going to be shot down."

"Banks suck," Glen said at last.

"Coming from someone employed in a zoo," Paige said, "I'm not sure I'd say anything."

Her routine question to him, in turn, refers to word from the dean. It's a question in which she retains the single degree of hope between them, for Glen retains none at all. "No, no word," he tells her, and adds, "When it comes, believe me, it won't be good."

"You never know," she says.

"Some things you know."

"At least I don't know who the other two are," she says. "I'm glad of that. Besides, I intend to win."

"Well, the bankers are scumbags in my book—setting you up like that and not saying anything. You be careful of those bank dudes on your visits there—I wouldn't trust those guys with a dollar bill."

"Your students—are they careful with you, when they stop by to discuss their grades?"

After a moment Glen says, "What's that supposed to mean?"

"Isn't it the same thing? Poor little women at the mercy of you big powerful men to give us what we need?"

"You know, Paige, that doesn't sound like you."

"Maybe I'm changing."

"It's what I hear all the time," he says, "how horrible men are. I'm a little tired of it."

"Or threatened by it?"

"Gee, what happened to the sweet little homemaker and mother of our child?"

With less humor than expected, she says, "Maybe the sweet little homemaker is finally wising up."

Glen looks at his watch, thinking he has to get back to work.

"I happen to be serious," she says. "If I get this job, there'll have to be some changes around here."

Glen takes a moment. "Such as?"

"I'm not sure. We'll have to see."

"Well," Glen says, "it's admirable of you—to call up some strength. But it doesn't have to be at my expense. I know I'm down, and I might be a little old in the ideal arrangement of things, but don't try to emasculate me just yet. I could always surprise you."

"I might surprise you," she says.

Glen hesitates, then says, "I have to get back to work—I'll talk to you later," and hangs up. He sits for a moment, telling himself not to think about it, they're only words. Don't think about it.

Near the end of the afternoon—when he has burrowed into the new translation, yet another article on privatization in the splintering East German economy—a call comes and a secretary tells him that the dean would like to set up a meeting. She offers times and Glen opts for the earliest, at nine the next morning. The end of the road is in sight, he thinks. It's time, at his age, to alter course.

Uncharacteristically for this hour—it's close to five and Paige will have picked Alice up by now—Glen decides to take a walk, to be alone in the air and see if he can think of how to proceed. For everything is going to change. His life will turn a corner, or it's possible that he might be entering space, as when nudged from the door of a moving plane. The word in the morning will be the official word, delivered in person. In time, he's been told, he'll also receive written notice from the president: "Your termination from the university is effective as of . . ."

Leaving his building, he crosses the bridge and turns downtown, where he only occasionally strolls at this time of day. Canned. Too old. Without prospects. However fit and capable he might feel himself to be, this profession he has known all along grants new places almost exclusively to beginners. Will he be able to rally himself and take a run at something new? Is it possible he'll end up like Preston Littlejohn?

Wandering into City News, a shop filled with two walls and a center rack of magazines, he's looking at the glossy covers and wondering what other professions might be open to him when Ecki, behind him, says, "You mingle with the masses, Professor?"

He turns to see her standing there with a young boy. "Robert," she says, pronouncing his name, as always, Roe-beart. "My favorite professor from the university, Professor Cady."

Glen shakes the small hand the boy shyly extends. "Hello, Robert," he says.

"I do wish to speak to you," Ecki says. "Is there a time when you are in your office?"

Glen is hesitant. "I'm not sure," he says.

"May I telephone—perhaps to make an appointment?"

Glen just looks at her, even as he'd like nothing more, he knows, than to say yes.

Then Ecki says "Goodbye," and at once she and Robert are gone. Glen knows he embarrassed her in front of her son, but this is less on his mind than the urge he felt to reach his arms around her and draw her to him. He looks dumbly at the wall of magazines, then wanders out the door toward home.

"How long have you known about this meeting?" Paige says, once they are lying in bed in the dark.

"Since this afternoon."

"You didn't want to call and tell me?"

"It was late, and I was coming home anyway. I don't see it as news."

"You don't know what he'll say, Glen. Nor do you know what the president will say."

"He won't say anything. He'll write. Let's just forget it for now."

"Will you call after the meeting and tell me what he says?"

"I'll try."

"You can be hurt only if you hurt yourself."

Glen lies there for a while. "I think there's truth in what you say. Still, I'm afraid your ego does take a beating when you're told to get out. The dean will tell me I'm too old for the university to invest in, something like that. And there you were, a couple days ago, suggesting that I start wearing an apron."

"I did *not* ask you to start wearing an apron."

"That was supposed to be funny, but I guess it isn't. I'd prefer laughing, you know, to moaning. One thing I can tell you, which *is* funny—I think—is that if I'd had a little thing with Monica, offered her favors, I wouldn't be in this situation. That's one of the curious realities."

"What would you have offered?" Paige says, not even faintly amused.

"I don't know. What would turn a woman on?"

"You really don't know, do you?"

"Tell me."

"Hearts and flowers."

"Hmm," Glen says. "I guess that's true."

"It's true," Paige says. "It's something I thought you knew a long time ago."

The dean is cordial. Inviting Glen into his plush office, offering a chair and coffee or tea, he adds at once, "I was also compelled to vote against you, and I'd like to offer any possible assistance as you look for another appointment."

Glen is caught off guard. There it is, he notes with some admiration, no beating around the bush. He's out.

"I'd also like to apologize for this Otto Gentz business," the dean is saying. "It isn't the first time I've had to deal with him, which is about all I'm allowed to say on the matter—except that I did speak with Monica and believe I have a handle on what happened. I assure you that we do not try to blackball people from the profession."

Glen feels himself liking him. He speaks clearly, and his candor seems genuine. His regard for Monica also rises. She could have hurt him for what he said, apology or not, and apparently she chose not to. He reminds himself: Go with dignity.

"You have your year of grace," the dean says. "And, again, if there's anything I can do to help—letters, calls, things like that."

"That could be helpful," Glen says. "Although I don't know if there's much out there. Language studies are dead in the water these days—German especially."

"Unfortunately true," the dean says.

"Which makes your offer a little hollow," Glen says.

The dean cannot help laughing. "Also true," he says. "But the Germans, they're tenacious. Maybe something will return them to prominence—economics, medicine, who knows."

"Possible," Glen says.

"I fulfilled my military obligation in Heidelberg, in the early sixties," the dean says. "Had a wonderful time, really—thoroughly impressed with the work ethic. People joke about it, but that doesn't make it any less real. The Germans took a terrible beating, as did the Japanese, but then they rolled up their sleeves. In the meantime, of course, this country has kept its sleeves rolled down. I'm always reminded of Erikson's theory of touching bottom being ultimately creative, for individuals *and* nations."

"I did time in Germany," Glen says, "as I mentioned before. The time of my life, in many ways."

"Well, the good old days," the dean says.

"Anyway—I'm off," Glen says, getting to his feet. "Thanks for your offer. Hollow, like I say, but you made it sound good."

The dean laughs rather hard. "Glen, I'm sorry we didn't get to know each other better—you have a wicked sense of humor."

"Well, goodbye," Glen says, shaking hands. "I'm not going to say thank you. I'll leave you to Otto Gentz, and wish you luck."

In his office—it's not yet nine-thirty—Glen sits at his desk and an unexpected elation comes up in him. He's free, he thinks, even as he knows he'll awaken to panic, surely before a full night has passed. What to do? Work, to be sure, a rolling-up of his own sleeves—but what kind of work? His only alternative, he knows, even as Paige would call it false pride, is to resign. Might the psychology of pride—it's real, too, whatever she may think—be a resource from which to rebuild their life?

Resigning would be risky, he'd have to admit. His office and telephone and university address—all this would help in ways both practical and abstract in finding another job. At the same time, if such pride is real, wouldn't each day spent within the gaze of Otto Gentz fritter it away?

He should call Paige and give her the news, but doesn't feel up to it yet and instead organizes his desk—papers to grade, an exam to write, chapters to review in preparation for his afternoon class, the ongoing translation. At least the question is answered, he thinks, which might be why he feels more high now than low. He's on his own and it's time to go out once more and play for keeps.

At last he dials his home number, but it's busy—Paige's bank work, which often has her on the phone.

It occurs to him, too, to call Ecki, not out of desire but because he should apologize for embarrassing her in front of her son. He doesn't, in any case, and sits looking away. The rest of his life. That's the challenge.

———

"You're going to terminate me, too?" he says to Paige as he gets a can of beer from the fridge. They're sitting at the kitchen table, now that Alice has gone to bed, discussing the future, at Paige's firm insistence.

"I've thought about this a lot, Glen, and this *is* the time to deal with it. Not after another routine takes over. Tonight—right now. I've taken a job and you're leaving one, being forced to leave. We have to make changes, that's all there is to it."

Glen looks at her and again sees—too clearly, he thinks—how opposite they are. Perhaps it's foolish, but he has always looked to elusive and romantic goals, not excluding his marriage to her, while she has seized upon immediate steps in realizable plans. Now she's taking charge of the future, unaware of his need—he has turned it over in his mind most of the day—to first find another dream, and to not surrender, not in this way.

At last, as he sits in silence, she says, "Aren't you going to say anything?"

He makes an expression intended to convey how offended he is. "You seem to want to punish me," he says, "but that's not going to work. Not for me—and it's not in your practical interest either. It's not in me to just give up. That's the most depressing, the most demeaning proposition I've ever heard. This whole business may kill me, but I'm not going to just give up."

"Please, do we have to be so melodramatic? I'm not sure I know what you're trying to say, although I'm not surprised. I knew you'd say something like this. I'll tell you: You've had your chance, Glen, and it's time for me to have mine. You've failed—which I am not intending to do, believe me—and if *you* choose to regard what *I* do as *you* being punished, then maybe it's what you deserve. We'll do this my way for a change. My father—well, I won't get into that. You've had your chance—for *years*, in fact."

"You're referring to my age?"

"Of course I am."

"Jesus, your sense of tact is shameful."

"Say what you like. Look, I know this is painful for you, and I'm sorry about that. But I'm not going to be dictated to by your delicate ego."

"I've worked hard all my life, important work, and that's all it means to you? Ego?"

"I'm going to have my say, Glen, no matter what, and we're

going to come to terms with this. Tell me where you're going to find another job. I have no intention of leaving here, believe me, and as far as I know, the only place around here that hires professors is the one that's giving you the boot! This talk about not working through your year of grace—that is ludicrous! I've never heard anything more childish! You have no choice, Glen—that's what *you* have to realize. No choice! Your job's always been the big deal—well, now it's going to be my job."

"It's more than a goddamn job I'm losing. You might try to figure that out."

She suddenly gets up, and stands behind her chair.

Glen looks at her, the feeling of depression choking him. "I don't want to talk about it anymore. But if you think you can just bury me," he adds, "you're wrong."

They stare at each other for a moment before she says, softly, "You can no longer afford to be the kind of person you think you are. That's where *you* happen to be wrong. Things have changed. I'm sorry, Glen, but they have."

"Fuck you."

"As you wish. I'm going to bed. Sit here and drink—that's more your style. I have work to do in the morning, and I'm going to bed. So good night."

She is gone and Glen sits there. Five minutes later he's still sitting there.

17

Ecki crosses the street in front of their car and Glen, at the wheel, is all at once alert. Paige is in the passenger seat, Alice in back, as on this Saturday afternoon they are on their way to the supermarket. The days have slipped by politely enough, but for Glen the space between them is as distinct as a wall of glass. Perhaps it's the same for Paige.

Ecki. He seems to have entered a state of doing nothing but looking for her, through classroom doorways, along hallways, sidewalks, even though he has no idea what he might do or say if they should meet.

He's been so intent on seeing her that it's hard to believe she's the young woman who just crossed the street. There goes someone I miss and need and adore, he imagines telling Paige as they roll along. I've tried not to, and I don't do anything about it, but that's the way it is.

Paige sits in the passenger seat staring ahead.

I had an affair with her, he would like to say—love, sex, everything. I want her still, not merely because she's a bright and sexual creature. I want her for the sweep of what she represents, and because she wants me, and makes me what I want to be. I want her, I have to say, because she is someone who counts.

Beyond the street where she passed, he glances in his mirror in hopes of seeing her again, but the sidewalk is empty.

Paige might not realize that he's in love with someone else.

Later, he imagines, she will see that she knew all along. But she is preoccupied with her job and perhaps, for now, attributes his distraction, his added glasses of wine and bottles of beer, to the distance between them and to the impending conclusion of his job.

Meanwhile, Glen is attentive to household chores. He fixes occasional meals, to allow Paige added telephone time during the evening; he washes the dishes and more often than not puts Alice to bed, as if fills him with relief to sit on the floor beside the tub or to lie on the carpeted floor in her bedroom sometimes, and the things they say and read provoke him to tears or laughter, even as all of it has him wondering if his daughter sees how emotional he's been becoming. Later then, on these chilly spring nights, he often takes long walks, and Paige is usually still working when he returns at ten-thirty or eleven.

Job prospects are all but nonexistent. He begins to follow *The Chronicle of Higher Education* and *MLA Job List*. The few ads that appear are for entry-level positions, or senior professorships for internationally known authors. Most of these listings are accompanied by "EOE" and "AA," and Glen wonders if reality should compel him to interpret these as "White Males Need Not Apply." Such is the prevailing belief, and one day in the hall he asks Monica, only half joking—he'd really like to know—if that's a reasonable reading of the two anagrams. As if to keep the exchange light, she says, "It wasn't so long ago that 'No Irish Need Apply' ran in all the Boston papers."

Glen smiles, but his heart only shrivels with added fear.

"Things are changing," he overhears Otto Gentz say one day in the faculty lounge. "This Gorbachev character—look at the rumbles in Eastern Europe, Poland, and East Germany. Who knows? Maybe languages will pick up again."

Glen runs into Ecki at last, on an April morning damp from daybreak showers but already turning sunny and warm. He's leaving the library, where he spent an hour in the stacks reading *Der Spiegel, Die Zeit, Stern,* looking again for photographs that could call up his past, but also for any possible interest on the other side of the ocean in an American trained in German language and literature.

Ecki is coming his way and sees him as he sees her, and both smile. "Hullo," she says.

"How have you been?" he asks as he stops beside her.

"Fine, I think. And you?"

"I have something for you. A small something."

"For me?"

"The truth is—I've been hoping to run into you. It's really nothing." He unshoulders his bag and retrieves a Swiss chocolate bar he'd bought many days before in a silly anticipation of meeting her. Smiling, she takes it from him.

"I hope you've been getting along okay."

"I am, yes. Not so many treats like this—but yes, it is all right."

"That's good to know," Glen says.

"And you? All is well with your wife and child?"

"Yes, life goes on. It's spring."

"I've missed you," she says. "There is no one with whom to be irreverent over German literature."

Glen looks into her eyes, her face. "Take care of yourself," he says suddenly, gesturing that he has to go on his way.

"Thank you so much for the treat. Tell me—how long has this item been traveling in the black bag?"

Glen is still looking at her. "If I told you, you'd see right through me," he says, turning to walk away.

The clash with Paige is colossal, even as it is triggered by nothing apparently greater than clearing the table. Standing up, Glen gathers Alice's dishes and his own to carry to the sink, and Alice follows with a handful of silverware.

"Isn't anybody taking my dishes?" Paige says, still sitting.

Glen is rankled less by the words than by her impatient tone, and doesn't bother to say he was about to return and finish the task he had begun.

"I worked damn hard today," Paige says. "And this isn't easy, believe me."

"Maybe it's news to you, but we've all worked hard," Glen says, adding to Alice, "Sweetheart, go on upstairs, I'll be up in a while."

Paige's tasks have been irritating her lately, and it's occurred to Glen that she has scant capacity for the unpleasant and tedious elements of work and in fact has been resurrecting the old resentment of having to work at all. She remains sitting while he sorts dishes and ignores her.

"I'd like you to clean my place, too, just as you did your daughter's," she says all at once.

After pausing for a breath, Glen says, "Did you really think I wasn't going to?"

"I don't know what to think. All I know is you haven't, and I'm sick to death of being ganged up on. Kindly clear the dishes!"

She would know how he'd react, he thinks, and in a perverse way must desire the inevitable response. "Let me tell you something," he says. "Don't ever tell me to clear a fucking dish from anywhere, at any time."

Half an hour later he's walking a cool dark street in town, believing that after all the bile and accusations and anger spewed into their kitchen he is justified in calling Ecki. Is this what both he and Paige intended? Not really, he thinks, as rattled as he feels. It was just an explosion, from both sides, of what had been held within for weeks.

The dirty dishes probably remain on the table and kitchen counter. None were broken or scattered on the floor, though his rage, even in retrospect—he was a breath away from breaking everything—is frightening. He might have slammed Paige, too, and broken windows and wept, while his daughter, upstairs in her bedroom, would have borne witness to her father going to pieces.

He walks for fifteen minutes, then more, and still doesn't begin to breathe evenly. In town he looks in windows, seeing nothing beyond the anger swirling within him, and ends up as he suspected he would, sitting on a stool at a low-life tavern that sells only beer and doesn't offer glasses. The alcohol will soothe his crazed edges, or so he hopes, and perhaps he's known all along that he is seeking a frame of mind which will allow him to make a forbidden call.

After two bottles of beer and half of a third, as his pile of change accumulates on the counter, he steps to a pay phone next to the door and turns his back to the interior as he dials her number. The woman who answers says she is out.

"Do you know when she'll be back?"

"Around midnight," the woman says. "Is there a message?"

"Thanks, I'll call later," Glen says, and returns to his place at the bar. Midnight. The woman, he guesses, is the neighbor with whom she trades baby-sitting. In another half hour, he's drinking his fourth or fifth beer when he realizes that his rage is settling down. He'll walk again, window-shop for a time, and, returning home, if the kitchen remains as he left it, will clean it up himself before going upstairs and slipping into bed. His marriage, he imagines, will stumble along.

In the morning, from bathroom to kitchen to breakfast, neither Glen nor Paige speaks except in exchanges with Alice, which remarks they make in ordinary tones. In the past they would have reconciled by now, certainly before Glen filled his book bag in the morning and left for school. His doing the dishes at last might have been mentioned, even joked about, or Paige might have asked if he was still mad. This morning, however, Paige says, "I have no intention of moving."

"Moving from here?"

"From this house, or this town."

"Meaning?"

"Meaning, that as you look for a job, I have no intention of moving. Meaning, that if you take a job somewhere, I believe we should treat it as a trial separation."

Glen nods, gazing more to the side than at Paige, then steps over to kiss Alice goodbye and leaves. The old hurts and fears swim in him along the half-dozen blocks to campus.

Thanks for your support, he thinks to have said. Or, in sickness and in health—but not if you lose your job. None of this has any sting, however, for he feels as unhinged as he ever has. Nor does he harbor the aggressiveness he knows is necessary to even imagine a move to do anything.

And when Ecki stops by his office, saying she guessed it was him who'd called last night, he's as surprised as she is when he hears himself say, "I'd like for us to be friends again. What do you think? I value your friendship. I don't have any friends."

"Your psyche can afford this?" she says.

"Probably not."

"I love you still."

"I love you," he says. "I shouldn't. But I do."

"I want you to."

Days later, he's in his office waiting for Ecki to call when the telephone rings and it is Paige saying she has some news that's both bad and good. "What news?" he says, fearing the worst.

"It's a letter recommending that Alice not go to kindergarten in the fall."

Glen sighs. "What does this letter say?"

"It's a form letter," Paige says. " 'Not Recommended' is checked. They say we should make an appointment to discuss fall placement."

"So what's the good news?"

"That is the good news. It only sounds bad, is what I think. Another year in nursery school might be just the thing, giving Alice a chance to learn how to get along a little better."

"She gets along okay as it is."

"She could always do better."

"That's what her teacher says, but her teacher's wrong."

"I'm not so sure," Paige says.

"I am," Glen says, "but let me think about it. Have you made an appointment?"

"Not yet, no."

Off the phone, Glen sits holding his head. It doesn't make sense. Has he somehow drawn Alice into his confused problems? Is he being punished for his selfish affair with a student? It just doesn't make sense, and he calls Paige back.

"They're wrong," he says, "and I'll bring Alice home from school today."

"Glen, don't make things worse now."

"They're wrong. That's all I know. I'm going over there to pick up my kid and to tell them so."

"They might be wrong, Glen, I won't disagree, but you better think twice about telling anyone anything. We do have to live in this town, you know."

"So fuck the town!"

"I should've known you'd act like this."

"I'm mad, but don't worry."

"Staying back has nothing to do with intelligence, as you well know. It's a question of development."

"Well, they're all wet about Alice. And she's *not* staying back."

"If that's how you're going to deal with this, you're on your own. I want no part of it."

"It would be different if they were even close to being right, but they're wrong, you know, and what they're doing could actually hurt Alice's self-confidence. I won't have it."

"Glen, you go marching over there, you'll come off like some father hung up on his daughter."

"Well, maybe I am. But I'll forget you ever said that."

"At least wait until tomorrow."

"Don't worry, I wouldn't dream of jeopardizing our life in this shitty little town."

Crossing the street, on his way to the nursery school, Glen wonders for what seems the tenth time about Alice. Could they be right? Don't they mean well? Is he that most objectionable figure—a father hung up on his daughter?

Entering the fenced-in yard through the gate, he thinks they want to make Alice into someone else rather than acknowledge who she is. And—his most compelling thought—he knows his own father would have come to his rescue. His father loved him, as he loves Alice, and not all the Mrs. Ouellettes in the world would have kept his father away.

"Mr. Cady," someone says as he approaches the door, and he turns to see Mrs. Ouellette and another teacher in a white smock coming around the corner of the building.

"I'm here for Alice," he says. "And I'd like to talk to you about the letter you sent home."

"Fine. Let's go in the office. It's cleanup time anyway and Donna's getting the children ready to be picked up."

Inside, he glances around for Alice, but doesn't see her. A number of children are milling around near the wall of cubbies and he imagines her among them. Following into the office, he feels like a blue-collar supplicant with a bad credit history entering a bank, and the thought angers him all the more. Nor does Mrs. Ouellette give off any sign of conciliation. From her desk, she says, "Please, close the door."

He does so and turns back.

"I disagree with your judgment of Alice," he says. "To hold her back while the rest of the world goes on would be a mistake, would give the wrong message. I'll tell you right now—she's not staying back. I won't have it."

"Let me tell *you* something, Mr. Cady. No one is saying your daughter isn't intelligent or capable. We try to be as objective as we possibly can, and the consensus is that Alice isn't quite *old* enough for kindergarten, not yet. That's all it is."

"Well, you're wrong," he says. "Alice is not *young*. She is not *slow*. She's quiet is all she is. Quiet Alice—it's what I call her. That's all it is."

The woman is watching him. "We see the children every day," she says. "As a matter of fact, we see some of them more than their parents do. Our evaluations are based on working with them closely, and objectively, every day."

"So are mine," Glen says. "So are mine."

"Alice Cady spends more time by herself than any of our other children."

"So do I spend time with myself," he says. "And it isn't, to my mind, a deficiency of character. She's quiet. She's four years old. She'll be a different person by the time school starts in the fall."

"We're well aware of that, Mr. Cady, I assure you. And she is, I would point out, just weeks away from being five. What we want to avoid is having a child have his or her confidence *stymied* by being pushed ahead before he or she is ready. If a child is going to stay back, it's much better that it happen earlier than later, believe me."

"Well, I don't agree that Alice *is* being pushed. And what you're suggesting, I think, might be more damaging—in terms of self-confidence—in ways that you don't seem willing to factor into your little recommendation."

Glen wishes his tone hadn't changed, but now the woman is glaring at him. "I'll tell you this," she says. "You can do with your daughter as you wish—that's your prerogative—but Alice completely failed the coin test. Her score was zero."

Glen is caught up short by this and knows his face is reddening as he says, "What's the coin test?"

"It's a very simple test, to see if a child knows the value of different denominations."

"Denominations? I don't know if Alice knows anything about money. I haven't taught her."

"Children going into kindergarten, we assume, should have an awareness of the value of coins and—"

"Alice failed?"

"Completely."

"Well, was she taught before being tested?"

"It's our experience that children who have a sense of money are more mature than children who don't. But no, it's not something that's taught *per se*."

"Test her again," Glen says. "I'd like her tested again. Right now, if you don't mind." Jesus, be careful, he tells himself. "I'll get her," he says. "And I want to show her what coins are. I'm not sure she's ever even looked at coins."

The woman's sigh is long and audible. "I do have other, regular appointments," she says.

"This won't take two minutes," Glen says, though he is laced through with uncertainty as he leaves the room. Don't play William Tell with Alice, he's telling himself. Just pick her up and take her home.

There she is, standing at the large table, drawing with other children, before a woman who appears to be a mother.

Glen crouches beside Alice as she turns to look at him. "Hi," he says, close by.

Her wide eyes reflect what she sees, he imagines. Fear and uncertainty. Here, he wonders, or elsewhere? But there seems to be no choice. "Alice," he says softly. "Put down your Magic Marker. This is important." She gently puts the pen onto the table, and he knows she's reading the tone in his voice without any difficulty.

From his pants pocket he withdraws a handful of coins, a paper clip, his red penknife, and turns the whole lot onto the table. No pennies. Nickels, dimes, a quarter. Not a single penny.

"Alice, listen. I'm going to tell you the names and the numbers of these coins. Then we're going to go into Mrs. Ouellette's office, and she's going to ask you questions about them. We don't have a penny, but you know what a penny is, right? Big and brown, not silver like the ones here?"

She nods vaguely, and he thinks again to carry her out, to walk away from all of this.

"A penny's worth is one cent," he says. "That's its *value*. One cent. Okay?"

Again, Alice nods.

He points to the others. "A nickel—that's five cents. It's big and fat. A dime's value is ten cents, and it's small and skinny. But a quarter's really big, and that's twenty-five cents. Do you understand?"

She nods each time, a little more firmly. He stands up and returns his props to his pocket, thinking he could give her a quick review, but decides it's too late now and might only make her nervous. "Let's go see Mrs. Ouellette," he says. Then, leaning down, he whispers, "Listen, we're in this together and I'll always be on your side."

When they walk into the office, Mrs. Ouellette doesn't look up from her desk, and Glen says, "She's ready."

Mrs. Ouellette frowns, though she does swivel her chair and pull out a letter board on that side of her desk. "Alice, step over here, please," she says.

Alice is a person, Glen sees again, and he's put her in a spot. Mrs. Ouellette pulls the center desk drawer open, scrapes something into her hand, and turns back to face Alice.

"It's the same test I gave you several days ago," she says to the face looking at her above the board. "What I want you to do is touch each coin, tell me what it's called, and what its value is. Do you understand?"

Alice twists her head to look up at Glen. He doesn't want to speak for her, so he barely nods.

Her hesitation surprises him, and he's about to panic. But then Alice raises the forefinger of her right hand above the coins, and he watches.

Touching each of the coins, she says softly, "Penny, nickel, dime, quarter." Moving her finger back over them in the other direction, she says, "Twenty-five, thirty-five, forty—one!"

Alice looks up at him again, and a faint smile is in her eyes. Glen can see that she wants to make a face now but is holding back, and he needs a second to take in that she identified the coins on the first pass—and added them up on the return.

Mrs. Ouellette sweeps the coins from the board. "You prepared her well," she says.

Confused, Glen doesn't know what to do. So he picks up Alice and hoists her to a seat on his arm. "I didn't," he says. "I just told her names and amounts."

Leaving the office, he avoids eye contact. They are outside—
he hardly registers leaving—and he's walking with Alice on his
arm and her face next to his own. He's telling himself not to be
smug; still, he wants to kiss and squeeze her. At last he lets his
eyes fill and brushes his face, nose, eyes, into her hair as he whispers,
"You little devil! You're so smart and I'm so proud of you! I love
you so much."

When Glen wakes up to a rainy Saturday, his sense of elation has
evaporated. The afternoon before, Paige had smiled as he described
Alice's triumph. But later she said, "What you did is so working-
class, and it's not how I want to live," and yet again a feeling of
isolation wrapped around Glen as tightly as a cocoon. By midmorning, he packs a sandwich and excuses himself to go to his office
and work. Given the blustery weather, Paige offers to give him a
lift—their first words since their exchange—but he says a walk
might help clear his head.

   In his office, once he has his computer humming, and in
anticipation of surprising her with a Saturday call, he dials Ecki's
number. He lets the phone ring several times, hangs up, and dials
again. No answer. She and Robert are out shopping, he thinks,
and works on the translation for thirty minutes before trying again.
Still no answer. He repeats the sequence. Working then until he
hears the twelve o'clock horn blow at the shipyard—no matter
where they went, they'd be back by now— he swivels and tries
again. No answer.

   Inadvertently then, he sees her. From a classroom window, at
a distance of fifty yards, he sees her with a young man with whom,
on parting, she exchanges a kiss, and he is stunned by the laughable
irony.

   He had wandered down to the basement, to buy a Coke from
a machine. Returning upstairs, allowing himself an indoor walk
as a break, he had paused on the first floor to read a bulletin board
and then made his way to the window of an empty classroom on
the second floor, where, standing and taking a sip from the can
as he gazed over rain-covered walkways, he saw Ecki in her yellow
slicker, near the administration building. She was with a young
man, hands clasped between them.

   Glen froze as their postures, even the rain itself, conveyed the
intimacy of a couple who had just made love, probably had spent

the night together while the woman's child stayed with a friend, and now it was time to part. Ecki and the young man touched each other's forearm as they moved together to kiss, then separated to say some words, and kissed again at greater length.

Ecki moved out of sight past the red brick wall, toward the library and Married Student Housing; the young man angled more in Glen's direction before he, too, passed from view. A graduate student, Glen guessed. Perhaps not as old as Ecki, but too old to be an undergraduate.

Minutes later Glen is seated once more before keyboard and monitor, and is working. Live by the sword, he is telling himself. She's an attractive young woman, so what did he expect? Then, as his eyes close and his head sags, he cannot help thinking of how easily she seems to have betrayed him. Still, once his emotions have raged and cascaded, he decides to do nothing. After all, he promised her nothing, walked out on her more than once. He will say nothing, but instead will wrap disappointment in under-standing, in the love he's known for her.

Sunday, living with what he knows, is even worse. He does some work at home, and when Paige, as usual, declines the invitation, he takes Alice to Wallis Sands to see the waves, hoping to divert his attention. Again he instructs himself—as he and Alice walk and comb the windblown beach—in how he will work to forget what he saw and knows.

His resolve fades after his morning class on Monday, however, when Ecki surprises him with her regular call.

"I have to tell you I saw you Saturday," he says.

"Saw me? I was home Saturday, most of the time."

"I saw you with a boyfriend."

"This cannot be. I have been here, with Robert."

Surprised that she would lie, he doesn't know what to say.

"Are you there?" she says.

"No need to lie. It's not necessary. I understand."

She is the one then to pause. At last she says, "I'm sorry you have seen me, but it has nothing to do with how I feel for you. I have been seeing someone, it's true. At your suggestion, as you may recall."

"Well, I'm not blaming you."

She breaks the following silence. "It doesn't mean I don't want to be your friend and be with you also."

He inhales.

"You will come to me this afternoon, as always?" she says.

"No, not this afternoon," he says evenly. "I couldn't do that. It's going to take me a while to sort this out."

"You have said you love me. Is it still so? Tell me, please, that you do. Please tell me, I feel so bad now."

"Of course I do. I'll call in a day or so."

"Tell me, please? That you still love me?"

"I do," he says. "I love you."

That afternoon, with Alice larger in his heart than anyone else, he writes two letters on his computer. So much has been lost that, above all else, he must clarify who he is to himself as well as to others. Only in this way, he can see by now, will he finally survive.

Staring into the screen, he carefully rereads what he's typed.

This is to say goodbye and to ask you not to contact me again. It's been a wonderful affair, and maybe it's possible and reasonable that you carried on another affair at the same time because I did, too, although with my wife. It's best, anyway, to part on a small note like this.

> With love,
> Glen

And in a note addressed, appropriately, to Monica with a copy included for the dean:

I present here my resignation from the university, effective at the end of the current academic year. I understand that I am forgoing my year of grace, and I resign in awareness that my resignation is irrevocable. Personal reasons compel me to take this action, and I trust that a replacement may be found without difficulty for the coming year.

> Sincerely,
> Glen Cady

He addresses the envelopes. In the department office downstairs, he makes a copy for the dean, then leaves the building to hand-carry the note to Ecki's mailbox and to give himself a chance to consider yet again whether resigning is the right thing to do. His instinct, as he walks, tells him he has no choice.

He'll miss Ecki, he thinks as he turns onto her street, and a moment later, having left the envelope in her mailbox, he is returning the way he came. At the Administration Building, he hands one of the remaining envelopes to the dean's receptionist, and, returning to his own building, leaves the other on Monica's desk.

Then, walking over West Bridge into the surrounding city, he is truly alone. It's done. He walks, and in time turns toward home, to confess to Paige the breadth and depth of all his offenses, to recommit himself, if she will have him, to their small family.

6

SHACKJOB
Winter 1954

18

In the Service Club entrance his eye is caught by a poster he's walked by a hundred times: "German I & German II/Six-Week Courses/University of Maryland Overseas Program. Earn college credit in your spare time."

Just like that he's hooked. His desire to study the language is at once thrilling and frightening. What if he took on school as he had never taken it on in the past? Education. The challenge is as enticing as anything that's ever crossed his mind.

German I. Given maneuvers and alerts, he'd have to miss classes now and then. Still, could he learn enough to surprise her by Christmas, at the end of the first session? Might he present to her as a gift the ability to speak some German?

The first evening arrives, and fearing he may be called on to speak, Glen climbs the stairs of the PX Building to Room S-221. It's Tuesday, just before 1900 hours. If it proves awful, he'll chalk the ten-dollar fee up to experience.

Other soldiers are there in fatigues, including a second lieutenant; combat boots stick into aisles from the small desks as the soldiers wait in awkward silence. Glen settles in. The man who enters and proceeds to a table in front is a German national. Small, with thinning hair, he wears an old double-breasted suitcoat a size or two too large. It's another postscript to the war—used clothing.

He places papers on the table, pauses, looks up at them, and nods as though bowing.

"Langvage," he announces. "Educashun. Langvage iss at vunce zee heart and nerve-zenter of all else! Hear me now! Eggsperience! Tinking! *Being*! All sings vee know! Langvage iss at dee zenter of *eggsistence*! Langvage—young friends—is dah secret of life!"

On the board he writes, *"Herr Doktor Professor Staudinger."* Turning to face them with a smile, he has them grinning with pleasure already. "In person," he adds, half bowing again, and the room explodes with laughter. The man is adored at once and Glen's eyes glow with the thrill of learning, of having a teacher.

The room quiets as Herr Staudinger raises his arm like a baton.

"Dilly-gence," he announces. "Ve vill vork vid dilly-gence! Vizz fuul concentrashun! Vizz forceful intelly-gence! Vizz much elbow grease! Ve vill learn to spheak—Cherman! *Ja?* Ve vill not, as I haff in München a sussern sergeant heard to say: 'Whoa is der latrine?' 'Whoa' is said to der horse, *ja?*"

"Ja," the class replies in ragged chorus.

"Ach so. Gut. You are, please, to address me: *Herr Staudinger*! Not *Herr Doktor Professor Staudinger*, but *Herr Staudinger, ja? Gut.* And vaht am I to address you? Perhaps you tell this to me now, *ja?* I am nodding and are saying, *'Guten Abend,'* and you are saying, *'Guten Abend, Herr Staudinger, mein Name ist'—und* giff to me your nama. *So.*"

Thus does he nod to each of the soldiers. Some give their rank, some only their name. As he starts down his row, Glen's anxiety ignites, but as he gets the words out it dissipates and he feels he has slipped into water and is managing to swim.

"Guten Abend, mein Herr."

"Guten Abend, Herr Staudinger. Mein Name ist Glen Cady."

"Gut, Herr Cady! Your accent iss *sehr gut*! May you tell to me vaht ziss means, ven I am saying *'sehr gut'*?"

"Very good."

"Very good indeed, Herr Cady! *Ausgezeichnet!* Do you know, my friends, iss coming a time ven translation does not occur. Only meaning iss occurring, as in vun's own langvage. *Ja?* Tell me, Herr Cady, vaht ziss osser vord iss meaning? *'Ausgezeichnet'*?"

"That word—I don't know."

"Gut! I am teaching you somesing. Repeat after me, please, all: Aus-gah-psych-nett!"

They repeat, *"Ausgezeichnet."*

"Excellent! Herr Cady, ziss word iss meaning?"

"Excellent," Glen says.

"Ausgezeichnet, Herr Cady! You are never forgetting this word—*ja?"*

"I don't think so."

"I don't sink so, *'Herr Staudinger.'* "

"I don't think so, *Herr Staudinger."*

"Excellent, Herr Cady!"

Herr Staudinger moves on to a black corporal in fatigues. Glen sits not entirely hearing the teacher question the corporal, but seeing Hedy in flashes and thinking, It's going to work!

The class ends too soon for him. Passing out small books, Herr Staudinger tells them to work "dilly-gently" for class next week. A new world has opened for Glen and he has no wish to leave, but he files out with the others. In the hallway the black corporal remarks, "Something, ain't he—like being home at last," and Glen says, "He's great, the time just flew."

He can't let it alone, not this first night, caught between wanting Hedy to know what is happening and wanting to continue the work of the class. It'll be a surprise, he decides, and by 2030, at a desk in the day room, he has begun reading every word of *Wir sprechen schon Deutsch!*, even the book's printing history.

"Die deutsche Sprache," he reads. *"Die erste Aufgabe." "Deutschland: Historischer Überlick."* He begins a list of unknown words and writes down seven of the first ten.

He reads "Pronunciation and Building Vocabulary/*Leseübung und Wortbildung*," and adds two more words to his list.

He turns a page and reads,

> *Ein Amerikaner oder ein Engländer kann viele deutsche Wörter verstehen, auch wenn er die deutsche Sprache nicht studiert that. Warum? Die Wörter sind germanisch. Die deutsche und englische Sprache sind germanisch und stammen von einer gemeinsamen Sprache ab. Diese gemeinsame Sprache man vor zweitausandfünfhundert Jahren gesprochen . . .*

and gets it. A word or two eludes him but still he gets it and is elated. He just *read* German! At least a little.

Lights-out is sounded and Glen studies on. Soldiers come in talking about the movie, stagger in drunk, pass in the street on their way to the taxi stand, and nothing distracts him. In language, as he has glimpsed it, one may be transformed, may become a new person, and so it is happening to him. Eleven bells sound, and he has no urge yet to make his way upstairs to bed.

Near midnight he looks up and imagines that the black corporal, saying "home at last," is also taken with a German woman.

He might love Hedy without fear now, he sees as he lies in bed. He imagines them here together, fantasizes lifting her to his shoulders and galloping outside like a horse. He feels six years old on the night before Christmas, waiting for language to open every door.

They could find an apartment, as she suggested. She would walk in her dirndl to the *Bäckerei* for *Apfelkuchen*, and music would flow from their balcony windows. Hedy with her slim brown arms and slim brown legs. He would be at home with her and, for the first time ever, at home with himself.

December arrives and Hedy is walking beside him on a Saturday night in Stuttgart. He has yet to tell her of his language study. His own surprise has been that making the leap from reading German to understanding what Germans in town are saying is more difficult than imagined, and he's learned why Germans with twelve years of English may speak with heavy accents. He continues to study—has signed up for German II—and feels all the more captive to his love for the woman beside him.

Does he love her too much? He's pleased to be with her this evening, coming from the Crossroads Theater in the heart of the city. The spacious theater, attended by civilians and officers, soldiers with American wives and German dates, is a place where Glen feels less anxious about guarding Hedy from an unprincipled officer or a gang of horny GIs.

They walk along neon-lighted Königstrasse in the bracing December air. Glen has had no experience with dates, and the nearness he feels to Hedy, the pleasure of having attended a movie together, is new to him. Is this what it was like for couples who held hands at autumn-night football games?

Walking beside her, he realizes she is not just his date but his girlfriend. For the first time in his life he has a girlfriend. He had some semi-dates at home—he and Marvin Stein took Judy and Janet Ackman to a circus in ninth grade, and he took Beth Hayes to a drive-in a dozen times to neck, but he has a girlfriend here in Germany, though one who is married and has a baby. First love, as in all the songs.

They chat as they walk. The movie was *A Star Is Born*, with Judy Garland, and they discuss it.

"Did you like the movie?" she says.

"I liked it," he says. "Did you?"

"Very much. It's such a pleasure to see a film in English."

In glances he is drawn to her and anticipates touching her stockings and silken underwear, sliding his hands over her and kissing her neck. He strolls casually, when what he wants more than anything is what he thinks of all week when they are apart, to make love to her, to kiss her from head to toe.

He doesn't walk with hands folded at his back like a German, but acts as if in a similar frame of mind: an American strolling with his German girlfriend. He takes pleasure in touching her arm when they turn to look in a lighted window, in having his arm held as they cross a street. They don't fear here, as they do in Baden-Baden, that someone will know her husband, and Glen is free to be himself. Even the hotel, where they have taken two rooms, was his selection.

So they are both surprised when a man recognizes Hedy, smiling and speaking at once, taking her hand in both of his. "Hedy, Hedy!" he cries as she laughs and speaks happily in turn. The man is an old friend and they have not seen each other in years, more than three years, Glen deciphers. At the same time, he doesn't catch any words indicating they might move toward a storefront, out of the flow of pedestrian traffic. "You do not have to stand apart, it is okay," Hedy says aside to him, tenderly.

Glen dislikes the man, who seems to be a friend of her brother, on sight. Perhaps forty, he is elegantly dressed and effeminate, with chiseled features and blond hair. A camel-hair topcoat hangs unbuttoned from his shoulders and he holds chamois gloves in one hand, slapping them into the other in bursts of unrestrained laughter. A paisley scarf puffs at his throat. To Glen he looks like an upper-class dandy. His teeth flash as he and Hedy laugh, and Glen believes he hears the man ask Hedy if this is her *"neue Mann."*

Glen is introduced, in English. "My friend, Glen Cady," Hedy says. "Please, Erich von Hebbel, here from Düsseldorf, an old friend and a shocking surprise!"

"My pleasure, of course," the man says with a curt bow, extending a hand from within the draped topcoat.

"How do you do," Glen says.

"Ah—a wonderful evening," the man says. "I have been remarking to dear Hedy how I am coming to enjoy the onset of the cold, as opposed in the past to having preferred but spring and summer. Mr. Cady, yes, what do you say? Is it cold or warm season to which you first respond?"

"I guess, well, spring and summer," Glen says, not very agreeably.

"Maneuvers in freezing weather," the man says. "I assume you are in the military?"

"Yes," Glen says. "Maneuvers in the snow. Can be tough," he adds.

Moments later, when they have shaken hands again, Glen and Hedy are walking again, although silently for a time. "I cannot believe I am meeting this acquaintance here!" she says, not unhappily. "Here, where we imagine to be free from all eyes!"

"He asked if I was your husband?" Glen says.

"Glen, you have understood this? That's remarkable. But no, what he has said is not this exactly, is only a certain joke."

"What kind of joke?"

"This man, he knows I am separated and to be divorced, you see. He is asking if I shall marry again soon, if, already—I believe it is a German sense of humor—yes, if you are to be my new husband."

"I still don't understand what's so funny."

"Oh, darling, I think you are jealous. It is not meant to be this way. It's more to say that in today's world, life is turned upside down and moving quickly. Do you see? Times are changing."

"What did you say when he said that?"

"I said that you are my American friend. It is true."

"You just said that *he* was your friend."

"Glen, please, jealousy does not become you."

"I was trying to be funny. Sorry."

"Hmm. We are at an impasse."

"He did say that, in front of me, because he didn't think I'd understand."

"Glen, please, it's a source of humor in Germany. The Americans *are* amusing at times. You see that I'm here with you, that I love you? There was some rudeness, you are entirely right. For this I apologize. But there's no reason to be jealous. Don't you know you have swept me off my feet like a silly schoolgirl?"

"I have?"

She smiles up at him as they pause by a storefront, and he sees again how striking she is. She holds his arm above the elbow as they cross a street—few things please him so much as when she takes his arm—and he wishes he had kept his mouth shut. "Sorry," he says again. And, "Will he tell?"

"I think this must be assumed," Hedy says. "Still, it shall prove nothing. It's dangerous only when my husband and his solicitor have learned this news. But this man, he is acquaintance of my family, not of my husband. For this we are fortunate."

"Your brother's friend, before he died in the war?"

"My brother's good friend, yes."

"How did he survive the war, someone like that?"

"Darling, this is von Hebbel," she says. "He is known as a hero of the war, one of the most remarkable. No, I think he is not what you have guessed him to be. Von Hebbel. He is in the Panzer Korps, you know, is one of few to survive in the East, although his injuries are not so apparent. He is many times—you know the Iron Cross? Von Hebbel is three times awarded the Iron Cross, and that he speaks of winter as he does is a statement of personal irony."

Glen is ashamed. Heroes, as he grew up knowing them, from movies and football fields, were not the same as heroes in Germany. "I feel like I've said something dumb," he says at last.

"Oh, you are entirely forgiven. I am sure von Hebbel would be only amused with your perception of him."

"My apologies to von Hebbel," he says then. "To you, too, and to your brother."

"This does bring to mind that I shall visit my family at Christmas," she says. "For some weeks. I have wanted to tell you this, that I shall be in the north for this time and ask if you may visit me there? I'm not allowed to introduce you so easily, because of the status of my separation, you know. But I fear I will miss you desperately. May you visit and stay in a hotel, as Ilsedore shall be with my family and I may steal away? Is it possible? Don't tell me now, but give some thought and tell me soon, that I may have a holiday treat to which to look forward?"

They enter the hotel separately. Hedy goes in and after a minute Glen glances through two thicknesses of glass. He glimpses her small shoulders and the parentheses of her hips. Then he follows through the polished doors. A luxury hotel, its lobby is large and people pass among plush chairs and couches, over soft carpeting. Their plan is to rendezvous in her room, but they end up in the same elevator, in the presence of a middle-aged German couple.

Hedy is aboard when he enters and they stand apart like strangers. As the car rises, Glen cannot suppress a giggle, which he covers by coughing, which makes Hedy laugh, too, though neither looks at the other. The car stops for the couple to depart and the woman of the pair glances back at them. As the doors reclose, they are choking back laughter, and Glen gets his lips to her neck at last, holds her, and feels the glide of fabric on her silken underwear. "I'm so nuts about you," he cries as they giggle.

He knows by now that when she presents herself in degrees of nakedness she is in a sexual mood, that it's another enticing instrument she plays for their mutual pleasure. He knows it as they lie in bed, sipping wine, the covers drawn to her thighs and the puff of fur between her legs partly exposed. The bed is made up of the cleanest-smelling sheets and feather comforter and pillows he has ever experienced. Golden light from a lamp across the room accentuates the tan color of her slim body. He wants to entirely uncover and touch the puff and reaches to do so with the back of his hand, though they are speaking at the moment of her trip to visit her family over Christmas.

"May I?" he decides to say after the fact. He glides his hand backwards over the puff.

"It feels nice this way," she says.

He touches her gently as they talk. She tells him about her family and how they've responded to the news of her separation and planned divorce. "My relief is that it is now known to them," she says. "I'll have to endure advice, I know, from my father, also from my mother. I think they do not understand the desire I have for freedom. Such as this," she adds. "To have you excite me as you do."

"It excites me to touch you," he dares to say.

He continues to caress her, and notices a movement of her eyelids in response. His erection is lifting and he pushes the comforter with his foot to reveal himself to her.

"It's a time when I know I must be by my family," she says. "I know now with certainty that one's own heart may not be directed by others, and I'm certain they will see what an unfortunate mistake it is to think so. I shall be free, you know, for the first time ever. Freedom is so crucial for happiness."

"He's a manufacturer, your father?" Glen offers, although his attention lies elsewhere.

"Parts for electronic equipment, yes. Shipped mainly around Germany, also to Holland and Denmark. Darling, would you kiss me there, please?" she says.

He carefully teases and provokes her. To him it's the closest they've been; she sighs, and her sounds are so exciting he cannot restrain himself, and later, exhausted, they joke about shots fired into the air in ecstacy and of the tangled mess made of the bedding.

In the morning, when it's time for her to retrieve her car, he is the one who wishes to talk. He will not see her again until after Christmas. "What would your parents say, if they knew you were seeing an American soldier?" he asks.

At last she says, "May we talk of this at another time? My mind is directed to recovering my dearest baby, you understand?"

"Sure, another time."

"Of the Americans, I will say briefly: My father is not without regard, you see, though it's the English he most admires. For the stiff upper lip, you know, and their courage. He has survived the war also, is a miracle and many lucky breaks that he has done so, and that he is able to rebuild his business is due not only to the economic miracle but to the Allies' policy of reconstruction. At the same time, on a personal basis . . ."

"Yes?"

"Of the Americans, I believe it may be said he is a snob, at a distance, though he is not an inflexible man. Anyone who has survived these years in Germany, they cannot be so inflexible or unintelligent. One has to accept reality and change."

"I'm accepting it," Glen says.

She smiles. "I will tell you," she says as they reach her car. "It's been so pleasant to be here, to attend the movie, and when we are making love. I think it will be impossible to wait all these weeks to see you."

They smile and touch. He doublechecks the address she has given him for writing; it's all he has, there's no way he can call her in an emergency. No more than a letter a week, she has warned. Two and two will be put together. "Perhaps the custody of my child is at risk," she says.

A last glance of her green eyes, and she is gone. Her VW turns the corner, and Glen pauses a moment before beginning to walk. He decides to stroll in the city and have a new look at Germany. He'll enjoy Sunday alone, and try to understand what is happening. In love with a married woman in a foreign world, and can't have enough of it. Whatever the future may bring, he thinks.

He passes two GIs in uniform and a string of German men and women in greenish-pink raincoats which exude an oil-on-water sheen. Then he imagines her on the Autobahn, and missing her comes on him like a fever. He imagines her passing Pforzheim, gliding into the depths of the Black Forest. Four weeks before he will see her.

19

He wants his Christmas gift to be perfect but has no idea what to buy. Jewelry? Something from the PX, Made in USA? An art object? He has bought gifts for his parents, but this is different. The gift for his first girlfriend ever needs to be more special than a gift may possibly be.

A set of books? The works of one of the writers she has mentioned: D. H. Lawrence, Henry James, Joseph Conrad? Chekhov, who died in Baden-Baden and after whom the street where she lives is named? Price barely matters, if only he could know the choice was right.

The post is becoming a ghost town in the holiday season. Officers and married NCOs are disappearing, duties are being put off until after the first of the year, and the troops are left on their own. A fierce, snowless winter slips in, turning the parade field to wind-whipped stone, and the frigid air keeps everyone inside the barracks and motor pool bays.

Music? A set of long-playing records? Sarah Vaughan?

His search continues, as he anticipates the trip north to Duisburg the day after Christmas. In the meantime he makes courier runs over the Autobahn, side curtains snapped tight, wearing a fur-lined field hat with earflaps, Mickey Mouse field boots, leather gloves with wool liners. With others he walks to the post theater for evening movies, and to the EM Club for beer, since everyone has time on his hands. He makes unauthorized trips to Robinson

Barracks in Stuttgart, to shop at the big PX there and to sit in the snack bar and hear Tony Bennett sing "Rags to Riches" on the jukebox. He also escapes down the long hill to shop in Bubblegum, and makes evening *Autobus* trips into Stuttgart, to walk neon-lighted streets and look in shops and specialty stores.

At last he decides. But then he un-decides and decides several times again before he really decides. Having a girlfriend is work. He returns to a jewelry store in Stuttgart for the sixth or eighth time, and at last says, *"Ja. Ja, ich möchte die gold Ohrring kaufen."*

The clerk, relieved, nods approvingly.

Leaving with a small box, Glen feels he's made the right choice, however minuscule the package. Gold earrings with teardrop rubies. DM 240. It's a month's wages for a German workingman. Riding the bus back to Böblingen, he feels that the gift is right, the task complete.

The next morning, however, standing reveille in cold darkness and returning to his bunk area to shower and dress for the day, he glances at the small package on his personal shelf and experiences doubt. He's in the mess hall, *Stars & Stripes* beside his coffee mug, when it hits him that the gift isn't right. It's too something.

Still, he tells himself—trying to read the paper—he'll go with it. It's what he bought, and he'll go with it. Maybe someday he'll tell her of his difficulty in buying her a Christmas present. If there is a someday.

Christmas shopping behind him, he lives for mail call. He misses her, although there are times—when cold air is whipping through his jeep's canvas top and his fingers and toes are freezing—when he feels relief that she is far away and he has the warm barracks to go home to and weekends when he may stay around the post if he wishes and read and study, or get into a poker game.

Then hurt and lovesickness come up in him, after dark and at daybreak, as they side-straddle-hop and hit the frozen ground for push-ups, as they double-time to the dispensary for shots. He contrives games of avoiding mail call, wasting time at Autobahn snack bars to play love songs on the jukebox, in the hope that on his return, doing maintenance on MC/5, he will hear, "Cady, letter for you in dispatcher's shed," and will feel saved.

Christmas Day at Panzerkaserne. The battalion commander

visits each company's mess hall to say a few words over midday turkey. As he speaks, the troops wait to dig in, eager to return to poker game or matinee, to take a bus into quiet Stuttgart. Word has it that northern Europe is in the grip of a deep freeze. But as Glen lies in his bunk that silent Christmas night, reminding himself that the day after tomorrow he'll see her, cold weather doesn't cross his mind.

The train he boards in Stuttgart is not warm, but offers some protection from the cold. Most compartments are empty. He selects a seat and stands near the chilled glass, watching and waiting. Fine snow swirls out of a gray sky. He's put together seven days, leave days and days off, before he must return to duty. Overnight up the Rhine Valley in wintertime. He heard someone say the weather is going to warm up, and he has placed his trust in light civilian clothing.

So far, so good. The compartment, with its stale tobacco smell, is warm enough. He has money in his pocket, and his awol bag on the overhead rack contains a carton of Camels, clean clothes, and toilet articles. He's never felt such anticipation. Under his suede jacket he wears a sweater he bought from a country woman outside the main gate for forty deutschmarks, but he has neither hat nor gloves, and figures to avoid the cold by slipping into train stations and cafes.

Head angled toward the cold glass, he reads a perpendicular platform clock. He's nervous that he might accidentally meet a member of her family, but still wishes the train would get under way. If he has to stand up to any of them or endure temperatures twice as cold to be with her, it's what he'll do.

The train is moving, the platform silently falling away. From under the overhang the string of cars passes into open winter air. He turns from the window as a couple in overcoats enters the compartment. Feathers extend from the woman's hat. *"Grüss Gott,"* they say, to which Glen replies, *"Grüss Gott."* The two whisper closely, however, and the woman departs. Nor does the man sit or lift their luggage to the overhead rack. In a moment the woman returns and the two slip away on weak, nodding smiles.

Suit yourself, he tells himself, and when he has stared for a

time at Stuttgart receding, he pulls out his German I book and
settles in to study. He slips his jacket back on against the cold and
a minute later zips it up to his throat.

His current chapter: *"Leseübung 13: Studenten gegen Hitler."*
Holding his hands under his arms one at a time, he stares at a
page, and then at the strange gray country rushing by.

With an hour to kill in Mannheim, he walks from the station into
the city in search of gloves. There are more American soldiers
and airmen here than in Stuttgart, in civvies and in uniform, and
he feels the urge to return to Panzerkaserne and forget it all. Each
American in civvies is recognizable and so is he, caught in the
hard German winter in flimsy pants and jacket. They are all given
away by their shoes and haircuts, hatless heads and gloveless, fisted
hands.

Some GIs pass—subject to citation by MPs—with hands in
pockets. Germans by contrast wear long overcoats, hats, gloves,
and scarves, and appear immune to the weather. As if to mock
them all, a flock of black-scarved old women works sorting bomb
rubble, ruddy faces exposed and rag-wrapped hands pushing
wheelbarrows, effecting the economic miracle. Wooden streetcars,
lacquered blue and blond, squeak around corners and take on
passengers, black Mercedes taxis, red flowers in their lapels, lift
orange directional-signal-arms as they do the same, and however
familiar the world, Glen's shivering reinforces his sense of not
knowing who he is or what he is doing.

In a small shop the thin leather gloves, *Handschuhe*, cost too
much of his travel money and he returns to the cold, suspecting
the shopkeeper was out to hustle a GI. Walking, he cups his hands
to his mouth, and the warm motor pool, barracks, and mess hall
south of Stuttgart seem increasingly homelike.

A red-lipped prostitute steps from a doorway. "Hey, Joe, vant
qvickie? Vaht you say—come on, hot to trot, gimme gud fuck
ja? Tventy mark."

A younger, prettier girl appears. "Hey, honey, vant qvickie
fuck viss me? Come on, go right up here, got nice room, come
on, you good-looking guy."

"Can't do it, I'm in love up to my ears," Glen tells her.

"Love viss me, honey—come on—hot pussy for you, come
on, girlfriend don't care you get hot pussy on the side, come on."

In a *Gasthaus*, where *Hofbräuhaus* music plays and GIs drink, Glen warms up at last with a half-liter glass of beer. His mind clears. When he leaves and is approached by a teenage girl, he says, "I'm on my way to see my girlfriend," and thinks that what he feels for Hedy is so strange and strong that if it fails, it could turn him to whoring and drinking, singing and trying to laugh unto the end of life's road. You got it good, and you got it bad, he tells himself.

He travels the night, sleeping in snatches and getting warm only now and then, mainly in the WC, until the train chugs into the mausoleum which is the Duisburg *Bahnhof*. When he deboards into the frozen predawn air, Hedy is nowhere to be seen.

He proceeds along the platform, thinking he'll see her ahead, but she is not there. He checks everything again, the time, the name of the station, even the day. Well, it shouldn't be a surprise that the mother of a small child is late before six o'clock in the morning, he thinks. It's okay, one occasion when she is the one to come up short.

She doesn't show, however, and he cannot figure out what to do. There is nothing like coffee available and he fears if he goes to the street to find a cafe and warmth he might miss her altogether. She could think he missed the train or did not make the trip, and return to where he'd be unable to reach her.

Bag in hand, in need of a shave, he stands bleary-eyed and waiting. The other passengers are gone and he envies them the warmth of their homes and hotels, their places of work. He feels as lost here as he's ever felt in Germany.

Twice more he circles the interior of the stone building. A man in a thick coat, mittens and hat, and a scarf wrapped around part of his face is selling newspapers and magazines from a kiosk, and Glen decides to try to ask if there is a place nearby where he can get warm and buy coffee. *"Morgen,"* he says to the man. *"Gibt es hier in der Nähe Café—für Kaffee? Verstehen Sie? Kaffee Geschäft?"*

The man's eyes squint and a hand waves as he sputters in unrecognizable dialect, something to the effect that he sells newspapers and nothing more!

Glen's angry impulse is to reboard any train headed south and get back to who he is and where he more or less belongs.

Could she be sitting in her car, waiting for him to come out? No, he's certain she said she'd meet him *in* the station. He stands freezing, hands in pockets. He's so cold that when he looks in one direction or another he pivots, as if his neck, turned alone, might crack.

Another train arrives and he watches its passengers disperse. A few buy newspapers from the kiosk, and several enter a doorway which, for the first time, Glen realizes could be a waiting room. Feeling foolish, he makes his way to the shallow stone alcove. Did she say waiting room in one of her letters?

Warmth. Relief is immediate as he passes through a doorway into a large haze-filled space. There are wooden benches, caged windows where tickets are sold, people sitting and sleeping, and mainly warmth, and an opening at one end where *Würstchen* and *Brötchen* are being sold.

He glances at lost souls sitting and sleeping on their sides, but Hedy is not here. She couldn't be; her color and beauty would stand out like a flower in a barren field. He moves at once to the opening, hoping to pick himself up with coffee. *"Tasse Kaffee?"*

"Wir haben kein Kaffee," the woman says.

"Shit," he says.

"Wir haben Tee," the woman says.

"Gut, ich habe Tee, bitte."

At a stand-up table, sipping tea, Glen takes stock. It's only been thirty minutes, according to a clock above the door. It's hardly daylight and maybe Ilsedore presented a last-second demand. After all, he's been late a few times himself, and he decides to be cheerful when she shows up. And isn't this the place to wait? Won't she— but there she is! The door has opened and Hedy is entering; she does pass for a flower, wearing a touch of red, and he has no need to generate cheerfulness as she has seen him and is coming his way.

"You look so great!" he says as she leads him out through the station. "I thought I'd missed you—you look like a dream come true!"

"I'm so damn sorry for being late," she is saying.

Glen wants to embrace her, but senses her caution, and little else is said as they go along the hard, cold street. "I was really afraid I'd missed you," he says.

"You do not have luggage?"

"This is it. Where do we go? Can we go somewhere?"

"It's so complicated, I can't tell you," she says. "I've been unable, my family and friends, I have been unable to do as I wish. Can you—"

"You're here," he says. "You don't have to explain."

It takes a moment, as they walk, under a nickel-colored sky, before she says, "Of course. I'm accustomed to my husband and family, you know, who must have explanation for everything." Her smile reassures him.

Inside the car, she embraces him and, with her faint smile and sparkling eyes, is the striking creature who has held his attention all these weeks. She is sexual, too, and he takes in her nylon stockings, the warm hollow of her neck and the pathway to her breasts, he inhales perfume and body warmth. He feels amorous at the prospect of being in the hotel room she would have reserved for him. But when he utters, "Let's go to a hotel. I want you so much, I love you so much," she answers, "Glen, you know, I'm sorry, I must return at once. To care for Ilsedore. There's a hotel, just on this street, where I may drop you and return, I think, in only one or two hours."

"Oh."

"You are disappointed. I'm sorry. It's so complicated here, with my family, and caring for Ilsedore. At times, I swear I'm not sure if I know what I'm doing, let alone going from one moment to another. I'm not so free as in Baden-Baden. Please understand. I long so much for the day I am free ... but for now I have no choice. I think in two hours I might come to this hotel. May we be happy with moments to see each other, as we have said?"

"Well, sure," Glen says. "I'd be, I'm happy to see you. I'll get cleaned up and have some breakfast. It's been a rough night."

"I knew you would understand. I'm so happy for this. My husband is known here, you see, and maybe it isn't wise after all for us to meet. Yet, for one hour, as you said in your letter. An hour may mean everything to me, too."

Two and a half hours later Glen is sitting in the warm lobby of the old hotel. He has shaved with lukewarm water at a sink in his chilled room, washed there, too, head to toe—a whore's bath, as if on maneuvers—and visited a dining room downstairs, the only patron present, to sit over a cold continental breakfast and small pot of coffee. Finishing the meal, missing the *Stars & Stripes*, he returned upstairs to where they might undress and sink into feather pillows and comforter, sat in the room's only chair, then went back to the warm lobby, waiting for life to proceed.

Time slips away without any sign of her. Nor, upstairs again, are there any buzzes from a wall instrument over which he makes a trial call to the desk, to be ready for whatever might come his way. Nothing comes his way.

Returning to the lobby, taking the stairs—in his increasing anxiety, he fears she may be carried up in the old elevator as he walks down—he struggles with drowsiness sitting next to a porcelain stove. A wall clock tells him that over three hours have passed. After they've made love and she has left to care for her baby, he thinks, he'll have a chance at last to catch up on his sleep.

Standing up to keep himself awake, he studies old paintings along the cooler lobby walls, and steps outside to have a minute in the frozen air. To arouse himself, he thinks of her silken undergarments and of the smooth skin he may in time touch and taste.

A fourth hour passes. He hadn't wanted to count, and tries now not to check the clock. Seeing a newspaper on a wooden spine behind the desk, he steps up—uncertain of the words, having left his pocket phrase book upstairs—and says, *"Darf ich,* the newspaper, *darf ich es sehen?"*

The clerk, a tall blond twenty-year-old wearing a jacket with a hotelier's "key" lapel pin, replies, "Of course you may see the newspaper, sir, without question."

"Thanks," Glen says.

"You are most welcome, sir."

Glen says nothing more, afraid the young man will give another elaborate reply, and returns to the chair near the stove. How is it that Germans are so adept at English, which, according to Herr Staudinger, is equally difficult? Well, they study, he allows. Foreign languages are taught in school from first grade on, exist on borders and in half of the movies. And language is merely the mechanism of everything, he thinks—as Herr Staudinger would have them know and which they were never told in school at home. No wonder some Germans, like that clerk, act so superior. They possess language, and it lets them see more. The bastards.

Glen can't read more than a word or two of the newspaper,

for not only is it printed in what his book calls *Fraktur*—wrought wire shapes he has yet to learn—but he has to face a sinking realization of how modest his progress has been. So he sits with the puzzling paper, thinking the clerk would really laugh if he knew that what he's doing is picking out letters one at a time, to teach himself the wiry alphabet. Herr Staudinger, at least, would be pleased. However, capital *D*'s and *O*'s appear impossible to distinguish from each other, as do lowercase *t*'s and *f*'s, and he wills himself to concentrate, not to be defeated.

He's awakened by the clerk saying, "Sir, excuse me, I fear you may fall from the chair. Perhaps you would like to rest in your room."

Glen stirs himself. "Thanks," he says. "Thanks—I'll go to my room. Yes, I'll be in my room."

The next time he wakes it is to a remote *click-bzzz*. He sits up with the vague sense of an irritating noise, which stops. He sits on the edge of the bed, is realizing, yes, he's in a German hotel in a sea of cold air, and as he is getting to his feet the *click-bzzz* sounds again.

He lifts off the earphone, speaks into the opening fixed to the wall. "Yes, hello?"

Her voice sounds as though it comes out of a tin can behind some adjacent tree. "Glen, it is you?"

"I was asleep, I fell asleep."

"Darling, I'm so sorry. I haven't had a chance."

"It's okay."

"May we meet then at last? I believe I have time. Are you too sleepy?"

"No, no, I'm fine. You're not here, at the hotel?"

"Oh, darling, no, I may not. It's too risky for me. Please don't be disappointed."

"Where are you?"

"From the hotel, you are turning to the right?"

"Yes."

"In this direction one hundred meters, yes?"

"Yes."

"There, on this intersection, is a tobacco shop. I will pick you up there. Yes, in thirty minutes?"

Replacing the earphone, Glen tries to synchronize his disappointed thoughts. What is he to do? Again he feels like a foreigner, but the fear in his heart is familiar. She doesn't want to show herself here—would the clerk know her?—and he must accept that her concern is reasonable. But lovemaking postponed has his insecurity thriving.

They exchange gifts in a second-floor cafe where they are not likely to be seen. The cafe is empty and quiet. He has the small box of earrings in his pocket, and as soon as they have been served wine in glasses with decorated stems he slides it across the table. "Merry Christmas," he says.

She removes a slightly larger package from her purse on the seat beside her. "Merry Christmas to you, my wonderful lover."

Glen thinks, there was no need to worry. She was late, but after all she has a baby and a family, their rendezvous time was at daybreak, and she has to be careful of being seen.

"We shall open our gifts at one time?" she says, and he realizes she is looking at him, waiting and amused.

"I'm sorry," he says. "I'm a little dopey."

"Dopey?"

"Maybe it doesn't translate. I haven't slept much."

"Darling, you must have a good rest."

"I want to rest with you."

"I know," she says. "Shall we?" she adds, taking up the small package.

"I'd feel better if we could go to bed together," he says.

"We shall. Not in the next moment, I'm afraid. But we shall. Now, please open your gift, young man!"

As each removes paper and peeks to see how the other is doing, he finds himself looking at a watch: Omega Seamaster. He's never before received a valuable gift and is a little shocked. "Gee," he says. "My gosh, a watch!"

She offers more elaborate remarks about the earrings, which, to him, seem all the more inadequate. He fits the watch strap, inserts the pin. Squeezing the instrument around his wrist in his free hand, he likes the grip of it, savors the look. "Your hand on my wrist, that's how I'll think of it," he says. She returns a pleasant smile, a glance from the unknown depths of her eyes.

Lovemaking is not to be, however. When they have spent some forty minutes in the cafe, she looks at his new watch and says she must return to care for Ilsedore. "I leave you to recover needed sleep," she says. "This evening, if I am able to get away, I'll telephone as before. Or leave a message, if you've stepped out. Which you must do, darling. Please, do not wait only for me to call. It's too hard for me."

"You'll try to get away?"

"With all my wits."

He ends up in the hotel room, waiting for the wall device to summon him again. Seeing her for an hour, whatever he said in a letter, has him in a state which makes sleeping difficult. He has never wanted lovemaking like he wants it now, less for sex than for reassurance.

He looks at the maddening wall device. What if he washes up and goes into the cold to find something to eat? But what if he misses her call and there's no way for him to contact her, even if she leaves a message? What if she leaves a message which says meet me at the upstairs cafe at 1900 and he isn't back until 1930?

In time he falls back asleep. When he sits up again, it's ten to eight and he knows he won't see her tonight. The preceding twenty-four hours seem to have passed under water. At last he thinks, to hell with it, and moves to the sink to splash cold water on his face.

The air is stinging cold, and every restaurant appears to be closed. He ends up in the *Bahnhof* waiting room, the only sure place he knows, where he buys *Würstchen und Brot* with a dab of mustard, his being the last purchase before a middle-aged woman slams down a curtain of rolling corrugated steel. After he's eaten, standing, he sits on one of the benches for a time, trying to sort out what to do. Maybe he'll return to the hotel to see if she's called; he doubts she has but doesn't know what else to do.

Hardly a hundred yards from the *Bahnhof* he is propositioned by a streetwalker who materializes from a narrow side street. He says, *"Nein, danke,"* but, glancing down the side street, spotting another woman in a doorway, he sees an orange light indicating a bar or cafe and turns that way. Das Nacht Lokal is sleazier than expected but inside he feels oddly at home. It's dark and most of the patrons are drunk, but they laugh and joke, no one corrects his Deutsch when he orders, and after two or three glasses of beer he feels comfortable. For the first time on this journey north he feels at ease, with Hedy and with the idea of expending such time and money to be with her for an hour.

He remains true to her, though the bar is full of prostitutes who tease and tempt with bargains. However many of the women pause at his table and however much he'd like to submit to the deals they propose in whispers, pronouncements, and mini-performances, he resists. One woman, leaning over his table, opens her blouse and presents a breast in one hand, to the hilarity of the patrons, who howl and call.

Drinking, declining other propositions, he tries to explain his lovelorn predicament and hears his explanation translated and called around. He's kidded by a bartender and others about *"Genauigkeit," "Geliebte," "Treuegelöbnis,"* and being held down by his *"Frau."* Only one sodden man is belligerent, but is hushed. When it comes out that Glen is an American soldier in love with a German woman, scattered clapping and hooting breaks out, then an explosion of applause when they ask her name and he says she is married and he cannot say. In response to a schnapps toast to *"alle Soldaten,"* not a little intoxicated, he stands and drinks. "To all *Soldaten* who paid the big price," he says. "To all the beautiful women and five-star cognac they left behind." He tosses off the schnapps to applause, and when he leaves, it is to handshakes and kisses. In the night air he weaves his way chaste and tittering back to the old hotel.

At dawn, hung over but relaxed, he feels at peace with Hedy, even if she wouldn't know they were at odds. And he feels less of a need to wait for her to call. He'll do as he wishes. All this he decides while lying under the comforter, before he lets his feet hit the cold floor like a recruit on field maneuvers. Pleased with the luxury of running water, leaning his face into the sink, he splashes with abandon.

"Screw it, be who you are," he says as he pulls off T-shirt and shorts and advances, naked, into a splashing hand bath. He proceeds, with soapy water, to scrub into his ears, under his arms, between his legs.

Shaved, rubbed dry with a towel, he drops to the floor for naked push-ups, side-straddle-hops, takes pleasure then—running in place—in the flying up and down of his lonely little pecker, and is tempted to induce swelling but for the old reproof of wasting ammo on the way to the field of engagement. "Hut two, fuck it all!" he sings and runs. "Ain't no use in goin' home/Jody's got your gal and gone. Sound off!"

He runs on. "Every time you stand retreat/Jody gets a piece of meat. Sound off!"

Dressed, Glen heads downstairs on a mission to have breakfast in something approximating an American diner, with bacon and home fries crackling on a grill, happy laughter and voices, Jo Stafford on a jukebox singing, "Fly the ocean in a silver plane. . . ."

To the clerk, he remarks, *"Guten Morgen—ich gehe aus—ich bin in eine Stunde zurückgekommen."*

The blond boy says something in response, and Glen feels that however he has mangled the language, he communicated his message. Be back in an hour.

Duisburg has nothing like an American diner, however, and he settles for a chilly *Konditorei* where, one of three customers, he sits at a tiny table over an expensive demitasse of espresso and a torte which had been fresh a day or two earlier. He peruses a newspaper, reviews his reading of *Fraktur*, and presses to distinguish the *P* from the *B*, and the *M* from the *W*. Don't give up, he tells himself, as he sees that he had been coming close.

Hedy calls at eleven; he notes the time on his new watch. She is cheerful, has taken him at his word that there is no need to explain, and wants to know if he has caught up on his sleep.

He sinks at the news that they may not meet until two, but they will not be restricted to a booth in a cafe. They will be guests of her friend Renate—his hopes sink again—for coffee. There is important news, too, but only when they are alone. Before the tobacco shop at 1400? The Seamaster will assure punctuality?

"What's the important news?"

"When we are alone," she says, "which isn't quite so on the telephone. Is happy, and news, I'm afraid, which is not entirely happy."

Replacing the earphone, Glen pauses. He tells himself not to be let down but he feels like a puppet on a string. Three hours again to wait.

———

She is beautifully dressed, wearing the gold earrings with small red rubies, and they kiss and embrace between the seats of her car. He told himself not to press, but asks anyway, "What's the news?"

"I will tell you soon, not just now. I must be certain in my own mind that it is news. Please?"

There will be no lovemaking this afternoon either, as they pass time visiting in the home of her friend Renate. Glen considers making a direct appeal on grounds of feeling foreign on this trip and, the truth, wanting her more than she may realize.

At the same time, he worries that asking directly would be base, even though it was she who introduced him to the wonders of such direct speech. Instead he listens to her talk about her friend, in whose presence, she says, they may feel free to speak as they wish.

Having him meet her friend, it's clear, is a higher priority to her than being in bed together. Still, as they roll along streets of large, stone residences, he touches her knee, leans over to kiss her cheek, her hair about her ear, and says, "Can't we make love somewhere?"

She glances, smiles. "Oh, darling, I'm sorry. I have so much on my mind. Concentration is difficult."

At Renate's handsome second-floor apartment he is received and introduced as the two women converse in German before shifting to English. Renate shakes his hand and smiles pleasantly. A young woman like Hedy, though plain by comparison, her English seems of less range than Hedy's. After a moment, Glen catches her studying him, as though to inspect Hedy's GI boyfriend.

The inspection continues as Renate serves coffee with glugs of cognac, and puts on phonograph records. It comes out that English officers have been befriended, at least by Renate, here in the British Zone.

Glancing at Renate another time, Glen smiles faintly, as does she, and their relationship as Hedy's friends seems to shift into place. Vaguely jealous of the English officers, he cannot help thinking that none of this would be taking place had the Nazis not taken over Germany. What a curious time in his own life. To be his age and to be here in the aftermath of a bloody war. Life goes on and to hell with the English officers, he thinks.

Praise be to the troops who paid the price, he thinks again, sipping cognac.

"Glen," Hedy says. "What is so amusing?"

"Nothing, just thought of something."

Both women look at him as, try as he might, he cannot restrain a faintly intoxicated smile.

"Glen, it isn't fair to not let others share the amusement."

He sees that he is embarrassing Hedy, and it is on his mind as they return to her car and drive back into the downtown area, when she says, "May we stop at our secret cafe, so I may tell you my news at last?"

"Can you tell me in my hotel?"

"Darling, it is simply too dangerous, and I must return in but thirty minutes to care for Ilsedore. Please, I know you wish to make love, as do I, truly so, but it's so damned difficult here. Please understand."

They sit in the same booth, and Glen waits to hear the news. First, it is established that she'll do all she can to be free tomorrow to see him for a last hello before he must board his train.

"It's important news," she says. "A crucial decision."

He looks at her and waits.

"In two weeks I shall go to Cambridge University," she says. "In England, where I shall remain four months for courses of study in English literature. I shall rent an apartment in Cambridge, while Ilsedore is cared for here by my family. It's arranged by my father, and is to do with the divorce and its proceedings. It's an appropriate step for me, as I must learn more of independence. It's necessary that I do this, though I know it means we may touch only through cards and letters."

Glen doesn't know what to say.

"I hope this doesn't disappoint you, that you trust in my love for you. Darling, may you permit me these special months? I shall return in May to Baden-Baden, where the divorce proceeding will be determined on a legal basis, and all between us may be as before. You will still love me?"

"Yes," he says, still not knowing quite what to say.

She removes a photograph of herself from her purse, writes "I LOVE YOU" on the back, and slides it to him. "I do love you," she says. "You've entered my life and it will never be the same. Please don't be too disappointed that I must continue to evolve in this way. My father, he's thought carefully on this, and while it is difficult, I believe it is right."

"Well," Glen says then. "It sounds like the right thing to do. You won't fall for some limey while you're there?"

"I think not."

"I'll miss you."

She smiles, reaches to squeeze his hand in both of hers as her eyes film over. "It's what I must do. It hasn't been easy to decide, believe me."

As if waking from a nap, Glen finds himself sitting once again on the side of the bed in the chilly hotel room. Hedy is returning to her home. He's a little drunk and the morning's impulse to turn the room into his bunk area has fled. He picks up the photograph and looks at her words, and everything seems gone from him.

Up at 0600, he takes his time dressing, going down to eat, getting through the morning—scans a morning newspaper as if he knows what he is scanning—and checking out of the hotel. By the time Hedy picks him up at eight-thirty and drives him to the *Bahnhof*, he's come to the awareness that he knows at least that he wants her to be happy, to do what she must do, though she's being taken away from him. He'll have to wait for her and see, and as he walks to the driver's side and she rolls down her window, he says, "Be good to yourself." He gives her leather-covered fingers a squeeze, turns, and walks off, and half an hour later is sitting in a compartment on a train rolling south out of the city.

20

Vera Lynn is singing "Auf Wiedersehen" on AFN Stuttgart, her voice filling the mess hall serving area. The grill is popping with heat, waiting for cracked-open eggs to sizzle, and the big toaster is revolving, empty as yet of the mis-cut army bread filling a stainless steel tub on the counter, next to the tub of help-yourself oranges. Back home in the army.

Glen is ten minutes early, and has no wish to wait. He wears clean fatigues and glossy combat boots, has an appetite this dark morning, and, thinking a brazen offense the best strategy, ducks under the chain, takes up tray and silverware, and calls over the grill into the kitchen, "Rusk, where the hell are you? Give me some goddamn eggs, get this show on the road! It's six o'clock!"

Rusk appears in white shirt and white hat, eyes wide, wiping his hands and ready either to growl or smile. "Man, fuck off, ain't no six o'clock!"

But he's smiling and Glen adds, "Come on, I'm happy to be home, don't wanna wait—time to feed the troops."

Rusk feeds him. They play poker together, and Rusk says, "Love my cookin', don't you, sweet thing?"

"Been going nuts without your cookin', darlin'."

Rusk howls, cracks an egg one-handed and lets it flow, cracks another and laughs some more.

"Sunny-side up, don't break 'em," Glen says.

Rusk howls again at the insubordination. "Make yoself some toast, man, shut yo mouff to me."

Glen moves two slices of bread from tub to toaster, waits to reverse the slices.

"First sergeant's there," Rusk whispers then, nodding toward the dining hall doorway.

"I don't care where that fucker is," Glen says, entertaining Rusk some more as he spatulas the eggs to one of the heated white plates. "Missed this place," Glen says, peeling paper from a pat of butter to lay on the eggs. "Missed you, Rusk, it's no lie."

"Reenlistment blues," Rusk says as Glen adds the toast, an orange, and a half-pint of milk to his tray and enters the dining room, walking away from the first three graders' table.

At his back, two steps along, however, there comes the roar: "Cady! Front and center, goddamnit! Trying to avoid the first sergeant? Get your candy ass over here!"

Glen takes a breath, and reverses direction. Thatcher, looking drunk, and Sergeant Hawk sit at the sergeants' table. "Sergeant?" Glen says.

"Have a seat, soldier, gotta talk."

"First three graders' table, Sarge."

"Sit your sorry ass down, goddamnit, do as you're told."

Against his wishes, given smoldering butts and ashes on the table, Glen lifts a leg over the bench, uses his tray to push away stained coffee mugs, and adds, enjoying insubordination, "Don't blow smoke my way, Sarge, spoils my appetite."

The two sergeants snort laughter, and Thatcher, as Glen should have known, leans to blow smoke over him and his breakfast. There are Thatcher's rheumy eyes and vein-broken red cheeks, his grinning, yellow horse teeth. "Cady, anybody tell you you gettin' too smart your own goddamn good?"

"Only you, Sarge."

"Careful, soldier." On a puff, Thatcher adds, "News, fuckface. Going to the field with S-3. Special request, Major Guptill. Cady's wanted in S-3, Battalion Headquarters."

"What's that mean?"

"Means you're TDY S-3, winter maneuvers. Driver, handyman, assistant to Operations Sergeant Doughan. S-3 has requisitioned one-each jeep and one-each driver Cady. Means you go to the field ten days ahead of everybody else, freeze your candy ass off. You'll love it."

"I have to do this?"

Thatcher cocks an eye. "Kinda question is that? Goddamn honor, you stupid fuck. They don't want Noyes or Nutter or Corporal Rusk, they want Cady. Good riddance, I say."

Glen gets up to draw a mug of coffee.

"Probably get promoted," Thatcher says as Glen sits down.

"You're kidding?"

"I don't know for sure. Report Battalion Headquarters 0900 for briefing, that's what I know. S-3 hotshots say jump, you know what to do, dontcha?"

"I've been told, Sarge."

"Wish you well," Thatcher adds in a different tone.

"Thanks," Glen says. "I guess," he adds, drawing more cackles from the two old soldiers whose arms are covered with stripes and hash marks.

Operation Fishhook. The battalion's mission: Provide communications to Seventh Army by way of radio, telegraph, wire, and messenger. DOD: Thursday, January 6, 0900. Exercise: January 25–27. Approximate date of return: January 30. His assignment, shown on a chart: Driver (Cady) and jeep (MC/5) assigned S-3 OIC Major Guptill, plus assistance to operations sergeant, SFC Doughan. Winter maneuvers, everyone knows, can be brutal, and twenty-five days in the field in January seems like a jail sentence.

"We do serious work," Jake Doughan tells him. "No room for mistakes or goldbricking. We take pride in what we do. You've been picked, given evidence general capability. Welcome to S-3, soldier. Understand that we run the show. Anybody gives you any shit whatsoever, anytime, tell 'em to contact me or Major Guptill. Questions?"

"Mail?" Glen says.

"Oh, shit," Doughan says. "Did you say mail?"

"In the field, will mail be delivered?"

"Major, sir," Doughan calls from the side of his mouth. "Somebody else wants to know if mail's delivered in the field."

The major appears in the doorway to his office, next door. "I got a girlfriend, too," the major says. "We're gonna get our mail, for sure, although Jake'd like to leave it all behind. Don't worry, you'll get your mail."

"Major's a widower, is madly in love with a teacher at the Base School," Doughan confides when the major has withdrawn to his office. "Me, I'm ready to leave the ole ball and chain behind for a while. Anyway, you'll get your mail, assuming it gets written."

"Cady, welcome to S-3," the major calls from his office. "Glad to have you."

Glen checks out arctic gear from supply, including a field-jacket liner and winter sleeping bag. He isn't likely to freeze this time out, unlike during his previous trip into the unknown. Which brings Hedy to mind and he is touched with the fear of losing her. His mail will have to be routed from Message Center Company or the dispatcher's shed in the motor pool to the field through S-3 and Headquarters Company. Screw-up possibilities couldn't be better. Assuming she writes.

He sits on his bunk and broods over being in love and over the chances of Hedy drinking with the English officers she knew from the Ruhr. Or were the English as formal and nonsexual as they appeared to be in American movies? Fat chance, he thinks.

Glen drives and listens. The major rides shotgun, talking with Doughan, who has the backseat to himself. They lead a convoy of ten vehicles—the main body will follow in nine days—and Glen learns that he was selected as "someone who can deal with the krauts if we have to." It's his language skill, such as it is, from the bakery visit in the fall, and their knowledge—he doesn't know how they found out—that he's been taking night classes.

Drafts whistle around the side curtains, and they wear rabbit-fur hats and gloves as they trace the Autobahn at plus-forty, though the major remarks once, "Don't lead 'em too hard, leave 'em some extra on the upgrades."

In time, the major has him pull over onto a widened road space where they deboard to count the vehicles roaring by, including two deuce-and-a-halfs pulling one-each generator and water tank on wheels. The drivers put up salutes, toot horns singsong fashion, and as the last vehicle, a monster wrecker, rolls by, Glen is given the satisfying task of taking to the passing lane to recover the lead. "Steady fast," the major tells him. "You know how to do it." Glen already regards him almost as a father and thinks how amazed they'd be, the major and Doughan, if they had a glimpse of the woman with whom their teenage driver is involved.

A minor incident occurs at a rest stop. All are outside their vehicles, smoking, talking, laughing—Glen stays close to MC/5, keeping an eye on his vehicle—when a captain says to him, "You, soldier, trot on down to the end of the convoy and tell—"

"Hold it there a second," the major says gently. "That's my driver, we'll keep him here with us."

"Sorry, sir, didn't know he was your man." The captain nods.

"Cady's the force that keeps us on track," the major says with a smile, to let the captain off the hook, and Glen feels a new rush of admiration for the field grade officer.

No mail call, no letters. He imagines his mail left lying in the motor pool or in his Company Orderly Room. He could not contact Hedy now if he wanted to, has to wait for her to send an address. No, Thatcher would send his mail on, he thinks, and the major or Doughan, who see to everything, had arranged for S-3 mail to be forwarded to the field. Still, he sees no sign, and concludes, well, that's the way it is: simulated war conditions.

"Ain't no use in goin' home/Jody's got your gal and gone," a cook sings from the open-air field kitchen one dark morning.

Day by day Glen thinks: Maybe not enough time has passed. Then: Maybe she hasn't written. Then: Maybe she won't, as her father knew all along.

"Every time you stand retreat/Jody gets a piece of meat."

Glen zips around every day in his jeep, makes runs from CP to Bivouac, a mile or so away in the woods. Instead of having to set up a pup tent, however, he has space in a field tent with a gas stove, overseen by Doughan, who, like a commanding officer, has brought along fold-out cot, air mattress, and garrison pillow.

"You live like a full colonel," Glen says to him.

"Which I oughta be," Doughan says, and adds, "Don't be a smart-ass, ship you back to the goddamn motor pool."

In the CP, a winding mile away over a dirt road, in thicker woods, Glen spends much time working in the vans, two olive-drab trailers with rear doors attached by an enclosed ramp. The center of operations, the heated, lighted vans are positioned on higher pine-needle ground and contain telephones and telephone jacks, a wall of chalkboards in which wire, radio frequency, and teletype circuits are entered, and a twenty-jack switchboard in each van. Teletype machines are sixty yards away in a field tent, a radio tent is separated by another sixty yards, and the cryptograph van is in a location all its own, surrounded by fir trees, barbed wire and camouflage netting, and guards with carbines at the ready. Trial runs follow in anticipation of Operation Fishhook, which will be seventy-two hours of a simulated attack.

Glen receives no mail as the days of preparation follow. He makes courier runs to other units and answers the telephones in the vans, "S-3, PFC Cady speaking, sir!" The work is easy enough and at times interesting; word will come that tanks in trial runs twenty clicks away have accidentally wiped out ground wires, that an infantry battalion, jumping to a new location, has lost radio contact, and the action in S-3, always in an excited, emergency mode, is to assign new circuits and frequencies, order installation, and, when they come in, to test and log connection times on the wallboard.

Visitors, senior noncoms, officers, civilian technical advisers— the colonel is a constant visitor—pass through the vans to study the board, to question problems, and, often, to get warm and swap war stories. The major says to him one morning, "Whatta ya think, Glen, like working in S-3?"

"Like it a lot, sir."

"Setting up's a piece of cake. When the war starts, it'll be so nuts around here you'll be lucky you get six hours' sleep beginning to end."

Glen jumps from sleeping bag into cold air in the morning, dresses, goes to the field kitchen for a helmetful of hot water with which to wash and shave, and the Bivouac Area becomes a comfortable home to which to return. He enjoys the relative freedom of life in the field, and the burning-gas and food and coffee smells of field stoves and garbage cans used for hot-water and mess-gear washing. His job is fine; he fits. Some troops long to return to base, and Glen knows that he will start to feel that way, too. But not yet. Not, it seems, until he settles something in his mind over Hedy. Still, on the ninth day, he asks the major in the morning darkness, "Any word on mail call, sir?"

"Mail's being delivered," the major says, and adds in a moment,

"Guess you're not having much luck or you wouldn't be asking. Tell you what, I'll make a call when we get to the CP."

Entering the van, the major draws a cup of coffee, calls Bivouac, and shakes his head to Glen as he speaks to the mail clerk. He calls the battalion mail clerk at base then, and says, to Glen's surprise, "Run a check on this man's mail and call me back within thirty minutes. Any screw-ups, I'm gonna have somebody's stripes."

Off the phone, he says, "Sometimes you have to strike a match up close."

The call comes back in ten minutes. "Sorry," the major says. "At least now they know where you are."

"Didn't mean to cause trouble, sir," Glen says.

" 'At's okay. Just don't worry about things like that *too* much."

He worries about where she is and what she's doing. He imagines her meeting someone of her class and education—an English captain at Cambridge working on an advanced degree—and dejection fills him. At the same time, an increasing work schedule forces him to give his mind to S-3. They go to twelve-hour shifts in the vans and he is assigned 0700 to 1900, grabbing chow before driving the major to the CP in morning darkness, and evening chow, kept warm in the field kitchen, on their return in the darkness of night.

Better to be in the field, he thinks, as fear and jealousy take over when he is idle. Better to keep busy. He keeps the jeep maintained and topped off with gas, answers and logs calls in the van, enters changes on the chalkboard, and, in added emergencies, calls a Wire Company or Radio Company substation to report an outage or problem. The offensive attack is always pending.

Handling one call, entering a new frequency on the board, he turns to see the major pointing a finger at him and saying, "Cady, next week you're going to night shift. You'll work with a junior officer, but you'll do fine. Time comes, best way to make the transition to nights is to work straight through twenty-four hours, dawn to dawn, hit the sack, and sleep a stretch, and then you'll be on schedule. Jake'll anchor this place days, you'll do nights."

Glen knows little about night shift, but he's pleased by the attention and slight distraction. Then, near evening chow time, a courier delivers an envelope and the major says, "Glen, sign for that."

Glen signs, and the major says, "Open it, check it out. . . . What's in there?"

"Stripes," Glen says, confused.

"Better put 'em on," the major says. "Battlefield promotion, congratulations."

"I'm promoted?" Glen says as a thrill runs through him.

"Orders came in this morning and we thought we'd get you some stripes," the major says. "There's a sewing kit in that drawer."

In his T-shirt, using a needle to break the threads of his PFC stripes, Glen sews on the new ones, and wonders if he's ever felt so happy. A corporal. If only Hedy would write to tell him her new address.

This last free evening, when he's gassed up MC/5, he makes his way to the Beer Tent for the first time, conscious of the new identity on his arms, where he sits over one and another brown bottle of German beer with ceramic/red rubber caps. Alone at a folding table, he focuses on a stopper, brooding over where he's going in life and wondering if her trip to Cambridge is a way of saying goodbye. If she wants to cut him off, he can understand.

He buys another beer and returns to the table. Screw it all, he thinks. She hasn't written and there's nothing to do but to say screw it all. Of all things, to feel like an old soldier at age nineteen. Screw it all.

Well, she did write "I LOVE YOU" on the photograph, which he'd like to look at but isn't going to with GIs coming and going in the haze-filled tent. He removes his wallet nonetheless, and, counting his money, peeks at her image and words and, staring away, sees clearly how she will go on her way and his life will be left to him. Staying in the army? Being sent to Georgia or Japan? Going home to the auto factories? He pours away a last glug and moments later is in the cold air with his flashlight, pissing beside a tree and pushing on to his tent, eager to burrow into the winter sleeping bag.

He survives the twenty-four-hour transition, though he misses Major Guptill and Sergeant Doughan. At night he is regarded not as an inexperienced corporal but as an enlisted man who should know all the answers, and doesn't.

Nor does the three-day war, when it comes, pause for his confusion. Activity in CP and Bivouac speeds up, roads turn muddy, and work within the S-3 vans intensifies, drawing him into the fray. Throughout West Germany, infantry, artillery, armor, even medical and graves-registration units are caught up in the offensive, pressing for the wire, radio, and teletype communications provided by the Seventy-ninth Signal Battalion.

There is a pause each morning during the 0700 shift change as the major, Doughan, and others arrive, and the night crew returns to Bivouac. Outside the vans is a quiet world of fresh winter air in a bouncing jeep drive over dirt roads, then chow and freedom for a time before crawling into a sleeping bag. Glen counts deer in the mist-layered fields, takes time to scald his mess kit in a garbage can of boiling water before presenting it for a serving of eggs. And, since regular mail call now exists, he listens to Corporal Latourette or Sergeant Thatcher call names before the field Orderly Room.

Glen receives ordinary mail for the first time, a letter from his mother and a solicitation from *Encyclopaedia Brittanica*. He also endures taunts about his "battlefield" promotion, Thatcher calling him "Audie" and asking if his next step, now that he's achieved status with Hitler, is to take over the company. Then, one morning, near the field kitchen, Sergeant Hawk says, "Cady, you know there're letters for you in the dispatcher's shed at base. Came in some time back, just remembered that."

Hawk is drawing coffee into his canteen cup and Glen says, "Letters for me?"

"Think so," Hawk says. "Couple of letters around there for a time. You know the basket on the dispatcher's desk?"

Glen sees Thatcher watching. "We have the courier pick up my mail?" he says to the first sergeant.

Stepping closer, Thatcher says, "Careful who you tell about this."

Everything changes. Coffee tastes better and deer and fields along the dirt roads appear more beautiful than wistful. She wrote! It wasn't him, wasn't his age, his lack of education; it wasn't his inability to speak the language; it was the fucked-up army.

The next morning Glen returns to Bivouac with a single passenger, Angelopoulos, a new second lieutenant, a man with whom
it has been an exercise in irreverent army jokes to work the night
shift. Glen has an appetite and he says, "Sir, how about a quick
stop in town?" The letters will be his this morning, and he hasn't
felt so bold in weeks.

"Quick stop where?"

"Bakery. I'll make a wrong turn up here, in case we run into
MPs. Ten minutes later we'll be on our way back with *Apfelkuchen*
baked fresh this morning. They're great. Sir."

"We get caught you know whose ass'll get scorched."

"Not mine, sir."

The lieutenant laughs. "You know there's a bakery?"

"Always a bakery, sir."

"Wrong turn?"

"Sir, it happens."

"I don't know why I feel at the mercy of a smart-ass corporal."

Glen makes the turn—he'd spotted the sign KLEINSDORF, 2.5
KM the first day in the field—and minutes later they're back on
the road to Bivouac and half a dozen squares of warm *Apfelkuchen*
are disappearing one after another from between sheets of tissue
paper. "It's what they tell you in ROTC," Lieutenant Angelopoulos
says. "Want something done, find a smart-ass corporal who knows
how to circumvent the rules."

"That's what they tell you in ROTC?" Glen says.

"Better believe it."

Corporal Latourette hands over two pale green envelopes, and
walking away, heart alive, Glen buttons them into his shirt pocket.
The return address included: "Cambridge, ENGLAND."

Over midday chow, he thinks. Or alone in the woods. He's so
tired now he decides to wait until he's rested, and he curls sock-
footed into his sleeping bag with the letters in his shirt pocket. In
the afternoon, washed and rested, he'll wander into the woods
where he can be alone and savor her words. She wrote. Her letters
were there all along and his life, derailed, is back on track.

Awakening at midday, he is filled by her presence. Other soldiers
are stirring in the tent, and he pulls on boots and pants to fetch

a helmet of hot water; whatever the temperature, he'll wash and shave in the open. Has anyone ever felt so good, or so strong?

As the day proceeds, however, he keeps postponing the opening of the letters. He'll tell her sometime about being alone in a magical German forest in a spirit of love! Chow under his belt and bunk area squared away, he does time in the motor pool. It comes to him as a discovery that he is fulfilled by the letters remaining unopened, close to his hungry heart.

Does he love her more in not opening them? He cannot resist prolonging the sensation a while longer, maybe another day, making believe Sergeant Hawk never remembered seeing them in a wire basket. Someday he'll explain to her the special pleasure of holding the unopened letters, that it was like having her in his sleeping bag, watching her sleep and waiting for her eyes to open.

A rumor comes over a van telephone at 0355 hours: General MacAuliffe may visit the CP at any time. The vans are busy, phones and switchboards ringing and buzzing, and the question arises: Should they call the major with a rumor at four o'clock in the morning?

"Not me," Angelopoulos says. "I get along fine without having Major Guptill on my ass. Up to you, Corporal."

Glen took the call and he outranks the other enlisted men working the night shift. He has a sense that the major would bust his ass more for not calling than for waking him up. Tomorrow is Day Three of the exercise and the major wants nothing more than to have the battalion sail through unblemished.

He dials before he can think anymore about it, hears the field telephone ring in the major's small tent in Bivouac. His voice a squeak, the major needs a moment and a cigarette cough before he says, "Captain Rodgers said a rumor?"

"Yes sir."

"General MacAuliffe?"

"Yes sir."

"Didn't say where he heard the rumor?"

"Didn't say, no sir."

"Guys got coffee?"

"Yes sir."

"Be there in a while."

Glen gets caught up again in the taking and making of insistent calls. Everything is a dire emergency now, and anything not immediately resolved is reported in a return call as an even greater crisis. Maybe thirty minutes later he looks up to see the major, unshaven, enter the van and pull off his field jacket. Telephone to his ear, he watches the major draw coffee and sidestep along the van to tabulate casualties, outages, unknowns. Without a word the major picks up a ringing phone and is soon handling two calls at a time and calling out instructions as Operation Fishhook turns into its final hours.

The major's presence alters the shift change and daybreak relief is ignored. Caught in the turn into the homestretch, Glen is flattered when the major points at him at 0700 and says, "Stay on a while, we'll get you back soon's we can."

Eight or ten soldiers are working in the two vans, and the tension increases. At the same time, the rumor of a visit from the commanding general, U.S. Forces Europe, keeps flaring. Someone recounts how, surrounded by German divisions in 1945 and ordered to surrender, he sent the reply "Nuts" to his German counterpart and fought his way out.

It's a blur of cigarettes, coffee, ringing phones, and shouted replies. A fresh gallon of coffee materializes, and it's clear to Glen that the major can't be concerned with anyone missing sleep or food; the man is constantly talking, walking to the end of a telephone cord, erasing a wall entry with a finger, adding a new entry with a stub of chalk, grabbing dog-eared, stapled frequency charts and flipping pages, covering a mouthpiece and calling to someone. Then, as an emergency involving V Corps is taking place, and the major, a receiver in each hand, is shouting from one mouthpiece to another, someone roars, "GENERAL MACAULIFFE'S IN THE AREA!"

"Shit!" the major says. Replacing a phone, he pulls open a drawer and comes up with an electric razor. "Cady!" he calls as he plugs in the razor. "Call teletype, see if he's been there—goddamnit!"

Glen logs an entry, dials three digits, and is off the phone at once, calling, "Hasn't been in teletype, sir—don't know where he is," and the major, shaving, says, "Check the door, see if you see him in the area!"

The major's electric razor is buzzing as Glen opens the small accordion door above the three-step stairway to the ground, and directly in his face is a broadcast of stars, three on a helmet, three on a shirt collar, and three on a field-jacket collar. He jumps back, snaps to, calls, "Tensh-Hut!"

"At ease, Corporal," the general says, squeezing by, followed by a string of field grade officers who look like movie stars.

The razor stops buzzing, followed by a roar from the major— "A-TENSH-HUT!"—as he jumps to his feet with the awkwardness of a recruit.

"As you were, Major, carry on, finish shaving," the general says, amused, as he makes his way through the van.

"Yes sir, Major Guptill reporting, sir!" the major says.

"Carry on, all of you, just having a look around."

Major Guptill's razor is left on the counter as he takes up another ringing phone, processing more calls as though there were no string of movie stars watching.

Glen wonders if he should squeeze back to the counter, but his problem is solved when the four men follow the general into the attached van, and in a moment someone calls, "All clear! They've gone out the other side! All clear!"

At last 1600 arrives and the exercise ends. "People are packing it in," the major says as phone lines begin to quiet down. By 1700 the ringing has stopped altogether, and Doughan says, "The son-ofabitch is over."

Relief. Glen sits waiting for another phone to ring, which doesn't happen. The major lets his head hang, as if allowing its parts to settle. No one seems to know what to do. "Personnel all relieved for now," the major says at last.

There is movement throughout the vans as enlisted men and officers take up jackets and weapons, walk to jeeps, and return to Bivouac to wash up, eat, drink beer, perhaps to sleep. The major sits in place, as do Glen and Doughan and three or four more.

"Smoke if you got 'em," the major says, and they all titter.

"We'll pack tomorrow, day after tomorrow we'll head for home," the major says. He continues sitting in place, however, as do the others. "Glen, go on for chow if you want," he says, "or stay here if you want to, because I think we oughta have us a little snort."

"I'll stay," Glen says.

"What we can do, on me," the major says. "Glen, you know along the road to the Bivouac there's a sign—"

"Kleinsdorf—yes sir, I know it."

The major laughs. "Won't ask how," he says. "Happen to have a *Lebensmittel* there?"

"Yes sir."

"You know what," the major says. "I think you earned those stripes this time out. Think so, Jake?"

"No doubt about it, sir," Doughan says. "Should make a move, get back to base, transfer Cady to S-3, assistant to the operations sergeant. Just what we been looking for."

"I think so, too," the major says. "Whatta ya think, Glen? Wanna transfer to S-3 on a full-time basis?"

"Nothing I'd like better, sir."

"He'll do fine," Doughan says.

"If the general don't write us all up," the major says.

"One second sooner, sir, I might have knocked him down the steps," Glen says.

They laugh as the major removes DM bills from his wallet and slides them, one, two, three, four green twenties along the counter. "I'm buying," he says. "Everybody did a hell of a job, came through with flying colors, want to thank you all."

"Let's roll," Doughan says, and as Glen takes up helmet and rifle, Doughan adds, "Forget the armor, war's over."

Half an hour later, they've returned from the village with two cases of beer, an eighteen-inch *Mettwurst*, half a stick of salami, two kilos of sliced cheese, plus pickles, pepperoncini, olives, and a sack of *Brötchen* and breadsticks. Seven of them sit around drinking and eating sandwiches prepared with pocket knives, talking and laughing in the afterglow of the job.

Glen listens to the just-hatching war stories, smiling and enjoying himself, and when the major notes that Glen nearly knocked General MacAuliffe down the steps, he draws an explosion of laughter by saying, "He didn't tell me to continue shaving—sir."

They infect each other with laughter. The major wipes his eyes and breaks into a new convulsion. For Glen it's the best time he's had in the army, one of the best times he's ever had. He also sheds tears of laughter, and only as the seizure is dying away does he realize he has forgotten to think of her, and only then does he

touch his shirt pocket, to be certain the precious unopened envelopes are still there.

The words fall short of expectation. He reads the letters in sequence
the next day, as he waits in the jeep, and a line in the second letter
stops him. "English officers I have met in Germany are also now
at Cambridge and proving helpful to a new person."

The first letter—short on words of love he had hoped for and
long on details of her journey—is a disappointment, and the second
revives his jealousy. What did he expect? Why wouldn't English
officers fall for her just as he did, as, on that day in the park, love
came to him on nothing else than the faint line of her smile?

The major and Doughan approach and Doughan says, "Wake it
up, Corporal, let's hit the road," though Glen, staring away, doesn't
feel sleepy.

"Tonight we'll get some sleep," the major says as they bump
along.

"Cady, you a thirty-year man?" Doughan asks then from the
rear.

"I don't know," Glen says.

"If you are, the major has something to tell you."

"What's that, sir?"

"Guess it's as good a time as any. Think so, Jake?"

"Yes sir. Need to reorganize, might as well get started."

"Reenlistment blues," the major says. "Glen, you say the word,
we'll process the papers and have you transferred to S-3. Assistant
Operations NCO, recommendation for promotion to staff sergeant.
Jake rotates—I rotate, for that matter—you'll be in line for operations sergeant and eligible for still another stripe. Right now, if
you made sergeant, you'd be the youngest noncom in the battalion,
probably on post, one of the youngest in the peacetime army.
You'd have to sign up for six, though, that's the hitch. And your
heart oughta be in it. Thing is, we'd like you in S-3 on a permanent
basis. You'd be good for the army and the army'd be good for
you. Whatta ya say, Corporal, up for six and a recommendation
for promotion?"

"Wow," Glen says, knowing that reenlistment flies in the face
of his prevailing dream. "Gee, six years," he says. "I'll have to
think about it, sir."

"That's not unreasonable," the major says. "Wouldn't be a smart person who didn't think about how he's going to spend his life. I can buy that."

"Go for it, Cady," comes from the backseat. "Opportunity don't knock twice."

"It's okay," the major says. "Nothing wrong with thinking about it. Take a couple weeks. What the hell are those lights?" he adds as they turn onto the dirt lane leading to Bivouac.

"Headlights, the war's over," Doughan says.

"Not headlights," the major says. "Hold it a second, Glen. They're jacklighting deer. That's what it is. They're on those platforms, jacklighting deer."

"Germans?" Glen says.

"Hell, no, rednecks," the major says. "Last night out—jacklighting deer to lug back home. See that light?"

Before them in the dark, lights flash high and low. "Let's proceed with care," the major says. "Throw your lights on high, flash 'em a few times. We'll run the gauntlet."

"Dependent quarters'll be full of venison," Doughan says.

Glen drives along and the lights in the trees cease.

"To the victors go the spoils," the major says. "It's the kinda thing, though, that really gets up the Germans' dander."

21

Munich on a Saturday night. A letter is on its way to Cambridge, a mild letter putting the world on hold, and Corporal Cady, would-be youngest sergeant on post, is staggering along a fog-shrouded street in the heart of Bavaria. Fog begins at knee level and car motors make no sound; headlights become visible at six or eight feet. Cobblestones, in the clear space above ground, seem polished with oil, and the smells of Germany ride the night currents. She's in Cambridge and he's at the end of a train ride in sodden, sexual, medieval Munich.

By himself, he thinks, and himself ain't sober. He's seen that he belongs to the world of stripes, and that he probably can't accept them. In his drunken heart of hearts, he's also seen that she will soon be done with him, and now he knows where the sad songs come from.

His drinking has him lost in more ways than one. She's there and he's here, and he has to say goodbye. He's been in one and another *Hofbräuhaus*, weighing Doughan's theory that German beer is happy and American beer is sad. One makes you sing, the other makes you brood.

Glen wonders if this is happiness. Porcelain street signs attached to buildings at corners mean nothing to him. He's lost and doesn't care. Beer halls and oompahpah music. Women and food and singing. Women with propped-up boobs and all but nipples exposed—where are those nipples?—women with half a dozen foaming steins of beer in one hand, platters of juicy *Krai-nerwurst* . . . a night out in war-torn Munich.

Someone passes in the fog, and he believes he glimpsed female legs. Headlights emerge ten feet away, preceding a near-soundless motor; taillights fade quietly away. Doughan seems to be right about the beer, he thinks, singing *"In München steht ein Hofbräu-haus . . ."* As dim lights pass he reads:

U.S. ARMY
MILITARY POLICE

Here in uniform and probably in an off-limits zone, and he could care less. At a corner underneath the lamplight a woman appears out of nowhere, beautifully sexual in her paint and perfume and proportions.

"Abend, Schatz . . . vant good hot pussy? Good hot pussy for you here." A leather coat opens, revealing legs, stockings, garter belt; naked pussy and ass swish and turn, and seem to him, as advertised, to be steaming.

"Les get married," he says.

"Achh, too much drink," she says, and instantly the long coat swirls away into darkness.

He wanders fearlessly, finds other women standing under tents of lamplight, leaning, walking away. The drunken corporal forges ahead, eager to punch any foe, outmaneuver and outdance any unrepentant Nazi gang. He could be in a forest of damp dreams, of elves and sirens, vampires, hags, and witches.

"Qvick hot screw, *Schatz? Komm!* Qvick hot screw vizz me. Tventy mark. Qvickie hot screw, hot to trot!"

He wants it and doesn't want it. The woman in the long leather coat was so beautiful, Lilli Marlene Dietrich underneath the lamplight, he wants love only from her. What he really wants, he knows, is to have someone to talk to. Where is Hedy tonight? Whose lips ride the veins of her warm neck tonight?

"Sirty mark, Joe. Qvick hot pussy like Momma giff you."

He stumbles along in the fog, and a young girl with red lips steps from a doorway. "Hey, Joe, giff me good fuck. Sirty mark. Come on, Joe, put it in hot pussy, sirty mark."

"Too much," Joe tells her. "Don't have that much."

"Vaht you sink, fuck for free?"

"Sure are pretty," Joe tells her.

"Vaht you got der, Joe? Got der bazooka? Show me see dat ting gettin' hard, Joe, come on."

"Twenty," Joe says.

"Sirty mark, come on, you good-lookin' guy."

"Twenty-five," Joe says and knows she has him where they both want him to be.

They climb stairs past closed doors. An Eighty-second Airborne master sergeant descends grinning, says, "Just found the end a the rainbow."

Fearless of the shadows, Joe follows the young shape before him, pulled by love and desire. She unlocks the door to a room with a reddish-yellow lamp at bedside. She sends home a lock, and turns smiling. "Sirty mark, *ja.*"

She's a lovely teenager, and he says, "What's your name? *Wie heisst du, Fräulein?*"

"Come on, Joe, sirty mark."

"How can I marry you I don't know your name?"

"Marry? Vaht you say?"

"It's 'thirty,' not 'sirty,' and 'marry' means to be in love and get married."

"Heiraten?" she says with a laugh, unzipping her skirt at the side. "Don't marry nobody, Joe. Come on, giff me da money I don't gotta call nobody. Vahtcha got der?" she adds, reaching to touch him.

He hands her two bills, and in a partial pivot, she tucks them into sleeve, brassiere, dresser drawer, it's hard to tell. Sliding onto the bed, she scoots back, raises her knees. "Here you go, Joe, good hot cunt. Take down dem pants, see vaht you got der. Come on," she says, rubbing between her legs.

In T-shirt, dog tags, hat, and socks, Joe is on the bed, resisting the sex she's offering. He touches her shoulders and would kiss her in spite of the warning never to kiss a whore, and for a moment she seems to relax. It is the sweetest part, has him touching her perfumed, soft upper body, has him trying to touch her hair. "Come on, tell me your name," he begs her.

"Katja," she tells him.

He presses his face to her breast and shoulder, closes his eyes, and believes somewhere inside that his move to kiss her neck and lips is his way of telling Hedy goodbye.

At Battalion Headquarters he stops to tell Doughan of his decision to reenlist and is surprised to learn he'll have to wait ninety days. Terms used are "freeze" and "quotas" and "peacetime army."

"I only have six months to go," Glen says.

"Listen, the army of the future won't be like the old army," Doughan says. "Top NCO in the new army won't be making his stripes on the parade field. It'll be brains and technology."

Glen hasn't told Hedy any of his thoughts for the future, perhaps because he doesn't know them himself. In his last letter he did mention sergeant's stripes and the six-year hitch, hoping she'd say something to help him decide. "Got the reenlistment blues," he wrote, but did not add that the blues would come from carrying a duffel bag aboard ship, as in a country song, to sail into the sunset and leave her to someone else.

As he's returning one night from a movie, the CQ on duty looks at him and says, "Cady, right? Phone call for you, all jumbled by a kraut operator. You expecting a call?"

"I don't know," Glen says.

A brief postcard comes from London, signed "Much love, Hedy." He doesn't know how far Cambridge is from London, and she doesn't say why she was there. "London more exciting than imagined." The words add more distance. Well, it's as it should be, he tells himself, and makes his way to a poker game he was going to avoid.

On a warm March evening, Glen walks down the hill into Bubblegum. In the weeks since his outing to Munich, he's hardly left the post. In Bubblegum, he sits in a hangout called Hillbilly Heaven where Hank Williams is singing "Cold Cold Heart" on the jukebox. Looking up, he sees Thatcher swaying above him with a drunken grin. A wet cigarette hangs from the first sergeant's lip and his Ike jacket hangs open. "Corporal," he says. "Invitation join me yonder table, buy you one each fuckin' beer."

"Sarge, no thanks, I'm just about to head back."

"Refuse invitation, hurt first sergeant's feelings, first sergeant hafta kick corporal's candy ass all over the fuckin' premises."

"Okay, can't argue with that," Glen says, knowing where drinking with Thatcher will lead, but welcoming the excuse.

"Momma-san!" Thatcher calls. "Knock mare beer, *bitte*."

Shackjobs. In a drunken pouring away of suds, staggering to and from the foul *Herrenzimmer* to piss down a tin wall, ordering round after round while the bubbling Technicolor Wurlitzer cries heartbreak, Thatcher tells about shackjobs, and tells Glen, jabbing a finger, that he's got just the one for him. "Cheaper'n anything going," he says. "Cleaner'n' better for the economy. Better'n wandering streets and throwing away money on whores and contractin' VD."

Glen barely pays attention. "Not me, Sarge," he says. "Got problems enough of my own."

"No no no no," Thatcher says. "You don't know what you talkin' about, soldier, and don't piss me off. You'll love it. I'm tellin' you, you'll love it."

"You got a shackjob, what you doin' here?"

"Don't hafta bring 'em out drinkin'. That's the thing, you dumb sonofabitch. They don't wanna come someplace like this! Nothing but trouble bring a woman goddamn place like this. Cady, you such a kid, don't know your asshole from a catcher's mitt. Getting me pissed here, too. Thing is, Ingrid *knows* I'll be there later. Saturday night, thas when I take her out. Get there, later tonight, she's all ready for my horny ass.

"Take you along," he adds, grinning. "Introduce you Ingrid *and* Marta. Don't give me no shit either. Marta's lonely as can be."

Glen laughs. "Not me, Sarge. Thanks anyway."

Thatcher grips his shoulder. "You got it wrong, goddamnit! These're good women! Don't think they ain't, gonna piss me off! They just trying to get along. Ain't whores, so don't think they are. DPs is what they are, fucked over by the war, thas all, so don't go acting better 'cause I'm here to tell you you ain't, goddamnit!"

"No offense, Sarge. But I already got a woman. Sorta."

"None taken. Just know these're good women, thas all."

"You get a commission?" Glen says, trying not to grin.

For a second Thatcher looks like he's going to come over the table, but then he smiles. "Give Ingrid hundred marks every payday," he says. "Two cartons cigarettes, one pound a coffee. Get all the ass I want, anytime I want. Once a while we go to a movie, a dance some country place. She knows I'm gonna ship out one a these days, she take on somebody else, or she don't, but ain't no bad woman, so don't think she is! Young punk making fun a people, tell ya, could get hisself hurt."

"Just making fun of you, Sarge, don't get all worked up. What's her name?"

"Ingrid. Goddamnit, I told you that four fuckin' times!"

Glen smiles.

"Friend's named Marta. She's the one I'se introducing you to—don't say a word! Old man shipped out months ago, Marta ain't got nothing and she's having a hard time. She's got the blues. Hear what I'm saying?"

"Don't hear a thing, Sarge. It's too noisy in here."

"Staff Sergeant Cullen, Wire Comp'ny. Good guy but he shipped out, it's all she wrote. You come along, introduce you, thas all. You ain't interested, go on your way. They ain't bad ole girls, though. Eighty marks, little something now and then from the PX, all it takes. It's like looking at a used car. Don't hafta buy you don't wanna, but she might still give you a little test drive."

Glen and Thatcher leave Hillbilly Heaven in a vague cloud of beer and schnapps, riding in the backseat of a clanking Mercedes taxi which disgorges them into darkness outside of town. A smell of manure marking the air, they weave over packed dirt into a concentration of shanties. Candles flicker here and there in the darkness. Thatcher pulls at Glen's arm every other step; he feels likely to collapse on the ground. Thatcher pulls, giggles, hisses, "Keep it quiet!"

"You're the one making noise."

"Shhhh . . . wake people up . . . keep it quiet!"

Next to a sheet metal wall, Thatcher trips over a bicycle and Glen falls on top of him. As they're laughing and snorting, a woman's voice hisses sharply from the side, *"Hinaus, Mensch!"*

Getting to his feet, Glen stumbles into Thatcher again, and through their stifled laughter Thatcher tries to whisper he's sure she lives right here somewhere.

"Who lives where?" Glen whispers back.

"Marta, goddamnit!"

Glen feels mud on an elbow and the side of one leg, and thinks drunkenly that he needs to avoid MPs between here and garrison.

"INN-GRID!" Thatcher call-whispers. "INN-GRID!"

Out of a shanty comes a flashlight beam and a sputtering of angry German. A woman's voice whispers harshly from a doorway where a candle is burning. "Villy!" the voice says. "Villy, shh!"

"Ingrid, *Schatz!*" Thatcher whispers back.

"She calls you Villy?" Glen says, trying to restrain his laughter. "She calls you Villy?"

A moment later Glen is inside in flickering candlelight, and Thatcher is trying to introduce him to Ingrid, is trying as he weaves to say he has someone for Marta but couldn't find her place. "Corporal Cady to meet Marta, corporal soon to be sergeant, looking to test-drive."

The two of them snicker as Ingrid tries to steer Thatcher to a cot—the only place to sit—before he falls. Glen finds himself being led by the arm back into the damp darkness and thirty or forty feet along until Ingrid, holding him, taps hollow wood. In a mix of German and English he tries to offer an apology, to say he didn't ask for this, can make his way back, but Ingrid, tapping, whispers something and is answered.

"It's okay," Glen says, only to be hushed. He can't help giggling as he imagines them negotiating, and checks his giddiness as he is himself led into a candle-lighted space so small he could touch both sides at once. Only a shanty in old Shantytown, he'd like to sing.

"Corporal, not der sergeant?" the woman says.

She is moving her small candle, trying to have a look at him, making it impossible for him to have a look at her.

"Just a corporal," Glen tries to say. "'S'all mistake. How do I get home?"

"Shhhhhh!" the woman tells him.

Glen feels himself swaying, senses he may topple, and the woman takes his arm and pulls him to a cot. Still his head sails, and as she whispers he thinks to try his German on her. She lifts his feet onto the cot while his head keeps sailing and the last thing he remembers is a candle and face floating over him.

A rooster is crowing. According to his Seamaster, it's ten to five, and Glen is out in the damp, cold air, staggering away from the shanties. When he woke he knew at once he was far from home, and wanted only to get back. Stepping over a shape on the floor he thought was Marta, he found the makeshift doorway and squeezed through into the morning.

He's still a little drunk, and his need to piss is immense. Through the mist he can make out the shanties; not wanting to piss on their dirt street, he pushes toward the road. He hoses then into a ditch of weeds, and it takes so long he imagines causing a flood. Walking left into the break of day, his head throbs and he thinks, Dear God, let it be the right direction. At least the cold air will sober him.

In time he hears a distant motorcycle and tries to determine its direction. He crosses the road to the side where he might catch a ride, and soon catches sight of the bike's single headlight. In an instant, though he waves, the bike passes him by, carrying a helmeted, leather-suited figure. Going to work in town, Glen guesses. The right town, he hopes, plodding along in the motor's lingering wake.

Suddenly and silently an old woman on a bicycle comes up behind him; she wobbles and nearly topples, barely missing him. *"Böblingen?"* Glen calls after her, but there is no reply as she, too, hurries away down the empty, lonely road.

He has no wish to return to Marta, but a day later he knows he's going to. It may be pity for her, or guilt for taking off; he hardly knows what he's thinking these days, if he's thinking at all. Maybe he can erase his longing for Hedy with a shackjob in Shantytown.

A rare card arrives from Cambridge. It mentions an outing to a London theater and is signed "With love, Hedy." Still she seems to exist at a distance, like words in a book. Glen places the card with others in his locker and goes to the PX to buy cigarettes, coffee, and candy for the woman, Marta, he has vaguely decided to visit.

Saturday at noon, as duty ends for the weekend, he works in the motor pool to be sure MC/5 is up to full field. He is leaving the jeep, too; on Monday he will finally transfer to S-3, though he has yet to actually negotiate with Doughan and the major the issue of promotion and signing up for six. Like others, like Thatcher, Tolliver, Gantos, many noncoms, Glen senses it could be his life's last turn. Doughan and the major would argue that a person could live a normal life, could marry and live off base in dependent quarters, but he knows it wouldn't work like that for him. He would end up with booze instead, both to purge her from and to keep her in his system. The future seems easy to read.

As he passes through the main gate to the taxi stand, he walks by street merchants selling photo albums and sweaters, as well as several women, standing apart and waiting. He notices the women—shackjobs, waiting for their lifer boyfriends—as if for the first time. The day is overcast and the women stand shivering in rabbit-fur jackets, berets, and fresh rouge. As he waits, Glen sees a white sergeant, a black SFC, and an old corporal, each bearing an awol bag, greet women, exchange handshakes and kisses, laugh and talk as they slide into the inevitable Mercedes taxis. As it turns out, he shares a ride with a sergeant he recognizes from Radio Company and the man's rosy-cheeked girlfriend, and as Glen tries to convey his destination to the driver, the couple laughs, with a rapid exchange in German. When the two deboard in town the sergeant says, "Careful out there, soldier."

As the diesel cab clatters on, Glen leans ahead to see the direction the driver is taking. His chest fills with anxiety as they leave town behind, and he thinks, Forget it, tell the cabbie to go back. Moments later the cab turns into the dirt entrance to the shanties, which look even smaller in the daylight. He pays, and the cab pulls away, leaving him not far from where he flooded the ditch.

He made no promises and she doesn't know he is coming; he could still turn around and leave. He doesn't know which shanty is hers, or that she is here, and he might have no choice but to leave. He walks a ways and pauses, filled with anxiety again. He decides that her place must be to his right and he walks then trying to see but not stare into the tiny residences. He glimpses a corner of window covering lift and drop but no one appears. All manner of lumber, tin, used wood, and plastic are assembled to make doorways, windows, and roof sections. There are even small "yards" near some entryways, including the flower of war-torn Germany, the potted red geranium, just coming into bud.

He has walked thirty meters when he meets a woman coming out of a shanty. She appears dressed to go out, in short beige coat and hat, pauses to look at him, and when she smiles he vaguely recalls her from the candle-lighted moments. She looks like a woman on her way to a Saturday night church supper.

"Marta?" he says to her.

She doesn't speak yet, though they shake hands.

"You come in here," she says. "Not out here, dey all vatch everysing."

As she turns around, he follows, ducking to enter her doorway. The bed where he passed out, no larger than an army cot, fills one end of her space. A make-do kitchen is to the rear and the rest of the space contains makeshift furnishings. There is no place to sit but the bed, and she points and says, "Sit der, is okay."

Hat on, bag in hand, he sits on the cot, though it seems discourteous. He settles the bag to the floor, and looks up to see her smiling at him. "You guy—come see Marta vunce more?"

He smiles a little.

"Dat hat," she says. "Off dat hat."

"What about your hat?" he says.

As he slips his hat off, she angles her head, removes a pin, removes the small hat, and shakes her hair a little. Her hair is full and when he says, "Pretty hair," her smile grows wider.

"Vaht you sink, vant to be togezzer now?"

He isn't sure what she is asking. "You were going somewhere?"

"Look for you, dat's all," she says, and raises her eyebrows flirtatiously.

Glen smiles in acknowledgment.

"I giff you trink?" she says.

"Good idea, could use a trink."

She laughs and, to his surprise, reaches to touch his hair. "Vaht you say?" she says. "You like Marta now?"

"Guess I do," he says. The contraband comes to mind, and he wonders if he should move to hold up his end of things.

She slides her hand down his arm. "My kinda guy, sink I already like," she says.

By instinct he touches her hip. It's the moment to cross a line, yet he holds back.

"Come," she says, taking his hand. "Take you home to Mutti."

He imagines that "Mutti" is her word for sex, and gets uncertainly to his feet, expecting her to unbutton her jacket and blouse. Instead she leads him a couple of steps into the makeshift kitchen and shouts, *"Mutti, ich bin zu Hause!"*

Behind a piece of hanging cloth, sitting in a straight-backed chair, is an ancient, white-haired woman, her mouth hanging open, gazing past her old hands where they rest on a blanket on her knees. Her eyes are vacant and the skin on her hands and forehead appears translucent.

"She was here, the other night?" he manages to say.

"Grandmozzer, *sehr alt*," she says. "Not to vorry, is okay."

Glen looks to Marta as she unbuttons her jacket and lays it aside.

"Dat trink," she says, pointing past him to a whiskey bottle and shot glass on top of a box.

"Come," she says. "Here, come, *Liebling*." She motions him back into the space in front of the bed, out of the old woman's view.

"Where was she?" he says as hc obeys.

"She sleep on da floor. She like dat. Sit, come. Trink dat trink, is okay for sure, no sveat."

As he tosses off the drink, Marta takes the glass and steps back to pour another, paying the old woman no mind. Handing him the glass, she says, "Is *alt*, ninety-two, *ja*. Sit der, is okay. Giff me dat coat."

He is still confused but unbuttons his jacket as instructed. "You were ready to go out, you wanna go out? What about your Mutti?"

"Pah! Is okay! Come, giff to me dat coat! Sit der."

Glen removes his jacket, trading hands with the shot glass, and sits on the bed. "Brought cigarettes and coffee," he says. "Candy."

"You vant dis coffee now, you sveet guy?" she says.

"Oh, no, just brought it, a gift."

"Vant some good time, *ja*?"

She stands above him. "Mutti no matter," she says. "Is okay." She lifts her large breasts in her hands and holds them. "Vant some a dese, *ja*?"

Glen smiles a little.

"Dcy pretty good," she says. "Shackjob dey say, but don't care about dat. Don't gonna sneak around, say dat for sure. Dey don't like it, say I'm da whore, go vid da American soldier, vaht do I care? Is some money for me, for sure, but da soldier make my heart go tump tump. I go vid da guy, make my heart go tump tump."

Glen is looking at her as she smiles.

"Like my Billy," she says. "Already like dat."

Glen doesn't know what to say or do.

"Feel dis heart," she says, moving to press her breast to his face, guiding him with her hands. "Hear dat?"

He lifts his eyes to return her gaze.

She unbuttons her blouse and pulls it from her skirt. Her breasts bulge out of a thick pinkish brassiere. "Potty der," she says with a nod to the side. She unhooks the brassiere and lets them fall, two footballs with pork-colored nipples. "Ain't bin vid no guy in a long time," she says. "Come on, off dem clothes, see vaht you got der. Come, see everysing now."

She continues undressing, seems to interpret his inaction as an interest in her performance. "Ain't so bad, pretty big here, guys like dat," she adds, lifting the two footballs once again.

Glen doesn't dislike her, likes the sweetness in her, but everything is wrong and something is knotting in him. "I can't," he says at last.

"Was ist—?"

"I can't, I love somebody," he says. Saying this makes him feel foolish but also makes his eyes film over and he feels he may neither wipe them nor look away.

"I love Hedy," he says, to keep from going to pieces.

Marta looks confused and lowers her breasts. They gaze at each other. "You crazy guy, vaht you say?"

"I just have to go," he whispers.

"You luff dis Hedy? Dat's okay, vee just having fun, dat's all."

"I have this stuff," he says. "I'm sorry."

"Such a boy. Luff dis Hedy, is okay have fun vizz me, is okay."

As he gets to his feet, she raises an arm to cover her breasts. He places his bag on the bed and takes out the things he brought. Concealing the gesture, he slides two twenty-DM bills under the cigarettes.

"No, no money. Don't gotta do dat." She moves to him, embraces his arm. "You kinda crazy over dat girlfriend."

He moves his shoulders to say he can't explain, and returns outdoors, back under the overcast sky. Reaching the road, he walks into the afternoon, welcoming the distance before him.

Thatcher is ousted from the army. Word is out like news of death and has soldiers clustered talking. Thatcher and a bus full of alcoholics have been shipped out. Most everyone has something to say, rumors and reports they've heard, jokes and theories to offer.

Thatcher is gone, and so is Mess Sergeant Roosevelt. Sergeants, old corporals, PFCs from around the battalion; stories fly about how they were called in at 0800, were informed in groups, were given two hours to pack gear, cleared personnel as a group in another two hours, were on an army bus bound for Rhein/Main at 1400. Destination: McGuire Air Force Base, New Jersey, to be followed by flights to home districts for forced separation. The reason, hinted at by the company commander at the 1300 formation: low IQ scores. The reason, everybody knows: alcohol. "A couple were illiterate lifers," younger soldiers keep saying, "but every last one was a certified drunk."

"Whatever Thatcher was," someone says, "he wasn't illiterate. Was a booze hound, no doubt about it, but he's a smart sonofabitch. At least he could be."

Glen is moving to leave the Orderly Room when Corporal Latourette, behind the counter, indicates a telephone receiver held to his shirt.

Under the counter, stepping to the desk and turning his back to the crowd, Glen takes up the receiver. Far away, through a world of static, Hedy says, "Glen, it is you?"

"Yes," he calls into the mouthpiece. "Yes, it's me. Where are you?"

"I've reached you at last. Has something been wrong? I'm in London, but returning now. You are okay? Nothing is wrong?"

"No, no, just me. I'm okay. I've missed you a lot."

"I've been worried, unable to reach you."

"I'm in a new company now. I'll write and explain."

"There is something to explain, darling? What is it?"

"There has, well, no, everything's okay. I've been dumb, not to write more than I have. I'll write."

"You love me still? May you tell me this?"

"Yes, I do. Yes. Always."

"I've missed you so. You know, in the beginning, so much is distracting. I've been so afraid you have found someone else. You haven't found someone else?"

"No," Glen says. "No. All I do is miss you. All the time. I'll try to explain."

"I'm happy to hear your voice. In four weeks I shall return to Baden-Baden, with Ilsedore. Divorce is to be granted. I shall be free. It will be spring, with flowers. I so wish to walk again in forest paths. May we have glasses of wine once more by Herr Günther? New flowers in the valley, doesn't it sound lovely?"

"It does, it's what I want."

"I shall write when I receive your letter, and in time shall relate my adventures among the English."

"Yes—"

"Until we meet, my dear one," she says.

"Yes, goodbye, till then."

Outside the building, crossing the quadrangle, Glen's eyes film over with happiness and confusion. "My dear one." He'll see her again. It's everything he knows. He's going to see her again.

7

GORBYMANIA
Summer 1988

22

"Is it irrevocable?" Paige wants to know.

"Is what irrevocable?"

Paige is so angry she swats a newspaper off the kitchen counter at him. "Your resignation! Is it irrevocable?"

Knowing he's never been in such trouble and deciding all at once to let it out, Glen says, "It's worse than that."

"What does that mean?"

"I had an affair," he says.

Silence. Paige studies him. "My God."

He says nothing.

"With who?"

Perversely, he says, "Whom."

"Jesus, don't tell me 'whom'!"

"It's not with anyone anymore."

"Who was it?"

"It was with a student, but it's over."

"A student?"

"An older student. Who's divorced. I love you, Paige, and I love our family. It happened, and I'm truly sorry. It's part of why I resigned. I messed up."

"I can't believe this. I knew you were capable of just about anything. . . . I cannot believe this."

"Please believe me when I say I'm sorry. I'll always be sorry. I had to tell you."

"Don't 'sorry' me. Who is this woman? Are you serious?"

"It doesn't matter who she is."

"Who is she?" Paige says.

"She came on to me," Glen says. "But I let myself get involved. Paige, I never meant to in my life. I don't mean to use it as an excuse, but losing my job messed me up more than I ever would have guessed."

"Involved? What does that mean exactly?"

"I had an affair! I got involved with her! It's over!"

"You went to bed with this woman?"

"Of course!"

"How long did this go on?"

"It went on—a few months."

"You went to bed with this woman for a few months?"

"That's what I said."

"Glen—my God! What is this woman's name?"

"Does it matter?"

"It matters!"

"I really don't want to say."

"What is her name?"

"Ecki."

"Ecki! Ecki what? What kind of name is that? Is that her first name or her last name?"

"Her first name. Ecki Reiff."

"Is that a German name?"

"Yes."

"Well, I'm not surprised. You are sick, you know that, you are *sick*!"

"I've never felt so awful, or so sorry."

"A German woman, of course. You make a fool of yourself. How old is this woman?"

"I think, twenty-eight. She's divorced. Has a seven-year-old son."

"Well, this is wonderful, Glen. You found yourself a young German pussy. How nice for you. A student in your class? A nice young German pussy from your class to fuck. How nice for you."

"I said I'm sorry. I don't know what else to say."

"When did this go on, exactly?"

"Three or four months, until a few days ago."

"You went to bed with her all that time?"

"Sometimes."

"Sometimes. Do they know at school about you diddling a little German pussy student from your class?"

When Glen doesn't reply, she says, *"Do they know?"*

"I don't think so."

"Maybe I should tell them. I imagine it's something they'd like to know."

"I'm sure they would."

"I cannot believe any of this. You quit your job and you have an affair with a student. . . . I wish I was surprised, but I'm not. I'm not surprised, Glen, you know, I am *not surprised!*"

"Paige—I didn't want any of this to happen."

"You quit your job without having something else."

"I had no choice, I was terminated. I had to quit."

"You had no choice."

"If I was going to have any self-respect, I had to."

"I see."

"It's how I saw it."

"Diddle a little German pussy and quit your job."

"I was fired."

"You know what you are, Glen? I've never wanted to say this. It's something my father told me when we first got together—if only I'd listened to him. You may be older than me, but you are an immature dreamer, that's what you are. You dream immature dreams, and you do immature things, because you are not grown-up enough, not manly enough, to do what has to be done in life. You are a husband, and a father. You put my father down because he's a businessman—well, my father has more manliness in his little *toe* than you have in that stupid thing between your legs. Do you *really* think you can say, 'Oh, I'm sorry,' and everything will be okay? Believe me, it isn't that easy."

"If I could have any of this not happen, I would. I could have lied, but I haven't. Paige, you have to forgive me. It's the worst thing I've ever done, and I *am* sorry."

Upon a pause, Paige says, "Saying it isn't enough. I don't know what is, or what to do right now, but saying you're sorry isn't enough. I do know that much. I'm going to bed, I have work to do tomorrow, and I want you to sleep down here."

Just like that, Paige goes upstairs. Glen wishes he could cry or shout but feels only dread and self-loathing. He takes a can of beer from the refrigerator and sits at the kitchen table. Maybe he is an immature dreamer, but he always thought it was his best trait. Calling him a fool would have been closer to the truth. That's his fear, at his age. Still—absurdly—he wishes they could have made up enough to sleep in the same bed.

He sips the beer and thinks about how little self-respect he's had in recent years. Now he has none whatsoever. Paige isn't going to forgive him, he thinks. He's given her what she may have dreamed of having, an opportunity to leave him behind, to go for a new life. And what about Alice?

Turning off the lights, he stands at a window in the dark living room and stares into the moonlit backyard. He can call up no forgiveness, least of all from himself. Paige is right: he's a grown-up with a wife and child who's been living on dreams.

There is a large cheap suitcase on the porch. Next to it is a cardboard box with an envelope marked "Glen" fixed on top with masking tape.

It's the end of the day and he's coming home from school. He's been full of regret and affection for Paige and his family all day. He wants to dedicate the rest of his life to making up for what he has done. Should he read the note? Its message is clearly: Go away. Should he go inside, throw the envelope away, and tell Paige he's not reading it? Should he tell her they're going to face the crisis as a family, are going to weather the storm, that he got them into this mess and he'll get them out and deserting ship is not allowed?

She needs to punish him, he thinks. She has to hurt him enough to even the score.

Where's Alice? Are they behind a window, watching him?

He pulls the envelope from the box and sits down on the porch. He sees the words "which car is yours . . ." and closes his eyes.

On his feet, stuffing the envelope into his pocket, he enters the house. "Paige," he calls, "I'm not going to read this. I can't. We're going to work this out."

No one is on the first floor and he heads upstairs, thinking to speak to her about the destructiveness of vengeance. But the house is silent and he realizes it is empty. In Alice's bathroom he pauses and experiences a heart-sinking sensation. Where's my little girl? he wonders. Don't take her away.

Downstairs, he looks through the kitchen window to check if the car is in the driveway. Inside the envelope he finds two pieces of paper, one of them a half-sheet in Alice's handwriting, which he forces himself to read:

Daddy,

It is mean to go with that woman and quit your job. Its a yellow belly.

Alice

He's either going to break down or break the furniture. Why do this to Alice? he hears himself asking Paige, as his eyes blur. I thought better of you than that. He scans Paige's letter:

... go ahead and take ... arrangements to borrow my mother's ... live by yourself ... explain to Alice ... should be aware that ...

He wads it up and whips it to the floor. "Cunt sonofabitch! Rot in hell, goddamn you!"

If Paige were here he doesn't know what he'd do. As it is, his anger recedes. Well, she's nailed him, he thinks. He had not thought she would use Alice, but she has, and she's nailed him.

Carrying box and suitcase to the car, fishing keys from his pocket, he slides in behind the wheel and tries to sort out what to do. To think that when he entered the house just minutes ago he was of a mind to take possession of Paige, physically and fondly, and now the thought of her repulses him.

Dear God, what a mess, he thinks with his forehead near the steering wheel.

Backing out, he drives toward the supermarket, for the appeal of happy families along the supermarket aisles, but in the parking lot he shuts off the motor and sits in the car. Papers: he has a stack to read for his class tomorrow. In his next thought he knows he couldn't put more than two phrases together.

Is this how it happens? Is he now separated and on his way to divorce? Paige is trying to recruit Alice, and it's clear she's recruited her family. How long has she regretted hooking up with an older man? How could she not have considered life with a younger man? Could anything have been more natural, have granted her better permission, than what he's done?

Little Alice. At least his record with her is unblemished. He's been a good father and knows that his love for her is pure. She won't forsake him, he thinks, not ever.

He drives to his office, the refuge soon to be taken away from him. Nor does it prove to be much of a refuge tonight—his ability to concentrate on reading student papers has the staying power of smoke on a windy day. He can force himself through no more than a couple of sentences before his thoughts give way to Paige, Alice, separation, his mother-in-law's Mercury, Alice, Ecki, losing tenure, alimony, Alice, Preston Littlejohn, Monica, Hedy, Paige, Alice. . . .

He rests his face in his hands. He made a life, and here it is just slipping away.

He rises, as if standing on his feet will steady his mind. He has to get through the night, has to be ready to meet classes tomorrow and hold on to teaching. Food. He hasn't eaten, but has no appetite. It's no time for booze either. His only chance is to rally some strength and begin—it feels beyond his capability—to work his way back.

Sleeping in one's office is verboten, but he imagines that if he leaves his desk light on he can get away with it for one night. To a security guard it will look as though he is only working late, taking a snooze. And no calls home and no driving by the house to see if they are there.

He spends the night not at his desk but in the front seat of his car. Nor does he sleep but dozes, changes positions, sits wadded behind the steering wheel, and at dawn, balled up on the seat and moments after he's heard five bells toll the hour, sees two hands place a ticket under his windshield wiper. Campus police. He doesn't know if he's been seen and doesn't care.

Ten minutes later, he removes the ticket and drives home. This doesn't have to be, he's telling himself.

Paige is in the kitchen in her robe. Neither of them speaks. Upstairs he looks in on Alice sleeping, showers, and dresses in clean clothes. On his way out she's just waking and he says to her, "Sorry you got drawn into the problem Mommy and I are having, but please don't make any more judgments until you have a chance to think things out."

"I'm sorry I wrote," Alice says down her front.

Glen blinks his gritty eyes. "It's okay," he says, and hugs her head to his side.

"I'm mad as hell that you brought Alice into this," he says downstairs to the back of Paige's robe. "That didn't accomplish anything."

Turning around, she looks so awful his immediate reaction is to go to her and help her, but then she says, "Did you spend the night with your little German pussy?"

"That's what you're thinking?" Glen says. "You think I'd say what I said and be lying?"

"Did you, or not?"

"Oh, screw you," Glen says. "Yeah, I did, fucked the night away. It was great, she can really fuck."

All of a sudden he is filled with regret over everything. "I slept in the car in the parking lot at school, and I got a fifty-dollar ticket," he says. "Paige, this is so foolish—we don't have to try to destroy each other. We can start over and put this behind us."

"I'm filing for divorce," she says. "And I intend to retain full custody of Alice. My parents will be here later today and my father's going to help me with a lawyer."

"Sleep on it for a day," Glen says. "You're being vengeful and not real thoughtful. Call them up and sleep on it."

"I've slept on it for years," she says.

Glen feels hopeless and walks out, granting her the final word. He wondered where she was coming from—well, there it is. He knows her parents' knack for taking charge, and is rattled all over again. Their response is easy to imagine: shifting into gear, engaging a lawyer, helping their daughter start life over again. And—the thought stabs him—regarding his child as their own.

Calm down, he tells himself. Do what you just told Alice to do. Think things out.

But as the day goes on, thinking eludes him. He has to read student papers over and over to take in what they're saying, and as he's addressing his classes, in German or English, the computer of his mind keeps going blank. On one occasion he says, "I just lost it, can someone tell me where we were?"

Four o'clock. Four-fifteen. There have been no calls or messages, and sitting in his office, he has no impulse to go home, feels
too tired and resigned to either attack or defend himself. What
he'd really like is to lie on Alice's carpeted floor listening to her
read, to gain some peace of mind.

He recalls one night months ago, falling asleep listening to
Alice read *The Tale of Peter Rabbit*, and awakening to find her
asleep. He made his way to bed, curled up beside Paige's warmth,
and in the morning he fixed his tiny child, in her belted housecoat
and slippers, her favorite breakfast of hot oatmeal with raisins,
walnuts, and brown sugar. Where would he be a year from now?

Certain his in-laws are at the house, he walks across campus
in the cool spring air to refresh himself if he can. The library is
unpopulated at this hour. Clerks stare at books on desks and
counters, actors in a dinner-hour still life.

On the second floor, in bound periodicals, he settles into a
pastime he hasn't turned to in months: looking for Hedy. The
habit started when he was a factory worker taking classes; he
would sit with stacks of magazines offering stories and photographs of places she might be. Of course he's a dreamer. Paige's
father is right. The first collection of black-and-white photographs
in his first college-level textbook made him into a junkie who
wanted only more of the same.

Two cars with New Jersey plates, a Lincoln Town Car and a
Mercury Cougar, are parked in the driveway. The wagons have
circled. Should he slip into his VW and drive away, or confront
his adversaries?

He aches with tiredness; the most appealing option is to find
a cheap motel along the shore and have something to eat in an
out-of-season restaurant, get a night's rest to the tune of waves
breaking on the rocks. At the same time, it seems unmanly not
to face his in-laws, and Alice is there—needing him, even if
she doesn't know it—and he climbs the small porch, wondering
whether to knock at the door of his own house.

Making noise to be heard, he enters the living room. Paige
and her mother sit looking his way, while Paige's father stands
gazing out the room's picture window. "Already eat?" he says.

His question draws no response. "Alice upstairs?"

"She's reading," Paige says.

"Ah, a voice," Glen says. Passing behind the summit conference, he makes his way upstairs.

Alice lies on her bedroom floor, dispatched, he imagines, to allow things to proceed downstairs. He sits on her bed and she turns to look up at him. "Hi."

"Hi."

"Are you still mad at me?"

She shakes her head no.

"If there's one person I couldn't stand to have mad at me, it's you."

"You going away?" Alice says.

"Well, not really. I may stay at a motel for a while, until Mommy and I settle our differences—we're having a serious fight, you see—but don't think for a second, no matter what anyone says, that I'll ever go away from you. Okay?"

She seems to nod.

"May I talk to you?" Paige says in Alice's doorway.

"Sure," Glen says, bending down to kiss Alice's frizzy hair. "Talk to you later," he says. "Don't forget what I said."

He follows Paige into their bedroom and she closes the door behind them. He waits for her to speak. She intertwines her fingers under her breasts, looking down. "My mother's on your side, if that interests you," she says at last.

"Really? I guess that means your father isn't."

"They both think you're horrible for what you've done. Mother thinks I should let it pass, though, and try to patch things up."

"Is that disrespectful to you or to me? What about your father?"

"He knows you'll do it again."

"Once a philanderer, always a philanderer."

"Please don't act smart—it just isn't the time."

"Well, I resent this whole routine. I went to you, out of love, and you try to turn my own daughter against me. That's right up there with philandering. Now you call in your parents as if—"

"Glen, I want a divorce. As quickly as possible. I'd like you to leave, and I don't want a trial separation or anything like that. I know I'm going to get the job at the bank, and I want a new life for myself. My father knew what he was talking about in the beginning, and I should've listened to him. What I'd like you to do—stay wherever you want, I don't care, stay with your little

German girlfriend, it's okay with me. I'd be just as happy if I never saw you again, although I know we'll have to work things out with Alice. Which we will, although I fully intend to keep custody. The marriage is over, Glen. I'd like you to please leave— get yourself a lawyer who can discuss these matters with my lawyer. Take the VW, it's yours. My mother's leaving her car for me to use in the meantime."

"This is what you want? You're going this far?"

"I don't want to talk about it. Get yourself a lawyer. Go see your little girlfriend. Please, just go."

"You've thought about this?" Glen manages to say.

"Of course. Now will you please go! Please!"

"I can't believe you've thought about this."

"Believe me, I've been thinking about it for a long time."

"This is just payback, you know, it's vengeance."

"Don't get off on vengeance," she says through tears. "I won't—I cannot live with you—and either you go or I go. I'll take Alice with me and I'll have my lawyer take you for everything you'll ever be worth. Believe me, I know what I'm doing."

Glen stands there. "You're sure," he tries to say, raising a hand to keep her from cutting him off.

"Glen, please just go, my God."

He walks out in a strange calm, and looks into Alice's room. "I'll talk to you tomorrow," he says. "I'll give you a call. Or you give me a call at my office."

Downstairs, not knowing the protocol of leaving one's house under such circumstances—do you say good night?—he bypasses his in-laws. In the driveway, in a daze, he thinks, You've been blindsided. Starting the car, he follows its headlights into the confusion of early darkness. Several blocks later, he pulls up to the curb and turns off the motor. He cannot call up a rational way to proceed.

In half an hour, he's rolling down Ocean Boulevard past motels, clam huts, and mom-and-pop takeout stores. Most of the eating places are closed for the off-season, while green neon VACANCY signs glow in front of many motels. He can't afford life in a motel, but has no choice right now. He has to settle in somewhere and pull himself together.

Feeling like an actor in an old TV series, he checks into a motel and carries in the suitcase and box. No space has ever seemed so drab; the TV is bolted and chained to the wall next to the bed, and the radiator under the drapes is making an angry hissing sound. He cannot possibly sleep—against growing claustrophobia, he has to get back into the air.

Thinking that he ought to be hungry, he drives down the highway to a restaurant-bar the size of a three-car garage. He's the only person there except for a woman and two men having drinks.

He sits at the bar and stares over his beer. The woman walks to a pay phone next to him, and tells a child, Lisa, that she's been caught in traffic and will be home in about an hour. "Tell Mindy to do what I said!" the woman suddenly snaps into the phone. "You tell her I said to get in that goddamn bed right now!"

Back at her table, the woman says she has time for one more. Glen wants to shake her. Lisa. It's Alice's middle name. You filthy, lying sonofabitch, Glen wants to say to the woman for telling her children she was caught in traffic. What he'd like to do is step across the room and throw the table and the woman and her friends through the window. And he might move to do so but for the surfacing again of his own lies and violations.

23

Midafternoon, in his office and unable to work, he calls Paige. "I'm sorry to bother you," he says. "I'm having a hard time, and I'm going to walk over and see Alice. I wanted you to know what I was doing."

"I'd rather you didn't go to her school," Paige says. "I think we should keep her out of this."

"Wait, Paige—I have no intention, believe me, of drawing her into anything. You should talk."

"I don't want you barging in on her at school and disrupting her. I don't want you doing that!"

"Well, I'm sorry I called. I'm only going—because she's my daughter, that's all. Because I want to. I thought I'd tell you so you wouldn't think I was sneaking around."

"I'd advise you to talk to your attorney before you do anything like that."

"Anything like what?"

There is no reply.

"I didn't call to ask permission."

"Talk to your attorney," Paige says.

"Jesus Christ, I don't have an attorney, what in the hell are you talking about?"

"Get one."

"I can't believe this is you," he says. "I'm having a hard time, and I'm going to go see my daughter, so screw you."

"Get an attorney," Paige says, and hangs up.

Alice is pleased to see him, which helps him a little. To Mrs. Ouellette, standing to the side, he says, "Came to see my daughter for a five-minute conference—outside."

Outdoors, he sits on the pine-needle floor under a large tree; Alice stands beside him and he wraps his arm around the backs of her legs. "I just needed to see you," he says. "If you ever just need to see somebody, you'll know what I mean."

"What's divorce?"

He laughs a little. "Well . . . I promised Mommy I wouldn't draw you into this, but I'll tell you what the word means. 'Divorce' is when people who are married decide not to be married to each other anymore. Husband and wife. Like Mommy and Daddy. Maybe we'll end up getting divorced, I don't know. At the same time, there are some people who never get divorced. Like you and me. Father and daughter. Mother and daughter, too. I hope we all get back together, but we'll still do okay if we don't. We'll have to."

She offers no response and he says, "It's nothing for you to worry about. Mommy and Daddy are having a giant-sized fight, but it doesn't mean either of us loves you any less. Probably more. It's why I came to see you. To say I love you. I came for me, too."

The restraining order is delivered over the phone. The call comes from Sheriff's Deputy Burrows, who explains the procedure and asks if Glen will stop by the County Courthouse to sign for the document. "If you're free to stop by," the deputy says. "You're willing to be cooperative?"

"I guess so," Glen says. "What's this order mean?"

"It's all spelled out," the deputy says. "It's fairly standard in divorce cases."

"Has to do with my seeing my daughter."

"I imagine so, sir. Not my business to interpret the details. My job is to see that you receive and sign for it. I can deliver it to you, as sheriff's deputy. But if you're going to be in the vicinity, and if you're going to be cooperative, you could stop by here and sign for it. So I'm asking, sir, if you're willing to be cooperative? It's going to be served in any case."

"Is there some deadline?"

"We'd like you in receipt within twenty-four hours. No later, say, than this time tomorrow. It'd be fine all around, sir, if you did it today."

"I'll stop by today," Glen says.

He knows that restraining orders restrict visiting and freeze joint accounts. As if there were anything in their account to be frozen. Another broadside in the ongoing offensive.

He walks to the payroll office to cancel direct deposit to their joint checking account. The request sends a sour sensation through him. In the credit union, he takes another step he doesn't want to take: application for a loan of two thousand dollars, to be deducted from his pay in increments.

Giving money they don't have to lawyers—she'll be supported by her parents, he'll have to take out a loan—seems such a waste that he goes back to his office to call Paige again, wanting to persuade her that they can handle things differently. Her father answers and is almost pleasant. "The women have gone shopping," he says.

"Shopping?"

"Well, we're helping Paige with some new things, if she's going to take this job."

"She got the job? I didn't know."

"I believe she has the job, yes."

"I've been notified of a restraining order," Glen says. "It means lawyers will have to be hired, which seems like a waste of money to me. We've been living on the edge anyway, so I don't know where the money will come from. Ed, can you persuade Paige, if you're helping her—isn't there a less wasteful way to do this? I don't think it should be done at all, although I admit that things need to be worked out between Paige and me. I'll have to borrow and job prospects at my age aren't the best, as you may have heard."

After a pause Ed says, "I'd have to say, at this point, my own advice to Paige will be to be represented by counsel. Makes things simpler in the long run."

Glen, taken by surprise, says, "Well, please pass on my request. Tell her I'd like—"

"You'll see, I believe," his father-in-law says, "that the restraining order instructs you to direct any such request to her attorney. She's being represented . . . let me see how the name is spelled. Carstairs, just as it sounds. He's local. You'll find his name in the phone book."

Glen absorbs the blows, realizes his father-in-law is enjoying himself.

"You're a good man, Ed," Glen says. He hangs up.

What a reactionary prick. He gave his in-laws an opening and they're letting him have it. Good Christian people.

Weakly, he flips through his telephone book to the heading "LAWYERS." He traces the columns and finds "Carstairs Law Offices" under "DIVORCE LAW." Divorce/Child Custody/Alimony.

Glen has no heart for this. The telephone rings; it's the credit union telling him his loan application has been denied. "Payroll says you're on a terminal contract," the man says.

Glen can't help laughing. "Four months left," he says. "I agreed to repayment by payroll—"

"I'm sorry, sir, I don't make the policy. Loans are—"

"It's okay," Glen says. "You don't have to explain."

Receiver replaced, he doesn't know what to do. The rules were made by the likes of Paige's father, and he's being put in his place. How will he not lose his daughter to the rules and forces of such people?

One night as a teenager Glen was sucker-punched on a porch. There were two group of teenagers, his and theirs, on the porch of a house where they had been drawn by girls, a party, some kind of action.

The porch was dark and all at once an unseen blow smashed his mouth and knocked him down. He got to his feet, tried to say, "What was that?" and got knocked down again. He took more blows and was knocked down again. Pushing up a fourth or fifth time, disoriented, whipped from out of the shadows, he was sent flying into the wall and the railing. He heard snickering, and a voice saying, "I think he's hurt," and the gang walking away. All his life he would remember their voices and their laughter as he leaned bleeding in the dark and their cars started and roared away.

In a dirty gas-station bathroom he washed blood from his face and gums. His friends told him they were afraid to help; the others were bigger and widely known. And the shame is in him again, he

thinks, as if it will never go entirely away. All that's missing are
torn flesh inside his mouth and slitted, plum-colored eyes.

Monica Beniquez stops by. His office door is half-open when she
asks if he has a minute, and he says, "Always have minutes for
you, Monica."

The semester has ended and it feels like summer. Grades
turned in just hours before, Glen is in his morning mode, the time
of the day when he is least despairing. He's moved from the motel
to a one-bedroom apartment in Kittery Point for the summer, and
is turning his attention to a job search.

Monica's presence on the third floor is rare and he smiles at
her. "Won't take long," she says, closing his door and moving to
the conference chair. "Unfinished business, really, some things I've
been wanting to say."

"Sorry I can't offer you coffee," Glen says. "Could be like old
times, when we had occasion to gab a little."

"Oh, Glen. One thing I do want to say is how badly I feel
about all of this."

"Well, nice of you, but . . . life goes on."

"You're checking help wanted ads? May I offer some advice?"

"I'd love some advice. As for these ads, well, I'm just taking
a look. Where do you begin, at my age? I thought I'd look and
see if I could get a feel for what the world's all about these days."

"You're thinking of leaving teaching?"

"Well, teaching seems to be leaving me. It's the one thing I
guess I've learned how to do. But as you know, no one wants to
hire old dogs like me. Not in teaching."

"You aren't that old, Glen. Don't feel sorry for yourself."

"The unfortunate truth is that I'm being realistic. I don't *feel*
old, for sure, but tell it to the rest of the world."

"It is ironic," Monica says. "In some societies, in other times
. . . well, mature men are taking a beating these days, and it's too
bad. In any case, for teaching positions: the *Chronicle* and *MLA
Job List* are the best. I'm sure you know that, but anything you'll
find in a newspaper you'll find in one of those. Feel free to avail
yourself of the department's copies, by the way."

"Thanks."

"I'll have Mary make copies of some good cover letters, vitae,
supporting letters, what makes a good package from the point of

view of a chair. If you like, I'd be glad to provide a letter myself. Have you thought, by the way, of trying the prep schools?"

"Well . . ."

"They emphasize teaching, and they'd be thrilled to land someone with your credentials and classroom skills."

"Truth is, Monica, sorry to say, I may be getting divorced, and divorced men apparently aren't very acceptable at prep schools. The group no one lobbies for—Jesus, I guess I am feeling sorry for myself."

"I'd try them anyway if I were you. They like Ph.D.'s and your teaching evaluations will speak for themselves—they're among the best in the college. And don't we all feel sorry for ourselves sometimes?"

"You're right, of course. And thanks for the offer to write. A letter from you would be a great help."

"The best possibilities at the college level are replacement positions. People going on leave, that kind of thing. People die. Problem is, these positions don't become available until the last minute and they're usually over in a year. You watch, though, in late August, there'll be ads for immediate, one-year replacements. Keep an eye out for those. They're better than nothing, and some of them do turn into regular appointments a year or so later."

"I'll do that. I appreciate your help, and I'm still sorry for acting resentful a while back."

"Apology accepted," Monica says, getting to her feet.

Glen's emotions are near the surface, and at the door, as Monica hesitates, he feels like they're about to embrace. "Glen, I need to ask," she says. "When will you be vacating your office and turning in your keys?"

He needs a moment. "My keys," he says.

"It's not a pleasant part of the job, I'm afraid."

He has to check his voice against cracking. "Monica, excuse me, I'm something of an emotional wreck these days." Hand visoring his eyes, he works to retain composure. "I'll get them to you, I'll let you know," he says.

"Glen, I'm sorry."

"Took me by surprise," he says. "Don't tell anyone, but I've loved my little office. It's going to be hard to leave."

"I'm so sorry."

"No problem, it's not your fault."

"You feel free to make use of any of the department's facilities, copying, stationery, anything ... postage."

"I don't mean to go to pieces here. I'll be fine. I'm sorry to embarrass you. I hope to be out, well, I don't have anything yet, but as soon as possible. Probably mid-August. I assumed I was allowed to use my office through the end of my contract."

"Of course, don't worry about it. We'll make do."

"Have you found someone to take my place? Is it inappropriate to ask?"

"We have a replacement. A young Ph.D. from Chicago. Next year we'll conduct a search, though she's coming with the under-standing that she'll be a candidate. And no, it's not inappropriate. We're friends, Glen; I hope we always will be."

"We will," he says.

"Send me a card from wherever one of these days," she says. "I know you'll land on your feet."

He nods.

"I mean it.... I'll get Mary to work on those things right away."

Glen nods and turns back, angry and determined not to lose composure again.

Moments later Monica taps his door, holding a pasted-together manuscript. "I have this East German publication, I guess that's what it is. I don't know if you're interested, if you're still doing translations."

"I have been," he manages to say.

"This is the quality of publication coming out of East Germany. I'm told—who knows if these things are true—I'm told this is an underground item, flies in the face of government policy, and so on; what doesn't in East Germany? It's by ..." She holds it up and reads, " 'Elizabeth Speyer-Weiss, working in public policy and economics, at Dresden.' If you're of a mind to do something on spec. It came from a Manchester businessman who visited Europe on one of those fact-finding things. It's yours in any case, if you want it. No one else around here—oh, Glen, I'm so sorry about all of this."

She pauses and they look at each other. "I'll have a look," he says. "I don't know about translating anything that sizable on spec, but thanks, Monica."

He stands there a moment before glancing at the homemade cover. The title is *Sandkörner,* which translates as "Grains of Sand." He fans the pages—all text, no illustrations—and places it on his desk as he turns back to the *Boston Globe,* to force himself to check the ads, to force himself to hang on.

Later, he dials attorneys and the minimum the first two will accept is a five-hundred-dollar retainer. The amount would wipe him out and he keeps looking. There are fourteen pages of listings. A sickness rises in him as he turns the pages, and all at once he decides not to do it. What can they take from him? His house, furnishings, pension? He'll lose what little he has anyway, so why waste the money and energy? There's only one thing he needs to keep hold of, and he doesn't believe, really, that Paige would try to exclude him in regard to Alice. Paige may be out to punish him, and may be succeeding, but he doesn't believe she'd twist the knife to that degree. In any case, it's a loss he wouldn't allow.

That afternoon his hopes rise some. Poring through half a dozen issues of *Chronicle* in his office, he finds five listings for assistant and associate professors of German. He embarks on a campaign: to create a new vita, eliminating references to his age, and compose a cover letter adjustable to imply an interest in living in upstate New York, northeastern Pennsylvania, southern Ohio, the Florida Panhandle, or western Massachusetts.

He works into the evening. He has no wish to return to the small apartment he's subletting, and no appetite. At half past eight, with the application materials ready, he sits back to take stock. At the moment, he thinks, Alice must be on her way to sleep, unread to, since Paige has never had much patience for reading. Paige has to be pleased with herself, he thinks. Who can blame her for seizing the chance to go it on her own. Independence and a new life. Romantic encounters over NOW accounts and CDs, mortgages and credit lines.

A mild spring night. The stack of letters ready to go gives him some buoyancy as he walks over the bridge into town to find a bite to eat. He'll sit somewhere and see if he can drum up ideas or images, the merest inroads into a new life. An adventurous thought takes him at the end of his meal, when the waitress offers coffee. "I guess I will, what's to lose," he says. "Coffee to go, large coffee."

"Decaf?"

"The real stuff," he says.

Back at his office, he turns on his computer and opens *Sand-körner* to page one. He takes a daring sip. He hasn't used coffee at night since he was finishing his dissertation. Maybe caffeine will be the drug to save him—caffeine and ideas. The life of a graduate student. Sleep only when it will wait no longer, and on waking, score another hit and keep going.

Within minutes of translating the book's opening paragraphs he laughs. While its subject is privatization, the book also treats the larger economic issues of Eastern Europe; it is, at least in its foreword, a work of outrageous prophecy. The author writes in compound sentences; Glen translates them whole, then breaks them down, striving as always to make them understandable to Alice. The author's message is simple. This will happen, she asserts, which will trigger this, which will trigger that, and Glen laughs as he translates:

> Thus, before the year 1989 concluded is, Mikhail Sergeyevich Gorbachev at home and abroad expectation defying is, through swatting as with the stick behind a mule the government of Poland, and to the consternation of the Politburo and Western leaders, also visiting Warsaw in person for the singular purpose of severing Soviet control as in the West ribbons are by heads of state given with scissors the triumphant *snip!*

The idea of Gorbachev severing Poland from Soviet control is barely plausible, and Glen is amused by the impassioned sentence building to the verb *"schnippen!"* Another audacious sentence likewise amuses him:

> Whereupon, ergo, the unimaginable following is, the grains of sand *two!* numbering are, as Poland a non-Communist government joyously into power, from its discarded collectibles, placing is!

His letters of application are answered without so much as a nibble. He speaks to Alice on the phone, takes her to lunch, and returns most evenings to his office to work. But exhaustion insinuates itself. During the night, when he's able to doze, he suffers in dreams as if he were awake.

Sunday is Graduation Day. Exams and grades are forgotten; all the students except seniors have left town, replaced by families with cameras, graduates in caps and gowns, and faculty in their regalia. The college band is tuning up somewhere within hearing, and the awarding of degrees and honors, farewell parties and promises, is about to define the day.

Glen has to admit that he loves the pomp and circumstance and the launching of bright-eyed young people into the world. Although he's invited, he has to accept that attending would be indecorous and, for him, certainly painful.

He arranges to pick up Alice on Sunday rather than the usual Saturday. Paige has no objection to the change; she seems to know that Sunday is Graduation Day. When Glen toots his horn, she calls from the door, "She's not quite ready, want to come in and wait?"

Glen isn't certain what he wants to do as he approaches the house. The Cougar is the only car in the driveway—mission accomplished, Paige's parents have returned to Seekonk. Maybe Paige is ready to effect a reconciliation.

The house presents its familiar smells. Paige goes back upstairs, where Alice is dressing. How many weeks have passed since he was in these rooms? He tries to count, as a way to contain his emotions. The kitchen desk is piled with bills and letters, and he resists an impulse to sort them. When he hears footsteps his eyes begin filming over and he looks away.

A hand touches his side in a way that says it's Alice, and he lifts her from the floor and holds her in his arms. "Think I swallowed something," he says. Seeing Paige over her shoulder, he tries to smile.

"What's the matter?" Paige says.

Well, she isn't made up for reconciliation in that floor-length purple robe. "Oh, it's Graduation Day," he says, as if it were the only reason. "I guess I'm feeling dealt out."

"I thought you didn't care about that stuff," Paige says. "If you feel that way, why don't you go?"

He looks at her, trying to steel himself.

"Glen, my gosh," she says.

"I'm sorry, I'll get a hold of myself here."

"You've loved being a professor, haven't you."

"I'm fine," he says. "I'm fine—I'll have Alice back at four."

Alice still in his arms, he wonders if Paige might feel left behind and if he should invite her along. They could drive to Lake Winnipesaukee, the three of them, or to Ogunquit for a seafood dinner overlooking the water. "You want to come along?" he says.

"Oh, I have some plans."

"Ah. How's the job—you like working?"

"A lot, as a matter of fact. Alice, don't forget, when you get back you *have* to get that homework done."

Glen carries Alice out into the summer air. "You have homework, the last week of nursery school?" he says.

"Kind of," Alice says.

"Mrs. Ouellette calls it homework?"

Alice nods.

"What kind of homework?"

"What we learned all year."

"Why didn't you do it yesterday?"

"Mommy didn't make me."

"You just *do* homework, you know. And it's not something you have to be made to do. It's the first thing you do, always, because it lets you feel free, allows you to be creative."

"Yes, Daddy."

In the car he says, "Okay, wise guy, we'll do this homework right now, together."

"Okay," Alice announces.

She is so agreeable she has him smiling. "We'll go to my office and do homework, because putting homework off isn't real smart," he says. "First things first. When'd you become such a wise guy anyway?"

He tries to keep an eye on her as he drives. "Put something off, what you do is worry about it. Big waste of energy." Not looking, he offers a palm to slap, and she slaps hard and laughs.

"Whatever you do is important to me," he says. "Polishing shoes, homework, I don't care, I like to know everything you do."

It's old banter and Glen offers a palm again, but Alice doesn't slap it this time. Out of the corner of his eye he sees her unbuckle her seat belt and move to his side to hug him as he's driving. She's the one crying now and he rolls to the curb and turns to hold her. "Oh, sweetheart, I miss you so much," he says. "All I do is miss you. I don't know what the hell is happening in this world."

Three replacement positions appear in *The Chronicle of Higher Education* in early July, as Monica said, and Glen sends packets to each. His job campaign is nearing the phase when he will have to look for almost anything—clerking in a bookstore, substitute teaching. He also begins reading ads for rooms and apartments, which he had put off on the chance that come August, he might be moving to Amherst or the Adirondacks.

Then two of his self-addressed envelopes show up in one day's mail, and the days slip by without any word from the third. The small college in western Mass. is the one he most hoped for and fantasized over at night: woodsy, hilly country, close enough for weekend drives to see Alice and to have her visit. Autumn in the Berkshires and blueberry pancakes with Alice in a Main Street diner on a frosty Sunday morning in November. Pleasant weekend drives to the coast and back. Job security. A new life.

Working into another night on "Grains of Sand," he turns off his computer and tries to face his options. Don't call the small college. Looking anxious would be the worst thing. Hope more openings come along, but don't sink to telephoning lost causes.

The summer issues of *Chronicle* offer nothing new. Apparently no old professors have knocked off just yet. It's time to turn from teaching and look for any kind of job. And it is then he makes the call to western Mass. He places the call twice. The first time he reaches an operator but gets disconnected. Then he gets through to a Department of Languages staff assistant, explains his reason for calling, and the woman says, oh, that position *was* advertised but before it could be filled a college-wide austerity plan went into effect. "I'll be glad to return your—"

"No rush, I just wanted to check," Glen says.

He makes one last call—feeling vague shame—to the dean at a famous prep school near Boston. "I'll tell you something," the man says. "We're staying clear of Ph.D.'s these days. They're generally overeducated for what we need and our experience keeps proving that where they really want to be is in a university system, not coaching lacrosse and receiving parents on Sunday afternoons.

There's a glut of Ph.D.'s on the market, at least in this neck of the woods. The cab I caught from Logan—"

"Thanks," Glen says. "Thanks, someone's at my door."

For a moment he sits perfectly still. Well, go out like a man, he tells himself.

He goes down to the basement of the administration building, looking for boxes. Passing Monica's office, he says to her assistant, "I'll be vacating my office this afternoon. I'll drop my keys off by the end of the day."

He carries the boxes upstairs, passing through hallways empty on a late summer day.

24

He works at a kitchen table in the sublet, four miles away in Kittery Point. He studies help wanted ads, jots entries on a pad he keeps by the phone.

His computer and printer rest on top of the bedroom dresser. Standing, he taps out new letters and tells himself he'll return to the translation project within a week or two. He's due out in three weeks. He doesn't know where he'll go; a job will dictate the move. His fallback plan is to rent a sleeping room for a month. The seaside motels, still in season, are out of the question; the tacky units which absorb the rock-and-roll rumble of Route 1-A are more than he can afford. He's limited to old rooming houses in town.

"Smiling Voices Needed," "Counter Person," "Automotive Sales Help," "Part-Time Janitorial," "T-Shirt Printer," "Telemarketing Coordinator," "Assemblers," "Medical Billing Clerk." Something is wrong on every call. Experience mandatory, ad should never have been run, position no longer available, once "This is a job for a young guy can sustain heavy lifting all day," and "Hey, fella, this is woman's work, we're lookin' for a young woman."

Told that an ad for "Assemblers" meant "building a list," he experiences undeniable relief. He knows in his bones the noise and smells, the tedium and clock-watching, ignorance and meanness of such jobs, knows he could not go back to them.

The closest he comes to anything—a full-time janitorial position at a high school in Portland—is turned down with genuine
laughter when he admits over the phone that his previous employment with the university, no, was not as a custodian but as a
professor. Pushing a broom, emptying wastebaskets, waxing floors
during the night: the calm, measurable nature of the tasks appeals
to him as well as the thought that he could also continue his
translation work during the day. Though he argues he would do
a first-rate job, the man keeps laughing, and says finally, "Naw,
sorry, sir, it's just—you wouldn't be happy here, we're looking
for somebody who really needs a job, you know."

"I do need a job," Glen says. "I don't have a job."

"Listen, I put a college professor on the floor, superintendent'll
ask to have my head examined. Wish you luck, though."

Hanging up, Glen holds against a wave of panic and dizziness.
He stands up and presses his hand against the kitchen wall. The
telephone rings. He breathes in and out; the telephone rings again
and he makes no move to deal with it, tries to bring his breathing
back to normal. By the time he is able to grab the phone, thinking
it could be the call he's been waiting for, the ringing has stopped.

Sometime later he looks up. It's okay, he tells himself. Just get
up. Take a walk. Something will come up.

He walks in the evening air, resisting the urge to drive by the
house in the hopes of glimpsing Alice in the backyard or through
a window. Knowing he looks suspect, he sits against a tree in a
town park. For the first time all day and week he feels a touch
of peace. The sky is clear and cars pass; life is being lived all
around. The temperature must be eighty. He tries to consider
those who have it worse—bad health, tragic losses—and sits until
darkness lowers and mosquitoes whine around his ears. Go try
again, he tells himself. It's all you can do.

He's granted an interview with a small company in York that
manufactures propeller windmills, a product with which he feels
rapport. The interview goes well and in a follow-up call he's
invited—one of three, he's told—to be interviewed by Mr. Westphal, designer of the windmill and owner of the company. The job
involves travel, sales, public speaking, modest engineering skills, a
sense of marketing, and, what appeals to Glen, a high degree of
independence. A man on the road, spreading word of the energy

to be harnessed from currents of sea and air. Maybe this is how it works. You try and try again, and something finally comes along. Perseverance, as he's told many students. Endurance and the quality of the work itself are the keys to hiking trails in the Alps and looking back on a record of achievement.

His interview is last, which seems a good sign, and Glen likes Mr. Westphal immediately. Unlike most people with whom he's discussed jobs, this man is older, by about a decade. A self-educated engineer, his slight smile is genuine and Glen wonders if his charm is a gift or something he's gained through work. Near the end of their half-hour talk, though, Mr. Westphal says, "Two things, one less serious than the other. You'd be around here correcting our grammar—who needs that when we're trying to market wind power—and as soon as something came along you really wanted, you'd be outta here."

Glen doesn't know what to say.

"Tell me the truth," the man says. "Teaching job came your way, you'd at least *want* to make a move, wouldn't you?"

"I need a job, in the worst way," Glen says. "Believe me, I'd do a good job for you, though I don't know the future and I wouldn't lie to you."

"I feel for you," the man says. "You're the best qualified of the bunch, no doubt about it, and to be honest, I think you'd do a heck of a job. I like people who haven't been handed life on a silver platter. I'm joking about the grammar, by the way, 'cause I don't give a rat's ass about grammar. Thing is, a man's gotta do what he loves, and a job like this ain't where you really wanna hang your hat. What you wanted came along, we'd be into training somebody all over again. That's the way it is. So I'm gonna have to say no. I'm sorry. If you want my advice, which is free: Stick with what makes you happy, and if you don't really love it, don't get married to it."

Over a stack of newspapers it comes home to Glen that he has nothing pending. No lines, no leads. His age, education, and limited experience are all handicaps he seems unlikely to overcome. He feels the onset not of a panic attack but of a numb loss of hope. Trying another tactic, to kill time, he makes a list from the yellow pages and calls bookstores, libraries, newspapers, every possible employer who to some degree is in the business of words.

Some say they aren't hiring, and a few take his name while saying they have nothing at the moment. Twice he's told the manager will return his call when he/she returns that afternoon.

The calls, to be sure, do not come. When the telephone does ring in the evening he hurries to answer it, thinking of a job reply or Alice. Instead it's another problem. The graduate student from whom he's subletting is returning a week earlier than planned and is wondering if there's any chance Glen might be leaving earlier than expected. "Thought I'd check and see."

"No, though I wish I were," Glen says. "I'll be out the last day of August, like I said, but I can't leave before then."

"I thought of that," the student says. "What I'll do, I'll sleep on the couch and cut your rent in half for the last week."

"I have the place rented; those aren't the terms."

"Hey, man, I know that, okay. I don't have any choice either and I need a place to stay. Don't worry, we won't get in each other's way and it's only a week. You take the bedroom, I'll take the living room, and we can take turns at the kitchen and bathroom. Listen, I'll see you Saturday afternoon."

Glen is left holding the receiver as "Hey, man" sounds in his mind. This is what his life has come to; a grad student in hotel administration feels free to address him "Hey, man."

"Hey, man, how'd you like to kiss my ass?" Glen says to the silent space around him.

He stands staring at the floor. When the phone rings again a man calling himself "Professor Baumann" starts speaking well before Glen can follow.

"Professor Baumann?" Glen says, the graduate student still crowding his mind.

"Professor Beniquez has given to me your number," the man says. "Apologies for calling at such an hour. I hope it's not an inconvenience."

"It's okay, no problem—who is this again?"

"The question, Professor Cady—we are in a fix here. An emergency. Is there a possibility you may teach two courses, commencing in nine days, Thursday next? Our man, you see, has left us dangling. I tell you the truth, Dr. Cady, you may save our hides. Two courses on a part-time basis. One introductory, one sophomore. Sir, are you there? What do you say? May you bail us out of our sorry mess? Kindly say yes."

Glen takes a breath before he can speak. "I'll be there," he says with a rush passing through him.

"You will be here?" The man is laughing. "Just like that, you will be here! Say you are serious. I cannot believe it."

"You need me, I'll be there," Glen says.

"*Wunderbar, Herr Professor!* A man after my own heart. Have gun, will travel, yes, say it is so."

Glen cannot keep himself from smiling. "I've been looking," he says. "Haven't had much luck. I'll be there on the ninth, whatever time. I'll do the best job you can imagine."

"You know, Dr. Cady, this I certainly like. Will you—"

"You're located where?" Glen says. "I didn't understand where you're located."

Professor Baumann laughs outright. "If I am to say Alaska, what then?"

"Sorry," Glen says. "I don't mean—"

"Boston," the man says. "Wentworth School, University of Boston. No need to be sorry. We are a faculty of six in German language and literature—I should say seven, though our distinguished colleague, only in the second week of August, has decided to spend the year in the Greek Isles! But you are found. The faculty will be astonished; I'm acting on my own as chair. Doctor Beniquez has given you the highest recommendation and I'm pleased to make your acquaintance, albeit by telephone. Are you interested in pay, Dr. Cady, or will your enthusiasm lead you to teach for free?"

"Pay would help," Glen says.

"Twenty-eight hundred per course. For which I apologize. It's an exploitation of gifted persons, an embarrassment to our profession."

"Could you make it three thousand?"

"I could not. The dean would slam the door."

"Well, twenty-eight should keep me alive," Glen says.

"Again, I apologize. Now, will you confirm an address, please, and I shall send at once a packet explaining everything, including courses you shall teach. You will be here Thursday? Not to stretch my luck, but may I ask if there is a possibility you may visit Wednesday, so I can guide you through Human Resources?"

"I'll be there Wednesday and I'll meet classes on Thursday," Glen says. "I'll do a good job."

"I believe you will, Professor Cady, I believe you will."

Off the phone, Glen sits in the darkness filling the kitchen. He has something, at last. If only the wheels would stop spinning; if only he knew how to proceed. He makes a fist and closes his eyes. A break has finally come his way.

25

Weeks later he sees with visionary clarity that his only remaining possession is the quality of his work. He is lying awake before dawn in the new studio apartment in Newmarket, trying to consolidate himself. He decides to get up and make coffee. He'll come to terms with what he's seen, will write it down and live by it. The part-time teaching job—or maybe just the steady work—is cleansing his mind and he decides to recommit himself to teaching and translating the East German book. Alice, as always, is his secret guide. Clarity and craftsmanship are all he owns and the only things that may bring him fulfillment and peace of mind.

He believes Paige is seeing someone. The signs haunt him: Paige asks that Alice stay with him on Saturday night; Alice mentions an unknown baby-sitter, Mrs. West. The suspicion rattles Glen's class preparation and translating.

Otherwise he's getting along, commuting three afternoons a week to the sprawling university along the Charles River. On the other days he works translating and preparing classes at home in his studio space: hide-a-bed, kitchenette, windowless bathroom with shower stall. As part of their financial agreement Paige is paying the mortgage from her new earnings, as a loan being charged to him at seven percent. Like other migrant wordpickers working the language groves of Boston, he is able to survive. At the same time, he believes that Paige's willingness to postpone mortgage payments has to do with her seeing someone.

Parking is not provided for wordpickers and commuting runs up
a nagging expense: Gas, tolls, and, inevitably, returning to his car
every two hours to wedge eight quarters between the pursed little
lips of an iron-headed monster whose impassive eye blinks in
response.

Time left on a meter is found money. Any meter marked "Out
of Order" adds a lightness to his step and length to his stride. He
buys ten-dollar rolls of quarters at banks; each day at UB takes
twenty-four. A broken meter is enough to take Alice out for fast
food on Saturday night, while, he can't help thinking, Paige has
dinner with some mortgage officer over candlelight, the prelude
to a hot scene in the old master bedroom.

Maximilian Baumann takes a liking to him. He often stops by the
office in which Glen is allotted desk space, chats about classes and
mutual acquaintances, trades irreverent witticisms about Brecht
and Grass, Goethe and Kafka.

Glen is predisposed to like him. He was on the last fingerhold
when Baumann came along, offering not just work but this feeling,
however temporary, of being at home. Glen has to ask, though
the terms were set and he believes asking is unmanly: "Any chance
this job might be renewed. Sorry to ask. I know it's a one-year
deal, but I have to start thinking about next year."

They are in Baumann's office and the burly man studies him
across the desk. "No need to apologize," he says, "but the answer is
no. One year only. Your credentials are excellent and I have already
heard that your classroom work is outstanding. Perhaps another
course, but unlikely. You see, only the last-minute emergency and
discretionary power has allowed me to hire a white male person in
the first place. It's not a world today for this subspecies, as you
must know. Women in this department—ah, it's no use. The
subject comes up and I begin to sputter. Forgive me."

Baumann invites Glen for a beer one afternoon after a meeting
of the part-time faculty. "On me, of course," he says. "I haven't
unwound over glasses of beer in years. Do me the honor, please,
as a new colleague with whom I feel rapport?"

A few glasses of beer appeal to Glen in spite of the constraints
of the parking meter and the hour-long drive back to southern
New Hampshire. Feeding the monster eight quarters, he meets

Baumann on a corner: two hours will be his maximum. They cut through the college buildings to a street lined with taverns, bookstores, and student hangouts. Baumann guides them down an alley to O'Rourke's, where they settle in at a chest-high table; one's feet either hang in midair or rest on a chair's crossbar. The glasses are small, and after one each, Baumann suggests a pitcher.

"All expense on me, not a word ... this time. One day, who knows, expense on you."

Glen laughs with him, although the joke suggests his own diminishing chances in life. Making light of his predicament allows him such surprising relief that he laughs again, inordinately loud. "Sorry, I haven't laughed much lately," he says. "At least not over my sorry state in the world."

"The world may be getting even with us white males," Baumann says. "A drink even, in this way, may be regarded as conspiracy. I hope we are not being observed, and I am only half joking."

They drink and chat, and as they dispose of another pitcher time slips away. The conversation covers work in Boston, the cost of living, parking, and public transportation, and then Baumann is saying, "It's something I have not spoken of in years," as he talks about being a boy in Bad Cannstatt during the occupation. Glen tells in turn of spending his army time near Stuttgart, and of passing many times through Bad Cannstatt.

"I think I have known this!" Baumann says. "I have known there is something speaking to me! Let me tell you, please, of a seminal experience. It is before your time, but indulge me, please; it is one of the pivotal experiences of my life. It is 1945, you see, and all is in ruins. It is cold, desperate, sad beyond belief. Germany has sunk to the bottom and I am a ragamuffin, age fourteen. At home, if it may be called a home, is my mother still and two sisters, both younger. We are without food, heat, have no wood to burn, and I walk every day into the ruins of Stuttgart. Jeeps go by. U.S. Army, also the French for a time. The danger is that I may look older than I am and be identified as Home Guard, which I was, of course, at age thirteen and fourteen, when the war is ending and all is in chaos. If I am ten, twelve, it's one thing; the Allies pay no mind. But fourteen? I am thin as a rail, but I may pass for a man when doing so is extremely dangerous in Germany. At the same time, I have become the man in my family and search for food and wood. There are many like me who are caught in the middle as boys and men. You understand, I know. If you are in Stuttgart in 1953 and are here now, teaching what you teach, you must understand.

"We beg for C-rations, for anything, when trucks and jeeps go by. Then, I'm returning one day, it is March 1945, I haven't even twigs to burn, and there comes from behind a jeep moving over rubble and crossing to where I walk. I tell you I am petrified. American soldiers are in the jeep and I fear being shot for no reason. But the driver, a staff sergeant, the words he says I shall never forget. 'Do you need food?' he says. What a question. He hands me a cloth bag with a drawstring which I later learn is an old laundry bag. 'Some food and stuff,' he says. 'Stuff'—I shall never forget this word. 'Stuff.'

"I'm frightened over what may be in the bag. Like an animal in the wild, I move into bomb ruins before daring to look, and cannot believe my eyes. C-rations. There is even a towel and also worn army boots, and a shirt. Santa Claus exists, you see. I'm insane with such joy you cannot believe, and I run home in tears to share this windfall with my mother and sisters.

"The contents of these cans, I can see them as if it is today: one package Lucky Strike cigarettes and one package Camel inside two of the cans. Invaluable in 1945, as you must know. A small fortune. Five cans C-ration, three pork and beans, two hash. The U.S. Army combat boots are worn, of course, but also invaluable, the khaki shirt with staff sergeant stripes, this becomes mine to wear, but for warmth and not ostentatiously, for the strength these soldiers have given me. They are mystical heroes to me, these soldiers in their jeep, and I am at once enamored of things American, of American openness and generosity. They are characteristics which had disappeared in Germany and I seize them, I tell you, with all my faith.

"On one occasion, for taking a branch as firewood, I've been thrashed upon legs and buttocks by Home Guard repeatedly over one hundred meters, till I collapse and cannot walk. This when my father and brother, plus two uncles from my mother, have all perished in the war. Of course it is the time of worst defeat, when invading forces are due to arrive. But there come then the American soldiers, and we learn they are not to be feared so much as they may be turned to for assistance. The occasion of the laundry bag is a crossroads in my life. Thus am I here today, in my

heart as American as baseball, apple pie, and Harry S Truman."
Baumann gestures with his glass. "To stuff!"

"A wonderful story, a story I'd like to drink to," Glen says.

Baumann laughs. "I haven't told this for years, but, yes, a story
to drink to, good of you to say so. I regard you as a friend at once,
you know, on the telephone. Forgive me my sentimental nature.
Is this what old men do? Drink to old stories? I have thought the
stories men tell tedious and boring; can it be they are wonderful?
Or is it that I am reaching an age? Ah—*prost!*"

They tap glasses and drink. "I gave a German kid a shirt
once," Glen says. "Corporal's stripes. He may have wanted it for
fashion, but he wanted it in the worst way. He offered me money,
offered me his own shirt, but I finally just gave it to him."

"You have done this!" Baumann says, wagging a finger. "My
instinct is on the money! With age there should be something
which improves, hmm? I tell you a secret," he adds, leaning over
the table. "The shirt with sergeant stripes, its patch Second Ar-
mored Division—I still have it. I've worn it at the time nearly to
threads, only one time an MP questioned me about it, and now
it is put away in a special place, as it represents a truc gift. I may
be buried in this shirt, I don't know."

"*Prost* to the shirt," Glen says.

He is deeply enjoying the feeling of intoxication coming on;
he needs this. Even if he'll have to drink coffee and sober up
before starting back, and earn himself a daylong hangover.

He tells Baumann about *Sandkörner* and its timetable, the dissolution of East Germany and reunification in the year 2000. Baumann laughs over the messianic prediction. "In the East, unless
they are blind, they have to know Communism will never work,"
he says. "Still, I cannot believe this timetable. Not in our lifetime
will the Soviets give up their hold on the DDR. This woman, she
may be a genius, and Gorbachev may be a visionary, as she says.
But, reunification in the year 2000! It is funny, unless, of course,
she knows more than we know. Workers in the East, they may
know from evidence before their eyes. Who is your contract for
this book, by the way?" he adds. "U.S. or Europe?"

"It just came my way," Glen says. "I'm doing it on spec."

"Say this again, please. You do not have a contract? What if
this economist is accurate in her prediction?"

"Meaning?"

"Meaning it may be taken from you in one minute and your work will be for nothing. You must have a contract!"

"I have something of an agent, a man who sends me articles for translation—but it's true, I haven't mentioned this book to him."

"He has not secured a contract? You must gain credit and earnings from your work, it is only fair."

"I could use some money, even if it isn't much."

"What if someone has contracted already for this translation? Really, you must be in touch with the author and gain permission. May I see this book? I have some connections, you know. May I see your translation, and offer advice?"

"Of course, I bring it in tomorrow," Glen calls over the noise in the bar, then adds, "I just said, 'I bring it in.'"

"You adopt my accent!" Baumann calls back. "I think we drink one more pitcher beer till this tendency is thoroughly ingrained!" They both shake with laughter. "It's true, I've made a friend!"

"*Salud!*" Glen says.

"Schnapps!" Baumann says then, as though recalling something long forgotten. "Schnapps! Yes! You give your shirt to this child! I'm astonished! I tell you, Cady, we will tell one another more stories! Drinking or sober. That is a friend, to hear every story!"

"Baumann, I think you are drunk!"

"Ah yes, wonderfully drunk! My wife is not believing when I am returning home! Hah! And that I have made a friend!"

Moments later the waitress delivers shot glasses, which they raise and tink and try not to spill.

"To words with which to mend the old ticker," Glen says.

"To all days gone, all days to come," Baumann offers. *"Wie einst."*

The firewater scorches Glen's gullet and glosses his eyes, and he reminds himself that a hangover is what he needs. Maybe booze will kill the fear in his heart ... maybe then he'll begin to live again.

"What is happening first?" Baumann is saying. "This woman's domino theory—she is not the only one to propose it, of course. What does she say will happen first?"

"The woman," Glen says. "Yes, Elizabeth Speyer-Weiss."

"What does the seer see?"

"To set it all in motion—well, it's *in* motion, that's her theory, based on economics and human nature. Lingering grains of sand. Undeniable grains of truth. The way she sees it, first something will happen in Poland. Poland is crucial to everything, as are Gorbachev's policies, his policies of—"

"Yes, Professor, we know Gorbachev's policies."

"Events, what she predicts, are very particular. So are her dates, which are all even. By 1990 Gorbachev will visit Poland and acknowledge, by his visit, the first non-Communist government in the East. That's a big domino, but it *is* starting to seem possible, given what's been happening in Poland."

"And what of the Soviet-backed Polish military? Solidarity may be snuffed in one hour. Why is Gorbachev allowing this? He will be ousted by the Politburo at the first syllable of such reform. I believe your DDR economist is a dreamer, you know, but still I would like to see the text. And you must enter into a contract! This is foolish beyond belief."

They drink on, Glen's neck growing rubbery. He hears himself confess that he's opposed to his divorce, that he loves his wife and little girl but violated his marriage and now is caught in a downward spiral. "Didn't mean to quite let that out, apologize," he adds. "It's what preoccupies me."

"Fight for them!" Baumann says. "You have no choice. In this proceeding, tell the judge you are opposed. Say you regret your conduct and desire preservation of your family. It is necessary to *say* these things! It is what all Germans have been taught by the lesson of Hitler: You must stand up and say the truth. There is no alternative. To which," Baumann adds, "we drink one more schnapps."

Glen laughs in agreement.

"Waiter!" Baumann calls, teary-eyed. *"Herr Ober!"*

Glen opens his eyes to an unfamiliar wall and a sliver of light. Only after a minute does he know where he is and remember last night: leaving the tavern too drunk to drive, flagging a taxi, climbing stone steps, Baumann giggling the entire time. Where? He thinks he's in the neighborhood of Beacon Street, Marlborough Street.

One worrisome thought after another pokes into his sour mind.

His car, parked beside a monster near Mass. Ave.? And Alice? Like his car, she appears to be at an unreachable distance. As he rolls over on the single bed and feels the pain inside his skull, he's taken with the need to know that she's okay.

Twenty past six. She should be up, preparing to catch the bus to kindergarten, as Paige is preparing to drive to Dover. Deciding to leave Baumann a note and slip away, he makes up the bed and treads quietly out of the room, only to detect an aroma of coffee and a movement, or a shadow, from a room at the end of the hall. Spotting a bathroom, he detours to relieve himself, cleans his mouth with a finger-glob of someone's toothpaste, and emerges to present himself, and make his exit.

It isn't Baumann in the kitchen, but a woman Baumann's age, maybe sixty, in a floor-length housecoat, standing in front of the stove. "Morning," he says quietly.

She smiles. "Mr. Cady, yes, good morning."

"I came home with Max. We had a bit to drink."

She makes an expression to dismiss his tone of apology. "Please, have some coffee," she says.

"I should go, really. Sorry to show up here like this."

"No, no, no problem, I assure you. I'm happy Max has found someone to have a drink with. Please, some coffee."

"I'd love some, then I'll be on my way. You're Max's wife?"

"Excuse me, yes. I am Margot. How do you do. Please sit down, Mr. Cady. No need to rush at such an hour."

Glen envies Max the good nature and companionship Margot seems to offer. He mentions his car, and Alice, tells her that he commutes from New Hampshire and though he's living apart from his daughter, he woke up worrying about her. Margot responds by telling him about their two daughters, Barbara a psychologist in New York, Kitty a Ph.D. candidate in literature at Chicago. She remarks that drinks may be what Max has been needing, given his state of mind recently. Ten minutes later, coffee and two pain-killers at work, Glen is walking along Marlborough Street looking for his car. The early air *is* refreshing; the sun is out but has yet to clear building tops. With great relief he finds his car is where he left it and without a fluorescent-red ticket. He wonders if luck, in some inexplicable consequence of his drunken evening, could be coming his way.

Twenty minutes later he has northbound 95 to himself while the southbound lanes are lined with commuters. Then he is motoring through the fall colors of eastern New England, still hoping that luck has come over to his side.

Paige has an answering machine. When Glen calls to check on Alice he gets three rings and a message in Paige's voice. He replaces the receiver. An answering machine for messages from her lawyer? Dates? Why an expense of the kind at a time when he lives largely on bread and pasta?

Well, it isn't his business and the real message is that her life is moving on. Is she leaving him behind?

Alice is more than okay, he learns in the afternoon. Paige surprises him with a call and says, "Interesting news about Alice. Good news, I guess."

"Good news? What's happening?"

"Something I'm sure you'll like," she says. "I had a call from her teacher, Miss Richards. In the Iowa Basic Test, in reading, how do you think Alice scored?"

A thrill starts to rise in Glen's chest. "Tell me."

"It's something you're going to like."

"Paige, come on."

"Seven A. Can you imagine, grade level seven A in kindergarten!"

Glen takes it in, trying to persuade himself that his own luck is not related to Alice's performance. "Is she there?"

"Not right now. . . . I hope the other kids don't take it out on her."

"Paige, really."

"Miss Richards says it's the highest they've ever seen here. Also, she has Alice helping two boys learn to read. They put a little table and chairs in the hall, and Alice tutors these boys for ten minutes each. One of the boys is Kevin Baker, you remember, the boy—"

"Old Toilet Stool, I remember him," Glen says.

"You make her into such a little brain, kids aren't going to like her."

"Paige, come off this, you can't be serious."

"I am serious."

"I can't believe you'd say what you're saying."

"I wouldn't say it if I didn't think it was true."

"People like Alice," Glen says. "She's a nice little girl. Don't say people won't like her."

"I bought your ideas for a long time, Glen—it's not like that anymore. I'm going to say what I think."

Off the phone, a fear passes over him of losing Alice, of Paige and her parents trying to separate her soul from his. The road to divorce. Whatever fantasies he entertained about reconciliation have just been blown away. They don't want Alice to be her own person, he thinks. They want her to blend in, to disappear.

26

Max Baumann walks into Glen's office in a state, speaking excitedly and gesturing with both hands. "You have not read today's *Times*, of course not," he says. "Why do I know this. It is not *big* news, no, but it is *there*, you see, lost in the middle on a back page. Just like your work is being hidden."

Glen doesn't know what to make of his circling and gesturing until Max says, "This Speyer-Weiss is *right*, you see! Her timetable is off, but she is accurate! Restlessness in Eastern Europe. Protests in Poland. In Czechoslovakia. And they are indeed being prodded by Mr. Gorbachev. Do you even know she is right, you bumpkin? Gorbachev, he *is* the key, and he *is* doing *now*, as she said two years ago! Who is expecting this even three months ago? This woman has read the future—history is validating her prophecy!"

Weeks have passed since he left "Grains of Sand" for Max to examine. He had assumed that was the end of it.

"Also," Max says, "why have you not told me this translation is brilliant? Are you foolishly modest or only naive? Imagine if other steps in her timetable are coming true? This book may become important, perhaps, in a year, indispensable! There is hope, you see, for mankind. A grain of sand. And your work—why have you not told me your translation is so accomplished? I had taken you for granted, and your work is outstanding!"

"You think it is?"

"My friend, you know as well as I that no one in this country, only a handful of people, is reading German. Would a translation of *Das Kapital* in 1860 not be invaluable? Two things you must think about. One: This volume could prove requisite to decision makers, to the media and intelligentsia. Two: The translation, not only is it yours but it is eloquent! You could make a name for yourself, not to mention some money also. Do you know we have a connection with the Mielein Insititute in Berlin? I *know* translations, and sometime I wish to know how you have acquired this skill. It heightens your employability, and also you could attend the Mielein for a session. But this is not important right now. What is important, what you must not hesitate to do, is secure rights from the author. I cannot believe you do not have rights. Immediately, or you may not receive the credit you deserve. Immediately!"

"I did mention to the agent—"

"Today at the latest. I could have left this on my table all year! Today you are in contact with this agent and he, by courier if possible, is in contact with Speyer-Weiss. And, a small fib soon to be corrected, you must represent the work as ready for publication, and then make it so! Work tonight, tomorrow, do nothing else but finish this work!"

"I have—"

"You are being sick one day, tomorrow. Have Emily assign a TA to your classes for one day. Communicate this urgency to your agent. From Berlin a contract may be prepared to go at once to Dresden. Dear God, it takes a German to get things done around here! One month, three weeks if possible, you *must* have the balance of manuscript ready. Assuming your agent has secured permission, he may at once present it to publishers. Your translation, Dr. Cady, it will not make you a wealthy man, but it will make a big difference to your life and career. Of that I am certain. An over-the-hill white male may come off the bench and show his stuff, his tenacity, his elbow grease, and that most singular attribute, *self-reliance*, from which murderous impulses but also masterpieces derive! *Sandkörner*, you see, shall be a masterpiece, twice over."

Glen sits smiling at Max's exuberant rhetoric. "I'll do my best; you inspire me," he says.

"If you should fail, if you miss this opportunity, I will drop to the floor and weep."

"I won't fail," Glen says.

He meets his classes the next day, despite Baumann's urging, unwilling to be neglectful where he's always been true. He works constantly to sustain Baumann's enthusiasm and his own determination in the face of his depression and loneliness. His efforts keep the painful emotions at bay, but if his concentration lapses for a moment his mind lets in the fear.

In the dreadful, losing moments, he thinks of Alice. He seeks her presence in the words, addresses phrases to her. When a copy is ready, no matter what Paige thinks, he will ask her to read the opening pages as the book's final test. If Alice can understand the dissolution of East Germany, then the translation might be half as good as Baumann claims.

To whom, as a middle-aged man, may one confess loneliness? Baumann has his own work and family, and not even Max, Glen imagines, would care to hear about all the demons still haunting him. Except when engrossed in the translation or his classes, he continues to suffer mini-breakdowns. A phrase of music as he makes coffee at daybreak, or a child playing in a yard he passes, may cause his heart to contract. His only hope, regardless of what experts say, is not to ask for help. Max is right: Self-reliance is the only way.

Baumann has problems of his own. His report: A professor whose weak tenure case he carried through a field of foes just five years ago—prior to the current disease, he says, of radical feminist insanity—has filed a report with the president charging him with multiple offenses against women, all verbal and delivered within the context of his lectures on modern German literature. Her method, Baumann says, has been utterly without fairness: spying by students. Under the guise of a class experiment she recruited two young women from her Women's Themes coincidentally enrolled in his Modern German Lit. She advised them to record, with the dates, references in his class which to their minds fell into categories "sexist," "offensive," and "insensitive." The charges tabulated by this professor and her hairy-legged *Hitlermädchen*, Baumann tells Glen, numbered forty-seven—including, under the category "insensitive," six references to himself as "chairman."

"Please, return to your labors," he says finally. "The book is approaching conclusion? Allow me to read the final chapters when they are ready, and thank you for allowing me to release steam which might otherwise have this Professor Napp under her desk in defense of her life. To think that the latest wave of fascism is women seeking wholesale power and the subjugation of men! It is astonishing. No more fascism, thank you, as Germans must say. And don't forget, one day soon we speak of the Mielein. I think you may attend at the beneficence of UB and DAAD. It could lead to something."

Telephone calls from Magnus Klein are like cortisone shots; they bring immediate and dramatic relief from worry. Progress is being made via East Berlin, he reports in one call. In another he asks Glen's permission to seek a full share of the author's English-language royalties, a tenth of the author's tenth, to which Glen says, Of course, seek the best possible share. "The alternative," Magnus says, "is cash payment, maybe three thousand to be paid at once by a publisher, three to five K, but maybe two, I don't know. Versus a share of the author's share. The risk, of course, is that your earnings will be minuscule. Or Speyer-Weiss may say *nein*, just like that, however clear I have made it that they will not acquire a better translation, or one which will be more widely read in the English language. Your translation is going to be read, Dr. Cady—because it has the secret advantage of being readable."

He calls up Alice and Paige and sometimes their exchanges afford him some comfort, especially when he can sense affection from his daughter. How is *he*? she will ask. Does he like his students? Is he—this from Paige one night, catching him off guard—seeing anyone? After a pause, he says, "No, are you?"

"What I am doing," she says, "is trying to persuade my supervisor that I can handle commercial mortgages."

"You didn't answer my question," he says, against his better judgment.

Paige, he knows, abhors lying, and into the silence he says,

"Sorry to embarrass you. Your job sounds okay. You're making strides in your work?"

"Were you unfaithful with other women?"

"No, just the one," he says at last.

"Nothing between you and Monica?"

"Maybe there could have been," he says. "But no, nothing."

"You wouldn't lie to me?"

Glen sits gripping the receiver, the old hurt and confusion in him again. Does she think he'd lie at this time in his life?

"Glen, tell me," she says. "I'd like to know. It doesn't matter now, I'd just like to know."

"Have to go," he says. "Talk to you some other time."

"Does that mean yes?"

He starts to speak, but a gasp fills his throat and he replaces the receiver.

Days later, Paige brings up Monica again and Glen says, "Maybe if I'd had something going with Monica, I'd be tenured now, and promoted, and we'd still be together."

"Be serious. I know she liked you."

"Is your lawyer telling you to ask these things?"

This time she is the one to hang up the phone.

Magnus calls upon receipt of the concluding pages. "They read with the clarity of the preceding chapters," he says. "I've been in this business for years and have never seen a better translation. I hope you're pleased?"

"Magnus, I feel happy every time I talk to you," Glen says.

"In this moment copies are being made to go to commercial houses, while I'm also composing a cover letter. Did you see today's news, that Gorbachev will address the UN in January, and will also propose a Peace Offensive to President Bush. These are events I'll be pointing out to publishers."

"If no one takes it?"

"Certainly it will be taken by a university press. Of that there is little doubt."

The commercial presses decline. Some editors extend praise for the translation, some are skeptical of the book's premise, and some pass without comment. An editor named Cale Holt, of the publishing division of Barron Bell Communications, telephones. Glen has heard the company called America's little BBC, and his hopes rise briefly. Holt says he liked the book but is passing, for the simple reason that he couldn't buy the premise. His words, as Glen recalls them to Max: "tremendously impressed with the writing." And: Did Glen have or know of other books or monographs by East German academics or intellectuals?

Three weeks later, good news strikes; the book is taken by University Press of New Haven. The semester is over and Glen is translating another article on perestroika. It's December 30, a Friday afternoon, when Magnus calls and says, "Professor, the book has landed."

"Magnus, call me Glen. Professor doesn't apply anymore."

"In any case, it's good news! We have a contract. Not New York, true, but a publisher of high regard. This press had great success three years ago with a book on the CIA—you know this book? Not much money up front, but they recognize the timeliness of 'Grains of Sand' and will rush to publication, by September 1. They promise to do everything possible to present the volume as a commercial book. As always, everything continues to depend on the vision of Speyer-Weiss and the actions of Comrade Gorby. Maybe more now on Comrade Gorby, though the earthquake in Armenia just as he is bringing his Peace Offensive to the UN is not helping his cause, or ours, I'm sorry to say."

Standing at the window, Glen tries to appreciate the news. If only he could believe the prophecy himself. He doesn't, any more than he believes his own life will come together again. Reunification of divided Germany is a nice idea. Having a new chance in life is a nice idea. But he fears they are as ethereal as the dreams of children, and he cannot really believe them. None of them.

27

Registered letters from Paige's lawyer follow in January, February, and March, telling Glen to respond by registered mail within ten (10) business days. The tone always gives Glen the feeling that Donald MacNair, Esq., is trying to jerk him around.

Re: Cady vs. Cady

Dear Mr. Cady:

Please be advised that your reply to this inquiry is to be received in these offices, by registered mail, within ten (10) business days of the aforementioned date. Please be—

"Screw you," Glen says to the second letter, and tosses it aside. He's defeated in the divorce proceeding, he knows; the letters are just more water poured on his sinking case. Follow-up letters issue more "Please be advised" demands, and he tosses them aside, too. He doesn't care, and says so to Paige when she asks why he's refusing to answer her lawyer's questions. "It's only going to look bad for you in court," she tells him.

"I care about Alice," he says. "I don't care at all about your lawyer's letters."

"Glen, you're going to make everything worse."

"How could it be worse?"

She doesn't say.

"I don't mean to be difficult. We'll get a divorce, though I believe it's a mistake. But tell your lawyer to stop trying to jerk me around. I'm not going to respond to his poor use of language."

Paige laughs. "How can you say divorce is a mistake?"

"It's causing damage to my daughter."

"Glen, you brought this all on yourself."

"Did you know that girls who have good relationships with their fathers have the best chances of becoming successful?"

"Please just answer the man's questions so we can get on with our lives."

"My answers—you tell him, because I'm not going to answer his letters. They're no, I won't be represented by counsel, and no, I won't contest the terms of the settlement, unless, when the bill's presented at the hearing, I think the terms are unfair. Then I'll challenge."

"I hope you aren't planning to attend the hearing."

"I don't have a lawyer—who's going to attend?"

"Glen, you know very well it's a rubber-stamp thing. You show up, the judge will think you're nuts. Please, answer the man's letters!"

Glen declines. He visits Alice as usual, and Max Baumann grants him courses for the two summer sessions. It would appear to be his final employment as a teacher. He studies want ads and continues to translate as many articles as Magnus Klein is able to assign him. Unfortunately he is limited to one a month, and he knows he's sinking again. He is worried that he won't be able to keep up his strength—not of his body but of his psyche. And the next place of vulnerability, the part to stop working, will be his mind.

Eventually Glen replies to Paige's attorney. The hearing is two weeks away when he receives another registered letter beginning "Please be advised that you are in receipt of the final . . ." Glen writes:

Dear Mr. MacNair, Esq:

No, I will not be represented by counsel at the scheduled divorce hearing in Rockingham County Superior Court. What I will do, representing myself, is ask the judge to reverse the proceeding and impose counseling with an eye to restoring my marriage and family.

Yours sincerely,
Glen Cady, GED, B.A., M.A., Ph.D.

Glen walks out to mail his note. It's Friday, the one day his summer school class doesn't meet, which meant solitary drinking last night and a hair of the dog this morning, before receiving MacNair's letter. He's pleased to place his view on record, and pleased to imagine MacNair popping his bagpipes.

MacNair's pipes do apparently pop, sometime on Tuesday. Arriving at UB to teach his class, Glen finds two pink "When You Were Out" slips in his mailbox, each checked "Urgent" and telling him to call Paige.

"Mr. MacNair is beside himself," Paige tells him. "If you're really going to attend the hearing, he has to know. Glen, why in the world are you making everything so difficult?"

Glen doesn't know what to say.

"Can I say that I talked to you and you said you're *not* going to attend?"

"I feel like I should. Don't I have to sign something?"

"Glen, you've agreed to terms. And there's no way counseling will ever take place, you have to know that."

"I guess I do."

"Get real then. It isn't funny."

"Paige, you know, everything's being taken from me."

"You brought it on yourself."

"All that'll be on record is the voice of your foolish attorney."

"I can't believe this!"

"I think about Alice all the time," Glen says, and is going to say more when the line goes dead.

Another morning, barely having slept, Glen finds himself staring out the kitchenette window in a state of nervous exhaustion. Well, it's happening, he thinks. Max said divorce was life's graduate school, and the hearing this morning is like an exam for which he is unprepared, as in his old nightmares.

At midmorning, he drives to the PSU campus and parks in

its half-empty lot. He takes a walk into town to have coffee, but what is on his mind is seeing Alice. As if he doesn't know her, he wonders if she's old enough to walk in town by herself, and wonders, if he should see her, if he might steal her away. Off to California. How far might he get before he'd be arrested? He sits at a dime-store counter until he sees two waitresses looking at him and whispering. How long has he been sitting here?

Later, driving into midday, he rolls past the exit which would have taken him to the Rockingham County Courthouse. He takes 95 south, as though on his way to another day of teaching, though the school closed two days ago for the rest of the summer.

He knows he's giving up now. Paige is lost to him, and Alice is lost to him, too, however much he will still see her. The warm, sunny day and the crowded, aggressive traffic are suddenly surreal. Now that his eyes must remain open, all he wants to do is close them. He stays close to the breakdown lane, to be out of the way of people who seem to know where they're going.

He comes to himself sitting in his car at a rest stop, and can't remember exiting the highway. Windows down, taking in the warm air, he looks over land, highway, trees, and weeds. He seems to have dozed. Leaving the car, he uses the bathroom and washes his hands and grizzly face. He sees "Gorbachev" in a newspaper headline but has no appetite for news. He sits on a bench where there is shade. These hours have slipped away; he doesn't know if he's in New Hampshire or Massachusetts or Rhode Island.

Massachusetts. A sign for Topsfield. Passing cars carry beach paraphernalia strapped to their tops, happy people sailing by on a warm day in August. Too late, sir, the door is closed and no one may enter when the courtroom door is closed.

He drives slowly and close to the breakdown lane. The hot summer afternoon is fading away; in the past it might have been an hour full of pleasure, returning from an outing to the beach or to a lake in Michigan. A sign for Framingham and routes 9 and 128 lets him know he's back on the highway for Boston.

Again he gets off at a gas-station rest stop, he thinks in Rhode Island. Leaving the car, he finds that his legs are weak, and against all decorum he sits on the curb. In front of him two gas-station jockeys, one a teenager, the other possibly his father, come and go, pump gas, check oil, take money. They talk and laugh and pay him no mind. Glen's eyes feel dry and he grinds them with his knuckles.

He buys gas. He likes to pump his own, but isn't allowed.

"What's ahead here?" he asks.

"Veer left to Boston, right to the Cape."

"Boston is south?"

"North."

He has circled into Rhode Island, south of Boston, and his route back will be through heavy city traffic. As he drives, the shadows of evening begin to fall and lights are coming on in the skyscrapers. He finds himself, as if in a dream, back on 95.

He exits at another unfamiliar area, and only when he stops, in a shopping-mall parking lot, does he sense that exhaustion may have led him to leave the highway. He lets the car roll onto an outer fringe of tarmac and turns off the motor. There are weeds here and stillness. It's hard to accept that he isn't moving.

The parking lot is vast but there are no cars or stores nearby; just a curb separating the asphalt from a hillside of brush. A highway sound carries on the evening air, maybe a quarter of a mile below. But right here it's peaceful. Maybe he could set up camp.

He sits on this curb as he sat on the other. In the distance he can see the evening activity of the mall. People and cars come and go, but none come his way. There is a telephone shell attached to a faraway wall and he thinks to call Paige and ask if the hearing is over now and they are officially divorced.

A warm August evening. Sitting on the curb is taking him back to childhood. Sitting with Blackie there beside him. Does he know any more now than he did when he was twelve sitting on a curb with his dog? Or when he was a teenager having a smoke and thinking of Hedy? He picks up sand pebbles, rolling them between his fingers and flicking them away. Then he leans over and rests his head on his arm on the curb, inhaling dirt and ironweed. He doesn't close his eyes, and at a hundred yards can make out the shadow of a figure behind the wheel of a black-and-white police car, watching him.

But Alice and Blackie are with him, so what does he care? Two friends in a lifetime, and two or three love affairs. If he sits up, he thinks, the cop will leave him alone.

He doesn't sit up. He lies on his arm, looking at pebbles of sand on the tarmac. There'll always be one to produce a pearl, sayeth Elizabeth Speyer-Weiss. He hears the cruiser approaching, and it amuses him to think about telling the cop he has his ear to the ground for grains of sand. The car stops and its motor idles with a faint drumbeat. He doesn't look up.

"We help you with something?" the policeman says at ten feet.

Glen sits up, feeling it is the polite thing to do. "No thanks," he says. "I'm okay."

"You're sure?"

"I got drowsy on the highway. I'm just resting."

The policeman studies him, maybe trying to decide if he should check his ID.

"I got divorced today," Glen decides to tell him.

"Ah."

"It happens."

"Guess it can be rough," the policeman says.

For a moment nothing is said, then the policeman says, "You gonna be okay?"

"I was thinking about my kid and my dog," Glen tells him.

"She got the dog, too?" the policeman says.

"No, I got the dog," Glen says.

"Good you got something. Sure you're gonna be okay?"

"I'll be okay. . . . I just had to get out of traffic for a while."

Glen realizes he's been sound asleep. The sun is below the horizon and the sky is darkening. It's twenty to eight.

He uses an unmarked john at a convenience store. Flimsy wooden door hooked, he rinses his face and neck with cold water and then strips to the waist and uses soap and water to wash under his arms and around his neck and ears. He uses one paper towel to pat himself dry, and tells his image in the mirror to get on with things.

Pouring coffee at a fix-your-own station, wanting it as though he had been sleeping for hours, he carries the Styrofoam cup back to his car. He sips and gazes over the car's hood to the west. The trees are black silhouettes and headlights sparkle between them from the highway below.

He buckles up and starts the motor, feeling better. On the highway he continues north. Goodbye to everything but Alice, he thinks. He's divorced now, he admits, and feels he's awakening to something different. It's music on the radio, however, which starts finally to transform him. Window opened to the warm night air, the radio issues a woman's song, popular a while back, whose lyrics and melody set loose emotions he seems to have packed away for the duration:

> Go on now,
> Walk out the door!
> Just turn around now,
> You're not welcome anymore.
>
> You thought I'd crumble?
> You thought I'd lay down and die?

But it's the news which follows that makes him choke with disbelief. The lead: "Poland, for the first time since World War II, today voted into power a reformist coalition, and the message from Gorbachev to Communist leaders is 'Go with the flow, tanks and attack dogs will not be called out.'"

Glen is touched with teary laughter. Elizabeth Speyer-Weiss knew it all along. It's just as she predicted, and his eyes continue to blur with emotion as he drives. He had not believed it would happen but it has. He had thought it was a child's dream and it has come true. He drives into the night and the music rides with him.

> You thought I'd crumble?
> You thought I'd lay down and die?

28

A bubble bag containing a book arrives at his apartment. Unprepared, Glen reaches between the bubbles and withdraws *Grains of Sand*. It's his first sight of the book. Its cover is white-into-blue, a new sky dawning. Under the title is the author's name in gold; under her name, in smaller black letters:

Translation by Glen Cady

He clenches the volume and gives another thanks to Elizabeth Speyer-Weiss. An editor's card is paper-clipped to the first page:

Glen,

We all think it looks wonderful. Be proud—tell us you love it. Author's copies to follow.

Wynn

Glen makes a spontaneous drive to Boston to show the book to Max but misses him and has to settle for a lunch opening six days hence. Driving back to his apartment, he walks in on the ringing phone. Alice. He was on his way to call her, to clear with Paige a visit to show them his blue-covered prize. He imagines telepathy will have his daughter on the line.

It isn't Alice, though, but a woman saying, "Cale Holt on the line for Professor Cady."

"Yes," Glen says. "This is Glen Cady."

Cale Holt of America's little BBC is not exactly on the line, however, and Glen is the one who ends up waiting. Then the man's crisp tone: "Professor, good to talk to you again."

"You have to call me Glen," Glen says.

"Of course," Cale Holt says. "Listen, I want to tell you how much—I really mean this—how much I've enjoyed *Grains of Sand*, and how I regret we didn't jump at it when we had the chance. Can't tell you how appreciative I am of the book's clarity. We're seeing translations all the time now, and we can tell the work that's gone into this one. A first-rate book, and given today's news, who knows where it could go."

"You've already seen it—I just got a copy myself," Glen says.

"It's okay, Professor, you want it read, don't you? I had an order in, since I last talked to you."

Glen laughs with him; of course he wants it read, even as he feels an invasion of something private.

"I have another reason for calling," the man says. "Telling you I admire your work is one, but there's another. I have a proposition to send your way—if your schedule will allow a brief trip. What we'd like to do is hire you as a consultant for a two-day seminar. We're interested in having our people get a better grip on the nuts and bolts of translation, whatever it takes to make them better writers and editors. The translators we use are mainly individuals working in English as a second language, and while many are good—some are brilliant in their fields—problems with clarity come up all the time. The material we see, at least half of it might as well remain in the original.

"Could you do this, Professor: come to New York and give our people a two-day workshop in translating from German into English? We'll pay for four days, assuming it would take two days to work up a seminar, and of course all expenses. The money isn't out of this world, but it's decent, seven hundred and fifty dollars a day plus expenses. I know the fall semester's about to start, but could you squeeze four days into your schedule?"

Glen pumps a fist in secret celebration, and hears himself say, "Could you make it a thousand a day?"

"I could make it eight hundred."

"Could I do it right away, next week?" Glen says. "Is that too soon?"

"Next week would be fine, any day but Friday. Which two days would suit you?"

"I could work up a program over, say, Sunday and Monday. How about Wednesday and Thursday?"

"Fine. If you could fly in Tuesday evening, we could start early Wednesday, say nine to twelve, then one to four. Twelve contact hours over two days? How would that be?"

"Would be fine, no problem."

"Excellent! I'll put Jackie on in a minute and she'll make arrangements for your flight. I'll be attending some of the workshop myself, and I tell you, I'm looking forward to it. This is great, good of you to make up your mind on the spot like this."

"You said today's news?" Glen says then. "You mean the new government in Poland?"

"No, no—you haven't heard? A trickle of East Germans has broken through the Iron Curtain. It could turn into quite a story."

"I hadn't heard."

"They're passing through Hungary on their way to Austria. The Hungarians are letting them use their borders. It's another line from *Grains of Sand*, of course, but who knows if it'll be allowed to continue? Gorby tells the Poles to go with the flow, now he's telling the Russians to look the other way, while the East German government wants to institute police action. It's happening earlier than your Elizabeth person said, but it is happening. Listen, make sure your publisher's getting the book out to the media. The timing couldn't be better."

Glen walks around his studio in exultation. Over three thousand dollars! It's what he made all summer. And, in the trickle through the Iron Curtain, a boost for the book. If only the door isn't slammed shut.

Television news shows the young East Germans, students and young families, passing through Hungary and entering Austria, yet to reach West Germany. Then there is footage of several young men and women arriving in Munich, being mobbed as dazed heroes, and the release of emotion matches the enormity of what's taking place. Hedy comes to mind. Glen wonders if she is still alive.

A less surprising surprise: The seminar in New York turns out to be his most successful teaching experience ever. He prepares carefully, though it is, after all, only a two-day event. The surprise is that he gives more than he may ever have given as a teacher, and that it takes and works better than he ever would have imagined. The six students are all are multilingual adults who work with the company's East European offices, and they are eager to excel. The rainy September weather seems to give the class cohesion, and even the snack breaks are given over to discussion of translation and of the news out of Eastern Europe.

On parting, Glen receives an ovation and a copy of the 1925 Knopf first edition of *Death in Venice*. At the end of the first day's session he went ahead and confided his experience of seeing Thomas Mann in Stuttgart and Erika Mann onstage, of reading the work of the other Mann offspring and dreaming (he did not share his wine-enhanced dinner affair with Erika Mann) of being part of a family so accomplished.

The students line up to shake his hand. It's the first time he's received such a response—he is overwhelmed—and on his return flight, still in the flush of things, he wonders if he shouldn't reconsider his chances as a teacher. He has a little money now, and if he can survive the year, he might find something for next fall. Could the events in Eastern Europe stimulate interest in language studies ... take him back to the classroom, explicating *Death in Venice* and the curious beauty of forbidden sex?

A call to Max in the morning brings him back to earth. "At your age and as a white male, your chances," Max says, "fall between nonexistent and zero."

When he picks up Alice on Sunday and they are rolling along in the car, she tells him she has a boyfriend. Glen is visited with jealousy. "You have a boyfriend, at school?"

"Neal Brusard."

"How is it you think of Neal Brusard as your boyfriend?"

"He said he is."

"How do you feel about that?"

"Okay."

"Other girls in first grade have boyfriends?"

"No," Alice says.

"You're kind of a trendsetter then, aren't you."

She doesn't reply.

"You like Neal Brusard?"

"Yes," she says.

"What is it you like about him?"

"I don't know."

"Forgotten what I said about saying that?" he says.

"No," she says, and they laugh.

"What do you like about Neal? I'd like to think you can tell me at least some of your secrets."

"His daddy's gone, too," Alice says.

"Ah," Glen says.

After a moment he says, "It's nice to have a friend," but Alice has no reply.

UB does come up with an opening at the Mielein Institute before the end of the year, funded by a West German grant that will otherwise expire. Over coffee in his office Max extends the invitation, and Glen says, "Really—no one else wants to go?"

"Everyone always wants to go," Max says, "but it's impossible to fit into anyone's schedule. You shall go. I've worked it out. What's possible is that this program may give you added insight concerning translation, and could lead to something. Who knows?"

"When would I go?"

"Whenever. October, November. Two weeks each month the program is offered, in, I believe, the Kurfürstendamm area. You have an up-to-date passport? Apply at once, on an emergency basis. Charge all expenses to UB. Keep receipts."

Alice is in first grade now, and on the day he agrees to attend the Mielein, Glen intercepts her at school, delighting Alice and saving her from two hours at Mrs. West's. He telephones Paige at the bank to tell her he has Alice and will deliver her home at dinnertime. Paige is so angry that there is screaming in her voice. *"This is a violation of visitation rights!"* she says. *"You are to return her to Mrs. West's, right now, Glen, right now!"*

"I'll drop her off at dinnertime," he says. "I'm going to buy my kid a book."

When they park at the mall, Alice comes around to take his

hand. She asks for a ride, and Glen lifts her onto his shoulders. He holds her ankles as he carries her. As he looks at their reflection in a store window, it is Hedy he seems to see and he lets her stay in his mind as he has rarely done before. Does she still live in Baden-Baden, in the house on the side of the hill? On a September day like today, would she walk in the green park and sit at an outdoor cafe?

In the morning, he decides with a rush, he'll call the German consulate, to find out how to trace someone's whereabouts after thirty years. Maybe, if she's still alive and still in Germany, he'll look her up. Overhead, Alice is leg-squeezing his neck, and as they enter the bookstore he puts her down and, confused with love, takes her hand.

8

GETTING ON AT CHEVY

Summer 1955

29

In 1955 there's a German joke that you can buy a new Mercedes in any color as long as it's black. Glen reads it in the *Stars & Stripes*, which comes out every morning for a paper nickel. Once a month or so he also buys a German newspaper to see how much he can understand before turning to his dictionary. He reads to himself, although he knows he'd do better to read aloud. He's in his fourth semester at University of Maryland, and has yet to disclose his language study to Hedy.

In Message Center Company his modest study earned him a sort of reputation as a brain, but in Headquarters Company language skill is not so rare. Many of the company's enlisted men are college graduates, among whom Glen holds his own in German, but the language masters are two PFCs, Keen of Harvard and Grandmaison of Columbia. Each enlisted for three years to gain assignment to the Army Language School at the Presidio. Both are near-fluent in Russian, having attended the six-month immersion program, fluent in French (Grandmaison was born in Paris), and are approaching fluency in German, with all but flawless accents.

The two of them are fast friends; they rent an apartment in Böblingen, where they escape the army on weekends and holidays, and even entertain students from the University of Tübingen. Glen secretly admires them. Their senses of humor are wonderfully

irreverent and the satisfaction they derive from daily life, so different from the grumbling draftees, is an inspiration to him. He
decides, at last, to try to befriend them.

He doesn't quite know how to do it, though the two are
congenial toward him. They pass on jokes and, if they're sitting
at the same table in the mess hall, will ask friendly questions, even
though they work in S-2, Intelligence. Only rarely, in a glance
between themselves, does a hint of condescension seem to appear.

A pretext presents itself. Privy to information about a midnight
alert, Glen goes that evening to their squad room and says, "C'mere
a minute, there's something I want to tell you."

In the hall he confides the scheduled alert to them and says,
"Anyway, let's go downtown, have a beer, and stay up for it."

Neither of them responds. Grandmaison says, "Again, please."

"It's easier to stay up for an alert than be called out of bed at
midnight. I thought you might like to go to town."

"Gee, I don't think so, no thanks," Keen says.

"It's what I'm going to do," Glen says. "I just thought I'd see
if you wanted to go." Into their silence he adds, "Don't say anything
about it," and walks away.

He could beat them up easily, he thinks, leaving the building.
Both at once if he wanted to. And he's the one who has Hedy,
he reminds himself. He's the one whose girlfriend attended a
famous university—a detail which, of course, he had been eager
to casually disclose.

It's in Stuttgart, on a warm May afternoon, that Glen sees Thomas
Mann. On duty and in uniform, he has maneuvered an afternoon
to himself in the city. Noticing two Mercedes limousines pull up
before the Staatstheater, he stops with others, hoping his uniform
is not in some way offensive. From beside him, as the dignitaries
emerge from the limousines, he overhears a whisper, *"Thomas
Mann . . . ist der Nobelpreisträger!"*

Glen wishes Hedy were here. He looks to the group of half a
dozen making its move. The central figure is easily identifiable.
He's a frail man with a narrow, lined face; Glen will read in a
newspaper later that he is almost eighty. He is in Stuttgart to
deliver an address in celebration of the 150th anniversary of the
death of Schiller—the author, Glen knows from grade school, of
William Tell. Thomas Mann is passing and Glen is so pleased,

with the day and with all things in his life, that he smiles—he alone seems to smile rather than stare—and their eyes meet (only later will he learn of Mann's U.S. citizenship and his having not only two sons but a daughter serve in the U.S. Army) and Glen is certain that he sees a conspiratorial glance of recognition and amusement.

A gift to take to Hedy, he thinks. A glimpse into history.

The *Stuttgarter Zeitung* piece he translates later makes mortal the figure with whose eyes he has exchanged a message. Living in Zurich, having moved there from Pacific Palisades, California, two years ago, Mann spoke out early against Hitler and was still accused of betrayal by some Germans. Only in 1952 did conditions settle enough for him to return to Europe to live out his remaining days. He was accompanied on his trip to Stuttgart by his wife of fifty years, Katja Pringsheim, and his daughter, Erika, herself a writer and actress. His older brother, the novelist Heinrich Mann, once more famous in Germany than the Nobel Prize winner, died in 1950 in California, while his oldest son, Klaus, author of *Mephisto* and a World War II writer for the *Stars & Stripes*, took his own life in Cannes in 1949 at the age of forty-two.

Glen is in the motor pool, working on the S-3 jeep, when a thin PFC in fresh khakis appears and says, "Corporal Cady, you're to report to the chaplain, in the post chapel."

"The chaplain?"

"Captain Harris. His office is to the right of the pulpit."

"What for?"

"Report at once, is all I know."

Glen secures the jeep and returns it to the line. Washing his hands in cold water in a small sink between bay doors, he informs the motor pool sergeant, in case someone from S-3 comes looking for him.

"You get some Fräulein pregnant?" the staff sergeant says.

The chapel is half a mile away, and each step of the way Glen wonders why he's being called in by the chaplain. He has a flashing thought of his mother and then wonders if someone, maybe Hedy's husband, might have notified army authorities in the course of her divorce proceeding.

As he enters the chapel the thought of his mother strikes him again. The stained glass windows, the pews and silence of the bright wooden chapel summon him to the Stateside world he's all but forgotten.

"Corporal, I'm afraid we have unfortunate news concerning your mother," the chaplain says. "I'm sorry to tell you she's been gravely injured in an automobile accident, which accident, we're told, occurred yesterday as she was driving to work. A vehicle apparently struck her car from the rear and forced it across the center line, where it was struck by an oncoming car. I must tell you that word from McLaren Hospital is that she's not expected to survive. I'm very sorry. I'm told the accident was so sudden that she's not believed to have suffered any pain. That's the report we've been given, coming from a Mrs. Ellen Foss. You know Mrs. Foss?"

"My mother's sister. Aunt Ellen. She—"

"Yes?" the chaplain says.

"I was just going to say she lives in Fenton, that's all."

Glen stands there. The chaplain is waiting for him to speak but he has lost the urge.

"Corporal, this is always difficult news to hear," the chaplain says. "Still, I need to explain your options. Ten days' emergency leave is *possible*. Should you wish to apply, I'll telephone Battalion Headquarters and you can leave within a couple hours. Nothing's guaranteed concerning travel, however. You can fly by commercial airline, at your expense. Or, which is what most people do, you can go to Rhein/Main and sign up for a hop to the States, from where you can sign up for another hop, to get you as close as possible to your home. Emergency-leave papers will give you priority on flights out of Rhein/Main. Thing to understand is that you bear responsibility for travel arrangements and expenses, and will be expected to return to duty at the completion of your ten days' leave. You're familiar with these regulations?"

"More or less, sir."

"Son, do you wish to apply for emergency leave?"

"Yes sir, I guess I'd like to apply."

"You have adequate funds to cover travel expenses, there and back, should you be unable to gain a hop?"

"Well, I guess not, sir, no sir. Not for a commercial airline."

"In all likelihood you'll get hops; still, it's your responsibility. You understand that?"

"Yes sir."

"Would you also like to apply for emergency pay?"

"Well, no sir. I'll go to Rhein/Main and if I get a hop, I'll go. If not, I don't know, I'll have to think about it."

"I'll initiate emergency-leave papers, which you can pick up in an hour at S-1. My driver will take you to the train station in Stuttgart. You can manage getting a train ticket, you're familiar with the German railroad?"

"Yes sir."

"Would you like to kneel with me, Corporal, and pray?"

"Ah, no sir, I guess not. Thanks, sir."

"As you wish. On your return, if you'd like to talk about your mother's accident, feel free to stop and see me at any time. It's what I'm here for."

When four hours have passed and Glen is on a train heading north to Frankfurt, the shock comes home to him. Telephoning Hedy, packing and picking up leave papers, the ride to the Stutt-gart *Hauptbahnhof* and waiting for a train—throughout it all he's felt numb. Then, while he sits beside the window, the events no longer seem to be happening in a movie, and he guesses his mother has died.

Why did he turn down the offer of emergency pay, which would have allowed him at least the possibility of a commercial flight? To save his money for later trips to Baden-Baden? He has maybe fifty dollars in his wallet, MPCs he'll have to change to greenbacks if it looks like he'll catch a flight. The train rolls on and he realizes he's probably going to the States. After being away for what seems like forever he's headed for every soldier's dream, the Land of the Big PX.

Aunt Ellen picks him up at Selfridge Field Air National Guard Base near Detroit on Saturday afternoon, and Glen puts it together that his mother had died before the chaplain spoke to him. He's surprised at how he falters into weeping on meeting Aunt Ellen at the gate. When he telephoned her, on landing, she told him when his mother had died and that the funeral was scheduled for tomorrow on the chance he'd make it back. She even got him to laugh, telling him drolly to look for "a piss-colored Pontiac assem-bled on a day when everybody on the line was either drunk or hung over." As soon as he saw her he broke down.

The factories. Over dinner, after they visit the funeral home, Uncle Jay says he's pretty sure he can get him on at Chevy when he gets out.

"I still got time to go in the army."

"Four months ain't nothin', you'll be home before you know it," Uncle Jay says.

"I'm not sure what I wanna do," Glen says, hearing his former Michigan self in his voice. "Been thinking I might try college."

"How can you do that when you didn't finish high school?"

"I have a certificate. I can do it."

"Won't make much more money going to college, tell you that."

"I gotta think about it."

"Gettin' any a that kraut stuff over there?" Uncle Jay says.

"Jay, stop it," Aunt Ellen says. "Good Lord, he just came from the funeral home."

Recrossing the Atlantic in a C-47, Glen feels relieved to be returning to the army and to Germany. He doesn't know if the attraction is one or the other or both; he mainly knows that it's summertime and he's going back to where he seems to belong.

The plane refuels at Gander and again in England, before its last leg into Rhein/Main. It's day eight of his ten-day leave. As the plane drones above Germany, he blinks back tears over his mother and tells himself to think out the future. Being taken on at Chevy presents not a good job but confinement, while on the other side of the world Hedy would walk in the garden park in Baden-Baden and along pine-needle paths in the Black Forest. He'd rather stay in the army forever than be on the line at Chevy thinking of her.

His immediate future is easy to sort out. Instead of returning to base, he'll make his way to a country *Gasthaus*, call Hedy, and report for duty Monday morning. His uniform presents the old problem of her being seen with a soldier, but maybe she'll be able to get free and drive to see him.

He's pleased with his plan and imagines she will be, too. His mother is gone now and he's on his own. He wishes she could know that he's become a person who can take care of himself.

Uncle Jay is right about one thing: His time is close at hand.

Aren't Hedy's plans the answer to his plans?

Stepping down from a military shuttle bus, he's struck at once by the richness and summertime color of Frankfurt; he feels he's come home. He's happy here, never happier than on this sad summer day.

Garden cafes are teeming with people. There is beer-drinking and food-cooking and music-playing. Everything is fast and sexy. At the thought of Hedy, love and desire shoot through him. No, he doesn't want to get on at Chevy. What he wants is to become the person he's dreamed of becoming, a person at home with Hedy on a street in Frankfurt, in Vienna, in Zurich.

Avoiding Baden-Baden, he travels by bus to a town called Gernsbach, on the Schwarzwald Tälerstrasse. Throughout the afternoon train ride he's been planning what to do. On his own, and liking it. In death his mother has set him free. And Hedy is there before him.

He could apply for discharge in Germany, although he's heard permission is rarely granted. He could marry her. What a thought! But he's a grown-up, isn't he? If she'd have him, they could get married. It was her idea in the first place, but all at once it's his and his heart is alive with it.

Gernsbach is a village from another century. There is a tight concentration of Tudor buildings with balconies and slanted red-tile roofs and overhangs; the room he rents has a flower box on its small balcony and looks down on an old stone street. No one in the world knows of his whereabouts. This time is extra time in which to live and think, and he decides to line up his thoughts before doing anything. He remains both terrified and thrilled by the idea of proposing to Hedy. Walking into live ammo would require half the mad courage of what he's been thinking to do.

He calls her from a telephone near the *Postamt*, and is reaffirmed in his dreams and plans when she answers on the second ring. She's surprised, but sounds pleased to know he's back and asks about the fate of his mother. She offers sympathy almost formally as he explains what has happened.

"Unbelievable—Gernsbach!" she says then. "You're here in the Black Forest area?"

He tells her he had no chance to return to base to change

clothes, and how he decided to bypass Baden-Baden to avoid the problems of being in uniform.

"Yes, it's difficult that I may see you," she says. "I can't do this until tomorrow, I'm sorry to say. Making arrangement for Ilsedore, being away, everything's difficult, and I haven't known you will surprise me like this!"

"Maybe things will change," he says.

"You don't mind waiting until tomorrow? You will forgive me? You are so close, yet—"

"Tomorrow's fine. I'd love to see you tonight, but tomorrow's fine. I'm sorry I didn't carry civilian clothes."

"I'll come to you there tomorrow," she says. "I'm uncertain what arrangement to make for Ilsedore, but I may promise to visit you there. Eleven is okay? Shall we say eleven?"

"Eleven's fine—I can't wait. I think about you all the time. More than ever."

Glen is excited, and when he walks in the village and settles into a garden restaurant to eat, the setting and evening couldn't be more attractive. The air is full of farm and flower smells, and the food is delicious. He walks out of town where a valley meets the forest, and sits on a hillside bench. He wonders if his excited boldness is a sign of manhood.

It isn't until the morning, standing on the balcony between boxes of geraniums, that he answers the question hovering in his mind. He's eaten a continental breakfast, has shaved and walked again, an impending happiness all the while alive in him. He doesn't know the answer, though perhaps he does. As he rests elbows on the flower box and gazes over the narrow street, it comes to him that he's going to go ahead and do it. He's going to ask her.

The location doesn't matter. He can see the three of them driving across the USA in a new Chevy convertible. They'd be madly happy, and what a thrill it would be to show her the USA. She'd love it, and they'd love California. Maybe they'd go to Pacific Palisades, where Thomas Mann used to live. He'd engage all gears and take the place by storm, that's what he'd do. If they were together, nothing in Los Angeles would hold him back.

Or, if it's what she wants, he'll stay here. Or go to the States to be discharged and return, although he'd have to get a passport

and work permit. He can't imagine anything but happiness anywhere. And if he decides to live and work in Germany, he thinks,
he'll really have to learn the language. He'll do anything, because
he loves her, and he's not going back to work in a factory and
will mark this moment on a balcony in Gernsbach as a turning
point in his life.

Tonight, he thinks. When it's dark and peaceful and they lie
together, he'll tell her what he has in mind for them and ask if
she's ready to take California by storm.

Hedy doesn't arrive at eleven, and at eleven-thirty he's still standing
in front of the *Gasthaus* looking for her green VW to appear over
the rise at the end of the street. That she is late doesn't bother
him; the circumstances are fresh and uncertain. But when twelve
bells sound throughout the forested valley he begins to worry.
He'd have liked to wait on the balcony with its view, but has
checked out, hopeful of spending the night in her hillside house.

At last there is her car, and in a flurry of apologies and explana-
tions he gets into the front seat, places his bag in the rear, and
removes his cap as he touches her and they embrace, and lateness
no longer matters. She looks and smells as beautiful as the flowers
in bloom, and all he wants is to keep touching her. "God, I love
you," he tells her. "I'm so crazy about you!"

They move apart and she asks if he is sad over the loss of his
mother, and he says he finds it hard to believe she's no longer
alive.

"At the same time, I've never felt so happy. I think it's because
I'm so much on my own, and can do anything now. It's because
I'm with you."

They sit in the car, the motor turned off, and she says, "You've
checked out? I have to tell you it's impossible to be in my house
tonight. I have been unable to make arrangement for Ilsedore,
who is with my friend at this moment, as I said, and it's also true
not only that my former husband is present to visit, but there are
other visits tomorrow from my family. It's so complicated, I don't
know if I'm able to explain."

"It's okay. You're divorced, it's final?"

"Yes, I, too, have independence I have not known. Still, it's
possible my husband may yet make trouble, concerning Ilsedore.

I must be careful. For this reason I'm not able to see you tomorrow. I'm so sorry for this, yet you have taken me by surprise."

"I should stay here, is what you're saying?"

"You won't be too disappointed?"

"It's okay. Main thing is I wanted to see you, and here you are."

"I'm so sorry. There have been so many things at once."

"I'll stay here. I'll take a bus to Karlsruhe tomorrow and catch a train back to Stuttgart. Right now, I'll drop off my bag and reclaim my room."

"In which time I shall park out of the way. May we have lunch and a drink here where it's so peaceful? I love the quietness, I can't tell you."

"I'll be back in five minutes."

Glen checks back into the hotel, carries his bag back to the same room, and returns to the street. Hedy is coming his way and one of two men passing calls out a remark. The two men laugh, going along, adding comments to each other which Glen doesn't understand. "What did he say?" he says to Hedy.

"It is nothing," she says. "They are having too much to drink. It is nothing."

"Tell me what he said," Glen says, angry with himself and the awkwardness he feels, knowing the substance of the remarks if not the words.

"Glen, it's *not* to be listened to for a moment," she says. "They are only foolish men having too much to drink."

He leads her to the garden restaurant he visited the night before. Flowers are all around and they touch sides in walking, and touch hands over the white tablecloth, and order local wine. Glen says then, with a smile, "Tell me what that guy said."

"He has said, 'There goes a hot number.' "

"Guy's right," Glen says. "You are a hot number. All I do is think about you, and there's nothing I want more than to be in bed with you, because I'm crazy about you, and there's something I've been wanting to tell you, too, to ask you."

She holds his hands across the table. "I think you have changed some," she says. She's smiling and his thought is that she could not be more beautiful than she is here in the shaded garden, but when a moment passes and she doesn't ask him what it is he wants to say, it comes to him as if on a current of summer air that something is different.

In the afternoon they visit her friend Lotte, to check on Ilsedore. They're having coffee in the living room when Lotte is all at once in a panic, looking out at the driveway and speaking rapidly to Hedy in German. To Glen, Hedy says, "Dear God, my former husband is here. Well, there's nothing to do. I shall introduce you as a friend. It's okay. There's nothing to do."

The doorbell rings, and with an expression of helplessness Lotte leaves to answer. "You are my friend, it's all there is to it," Hedy whispers.

Lotte returns with a man who is squarish, balding in front, a man in his forties dressed in suit and tie, smiling, taking Hedy's hand and leaning to kiss her cheek near her ear—did he whisper something?—as spurts of German are exchanged. He extends a hand to Glen. "Yes, how are you?" he says pleasantly, and they shake.

"Fine, how are you."

They stand by the window, looking at the view, and an awkward moment of silence passes, until Lotte says, "Hans, you shall like coffee, or are you liking another drink?"

English is the language of conversation, for Glen's benefit, impressing and depressing him at the same time. Well, it isn't going to be a fistfight, he thinks, but polite conversation.

The chitchat is neither rude nor unfriendly, yet there is an issue over nothing more than sitting down. Glen stands silent near the windows while Hedy and her former husband make small talk in English. Lotte, returning with Hans's drink, invites them all to sit down and Glen surprises himself by saying, "I'll stand, that's fine."

He has no idea why he said it. It seems like an attempt to assert manliness, although he's aware of it doing the opposite. "No, come, sit down, please," Lotte and Hedy say, but he's committed himself and can't change his mind without seeming even more foolish. "It's okay, I'll stand," he says.

The others ignore the awkwardness; they are three adults and they move to the coffee table. Why should they remain standing on account of the curious behavior of a young American soldier.

Not even a lieutenant or a captain, but a nineteen-year-old corporal. Is his age as apparent to Lotte and Hans as it seemed, long ago, to be unapparent to Hedy?

They sit and Glen stands. He's by the windows and they are sitting around the coffee table across the room. The situation grows inceasingly awkward as time goes on. "Glen, join us," Hedy says— bravely, he thinks.

He fights the impulse to say, "It's okay, I like to stand." He crosses and sits down, feeling even worse for having given up his pose on a word.

The moments are the longest he's ever endured. Since the others are smoking he brings out his Camels, takes one, and places the package on the table. "Please," he says. There is no response. Conversation, such as it is, seems to have to do with a World Cup team of which Glen knows nothing. To ingratiate himself, he says, "I saw Thomas Mann a while back."

There is no response, and Glen doesn't know what is wrong, if it's the subject, or his timing.

Hedy says, "You are joking, yes?"

"No. A few weeks ago, in Stuttgart. I was walking. Two limousines pulled over, where people were waiting, and Thomas Mann got out to go into the building. The others—one was his daughter, I read in the paper—I don't know who they were. His wife."

Again, there is silence. Did he say something he wasn't supposed to say? Do they think he's lying?

"The author, Thomas Mann?" Hedy says.

"Yes, the Nobel Prize winner."

No one speaks until Hans says, "Yes, he has recently moved to Switzerland, from California, I have read of this." It's like a remark extended in sympathy.

In another minute the get-together concludes, leaving him relieved and eternally dissatisfied with himself. Everyone else appears equally relieved. There are quick handshakes; Glen nods and shakes and still feels a fool. He's in over his head.

In his continuing embarrassment, he doesn't know what to say in the wake of Hans's departure, cannot think of a way to salvage things. In time Ilsedore awakens and Hedy has to return him to Gernsbach. Outside he says to the air, "I acted like a donkey."

She says nothing to this as they drive. Glen has no idea how to shed his embarrassment. When Hedy says, "I'm so sorry, I must attend now to Ilsekind," he feels only more distance.

"I'm sorry," he says, as she stops before the *Gasthaus*. "You can't stay for a while?"

"Really, I must go back."

"I don't know what to say."

She smiles pleasantly. "I know," she says. "You'll feel better in the morning."

He kisses her goodbye, wanting to hold on, hating himself. He moves across the seat to get out. "You're right," he says, "I'll feel better in the morning," and outside watches the green VW drive away along the narrow street. He waves, waiting for a wave, a toot for love, knowing none will come.

30

He's encouraged about reenlistment. In the S-3 jeep, returning to base after a week in the field, Major Guptill and Sergeant Doughan tell him he may have put it off too long already. They're returning in convoy, side curtains off, summer air blowing throughout, and Glen is oddly pained by the attention of the two men who like him and whose company in the army, he's come to realize, he most enjoys.

"Don't let it go until the last minute," Doughan says from the rear. "Who knows who'll be in charge of S-3 a month from now."

Glen drives, vaguely aware that he's about to become a short-timer, more aware of other unanswered questions in his life.

"You're how old now?" the major says.

"Almost twenty, sir."

"Your birthday?"

"August 1, sir."

"You enlisted when you turned seventeen?"

"Yes, sir."

"You couldn't have a better handle on retirement."

Glen keeps following the colonel's jeep. He'd like to talk about his problem, but cannot. He's tanned after the outdoor time in the field, driving along dirt roads with the jeep-top removed, and should be going back in high spirits to a long shower and an evening of freedom in town. But he keeps thinking as he drives that he would go awol, whatever the consequences, to see Hedy for one minute. For a day and night with her like it used to be, he feels capable of anything. Why hasn't she written? he wonders. As if he doesn't know.

"Did thirty," the major says. "You could retire, full pay and benefits, at age forty-six. That might be hard to appreciate until you're in the neighborhood, but take my word for it, it's a big deal. Not just pay, you'd retain full privileges; could live in Europe like a king. Could live in Florida, the Caribbean; you'd have time in your life to do a whole second career. Could go to college at that age, too, because you'd still have the GI Bill. Could just deep-sea fish every day if you wanted to."

Doughan leans forward. "Whatta ya say, Corporal?"

"I hear you talking," Glen says. "I appreciate it. I just have to work out something personal before I know what to do."

"Hell with him, sir," Doughan says, sitting back. "Too dumb to see what's before his nose, living all around the world, always doing something different."

"Sleeping in the mud, soggy rations and no toilet paper, running out for alerts at midnight," the major says.

"I'd still rather do that, any day," Doughan says, "than be tied to some two-bit job half my life. Whatta ya do, you retire when you're sixty-five goddamn years old? Imagine, working in a smelly factory, some dried-up office, punching a clock and doing the same thing day after day. That's what draftees do, most of 'em, spend their lives punching a clock like fucking sheep. What's this personal shit anyway? That's what I'd like to know."

"Don't overdo it, Jake," the major says. "I think he's got the message."

"Got it, sir, loud and clear," Glen says.

"So what's this personal shit?" the major says.

The three of them laugh as Glen drives along, hoping for another mix-up in the mail room but knowing better.

He tries to believe Hedy went north to her family and has yet to receive the two letters he wrote in the field. Then he wonders if she's punishing him for the embarrassment he caused in the presence of her former husband. Maybe he should let her know he'd planned to propose the day things went wrong. Maybe he should reenlist and get a promotion while he can, seek a transfer Stateside and begin living without her.

Another day, after the 1300 hours Work Call formation, he

places a call. Don't, he tells himself, and even as the woman is placing the call, he thinks he ought to wait another day in hopes of receiving a letter.

"I haven't heard from you," he says when Hedy is on the line. "I've been worried that something's wrong."

"Oh, it is my fault—I'm so sorry. I will write soon and explain everything. I'm very sorry, Glen. I don't mean to have you worry. Things have been busy like no other time."

"Things are okay?" he asks, knowing that they aren't.

"Please, let me explain in a letter, please. And I must go now— I'm sorry—Ilsedore is walking and reaching and I must look to her at once, that she is not hurting herself. Please, I will write soon."

"I love you. That's not going to change."

After a pause she says, "You sound so downcast, you know. You're too young for this. I'll write at once, I promise—now I must hurry—goodbye for now."

Returning to the motor pool to work on the S-3 jeep, Glen feels a little reassured for having spoken to her. She was right that he's too young to be so downcast, although he knows the reasons why. When the afternoon hour is close to retreat, someone speaks to him as he is head and arms in the jeep's motor. He looks up to see Doughan leaning under the hood. "Don't move an inch; I want to talk to you," Doughan says.

Glen looks over the engine at Doughan and his array of ribbons and stripes.

"I don't know what's going on with you, but I know I don't like it," Doughan near-whispers. "Pains me to see a person fuck hisself up for no reason."

Glen holds within the shadow of the propped-up hood.

"So what the fuck's going on?"

"Nothing," Glen says. "Nothing really."

"Come on, don't waste my time."

"I have a problem with a woman," Glen admits.

"Might have known. She pregnant?"

Glen shakes his head no.

"Married?"

"Not anymore," Glen says.

"German?"

Glen nods.

"What's the deal, she want to get married and you don't?"

"Not that, no."

"She got you by the balls?"

"I guess that's what it is."

"She squeezing?"

Glen shrugs vaguely, smiles thinly.

"Is she?" Doughan says.

"She's too high-class," Glen says.

"What's that mean?"

"She's too high-class to be with an enlisted man."

"How'd it happen?"

"I don't know, it just happened."

"Shake loose."

"I haven't been able to."

"Have to," Doughan says, and straightens up. "You got a hell of an opportunity here. And you gotta know you'd never be happy with a woman like that. Be a man. Walk away from it."

Then it's Friday. In the past they would have set up a meeting for the weekend. Then at mail call he's handed one of her pale green envelopes. She's written and he knows what the letter is going to say.

He walks from the quadrangle to be by himself, wondering if he should carry this letter like he did the others. Not this time.

Wandering past the closed post theater and bowling alleys, he settles on a spot at the side of the Service Club, where a stone wall extends into the shadows from nearby trees. He lights a cigarette, and tells himself that he'll hold to whatever amount of pride he has left. He snuffs the cigarette between his fingers, takes the slight burn as if for mettle, field-strips, and scatters the remains.

Dear Glen,

I hope you are not angry with me when you read the following words. I guess you have expected this after the last time I saw you. I could explain a hundred things to you which I should have done or should have let you know before now. But I could not, because I have not been able to make up my mind until this week, when I was having a day's rest.

What I want to tell you right now is that I'll marry again. Not today or tomorrow, but someday. But before I take this step I have to do an awful lot of thinking. That I wished to see you again was because I had to make sure that I was not in love with you anymore. I wanted to tell you that day about all of this but I did not have the nerve and, besides, could not make up my mind for anything in the world.

Glen, I don't mean to hurt you. What I hope is that you'll forget me soon and find a sweet young girl who really loves you. Anyway, you go back home. There are so many things for you to see and do. It's a change and I believe it may help you. Please forgive me, Glen. I wish you all the best for your future. Goodbye and good luck.

Hedy

He returns the letter to his shirt pocket. He doesn't blame her, he thinks as he gets to his feet. All that pains him is being told to find a sweet young girl, being told to go back to where he belongs.

He didn't want to get married anyway, he tells himself as he walks awkwardly on his way. What a dumb thing to want to do, when he hasn't even turned twenty. Then it comes to him that he's back to being nothing more than another soldier, another worker, and he'll never see Hedy or walk with her or touch her again, and his legs seem for an instant to lose their strength.

31

August 1, 1955, is Glen's twentieth birthday. Traveling by bus to Stuttgart, he goes to a movie at the Crossroads, trying not to look around for Hedy. Movies and bus rides have changed for him. He takes a look at a calendar and counts his handful of days left in the army.

A day comes when he is turned back to the company. The major has shipped out, and on a Monday morning Captain Cahill strides into the S-3 offices with a clipboard, looks at Glen, and says, "Corporal, I don't like short-timers on my team and you are hereby turned back to the company. Want your desk cleaned and you out of this office, twelve hundred hours today."

The captain walks into what had been the major's office. No one speaks, and activity starts up again. Glen knows it is about fifteen past eleven, but he looks at his watch anyway, to keep himself moving. He gave his best to the army and this is the end. Jobs well done are not given thanks.

Opening drawers, he deposits pens, lighter, small personal items in a manila envelope, and five minutes later walks out of the office without looking back. He thinks, Well, another day is passing; he'll do work details in the company, pull a lot of guard duty, and nothing will alter his move toward discharge and civilian life.

The tedious detail of guard duty will be his final reward from the army. Also, since there is an abundance of corporals on post, he has been assigned as a private, along with corporals from other companies. Some are short-timers and some are lifers who have fallen low, blue veins decorating their cheeks and noses. They are all at the end of things, and have little to say to one another.

He'll go home and try to get on at Chevy, Glen accepts at last, as he prepares for another tour of guard. Maybe stay with Ellen and Jay for a couple of months until he figures out what to do next. He'll check out the possibilities of going to college, and maybe he'll go to California by himself. But maybe not. What is he, anyway, besides a twenty-year-old high school dropout who has spent three years in the army?

Things could be worse. He could have ended up like one of these lifers, he thinks as he snaps to for inspection. Whether he'd blazed through to staff sergeant or not, another Captain Cahill would have been waiting for him. He would have wound up tipping bottles, humming sad songs, and thinking about a German woman and what might have been.

The officer of the guard, a first lieutenant, steps before him and Glen presents his rifle, chamber open. "Looking sharp," the first lieutenant says, and the sergeant of the guard, sidestepping with him, issues one-each clip live ammo. Up and down, Glen thinks, eyes ahead.

A twig breaks and his ears perk up. The sound came from brush to his left, and reaching a hand to the ground, he presses himself upright. Something—an animal, a person—had to have broken the twig and Glen continues swiveling in slow motion and raising his rifle in the direction of the sound. The day's officer of the guard is First Lieutenant Cohen, a West Pointer and an officer Glen knows from his S-3 glory days in the field. Cohen could be testing the guards in some West Point exercise.

There is a crash of twigs, then silence. Someone is there, though it's hard to tell how far away. Has to be human, Glen thinks, or it wouldn't pause like that. Still, he wonders if it could be a wild boar. Silence. He presses his rifle to his shoulder without entering a round into the chamber, sights down the rear sight, and looks for movement through brush and branches.

Twigs break again, closer, and he sees a shadow of movement, thirty feet away. In the distance, in the direction of the sounds, is the fence.

There's a flash of red, red and yellow! Someone is moving closer and Glen knows it's likely to be a GI without a pass, but at every guard formation they are warned to be alert for nationals, saboteurs, thieves trying to get on post, and he lets the red-and-yellow figure continue, knowing that in a second he's going to send a shock of fear into its system.

"HALT!" he roars.

The figure holds—Glen can see it's a man. In case he's being tested by Lieutenant Cohen, he adds, "ADVANCE TO BE REC-OGNIZED!"

"Easy now," a voice says.

The voice is oddly familiar, and as the figure ducks under branches and comes into view, Glen's thoughts seem to go blank. "Thatcher, my God, what're you doing?"

In the next moment Glen realizes that former First Sergeant Thatcher, his eyes liquidly red and something leaking from a corner of his mouth, is loaded. Not staggering drunk as in days past, but deeply juiced. They have sat down and are smoking Glen's cigarettes by the time Glen, still astonished that Thatcher is here, asks again what he's doing, where he's going.

"Jus' wanted a look-see," Thatcher says.

He sits there, more disoriented than seems possible for the cocksure first sergeant of only a year ago. A smile forming, he says, "Cady, you'se a goddamn corporal *last* time I saw you."

"Where'd you get that shirt?" Glen says. "Could spot you a mile away."

"Make my way to NCO Club, everybody jus' think some no-account off-duty NCO having a little drink."

"Get caught, you'll get thrown in the brig."

"Wish they would, is the truth. I'd rather be in the brig than where I been, I'll tell ya that. Logged more goddamn Greyhound miles you'd believe—ain't worth a shit nowhere, thas what I know. Thought I'd come back and see how things're going."

Glen has to hold a match for several moments, nearly burning his fingers, before Thatcher, trembling, pulls flame into the tobacco of another cigarette. He comes up grinning, and Glen notices again how drunk he is.

"What the hell you doin' on guard duty? Thought you'd be a goddamn three-star general by now."

"Man, you got it bad," Glen says.

"Tell ya what I don't got, is goddamn money," Thatcher says. "Maybe got some somewhere, but I don't know where."

"What're you gonna do with yourself, Sarge? I don't get it."

"Goin' to the NCO Club get a drink, if I can get you to loosen up and loan me some fuckin' MPCs."

"You look up Ingrid?"

"Don't want nothin' to do with me."

"You're hittin' the skids, Sarge, who could blame her."

"Hit the skids long time ago. Loan me five? Jesus, I gotta beg?"

"I'll loan you five, but what you oughta do is turn yourself in at the dispensary. They'll take care of you."

"Gonna give me this five today or should I come back tomorrow?"

Glen removes his wallet, sees that it contains a ten and two singles, and gives over the ten. "Owe me ten," he says.

Thatcher pushes to his feet. "Ain't gonna shoot me, are you, an' take it back?"

Glen gets to his feet, too. "It's not a bad idea," he says.

"Make it count," Thatcher says. "I wouldn't mind the shot, but I don't care for the sight a blood."

As Thatcher moves off on a no-look wave, Glen sees that his quiet movements had less to do with stealth than weakness. He's weak and broken and has to move one uneven footfall at a time. He calls without looking, "Stop by NCO Club, buy you a drink."

In another moment the Hawaiian shirt has vanished and Glen imagines Thatcher on the dirt road which leads to the Service Club and PX, looking like another off-duty lifer down on his luck. And when the day ends—maybe a second day if he doesn't slip off post—he'll be reported, or stopped and charged by the MPs, probably escorted to the gate and once again shown the door.

Days later at a Work Call formation word comes that Glen's orders are in. Even as it had to happen, it's a shock to think of being shipped home for discharge. He's twenty and getting out, merely a lifetime after he arrived. Is it what he really wants to happen?

Operation Flyaway. The luck of the draw has him scheduled to return by plane rather than troopship. Twenty-three August 55, 0900 hours, he will gather before Battalion Headquarters with other EM on orders, and they will be transported by army bus to Rhein/Main. From there they'll be redeployed by plane to the Zone of the Interior for discharge from bases nearest home. Glen's orders list his destination as Fort Sheridan, Illinois. From there, he's told, he'll be issued one-each train or bus ticket to his hometown. His army time over, he'll be on his own.

There are a few days left. He clears post, ships a box of personal items to Aunt Ellen's, and reduces all possessions to what will fit in his duffel bag. The stack of mail from Hedy he takes outside to the Dumpster in the bulkhead, lights the corner of one of the envelopes, and uses it to light the others, the telegrams and glossy cards. As the words turn to ashes he tries to think of nothing at all.

Sunday morning, buying the *Stars & Stripes* as he enters the mess hall, he reads that Thomas Mann died in Zurich on August 12. The Nobel Prize winner was eighty years old, the article reports, and Glen wonders how the news is being received elsewhere and what it signifies anywhere around the world.

On Sunday afternoon, in khakis laundered and pressed enough to reveal time in grade, he walks down the long hill into town for the last time, to have a bite to eat in a German *Gasthaus*. In the morning he'll bring his duffel bag to the bus which will carry him on the first leg of the journey home.

He strolls in town with little appetite. Had he stayed it would be time to add a new uniform to his wardrobe, maybe new stripes, too.

A sunny afternoon in August. He reads glassed-in menus, making his way, he knows, in the direction of Der Baron. There, he takes the table where they sat the night he fell victim to himself and the duplicitous *Festbier*. Why did she wait so long to do it?

In memory of his first meal in a German restaurant, when *"Beefsteak"* was the only German word he recognized on the menu, he orders *Beefsteak Tartar* and half a liter of beer. Surprised that first time to see a cup-shape of raw ground beef presented on a plate, he found the raw seasoned beef tasty and exciting. Here again he follows with a sip of beer, savors the mix of flavors, and gives in to a stray thought or two, glances around, wonders where she is today.

DINING OUT WITH
ERIKA MANN
Fall 1989

32

Hedy is living in Bonn under the name Andreas-Kahler. Why she would have kept and hyphenated her first married name in a subsequent marriage is a mystery to Glen. But the search procedure by the German consulate has verified that the woman living in the capital city is the Hedy Andreas he once knew.

For his three-week stay in Berlin, he's limited himself to a single carry-on bag. A Lufthansa Boeing 747, overnight from Logan International to Frankfurt. From Rhein/Main, after a two-and-a-half-hour layover, he'll fly across East Germany to Tegel Airport in West Berlin. He's traveling light for the freedom it allows and in case he'll want to walk distances—in case, really, he'll want to leave a train or bus to run after someone seen passing on a platform or sidewalk. It's a dream he's had all his life. If he doesn't catch the person who passes by, how will he ever know if it is her?

When he left home thirty-seven years ago he carried a toilet-articles kit and nothing else. The kit and a ten-dollar bill were gifts from his mother. He had been seventeen less than a month and had completed the tenth grade. The day he left—his mother said goodbye that morning before leaving for first shift—he stopped at the army/navy recruiting office for his bus ticket and walked two blocks along a street of dirty plate-glass windows to board a Greyhound bus on its way to the Fort Wayne Induction Center in Detroit. In addition to the kit and ten-dollar bill he carried cigarettes and a book of matches in his shirt pocket. He did not carry a pen or pencil there.

His departure tonight has him caught up in reflections on time and age. Just ten days ago he learned that Hedy was alive and located in Bonn. The tracing procedure, its forms and fees, did not daunt him. But the form he received, with her current name, address, and telephone number, did not reveal how many times she may have married, or if she remained married, or if she would mind a surprise visit out of the past.

What kind of person has she become? Has he been forgotten? Is it possible to forget love letters, secretive phone calls, and secret meetings? Maybe but one member of a pair chooses not to forget.

He hasn't written to the address in Bonn, and wonders if he should even think about trying to contact her. The question has visited his dreams, some of which have been accompanied by nearly forgotten sensations. Should he go close enough to 36 Aindorfer Strasse to see her from afar, as in an old Russian short story? Might he arrange a public encounter in a nearby *Lebensmittel* or *Apotheke*? Would a telephone call out of the blue stun her with embarrassment? Has she aged, or is she as fit and lovely as a movie star living in Switzerland? Would she agree to meet in a side-street cafe, or on the deck of a streamside tavern? Would she care to know she has remained in his imagination all these years? Would a woman of her age indulge him this way?

The Boeing 747 jets into the dark, foreshortened skies and Glen is too anxious to relax. There are magazines and newspapers, and a movie, but he has no wish to escape. He feels renewed, given the turns things have taken in recent weeks, and tries to settle into this magical dimension, as if he's been tending, always, toward this vortex. An alignment of stars and planets occurring once in a lifetime.

The thought of actually seeing her terrifies him, and so does the thought of her seeing him. Sexlove in a previous lifetime. In any narrative of the kind, do such youthful emotions survive? And what if she is not up to *his* standards? Could he be disappointed with the quality of her mind, after decades of recalling her sophistication? Could she turn out to be a most ordinary woman who once had a passing affair with a teenage American soldier?

The best turn of events would find her happy and secure enough in her life for them to smile over the past. Or would it be best, he wonders, if she were free and a spark between them reignited? Could they like each other and call up an exotic flavor of lost life and love? He has always thought that Hedy would be of a mind to employ what works—in a German way—if it meant squeaking latex, open-ended black brassiere, or provocative language. The old sexual call of Germany; it has him feeling younger as he hurtles in this constant hum through space and time. As an hour is lost, a new hour is gained.

Hedy is down and out, but beautiful still. He's her lifesaver, though there is nothing melodramatic in their encounter. She works as a waitress to get along, and there is curiosity over how each has fared in life. New friendship arises, a new rainbow of options presents itself.

Later, she is less lovely but has a heart of gold. A heavy smoker and drinker, she is wan and thin. Yet her eyes glisten and her smile is mischievous; she possesses generosity and wisdom and could not be more appealing. He finds her in a tavern and they sit in a booth and drink and talk. They talk and laugh into drunkenness and into one day and another, engage in a smoky-boozy affair, sleep soundly, and awaken to inebriated wisdom and sweet old songs, to freedom and happiness. They seize some time together, until the century clicks up a new row of zeros, and on a last drink she rests her head on his shoulder and his hand cradles her body as they let the world go on its way.

Der Spiegel, Stern, Die Zeit, Frankfurter Allgemeine Zeitung, Süddeutsche Zeitung, Le Monde, the London *Times, The New York Times*. All are available, but taking a look, Glen realizes he is still too distracted to settle down. All carry front-page accounts of events in East Germany, but having already followed the story closely, he decides to leave the news for catching up when he arrives in Berlin.

A professor? The possibility falls immediately into place. Literature and Cambridge. Professor Hedy—as he imagines her being known to students and colleagues—fools around a little still, and smokes and drinks. She affects the intellectual style of Simone de

Beauvoir; glasses hang from her neck and she smiles readily, which green-eyed glances have *Bierkeller* literati stealing looks. Her writings on sexual psychology in D. H. Lawrence have set standards for the psychoanalysts themselves. She was always her own person, Glen thinks. What would have stopped her?

The abridged night slips away by two a.m., when the captain's voice on the intercom announces the new day in English and German: "*Guten Morgen, meine Damen und Herren....* Presently it is eight o'clock in Frankfurt, where we will be landing in one hour fifteen minutes. The morning weather is overcast, sorry to say. The temperature at present is twenty degrees Celsius, sixty-eight degrees Fahrenheit. Yes, a damp autumn day in Frankfurt, but what do raindrops matter to Oktoberfest in Munich? Hot towels will be provided momentarily, with continental breakfast soon to follow...."

Glen hasn't slept, but no matter. The wadded hours have been tortuous, but he takes the hot, damp towel, refreshes himself, and lowers his tray in anticipation of juice and coffee, of touching down and stepping from the plane. Small window curtains go up, letting in morning light, and here and there voices have begun to speak softly in English and German. He wishes Alice were here.

Frankfurt *Hauptbahnhof* and its surrounding streets, where Glen travels by train during the layover, are disappointing to his romanticized memory. The area is dirtier and more crime-ridden than he remembers, and appears to have lost its gaudy vitality. The drabness makes Europe seem less exotic and makes Hedy less possible. They met here once for a mere thirty minutes, at the V corner opposite the *Bahnhof*, and Frankfurt was more vibrant then than stagnant.

He doesn't feel like sleeping during the seventy-minute flight over turbulent East Germany. His instinct is still to discover new life, and he determines to forgo the day's sleep he's missing altogether. He'll awaken rested tomorrow, adjusted to Berlin time and ready to start afresh.

Exchanging greenbacks at Tegel—appreciative in his weak, sleepless state of the light bag he carries—he rides the S-Bahn into central West Berlin, to the station called Bahnhof am Zoo. He walks and has a *Wurst* and glass of beer at a cafeteria-style

restaurant on the Ku-Damm and—is he coming or going?—
returns within the hour to Bahnhof am Zoo. There is no rain in
West Berlin and the autumn air is balmy.

Day is turning at last; a clock before the *Bahnhof* reads ten
past seven. Using his guidebook and a nine-dollar street map
bought at a newspaper counter, he returns along the Ku-Damm
in search of Hotel am Zoo, where Thomas Wolfe stayed in 1938.
In the hotel lobby, taking his time, wanting to stay away from
beds and awake until Berlin's bedtime is closer, he learns that the
Mielein Institute is twelve kilometers away, in a district called
Zehlendorf. The Wall, he learns, is two or three kilometers in an
easterly direction. Be careful in the vicinity of the Wall, he's told.

Returning to the wide Ku-Damm sidewalk, he strolls again,
caught in an out-of-body feeling. He feels as though time has
skipped a beat.

He'd like to see Checkpoint Charlie and U.S. soldiers on duty,
for sentimental reasons, and plans to do so early in the morning.
Like an old grad returned to his alma mater, he looks forward to
glimpsing the past. He has yet to see a single American in uniform,
and only later will he learn that Germany has become too expensive
for GIs, that they live in pockets and ghettos.

Returning for the third time—the fourth?—to Bahnhof am
Zoo, he asks at the hotel registry whether Zehlendorf contains
pensions and is reachable by S-Bahn, and is told "Absolutely."
Presented with a list he selects Pension JFK, and is handed a slip
of paper bearing its address.

Pension JFK, what a name, he thinks, as he walks to the S-
Bahn platform. He's read that Berlin is home to no less than five
thousand taverns, called *Kneipen*, that Berliners have a sardonic
sense of humor and love JFK. Is a Pension Gorby next? It's a
pleasant thought.

Downtown Zehlendorf is attractively lighted with store windows and cafes and he decides—it can be no more than half a
dozen blocks—to walk to Pension JFK. Thus does he bypass a
row of taxis, and for the first time since the beginning of his
downward spiral, walking along, he experiences relief at being
divorced. Here at last, he's starting over.

33

He realizes, not for the first time, that he could look up and see her face. It also occurs to him that he could take up smoking again—it would make him feel young. He's tempted as he sips coffee at an outdoor stand. A cigarette and her certain smile. He slept for ten hours and feels younger and lighter than he can remember.

Waiting for the pension dining room to open at 0630, he walks around the world in which he will spend the coming weeks, looks over fresh baked goods and Sunday morning newspapers, and takes in the *Berliner Luft*, sixty degrees on his legs and seventy on his face. The smell of tobacco also marks the city air, but he has no inclination to really light up a strong German cigarette, not just yet. It would probably take extreme joy or extreme despair for him to give in to the urge.

After breakfast he's also eager to make his way back to the central city and to East Berlin, and his vitality continues to surprise him. It must be the famous Berlin air.

He walks in search of W. H.-Auden-Strasse and the building housing the Mielein Institute, passing along the way Trumanplaza and Clay-Allee. The institute, surrounded by lawn and lush green shrubs, is built of thick-walled beige stucco, four stories high, perhaps at one time a residence of eighteen or twenty rooms. It looks the way Glen imagines New York publishing houses once looked.

As he sits at a table in the pension dining room, pouring coffee from a ceramic pot, he's struck: he's forgotten the second of two postcards promised to Alice. A card from Frankfurt is on its way, but words from West Berlin have yet to be written.

Their game of cards making their way to her is a small thing. He'll buy one at once, pen a message, and get it on its way. A card to Max, too. But within the modest oversight he sees an unpleasant reality. A space between him and his daughter has begun to open.

In his room, clearing his pockets and wallet in preparation for a half-day excursion into East Berlin—his guidebook advises against giving border guards any excuse to detain and question—he watches a CNN-TV report of demonstrations in Leipzig and East Berlin. History is taking major turns just a bus ride away. World War II is concluding at last, and he must look to final chapters of his own. Life itself punishes those who lag behind, Gorbachev remarked but a few weeks earlier to East Germany, and Glen believes he must adopt the slogan as his own.

Leaving, he's intercepted by Herr Schultheiss, the proprietor, who insists on speaking English while Glen insists on speaking German. Herr Schultheiss wants him to know that a typical Berliner is always quick to satirize. Also, that Americans are more popular in Berlin, with its sense of the sardonic, than in the Federal Republic, with its sense of the deutschmark. He compliments Glen on his accent and warns him to be cautious in the vicinity of the Wall. All-inclusive demonstration for reform again today, Herr Schultheiss wants him to understand. Who knows if this Krenz is not also turning to violence? Freedom is in the air, but so is the smell of blood.

"Will the Wall be taken down?" Glen asks on his way out.

"The Wall dismantled? Not ever. Not in our lifetime. There will be always East Germany. Those—I have heard this—those who imagine reunification have no sense of reality. In the two Berlins today, Professor, is the reality of tomorrow!"

On his way to the S-Bahn and Checkpoint Charlie, Glen detours to attend to something which has been on his mind all morning. At the *Postamt*, by the row of hanging directories, he swivels and opens a volume labeled "Bonn." Looking under *K* for 36 Aindorfer Strasse, he finds "Kahler, Ernst."

Of course she has a husband. What did he expect?

Passing through Checkpoint Charlie at 0900, he is one of dozens and the U.S. Army MPs are hardly different from policemen anywhere. He walks another fifty yards to the DDR border, where he spends more than an hour in line, waiting to be issued a one-day visa and to exchange the required twenty-five deutsch-marks for nonrefundable East German marks. On the East Berlin side, immediately in the midst of pedestrians, he feels anticipation in the air, like Kenmore Square before a Red Sox game, or Ann Arbor on a football Saturday. There are few cars on the wide boulevards, and people, many of them, keep surfacing from underground, emerging from buses and side streets in pairs, trios, foursomes, walking hard, talking, and tending toward that gathering ahead. It's nearly eleven a.m. and the sun seems more hazed with industrial and cigarette smoke than in the West. He's suddenly passed by three young men, one to the left, two to the right, striding hard without speaking to one another.

He moves with the flow along Friedrichstrasse to the intersection of Unter den Linden, where still more people are converging from other directions. Thousands, tens of thousands of people are congregating for a demonstration, just as he's seen on television. He takes his time to circle among the crowds and observe, looking over the Reichschancellery and Hitler's bunker, an open space covered with rubble, and recalling in a blur the near-half-century of books and movies he's seen depicting the rise and fall of Nazism, the photographs of the horror and the near-obliteration of Europe and Germany. Amazing that this is the concluding chapter of an era so infamous.

Sidestepping a stream of pedestrians along Marx-Engels-Platz and Palast der Republik, he sits over coffee in a smoke-filled cafe to rest his legs, to spend some of the East German marks, and to write more cards to Max and Alice and, since as he seems to recall that, yes, she was his wife for ten years, to Paige, and also to Monica Beniquez. What will he do about Hedy, he wonders. Mrs. Ernst Kahler. How much better if she would be drawn to him, if he could appear at the Frankfurt Book Fair as a figure of achievement, say, and she would read an announcement in a newspaper and stop by to say hello.

In the hazy autumn sunlight, exploring side streets, he stands at a table-on-a-post at the entrance of a supermarket to eat *Apfelkuchen*, noting that nothing in the East is as glossy and organized as in the West. An hour later, where Unter den Linden becomes Karl-Liebknecht-Strasse, he sits on a park bench to rest his legs once again. What does her husband do in Bonn, he wonders. Might he fly there over the weekend, have a look at 36 Aindorfer Strasse, and fly back on Sunday? Might he catch a glimpse of her without being seen? Or would he want to run into her, as if accidentally?

Still more people are gathering along Unter den Linden. Few cars move along the wide boulevard, a rare Wartburg or Trabant chugging along hardly faster than on foot. Glen is reminded—how could he forget?—of people overflowing into downtown streets on VE and VJ days.

Is Elizabeth Speyer-Weiss part of a similar demonstration to the south in Dresden? As he hears a voice calling *"Guten Tag, Guten Tag"* over a loudspeaker, he wonders if she has already escaped to the West. Or would she stay back to bear witness to her prophecy?

The translation program is pointedly prescribed; Germans will be Germans. Glen welcomes the diversion of history unfolding in their midst. Institute faculty are also caught between their obligations to the sixteen students and the reports from the incendiary world twelve kilometers away. Domino fashion, one thing follows another in East Berlin, East Germany, and Eastern Europe. Broadcast in color from a television in the institute lounge, and visible in store windows all about Zehlendorf, the uprising has the pull of a morality play. A ragtag collection of men and women keeps defying suppression, confronting and defeating bewildered professionals. Witnesses about them are increasingly stricken with emotion and disbelief. The underdogs score one devastating blow after another, and few can resist monitoring the dramatic events. The Mielein faculty are at times beside themselves with checked excitement as they address students. All the while they direct their ears to doorways for news dispatches and emotional gasps from secretaries.

Every hour brings a new turn. At one point Glen picks up a partial message from the opened doorway, something about Gorbachev, and he looks to Professor Kiesler. The man is only too happy to fill him in, as he appears to wish that the entire class would abandon the charade of analyzing translation skills and embrace the drama unfolding about them. "Gorbachev!" Professor Kiesler says. "It is not real—Krenz has appealed for Soviet military support and has been refused by Gorbachev! Once again it is incredible!"

Professors and students try to keep concentrating but no move is made to close the door. Professor Kiesler looks back and remarks more or less to Glen, the most experienced of the group, "It is crucial: Gorbachev *refuses* to countenance police brutality! He suggests East Germans have much to learn from Kremlin-style reform. When will these events end? Something vast is happening here! It is!"

At the institute's *Kneipe* hangout, Ein Tag Wie Ein Anderer, which name— "A Day Like Any Other"—Glen enjoys and attributes to Berlin's sardonic nature, TV screens carry nonstop live reports from East Berlin and East Germany, with updates from Moscow, London, Paris, Rome, Washington. Emotional responses erupt from the tavern's patrons. No one can guess what the culmination of events will be. But the rush toward climax is so clearly an impending victory for something good that goodwill, for now at least, fills the air.

By virtue of his seniority, Glen is increasingly invited to comment and participate in class. Placed before the group to conduct an exercise while Professor Kiesler takes a seat to observe, Glen manages the group like one of his own, gets the students talking and laughing. Professor Kiesler remarks later, "In this session perhaps I'm coming to understand the success of American universities. Do you know they are among the world's finest—a rhetorical question. I surmise it to be their openness, wherein learning occurs in participation. In Europe learning is imposed, and as Professor Cady is displaying, learning when imposed may not be so successful for all."

The drama out of the East continues. Thursday, November 2, returning from Moscow, Krenz offers a new concession to the

East Germans, concerning the Czechoslovak frontier, and there is another surge in the exodus. Now escaping are doctors, teachers, and engineers. Experts everywhere speculate that the hemorrhaging will have to be stopped. Still it continues.

Thursday evening of the first week, assisted by the program's administrative assistant, Frau Lowe, Glen connects by telephone with Elizabeth Speyer-Weiss in Dresden. When Frau Lowe establishes identities and hands him the receiver, he says, "Hello," fairly amazed that the woman could be on the line. He congratulates her on her foresight. He avoids the title of the book and tries to speak as if the subject were nothing more than a child's report in school, in the event of eavesdropping by the Stasi, which, Frau Lowe forewarned, "may be overwhelmed but can be expected to continue its sneaky business nonetheless."

"Thinking of getting away at all?" Glen asks the young woman.

"No," she says. "To do this, for me, would be an expression of disbelief. With my family, I shall work at home."

She describes her family—one daughter, one son, one husband—adds, "Of this we may speak directly," and Glen relates that he has a daughter who is six, although she lives with her mother, while he's attempting, age fifty-four, he says, to make a new life for himself. In response to her invitation to visit her and her family in Dresden, he says it will have to be at a future date, tells her how meaningful her quality of mind has been for him, and adds in closing that he will keep in touch and, please, to send a note his way in the event she or her friends come up with new ideas in need of a helping hand.

At the institute's Friday evening cocktail party, as the TV in the lounge reports the ongoing dramatic disintegration of East Germany, Glen realizes that a classmate is coming on to him. The woman, from Stockholm and prematurely gray, has been managing for at least two days to be in close proximity to him. As he stands in a small gathering drinking champagne, she says at his side that he reminds her "of the younger Bergman," which makes him sputter champagne in laughter. Moments later, closer and more intimately, she adds, "Our program format is ideal for a brief affair," and it occurs to Glen that she is the woman Ecki predicted.

He'd like to explain that if he were married still, he'd be more interested, but that he's single now and his heart belongs for the moment to a bewitching figure from the past. She remains close by him when he partially shifts to an adjacent circle. He takes occasion to extend his glass for a refill and to wander from the lounge to the building's darkened entryway. Small leaded windows on either side of the main door admit fractured light from outdoors, where, of all things, Puccini's "O Mio Babbino Caro" issues softly from a speaker of unknown location. The gray-haired Swede appears beside him. "Do you escape or initiate a rendezvous?" she says with a smile.

Glen would like to have the woman in his bed at Pension JFK. His loneliness has been palpable for months and he'd love to talk and laugh, would love to be sexually intimate. But his commitment elsewhere is too alive. He thinks he might explain that he's flying tomorrow to Bonn in pursuit of an old dream, and then, under the influence of Puccini and perhaps Speyer-Weiss's apparently warm family, he hears himself say, "The person I'm strong for is my six-year-old daughter."

Upon a pause and a laugh, the woman says, "Dear me, not one of those," and leaves him to make her way back to the lounge.

34

On Saturday morning, rain is misting from a dark sky over Berlin and the temperature is a cooler thirteen degrees Celsius. With time to kill before his flight, Glen paces the streets, trying to come to terms with what he's about to do. The overnight excursion makes him feel like an agent picking up sealed instructions at one point, to have his heart learn of its mission at another. He can't really believe Hedy exists and that he might see her.

Pausing now and then to look at Zehlendorf storefronts, he's tempted again to have a Camel to light. The city where Hedy lives. After all these years. He's going to walk on her street and have a look at her house, peer at its doors and windows.

From his room he gazes through sheer curtains over Martin-Buber-Strasse and tries again to understand the consequences of what he's doing. He might see her and his old dream could be blown away. A silly rooster crowing at the shadow of a memory! What a pathetic old cock-a-doodle-doo!

He'll fly directly to Bonn/Cologne International, an airport near the Rhine and between the two cities. Then he'll go by bus or train to Bonn's *Hauptbahnhof* and explore from there. He'll walk where Beethoven walked, seek inspiration from the visceral Ludwig, and secure a quiet hotel before venturing out to look around.

If he should actually see her and recognize her? The question floats in his mind as the airbus traverses the two Germanies, yet seems so impossible that he cannot imagine a valid answer. No, he will not speak to her. He'll merely have a look at her, if possible, and a look at where she lives. But what if she appears on a sidewalk coming his way? He doesn't know what he might do.

In Bonn the sky is the color of tarnished silver. Too nervous to search out bus or train, he slips into a cab at the air terminal like a flush young GI. *"Bonn, Hauptbahnhof, bitte."*

Raindrops begin striking the taxi windshield and he recalls long-ago Saturdays at this hour, heeding the magical call to the hillside house near the Black Forest, a spatter of rain against her bedroom window on a Saturday afternoon. Here he is making his way back a near-lifetime later. Not far to the south on the Rhine is the Lorelei, the rock formation where throughout time the siren has lured sailors to their doom. Soldiers, too, although it wasn't mentioned by recruiting sergeants. Stormy seas against which one knows, or desires, no defense, will trade anything for the sight of her.

Exiting the taxi, he moves nervously toward the *Bahnhof*, trying not to fear that he may look up and see her green eyes. All around is the movement of people, cyclists, vendors, a blur of streetcar platforms and bus shelters, flowers and banks of greenery. He instructs his breathing to return to normal. Take your time. You're only here to look around.

The air smells familiar—diesel fumes, maybe cognac and cologne, a Saturday afternoon combination which is erotic for him still. The sidewalks and pedestrian tunnels, tiled and curved and colored, are places she may walk every day; at any moment she might come out or go into a shop or cafe or tavern.

He finds no relief in the vast station. Everyone uses the trains, and why wouldn't she be returning from an outing to Frankfurt, from a visit to her family in Duisburg? He stands aside to sort out what he is doing.

First things first. Figure out how to act. Don't look at people, especially at women. Doing so, you may walk into a speeding VW and the Lorelei will scratch up another score. Don't look at women's eyes, or at their shoes, and try to breathe normally.

He buys a map of Bonn. Another expensive but elaborate red-and-yellow RV Verlag map, which he slips into his raincoat pocket as if it means nothing. No actual looking for her! he reminds himself as he leaves the station. You aren't here to spot her. Take a walk, and find a room for the night. Go out and have a look around.

What if she looked his way and said to herself: Glen Cady? She would go along thinking, No, it couldn't possibly be. Or perhaps she would remark to a companion, to her husband, Ernst: "The man standing back there, he closely resembles someone I once knew."

Glen crosses to the narrow, older streets of the country's capital, unable to keep himself from stealing a glance at an occasional face. Once he finds a hotel room, he thinks, he'll take a look at the local telephone book. He'll allow himself a peek at the street map, too, and in a Thomas Wolfe mode will go out to randomly haunt the city and wander into the approaching evening. He'll stop at a *Gasthaus* then for dinner and consolation. A look around and a return flight to West Berlin tomorrow afternoon. Nothing more.

Checked into a side-street hotel, street map left behind, he wishes he had brought the map and could go directly to her street. His confusion is close to panic. He does not even know what he stands to gain or lose. Should he give up the search at once and preserve the old dream? Is it a dream which has kept his heart alive all these years? Aren't journeys as rich in themselves as the prizes waiting at the end?

Bells ring out five o'clock. His legs have logged half a dozen kilometers and he has intentionally gotten himself lost in the city's maze of streets. By now, crossing bridges and crossing back as darkness falls, he's letting himself glance more directly at the faces of women going by. None have looked like Hedy.

He decides to forgo his constant anxiety and make his way back to *Bahnhof* and hotel. He's an adult, and enough is enough. He'll return to Berlin tomorrow, to the institute on Monday, and in the coming days will reconsider what to do about Hedy. It's at this moment, as he turns in the direction of the city center and abandons the idea of looking, that he reads a sign attached to a building, looks away and looks again. AINDORFER STRASSE.

He's on the street where she lives. He's in Bonn, as if in a dream, and is on the street where she lives. This street.

The number is 36, but he is determined, again, not to search it out, not, at any cost, to stand and stare at her windows. No way. He must hold to his plan and must retain his dignity.

Well, it's a prosperous street, he allows. Glancing each way, he sees two- and three-story residences, although he knows that within a block the large stucco buildings with wrought iron gates could give way to sleaze and neon. The lights at a distant intersection suggest commercial establishments, but more bakery or apothecary than nude dancing and porn. She could still prove to be poor and in need, he thinks, in spite of the street's apparent opulence.

As two couples pass, he tries to look at the women's faces. The couples are well dressed, walking and chatting this damp autumn evening, giving off a jingle and sparkle of jewelry and whiffs of perfume. A dozen yards along, a burst of laughter erupts and leaves Glen feeling excluded and bewildered.

Hedy could actually appear. She's an ordinary human being after all, and lives on this street just as everyone lives on a street somewhere. He grants himself a compromise. He wants to see where she lives, but continues to regard peeking as wrong and fears he would regret it. His compromise is to walk Aindorfer Strasse in one direction only. Only in the direction of the central city, he decides. Should the house numbers be going in the wrong direction, he will absolutely not turn around. He's been out for a walk and is merely returning, dignity intact, to his hotel.

His heart sinks at the first numbers, 67 then 71. The first cross street, a lamplighted lane hardly wide enough to accommodate a passing car, is Allee LeKarre. Feeling observed, if only by his rattled conscience, he pauses at this intersection as if to give number 36 a second chance. He is not going to give in to stalking Hedy here where she lives, but looks for another number anyway, to give the sequence one more chance to be backwards.

The next number is 79. The person who slaps his pockets then in a gesture of having forgotten his keys and pivots to return the way he came seems to be someone else. The person scans eagerly for numbers on the stucco residences which stand shoulder to shoulder two and three stories high. Number 49 glistens in the dark. He looks across the street to other houses, some dark, some with golden windows. One of them is hers.

Numbers 39 and 35. He doesn't stop, feels he cannot stare

outright, and looks at two houses across the street, one with lighted curtained windows, the other dark.

He still cannot be certain, however, and he crosses to a lighted three-story building to find its number on a wrought iron gate near the sidewalk: 34. He continues on his way, affirms the brass numbers on the gate of the dark house: 36. A large dark house with a mini-garden. Three or four steps lead to a wide and glossy wooden door. Three stories. He has barely paused and, glancing over his shoulder, has no choice but to resume walking away.

The next morning he believes he sees her. It's an incarnation he did not imagine: a woman passes on Aindorfer Strasse on a bicycle, wearing a helmet. He is astonished and thrilled. Not walking, not in a car, but pedaling smoothly by on a bicycle, moving with faint effort and deceptive speed.

A bicycle. It falls into place as the woman disappears. She was, after all, a cyclist; why wouldn't she be riding a bicycle now with the smoothness of an athlete? It brings a lump of joy to his throat. Hedy pumping a bicycle, as trim as a movie star. Of course.

It's close to eleven, however, and in only moments he must leave for the airport. Checked out of his hotel, carrying his bag, he's in a cafe at the street's intersection with Allee LeKarre, where there is a two-story *Konditorei*. Baked goods fill cases at ground level, and up a twisting staircase is a small cafe. Throughout the morning he allowed himself to pass number 36 twice before positioning himself over coffee at this table with a view back along the street. Until the woman rolled by he had given no thought whatsoever to cyclists.

He tries to recall what he saw. Hair around the helmet? He isn't sure. Slacks? Not slacks, stretch pants. His attention was drawn to her face, as he noticed something familiar, and strained with sudden excitement to ascertain features. Her shape, something about her—the angle of her eyes, her movement; an exalted sensation continues in his chest at the possibilities.

What to do? He rests his forehead in his hand, keeping an eye on the street. Boyish hair? Did she have boyish hair under the helmet? Glasses? Now that five minutes have passed he isn't even sure if she wore glasses.

However foolish he may appear to the handful of patrons in

the cafe, he shifts to the other side of his table for an easier view in the other direction. Newfound admiration for her keeps racing through him. As the woman rolled by and her trim legs so smoothly advanced the wheels, was there a faint smile on her face? Although he's unsure about her wearing glasses, he believes there was.

Where could she be going on a Sunday morning? Could it be that she's divorced and lives alone, and was going to visit friends? After three decades a woman who could have been Hedy has just pedaled by with a faint smile on her face, and he is foolish over her still.

35

The uprising in the East holds everyone's attention. The exodus through Czecho-slovakia continues and West German TV is filled with footage of refugees arriving, tearful reunions, of assistance programs going into effect, and the revolt in the East heading toward an apparently inevitable explosion. Institute activities move along. But news reports are directly accepted in the classroom now, as if everyone is of a mind to pause at any moment, at any new disclosure.

Tuesday, November 7. News out of the East is more frantic than yesterday and demonstrations demanding reform are more insistent. Something has to give. The East German government rushes forth a draft of a new law allowing thirty days' travel to the West each year, and the impression on ZDF, ARD, and CNN is of bureaucrats racing madly along hallways and making calls, trying to come up with anything which will keep the rising tide of revolt at bay.

Late Tuesday: The entire forty-four member East German Council of Ministers resigns. The proposed thirty-day travel law is rejected by the parliamentary committee as too restrictive. In five days, since passage through Czechoslovakia was granted, fifty-eight thousand East Germans have crossed to the West.

Wednesday: All twenty-one members of the ruling Politburo resign and are replaced by an eleven-member group containing four reformers. It isn't enough; by midday tens of thousands are demonstrating in East Berlin for free elections and an end to one-party rule altogether. Early afternoon: West German chancellor Helmut Kohl offers aid to East Germany in exchange for reforms in its state-planned economy.

Every time Glen hears the word "Bonn" he starts. Is Hedy captivated like everyone else by the story unfolding hour by hour, moment by moment?

No one anticipates that Thursday, November 9, will be a day of destiny. Reforms are granted into the afternoon, as East German leaders scramble to save their skins. By late afternoon free elections are approved by Egon Krenz while rumor has it that East German police are preparing to take control of the city. Then a report follows that the East Berlin policemen are themselves defecting to the New Forum.

A debate continues on television: Reunification in our time? No. Reunification ever? Never. The Soviets will never allow reunification. East Germany is a sovereign state and people need to accept that it will always remain sovereign. A united Germany will never exist. It is every expert's opinion.

Removal of the Wall? Possibly in a decade. No sooner.

Reaching with one hand to touch the Wall, a West German commentator says, "Remember the words of Erich Honecker just ten months ago: This structure will be standing in fifty or even one hundred years." The experts hold firm.

Institute activities continue through Thursday afternoon, with recesses in the lounge to hear ongoing reports. The concessions are analyzed, discussed, dismissed. Word comes that yet another key announcement is being prepared for broadcast later in the day. But so many key announcements have been prepared that this one receives no more attention than any other.

As the day's classes conclude and students and faculty leave, Glen stays behind to update materials for his report to Max and UB. It's after six and the building is all but empty when he takes up his raincoat and looks at the TV broadcasting to an empty lounge. Dinner at Pension JFK is on his mind, and he's getting an arm into a sleeve when he hears a commentator say, ". . . the most stunning pronouncement yet from the East German government."

Glen tries to sort out what is stunning. The woman commentator is saying in a voice far more excited than usual: "Free elections in Poland after two years, in Hungary after nine years, while East Germany by contrast entered the game but one month ago. . . ."

He strains to understand and there it is at last: "Again, this stunning concession but moments ago from the East German government: All travel restrictions have been lifted! Effective immediately, all citizens are henceforth allowed to travel, to emigrate if they wish, directly to West Germany! A minimum of bureaucratic delay is assured. Concrete and wire remain," the woman adds, "but the Wall separating East and West, as of this hour, is open! Repeat: As of this moment, November 9, 1989, the Wall is open! Citizens wishing to make private visits to West Germany need only present identification cards at border crossings to obtain exit visas. Passports are no longer required! *The Wall is open!* It is the biggest story ever out of East Berlin, as an atmosphere of hesitation and confusion, not yet of jubilation, prevails at the Invalidenstrasse crossing point. . . ."

Thus, at last, the climax.

Glen leaves the building and each move he makes into the evening, every conversation or report he overhears, carries an emotional, unbelievable message: *The Wall has opened!* East Berliners, confused, cautious, curious, are shown on TV passing through gates to see what they have not been allowed to see, to walk where, for twenty-eight years, they have not been allowed to walk.

Reports come into the night from leaders worldwide, from archives and studios, and live from the Wall itself. A Wall obituary is presented: There is its origin in 1961 as East German police rush into streets after midnight to unwind rolls of barbed wire. A photograph of an East German border guard, rifle strap in hand, leaping the barbed wire with the grace of a dancer. Sudden rifle shots in the night, bursts of machine-gun fire and slow deaths within beds of wire, all caught on camera. Presidents Kennedy and Reagan are shown pointing and issuing declarations. The architect of the Wall, Honecker, is shown two months ago gesturing and predicting: "This Wall shall be standing in fifty, in one hundred years!"

Then, live, a government spokesman from London: "Travel restrictions have been relaxed, but make no mistake about it—the Berlin Wall will stand." And Egon Krenz live from Moscow, where he has flown for assistance: "The dismantling of the Berlin Wall and reunification of Germany are an illusion." Granting a concession, the experts again close ranks.

In the morning the atmosphere in Zehlendorf is one of enduring tension. Television shows East Germans making their way into the West, having lined up at border checkpoints throughout the night. Germans on both sides are skipping work and gathering at the Wall. A feeling of celebration has begun to spread on both sides of the vast divided city.

   Then a spontaneous act is reported: Someone has begun to hammer and chisel. A workingman has apparently taken his tools to the twelve-foot-high graffiti-marked surface and his action unleashes an unforeseen, emotional attack. People are using pickaxes, pipes, and jackhammers in political expression. The Wall is no longer being circumvented but chiseled and smashed as jubilation takes hold.

The institute cancels the balance of this last day, gives in to the spontaneous holiday, and Glen stands with the others before the flickering television screen. Border guards are watching the smashing of the Wall. Suddenly, as he looks at footage of a man throwing grappling hooks to the Wall, a desire to be there overtakes him and he leaves to join the crowds, to be with others at ground zero.

   At Zehlendorf's overhead S-Bahn station, inside a flowing mob, he catches a report from a portable radio: "East Germans are gathering by tens of thousands to pass through checkpoints to the West! West Germans are gathering in equal numbers to receive them, to reunite with brothers and sisters! Even the ID card requirement is now waived! Word from eyewitness accounts is that the Wall is under attack from both sides with hammers and axes and battering rams! The Wall is being torn apart!"

   "The crush of East Germans attempting to enter the West is so large now that all crossing points are jammed."

   "East German border guards have themselves begun to bulldoze the Wall from the East! Repeat: East German border guards themselves are joining the people in tearing down the Wall! West Germans are hammering from the West! East Germans are hammering from the East. Gates be damned! The barricade is being dismantled!"

Glen pushes aboard a train car, as eager as everyone else to reach the center of activity. People sing and shout and laugh. Glen grips an overhead bar as the train flies, taken with an increasing desire to taste history, to see the Wall being hammered apart.

Above ground at last, he is swept along by the force of the crowd. The air is noisy and smoke-filled and people move toward the Wall from all directions. A sea of people, of sounds and voices, shouting and talking, flows in one general direction. He sidesteps among voices and shoulders, arms and legs, some all but running as if not to miss the kickoff, the first pitch, the pinnacle of history. Shouts go back and forth between friends pushing on in tandem, singular exclamations are sent into the air as the surge continues. Smoke is everywhere, acrid burning smells, dope smells, painted wood burning, and music is booming, sailing on the breeze.

Boom boxes duel to be heard; crazed people sing in pockets with crazed street musicians. The noise is so great that all words are shouted, all gestures wild. People of all ages, families, workers, businessmen, women in high heels, are part of an intoxicating street party. A man cries to the heavens, "Oh, what a wonderful day! Dear God, what a wonderful day!"

Glen weaves on, seeking the Wall, bypasses and sidesteps. Apparent strangers, mature- and dignified-looking persons, embrace, shake hands, cry out, *"Was für ein Tag!"* and *"Ein wunderbarer Tag!"*

Glen has his hand shaken ten times, is embraced by men his age, kissed on the cheek by a gray-haired woman as he pauses and moves within the racket. There are young men and women up high, sitting and standing overhead, and there it is, in and out of sight between heads and shoulders: the Wall.

People are being hoisted to the top, boom boxes are held aloft and bottles are passed atop the thickness of graffiti-marked concrete. Glen holds at last where he can look at dozens of people hammering the Wall, and to one side dozens more sitting, standing, holding each other, and crouching along the Wall's semicircular top. He has an urge to be hoisted up among the others, but fears he is the wrong nationality and wrong age. He stands and watches the mad scene, sidesteps to allow passage, strains for a view of teenagers, young men and women in their twenties, some in their thirties, squeezing to the Wall to gain a footing and stand at last to reach skyward. They raise hands and arms and sing and shout, crouch for more bottles handed up, more people climbing up, all having the truest of all parties, he thinks, a celebration of liberation, a party never to be forgotten.

East Germans coming through is what he'd like to see, and he moves between people and through smoke and racket toward a gate. On a radio he hears that Chancellor Kohl has interrupted his historic first visit to Poland to fly back to West Berlin, while riding the air from another direction, blaring in full volume, is the Beach Boys' "Help Me, Rhonda."

Finally, to the strains of "Good Vibrations," he catches sight of the Brandenburg Gate. Here, stretching for a view, he sees men using lead pipes as battering rams to hammer the Wall and send fragments of painted, pebble-filled cement flying. Others, one a woman, are using hammers and chisels. Elsewhere is similar, more extreme action, a section of the Wall under strain by grappling hooks coming from the other side. People work madly, emotionally; nearby others cheer from tear-stained faces. The Wall is being toppled; nothing short of massive military force could stop what is about to happen.

From a bullhorn, there comes an announcement, repeated several times, that new crossing points are being opened. It has no effect on those hammering at the cement, however, or on the shouts and applause coming from spectators. Glen skirts concentrations of people too thick to weave through, using the Brandenburg Gate as a landmark, until he is near a checkpoint. People are turning aside and gripping each other in tears, and he knows these wide-eyed, dazed men and women walking his way in antique clothes are East Germans entering the West.

The scene is subdued, even as bystanders clap hands and call out, lift their faces up and cry, while some withdraw to bow their heads and sob. Others clap their hands over their heads, let tears flow and turn to hug strangers. East Germans come walking through, looking about as if they don't know what to do, are looked at in turn, embraced tentatively by emotion-stricken adults, moved along, embraced by others. Glen takes a minute to realize that the small transactions taking place are the pressings of folded bills and coins into the hands and pockets of the frightened East Germans. The fifty-year-old nightmare is ending.

A young man with a little girl riding the handlebars of his

bicycle passes, and Glen's heart is checked; he misses his daughter and wants her back. The man lifts a hand to wave shyly and draws near-reverence from West Germans who touch his shoulders and arms, touch his child, and press money into their pockets.

Evening descends at last. In enveloping darkness, Glen finds himself in the heart of affluent West Berlin walking with the crowd along Kurfürstenstrasse. The party at the Wall is still going on and here a mass of people have paused on corners and in doorways to sing and drink, smoke dope and laugh and talk. Leg-weary, Glen leans against a wall and watches three polluted street musicians slash at guitar strings and toss wine at their mouths, and remembers being a child in a mobbed celebration in 1945.

At the Thomas Wolfe hotel, he looks to enter the bar, but bodies are packed like blades of grass and he returns outside. People are everywhere, passing beer and champagne bottles, calling and singing in groups, overflowing the sidewalk. A tabloid with the headline "NOVEMBERFEST!" showing the crowd at and on the Wall, is already on the street, and Ku-Damm shops appear confused between being opened and closed.

Walking to escape the mob, Glen turns along Düsseldorfer Strasse, a tree-lined street removed from the main flow. Here as elsewhere are two or three *Kneipen* per block, and he selects a warmly lighted establishment with a sparsely attended bar and empty tables. He goes to the bar to stand and watch the overhead television, to take in the latest.

Ordering a half-liter of beer, he stands watching TV and tries to sort out all that's been happening to the world around him and to himself. That he's here and has seen the Wall being smashed. Turning points in history.

He wonders what Hedy is doing tonight in Bonn. He's lonely, to be sure, and wishes she were here to tip glasses of champagne with him. On the screen, Secretary of State Baker is describing how West German Foreign Minister Genscher called to thank America for its help over the years, is telling how the secretary who greeted him said, "Just a moment, sir, thank you for everything, God bless America, and here's the minister." It brought tears to his eyes, Baker explains, as the minister came on to express gratitude for what America had done for Germany, particularly for Berlin, from the time of its lowest and darkest hours.

Glen's eyes fill up, too, over everything. The bartender, looking his way, raises a schnapps glass, nods, and says, *"Prost!"*

Glen says, *"Prost!"* in turn, and tosses off a drink of beer.

He feels daring. The time has come and he sees a blue-lighted bulb and arrow: TELEPHON. He moves as if casually; leaving his glass of beer, he walks to the back into an alcove. He empties a pocketful of DM coins on the shelf. Striving to remain detached, he removes his small address book, folds it open to her name, and takes up a coin. German telephone technology has far advanced since his last call to her, and when he has pressed the string of numbers, a telephone rings clearly. In sudden doubt he is tempted to hang up and leave things alone once and for all.

A woman says, *"Hullo."*

"Hedy?"

"Ja?"

He needs to swallow. "It's Glen Cady, from the long ago," he says at last.

Half a minute of silence passes before she says, "Glen Cady?"

"I'm in Berlin. I just wanted to say hello. I hope you don't mind."

"Yes, no, of course. You surprise me. Glen? It's been so long. Yes, you've surprised me."

"I'm sorry to surprise you. This hasn't been easy. I've been here today, at the Wall, and I had to pick up a phone to see if I could call you. Forgive me, maybe I shouldn't have, but then it's a rare day."

"You have startled me, certainly. After all this time. You are in Berlin? At the Wall?"

"I've been attending an institute. I return to Frankfurt Sunday and fly back to Boston Tuesday morning. I don't mean to impose, and I hope you can say so if I am. The truth is, you've always meant a lot to me and I wanted to hear your voice and see how you're doing. It's okay that I've called—you don't mind?"

"It's okay, yes. You give me a shock, into my knees, to also say the truth. I do not mind, though, not at all."

"I've thought of you a lot over the years and wondered how your life has gone. I became, of all things, a professor of German. Language and literature. You see the influence you had on me. I married, too, although somewhat late, and I'm divorced now. And

I have a six-year-old daughter, Alice. That's about my life, such as it's been. Right now I'm between jobs."

"Glen, you know, I have a six-year-old granddaughter!" She offers this pleasantly, and Glen is more relieved than he could have guessed.

"Not to mention a nine-year-old grandson!" she adds.

"Just one child of your own? Ilsedore? You didn't have other children?"

"One proved complicated enough, although Ilse has been a wonderful daughter and friend to me. Is so today. How have you found me? This is puzzling, isn't it?"

"It wasn't hard. You know the Germans. There's a service— if a person hasn't requested *not* to be listed, a process of tracing records. Does Ilsedore live in Bonn?"

"She is living in Mainz and is on her own with two children, but this is not unusual now."

"Divorced?"

"Twice divorced, yes."

"Little Ilsedore—that's hard to imagine. You're married now? May I ask such questions?"

"You may ask, and yes, I am married. Number three also. The daughter is not so unlike the mother."

"Are you—do you work—are you content, and happy? Do you mind my asking?"

"I don't mind, and I am content, yes. My husband, he's in sessions now every night while all is in turmoil over what is happening in the East, as he works in government. Happiness? I don't know—it's not so easy to know, is it? Is it known at the time or only afterward? I think only afterward, when one is older, is happiness known. And you are happy, Glen? You say you're not settled?"

"I'm not unhappy, I guess. I've had some ups and downs. And I'm not quite settled, no, though most of the time I wish I were. One of the reasons I'm calling, I suppose, is because I'm unsettled, so maybe there's a silver lining. Separation from my daughter has been difficult. My divorce happened this year, and that was hard, too. But new adventures come out of hardship, and I'm doing okay, more or less. Here I am, talking about myself, which I didn't mean to do. What I wanted to say, after all this time, is how much you've meant to me. I don't know how you put up with me, back then, as long as you did—I was very young—yet, of course, I loved you and am happy you did put up with me for a while, because it's meant a lot over the years."

"You know, Glen, I haven't forgotten you, and I can say that I loved you at that time also. Perhaps I have been not so fair, while my life was in such a state. At the same time, of course, you were very important to me. I shall always recall your youthful attitude, and how it was so encouraging to me."

"Now this is what I wanted to talk about!" Glen says. "I was certainly young, by the way," he adds, "two or three years younger even than I said I was."

"I found, your affections, they were cute, yes? And loving and genuine."

"Maybe cute is what they were," Glen says, wishing he had carried his glass of beer back here with him, wishing, too, that he had cigarettes to smoke as he talks and listens.

"Certainly youthful," she says.

"Unfulfilled," he says, and laughs through a faint catch in his throat. "I've always regretted that I wasn't experienced enough to appreciate more than I did. You were the first woman I'd ever known, and what I've learned since is that we had a story as wonderful as any. At times, I look back and regret that I wasn't better. It's something I've always wanted to tell you, so there it is. A late apology for not being better."

"Glen, you know, we all have regrets."

"Tell me something, if you will. I've tried to imagine what kind of person you are. You're not by chance a cyclist, an active cyclist?"

"A cyclist? No, no, I am not, sorry to say, but perhaps it is not too late?"

"What are you? Can you say? May I ask?"

"I—I'm not sure if it's so easy to say."

"You aren't a professor?"

"No," she says, laughing again. "No, I am not this, even though literature is still a favorite pastime of mine."

"You can't say?"

"Tell me, Glen, what you would say of yourself?"

"Well, I'm youthful still," he says. "I can say that. And something of a dreamer still. I'd say, too, that you, as an unfulfilled dream, you're at least partially responsible for what I am. I'm trim, have most of my hair still. As a person, well, I guess I became a professor type. Language and literature. Reading, ideas, what Thomas Mann called the manifestation of the mind? And you?"

"I think it is easier, for men, to center upon one's occupation; this has not been so for women. I'm youthful, too, I believe in all honesty, and also have good health."

"Do you smoke?"

"Not now for years."

"I don't either. You don't work?"

"I do not work, no. I am, what shall I say, the world where I exist, it may be called elegant, I think, if I am to be candid. Perhaps I may say that I assist my husband."

"In his work?"

"In his work, yes."

"Elegant?"

"I think so. Aerobic exercise each day, and nice clothing—this is elegant, yes? The theater is important, the symphony. A circle of friends. I do not mean to portray myself as shallow, only to attempt to say the truth."

"Do you drink?"

"Yes, a little."

"Your life has been okay?"

"I think so, satisfactory. What of your life, Glen? It's been satisfactory?"

"I guess it has, I'm not sure yet. What is it that finally counts? I don't know if I know. I count my daughter. I count you. I don't know if there's much else. Teaching. The army. They've counted for me. Marriage has been a disappointment, and now life's slipping away. That's what I know—it's why I'm calling you, because I'd like my life to have some meaning."

"I understand this."

"What I'd really like, right now, is to meet you somewhere," Glen decides to say. "I wish you were here, so we could talk and drink a little too much, even smoke a few cigarettes. A forbidden moment out of the past, that's what I'd kill for."

"Glen," she says, as if thoughtfully. "You know, I may meet you in this way. I will confess, I'd like to have something of this in my life also. Is it—does your position bring you again to Germany? We may meet at one time and have a nice talk?"

Glen is alert to what she has said and wants also to be thoughtful. "I have Saturday night, Sunday, and Monday coming up," he says. "My plane leaves Tuesday morning; I'm told I have to be at Rhein/Main by eight o'clock to get through security checks."

"Saturday and Sunday I may not hear from you. Monday is possible? Shall we meet—you will not be shocked that I'm not so young today as in the past?"

"I won't be shocked. I'd love to meet you. In Bonn? Tomorrow I fly to Rhein/Main, and I could go by train to Bonn. I'd love to do that. I'd really love it."

"I should tell you this: Mainz, only beyond Rhein/Main, is better to stop. In this way the train is direct to the airport at early hours and you will have no trouble meeting your schedule. From Bonn, from Koblenz, the schedule is not so convenient. You may telephone me on Monday?"

"There's nothing I'd like more than to telephone you on Monday. It's what I'll do."

"I must think. It isn't that I wish to deceive my husband, please understand, only that I'm uncertain in this moment. Until noon, I think it is better. May you call this number at one o'clock? And if I am free to answer, I shall."

"If you don't answer?"

"Yes, if I don't. Or, if another—with all the political turmoil, you see, it's impossible to know of a time, and I'm trying to think how to proceed."

"If you don't answer at one, I could call back."

"May you do this? On the hour, perhaps—no, at two hours, that I may know it is you? At three o'clock?"

"At three?"

"Perhaps at one and at three, it's okay? At five also? You may visit so long? At one, three, and five? I'm so sorry, because I do not know quite how to, how this afternoon shall occur. You may wait so long?"

"I'll look around, and read. I'll wait. It's not a problem."

"Please do not think this is what I have dreamed each day to do. Please do not think that. Still, you do have my heart moving faster now, it's true."

Glen pauses, says, "I'll call on Monday. One, three, and five. After five?"

"After five isn't possible."

"I'll call," he says.

"Goodbye then, till Monday."

Glen replaces the receiver and stands there, to regain his bearings. Yes, he's in Berlin and calling her wasn't impossible after all—now that it's been done. To think that he had made her into an unreal person in his mind—and just spoke to her on the phone. And managed to let her know she had counted for him.

Back at the bar the Wall is on the screen again, its surface being bashed by a powerful man swinging a sledgehammer, and this and all else in Glen's mind is touched with disbelief. He's going to see Hedy.

36

Sunday at midday, checking out of Pension JFK, he walks through Zehlendorf. He already misses the small city, for its colorfully paved walkways, its shops and cafes, and the new possibilities it has suggested to him.

Entering Tegel Airport, he feels yet again like a character in *The Third Man*, in spite of the Technicolor events in Europe and in his life. A rendezvous with Hedy is irresistible to him and he knows his lifelong dream will end now, for better or worse.

Deboarding from the shuttle at Rhein/Main, he rides the S-Bahn into nearby Mainz. Taking a hotel room near the Mainz *Bahnhof*, with the evening to kill, he sets out to tire himself in the brisk November air, hoping to sleep soundly before the special day tomorrow. Bonn is more than an hour north along the Rhine and the train he's selected departs Mainz at 10:08.

As darkness settles here close to the Rhine, hunger eludes him and his heart feels knotted like a teenager's. He's tempted to buy cigarettes, life's final pack, to see him through the coming twenty-four hours, but resists.

Would this be his last date? He hopes the kilometers he's walking will thin his old kisser, that the November air will add some ruddiness to its lineaments. On an impulse, he turns into a porn palace where, from a wall of cassette covers, he selects a black latex offering: *Lust am Schmerz*, an erotic specialty of Germany, he read in a Berlin tabloid. He proceeds to Booth 23-A for a viewing session in readiness for whatever turns fate might send his way tomorrow. Should he take a room in Bonn ahead of time? Strong drinks and strong tobacco in an out-of-the-way cafe? A taste of *Beefsteak Tartar* and a side-street hotel? Would touches of the tawdry kindle her blood and make her a little crazy at heart?

In Bonn, when he calls at one o'clock, a man answers, and he hesitates a moment before replacing the receiver. He wants to call back at once and has to force himself to walk away. Just like that, two hours to wait. Something sinks in him as he passes through the tavern and returns to the street. Six doors along is an inconspicuous hotel he had checked for vacancies. A small entrance, a counter, and a stairway.

What to do with two hours on his hands? He slept well enough, awakened once to pointed desire, but as he walks now in these near-familiar streets of Bonn, his excitement keeps faltering.

Hedy doesn't answer at three, when he calls from a newly selected tavern rendezvous, and hope stumbles again. No one answers at all. As before, he pressed the digits carefully, not to make a mistake. Double-checking the telephone book, he tries again. It's the same ring and he lets it sound twenty times throughout the house on Aindorfer Strasse before hanging up. Is she there, mind changed, waiting for the ringing to stop?

What to do but walk and spend time until five, as agreed, then call again. The plan seemed right on the phone in Berlin and yesterday evening, too, as he walked in Mainz, when he believed she would answer and believed in himself. Now it all feels wrong. He doesn't seem to know anything of love, while yesterday he believed he knew all there was to know.

Did Hedy have a change of heart? He doesn't believe, at last, that she did, believes rather that something came up. Maybe, he thinks, she's involved in date anxiety of her own, is having her body made more supple and firm, and nothing will keep her from answering at five. Even if her husband has returned from those sessions in government, she will have a plan, a reason to slip out; on the phone he'll utter an address and in ten minutes she'll appear, and it will be as in his dreams. *Wie einst.*

At three-thirty and at four he tries again. Still no answer. An hour more to wait. He tries again to believe she had to make an arrangement in anticipation of taking up the phone at five, perhaps of being able to say they might have the night together, or even that she might go with him to Mainz, to talk away the night and see him off in the morning. He sets out walking, to shed the last hour, and thinks not to give up. He'll find another small tavern in proximity to another small hotel, and will dial again, carefully.

Strolling, he passes through the *Bahnhof* and reads train schedules again, to reconfirm his possible moves. There are only two late trains, as he well knows by now, pausing before the glassed-in schedule for the third or fourth time. The first, at 22:18, will return him to Mainz in an hour and twenty-five minutes, while the second, departing at 00:46, is a train with many stops and will take an hour and fifty-nine minutes. Another train, one he has been unable not to notice, departs Bonn at the very time he should press the digits to place his call: 16:59. Among this train's symbols are a crossed knife and fork indicating a dining car, a glass indicating cocktails, a bed in profile, and even a telephone indicating on-train service. The thought of placing his third call from a moving train, going away, makes him shiver.

He walks once more into the darkening sky of the fading day. Twenty past four. He calls up the location of the third tavern and small hotel he had identified, however futile by now he feels his legwork to be. Thinking for the first time of November at home, he wonders what he will do this year at Thanksgiving. Car and bus lights are on now, and by five o'clock full darkness will fill the sky. If she arrives by taxi, it'll be too dark to see her legs reach to the pavement, or to be sure it is her, not until he's close enough to see her face and eyes.

He sits at a small table in a cafe. At street level, a hundred meters from the *Bahnhof*, the cafe is dimly orange-lighted, its windows covered with moisture. It's an old cafe, and recorded violin music, peculiarly German and reminiscent of the past, is playing. He sips cognac and strives to make things fall into place. The music touches him, and he thinks again of Alice, misses her and misses her presence within him. He wonders if his dreams are departing him now, and guesses they are. Ah, November.

———

As the train begins its soundless rolling, he looks out his window at the flow of people on the platform as if over his own history. He's decided to go on his way.

Maybe it's his only chance; he was aware that if Hedy had answered the phone he might have seen what he had no wish to see. If the times and places were wrong or right over all the years, he doesn't know. There is at least this movement of the train rolling away, which may not be denied. As the string of cars gains speed, his view is replaced by a reflection of the interior of the car and he thinks of Alice, and wonders where his little girl is tonight.

In time, when the conductor has paused to punch his ticket, Glen makes his way through the aisle of a swaying sequence of cars to a WC, and washes his hands and face. He touches some water to the back of his neck, as in the past, and moves then to the dining car, which has tables for two and four. He takes a place on the left, the only smaller table available, and in a moment a white-jacketed waiter presents a menu. *"Guten Abend, mein Herr, kann ich Ihnen etwas zu trinken bringen?"*

"Ja, bitte, ich hätte gerne eine Flasche Rhein wein."

Waiting for the bottle of wine, Glen surveys the other patrons who have settled in for a bite to eat on an evening train speeding south along the Rhine to Mainz and Frankfurt. There is a mother and two young sons at a table on the right, beyond her, two young couples apparently traveling together. Others beyond are lost to the darkness of the dining car.

A woman in a black dress appears, moving in the aisle to the sway of the train. She is an attractive woman, but just then a train explodes past in the other direction, and when Glen looks back, as he's always looked to see if it was her, the woman is gone from view. There was a resemblance, however illogical her presence on the train might seem to be.

He sips wine, orders a sandwich, and is beginning to feel a faint, pleasurable intoxication, an opening for a sensation of happiness, of music, although none plays. He'll sit and drink this bottle of wine, for the pleasant music and company it provides, and in any case, a sizable gratuity will cover for taking a table to himself.

There are sixty minutes left on the train speeding south, a time capsule on wheels. He recalls how drinking German alcohol, as reported, always raised rather than depressed his spirits. The woman in black passes, going the other way, and he sees what caught his eye earlier. The woman's shoulders, with their pads, make her appear sexual in the androgynous way of Marlene Dietrich. *"Wie einst, Lilli Marlene,"* he hears at a distance.

A voice speaks above him and he looks up to see not the sexual woman in black but another woman, asking if she may take the seat vacant at his table. Yes, of course, *natürlich*. As the woman seats herself, he adds that he's spending some moments in the company of a bottle of wine and should not be long, to which the woman replies politely that surrendering his place is in no way necessary.

She orders a sandwich and mineral water, and in time, his bottle of wine finished and wishing above all else to have more, Glen inquires if she minds his ordering another, remarking that he's having a pleasant time. Certainly not, the woman replies, implying with tone and smile that she sympathizes with his pleasure. Not an unattractive woman and one who seems blessed with education and a sense of humor, perhaps a professional woman, Glen thinks, a writer or composer, an editor of literary works.

A second bottle of wine is delivered.

It is neither Hedy nor Marlene Dietrich that Glen imagines the woman opposite to be, but Erika Mann. Who else, he thinks. He smiles to himself as he dines once again with the Nobel Prize winner's daughter, with history and with shadows of Hedy also in the air. It's a warm dining occasion, more satisfying than the last.

Erika Mann is an enjoyable companion in any case, gifted with memories and stories, a sense of humor, and a heart filled with tragedy, and as they dine she tells anecdotes of her father and brothers and sisters, moments in Bad Tölz and Switzerland, in Pacific Palisades, moments of exile down through the middle of the twentieth century. She hears fondly, too, of the teenage corporal's acquaintance with romance and laughs warmly as she admits him to her heart.

"May I ask you to join me in a glass of wine?" Glen hears himself say across the table. His smile is genuine, he is certain, while the image in his mind is of the train's golden windows sliding rapidly by, and of dust swirling in its onrushing wake.

A NOTE ON THE TYPE

This book was set in Granjon, a type named in compliment to Robert Granjon, a typecutter and printer active in Antwerp, Lyons, Rome, and Paris from 1523 to 1590. Granjon, the boldest and most original designer of his time, was one of the first to practice the trade of typefounder apart from that of printer.

Linotype Granjon was designed by George W. Jones, who based his drawings on a face used by Claude Garamond (c. 1480–1561) in his beautiful French books. Granjon more closely resembles Garamond's own type than do any of the various modern faces that bear his name.

Composed by Crane Typesetting Service,
West Barnstable, Massachusetts

Printed and bound by R. R. Donnelley & Sons,
Harrisonburg, Virginia

Designed by Cassandra J. Pappas